THE STEEL SERAGLIO

MIKE CAREY, LINDA CAREY & LOUISE CAREY

ARTWORK BY NIMIT MALAVIA

ChiZine Publications

FIRST EDITION

The Steel Seraglio © 2012 by Mike Carey, Linda Carey & Louise Carey
Interior Illustrations © 2012 by Nimit Malavia
Cover artwork © 2012 by Erik Mohr
Interior design © 2012 by Samantha Beiko
All Rights Reserved.

Library and Archives Canada Cataloguing in Publication

Carey, Mike, 1959-
      The steel seraglio / Mike Carey, Linda Carey, and
Louise Carey.

ISBN 978-1-926851-53-2

      I. Carey, Linda, 1959- II. Carey, Louise, 1992- III. Title.

PR6103.A72S74 2012   823'.92   C2011-907698-5

CHIZINE PUBLICATIONS
Toronto, Canada
www.chizinepub.com
info@chizinepub.com

Edited and copyedited by Sandra Kasturi
Proofread by Chris Edwards

Canada Council   Conseil des Arts
for the Arts   du Canada

We acknowledge the support of the Canada Council for the Arts which last year
invested $20.1 million in writing and publishing throughout Canada.

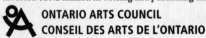
ONTARIO ARTS COUNCIL
CONSEIL DES ARTS DE L'ONTARIO

Published with the generous assistance of the Ontario Arts Council.

Printed in Canada

To Davey and Ben, with all our love

THE STEEL SERAGLIO

ℭℛ

BOOK THE FIRST

ᛒ

ᛒ

Book the Second

ᛒ

PROLOGUE

Once there was a city of women.

Its rulers were women, as were its judges and advisors. Female architects had laid out its streets and houses, and female masons had raised them. Its army was well provided and well trained, for though the city was isolated, in a remote desert region, it had had enemies in its time. And its arts and sciences flourished. Though there were few reports of anyone having visited the city—few, indeed, who could say in what direction it lay—its productions were well-known. From where else could they have come, the scrolls of poetry, the calligraphy and silk paintings, that circulated among the wealthy and earned exorbitant prices for any merchant lucky enough to get hold of one? Words and images to equal those of the masters, but no master laid claim to them, and where the master's imprint should be there would appear a woman's name: Soraya, Noor, Farhat; or an unfamiliar symbol of feather, leaf or flower.

The stories of the city spread far and wide. It was said that there were women physicians there with the skill to cure all diseases; even (though some called the notion blasphemous) women philosophers, scholars and divines. And some went further—in that city, they said, was the source of wisdom itself: a book containing all knowledge.

It was this rumour that prompted an adventurer to set out, without any map or more directions than could be found in drunken travellers' tales, to search for the city of women. A book of all knowledge! What long-tormenting questions could be answered, what hidden treasures discovered! And, he concluded, if this book of knowledge could confer such benefits on a commune of women, what vistas of opportunity might it open to a hero?

He took only two camels, and travelled for many months: at first confidently, following the hints and directions of the old men's stories into the deep desert. When the landmarks failed and the sun began to scorch his eyes, he slept by day and found his way by the stars. One camel dropped in its harness and died, then the other. And there came a day when his last skin of water was empty, and wandering on an endless plain of sand and rocks which was unmarked by so much as a thistle, he came at last upon his own tracks. The horizon was a vast circle around him: ochre and dun on all sides, pitiless blue above. The heat pressed him downwards. He fell to his knees, and then onto his face beneath the unblinking sun.

He awoke to a gentle rocking motion and a glare of light that dazzled his eyes. He was being carried on a litter by four black-robed figures, while a fifth walked beside him. As he blinked upwards this one held a little flask to his lips, bending towards him solicitously as he drank. Above her veil, her eyes shone black as olives. The drink was sweet and searingly strong, and the traveller spluttered and tried to rise, but his companion laid a hand on his arm and told him to be still. We have carried you for two days, she said. If you give us no more trouble we can reach the city by nightfall.

Her voice, though sweet, was full of command, and her hand was strong. The traveller obeyed her, and as he lay and listened to the quiet talk of his bearers, it came to him that all five were women, though they carried him along with no more trouble or ceremony than a sick child. He could not make out their speech, or his delirium prevented him from understanding them. He lay still, shielding his face against the sun's dazzle and watching the women's slender figures out of the corners of his eyes. Many times he slept and woke again; his bearers disturbed him only to give him water. It was darkening towards evening when the women finally slowed, and the horizon on all sides burned with sunset. He strained to see the position of the sun, but it was behind him, or else cut off by the shapes of buildings that rose like a mirage to block the horizon beyond his feet.

They entered the city as night was falling, and its walls blazed like gold in the low sun and in the light of a thousand torches. Two women pulled the heavy gates closed behind them; the traveller saw with wonder that both were uncovered: bare-headed and bare-armed. And his escorts, after setting his litter on the ground and helping him to rise, took off their own veils. At first shame overcame him and he could not look at them—but was he not a hero? Had he not faced death itself to gain this place? Taking courage, he raised his eyes to the woman nearest to him, who returned his gaze gravely. Her face was of surpassing loveliness, though her hair was threaded with grey.

Is this . . . he asked her, and his voice was a dry chirp like a cricket's. *Is this the city of fair ladies, of which I have heard in legend?*

This is Bessa, she answered. *As to what you have heard in legend, I cannot tell.*

Bessa was one of the names the traveller had heard from his drunken informants. In his head the book of knowledge was already opening its pages to him, but he managed to guard his tongue and asked only that he might see something of the city. His voice was still harsh with lack of use, and his compliments and courtesies sounded strained in his own ears. But his hosts seemed unconcerned, and one of their number stepped forward and offered to lead him. The girl's mouth made the traveller think of rose petals, and for some time he found it hard to look away from her face at the marvels around them. But they were marvels that she showed him.

He saw domes and towers there, he swore afterwards; gushing fountains, houses hung with vines and gardens of jewelled fruit. The torch-lit streets were filled with a cheerful din of voices, like the marketplaces of the towns he knew at home, with merchants, citizens, idlers each holding on to the last light of the day and a little beyond, to drink one last cup, make one last bargain before going home. But here the voices were all of women. He saw them packing up stalls, leading camels, selling wine and drinking it at outdoor booths: women of all ages and kinds. Some were round-breasted and slender; some stately, as tall as himself. All were uncovered; all, to the traveller's fevered eyes, as beautiful as the stars. Yet they were dressed plainly, some in desert robes, others in what seemed men's working clothes. There were silver-haired matrons, young mothers with babes, small children who giggled and pointed at the stranger.

How do you come by children, in a city of women? he asked his guide. (Like many heroes, he was a man of little discretion.) The young woman laughed, but gave him no reply.

She took him further into the city, and his wonder grew as he walked. She told him a little of this and that: *here is our square for dancing or disputing, there the schoolhouse, this garden is reserved for those who need to rest their spirits.*

But no word of what he had come so far to find. At length he could bear the uncertainty no more, and he stopped and asked his guide outright. *But the book*, he said, *the book of all knowledge. Where do you keep that?*

She stopped too, looking not angered at his rudeness but thoughtful, and maybe also amused. With a courteous gesture she turned, retracing some of their path, and led him into what seemed the outskirts of the city, to a low, stone house set apart from the others. Gesturing to him to wait, she slipped inside, and he heard quiet voices. *This is what you seek*, she told him when she reappeared.

He had to duck beneath the arch of the door. His guide drew the curtain behind him and left him there. The room was cooler than the warm evening, darker than the torch-lit night outside. A lamp cast its small circle of light, and in the light sat a thin woman with a book in her hands. His heart leapt at the sight. It was a small volume, but thick and richly bound: as she turned a page its cover glinted with the colours of jewels. An urge seized him to take the book now, grab it and run into the night. He had taken a step forward when the reader, who till now had not seemed to notice his presence, lifted her hand in a gesture of welcome.

Sit down if you wish, she said, without raising her eyes from the book.

There was a second stool by her own: he took it and risked a glance over her shoulder. The book was in no language he had ever seen: even the characters were strange to him. He could not make out a single word. He sat motionless, at the end of his road, while the woman read quietly beside him. After a while she sighed, closed the book and looked at him. Her eyes were black as ink, and as unreadable as the characters in the book.

You have come a long way, she said at last.

At that, all his frustration burst from him. *And all for nothing!* he cried, leaping to his feet. *Lady, how . . . ?*

She smiled and laid the book aside, and he saw on the low table beyond her, a heap of other volumes. She gestured into the darkness around them, and he saw for the first time that the room was lined with cabinets, each one filled with scrolls, tablets, leather-bound spines.

Not for nothing, maybe. I am the librarian of Bessa, she said. *And I am also the book you seek; there is no other.*

Before first light the women who had found him came for him again. They gave him dried dates and all the water he could carry, and two of them led him away from the city. The wind covered their footprints. By dawn they stood on a featureless plain; the women pointed to the south where he could see, many leagues off, the bushes that marked a waterhole, and they watched him as he made towards it.

He never looked back, he said. He knew as he walked that he would never return to the city of women, and no persuasion would make him tell any man the way there. Sometimes, when very drunk, he would hint: over such-and-such a mountain; west for three days, or maybe five . . . but no more. Nor would he ever say what he had asked the Living Book, or what she had told him during their time together. Some wisdom is too precious to be revealed, he said. But for the rest of his life, as he wandered from town to town, he was assured of a drink and a bed everywhere he went, just for the story.

REM SPEAKS OF THESE MATTERS

The truth opens gradually, like a flower. Or else it falls on you all at once, like a bag of spanners.

The city of women was both greater and less than you imagine.

I am a book, in which the future is written: I am a woman whom you might pass in the street without noticing, and never again be able to call to mind.

My name is Rem, and I can see the future. It's my gift. The Increate parted the veils for me and bid me look, which I did. Am doing. Will do. Tenses get a bit confused at that point, as I'm sure you'll understand, and unravelling them again can be a bitch.

I can be a bitch, too: I was taught by an expert. Unlike the sight, it's a gift I've come to value more and more as life goes on.

The sight has its upside and its downside. On the one hand, it gives you a kind of perfect sense of your own location. You can never lose yourself in the ever-branching forest of cause and effect, because you can see the invisible threads that link every effect back to its cause, at one remove and two and three and four, and so on back to the effect that had no cause and caused all things. On the other hand, that very certainty as to where you stand can be paralysing. Any motion you make, any degree of freedom you have, is—from the standpoint of eternity—infinitesimal, so you might as well not move at all.

I only ever knew one human being of whom that was not true, who seemed to move with perfect freedom, and around whose actions all things wheeled like the tethered tracks of an astrolabe.

But I'll speak of those things in their place.

In the meantime, and for the sake of context, imagine me against a backdrop of dry and baking sand. Shallow waterholes, of the kind called camel-licks, are spaced a hundred miles apart in the desert that seems to have no end: sky-blue eyes that stare up at the Increate in unblinking worship. When those eyes close in summer, the desert is impassable. There are deeper wells too, of course, but these cannot be seen because wherever one was found a caravanserai sprang up, and then a town, and then in some cases a city. Water, for all that it pools and flows and has no shape of its own, is the wheel on which we are shaped. In Bessa, where I was keeper of the books, there is a day of observance when we show our gratitude to Heaven for its liquid bounty by not drinking from sunup to sundown. Our parched lips move in prayer, but the only words we speak are "thank you."

It won't always be like this: the deserts, the scattered cities, the model of a civilization laid out like a string of pearls across the silent immensity of *As-Sahra*, the great nothing. One day we'll be gone, and the sands will close over us. One day the sun will set in the east and rise in the west. Not literally, you understand: that's just a poetic way of saying that sooner or later the Increate is going to decide to park his car in someone else's driveway. The power of Persia and Arabia will wane, and the infidel kingdoms will have their day.

Oh, don't fret. This will be a whole sackful of centuries from now, and despite the Earth tilting wildly on its geopolitical axis, nothing else is going to change very much. Oh, except magic. Magic just stops working somewhere along the way, more or less overnight. Quantum physics steps into the gap, strutting like a rooster.

What else? In fifteen hundred years someone will figure out a way to squeeze black juice out of the yellow sand, and that will get everyone very excited. Some people who were rich already will get a lot richer, and some people who were poor will be told that they're richer but will be pretty sure that they're not.

A century or so after that, the desert will become a sort of prophet in its own right, preaching to the nations of the world and telling them that to be barren is their inalienable destiny. Into every land, the heat will march like an army, build ramparts of baking air, defying humankind to come against it.

I'm hitting the high points here, you understand: missing out a lot of stuff that's mostly in a similar vein. And I'd like to make it clear from the outset that despite the male pronoun that slipped past my inner editor earlier on, I don't really think of the supreme being as a man. It's just a habit, a linguistic default built into me during the years of my childhood, and even though I lived in a place that came to be called the City of Women that's still the way my mind works when I slip it into idle and let it coast. I'd like to break the habit, but I'm a realist: I know that if I start off by referring to the Increate as a woman I won't keep to it, and it's a pain in the base of the spine to scrape ink (especially the indelible ink in which I write) off limed and scudded calfskin.

However that might be (and I could write a treatise on equivocation and compromise), sex—sex in all of its senses—is at the centre of this story. It's at the centre of everything, isn't it? Assuming you're of post-pubertal age in your own personal where-and-when, you probably have a few opinions on the subject yourself, and whether they're for or against I'll bet good money that they're intense. Intensity is part of the package. Sooner or later our souls find their centre of gravity in a hot, salt-tasting kiss and a trembling touch. Trembling is a good sign: it means you're open to a world that knows you're coming.

I reached for the shaving knife there, intending to banish that last sentence from the calfskin because it sounded so much like a tired, dig-in-the-ribs play on words. But let it stand. So many terms denoting orgasm also mean arrival, and that's a trend that will continue through all the ages of man (and woman). Ich komme. J'arrive. Vengo. Only the people of the far north, in a land that will be called Hungary, will choose to express the sexual climax in a word that means "I just left."

For me it was coming, not going. Arriving, not leaving. I'm here now, aren't I? I'm not going anywhere. And in spite of all I've lost, all the friends I've said farewell to when I'd barely learned the inflections of their names, I cannot envisage, and could not endure, a Hungarian orgasm. Give me excess of love, whatever it costs. We pay with our souls, and if we die with our souls intact we know we haven't loved enough.

But here I am, going on about myself and my own business as if I was at the centre of this story, instead of out on its edge. I promise not to do that too often. The next time I walk on-stage, I'll do so quietly and demurely. I'll try not to draw any more attention to myself than I strictly deserve, which—if I'm brutally honest—isn't much.

This is not my story. It's the story of Zuleika and Gursoon, Hakkim

Mehdad, the legate En-Sadim, Imad-Basur, Anwar Das, Bethi, Imtisar, the Lion of the Desert and the seven djinni. It's the story of the City of Women; of how it came to be, how it flourished, and how it was destroyed by a reckless and irrevocable act of mercy.

A curiosity: my name, Rem, will someday come to mean a line of text in a language spoken only by machines. Specifically, it will mean a line that the machines can safely ignore—one that's only there as a mnemonic, a placeholder, for the people who give the machines their orders. A REM line might say something like "this bit is a self-contained sub-loop" or "Steve Perlman in Marketing is a shit." The program as a whole rolls on past and around the REM lines, ignores them completely as it takes its shape, moves through its pre-ordained sequences, unfolds its wonders.

My mother named me well.

Book the First

Bokhari Al-Bokhari
and His Three-Hundred-and-
Sixty-Five Concubines

Once, long ago—so long ago, indeed, that historical records of any accuracy are almost impossible to come by—in a land of endless desert where water was scarcer than gold and truth scarcer than water, there was a city.

The name of the city was Bessa, and its ruler, the sultan Bokhari Al-Bokhari, was a man of no account at all. Al-Bokhari was strong neither in virtue nor in vice: he used his position primarily to gratify his sensual appetites, and left the running of the city to his viziers and other court officials.

These latter were a mixed bag, as such people tend to be. Some enriched themselves from the public coffers, flourishing in the sultan's benign inattention like flowers that grow best in shady corners. Others lay back and let the current carry them through an easy and unreflective life. Some few did their job to the best of their ability, setting up oases of justice and good governance in the city's general ruck of disorder.

It should not be assumed, by the way, that this was widely lamented. Bessa had had its share of tyrants, and most people who had an opinion on such things felt that a lazy hedonist was a comparatively light burden to bear. The risk of being flogged or beheaded for a minor misdemeanour was greatly lessened: heterodoxy in matters of faith and pluralism in the arts were alike tolerated, if not exactly celebrated. There was even a move afoot to allow women to officiate in the temples of the Increate, but this was unlikely to succeed. Who would follow a woman in prayer? Dogs? Camels? Other women?

So Bessa enjoyed its minor efflorescence, while the sultan enjoyed the rights and privileges of his exalted position. Chief among these was his seraglio.

The seraglio numbered three-hundred-and-sixty-five concubines, most of whom were young and comely. They had all been young and comely when they first arrived, but time takes its toll, and the complaisant sultan did not trouble to weed out from the throng those women who had declined in the vale of years. He just wasn't that efficient—and furthermore he knew that in the great game of hanky-panky, youth was far from being the ace of trumps. Some of the older concubines were still very definitely on Al-Bokhari's things-to-do list, while the Lady Gursoon was like an unofficial vizier, routinely consulted by the sultan on matters of state, up to and including treaties and trade negotiations.

Oh, he had wives, too, to be sure. Only ten of those, but because they were wives, with contracts and nuptial oaths to their credit, they had rank and privilege far above mere concubines. Their children were legitimate, and stood in line for the throne. They stood in line for a lot of other things, too, because there were dozens of them and the palace was only a modest two-hundred-up-and-two-hundred-down number with a view of the artisans' quarter and the Street of Cymbals.

The seraglio was a separate establishment within the same walls, and by and large was a fairly cheerful one. The concubines were allowed to keep their children with them, and they lived in luxury, with storytellers and musicians to attend them. Their sole responsibility was a little light sexual putting-out from time to time, and for most of them that chore did not come more often than once in five or six years.

The concubines' children, of course, were not legitimate and stood in line for nothing. But the girls were assured of a good dowry when they came of age, and the boys of a leg up in any reasonable career they chose so long as they took their leave of Bessa once their height topped four feet. Bokhari Al-Bokhari wanted no arguments about the succession, and bastards can sometimes complicate the issue without even meaning to.

There is more to tell about the sultan, which might be of some trifling interest, but I will forebear to tell it because he's going to be dead very shortly, and thereafter plays no part whatsoever in our story.

In Bessa, as has already been said, there was a fair degree of religious tolerance. The Jidur, the garden of voices, was a proud institution in that city, and anyone was allowed to preach there. This was not Bokhari Al-Bokhari's innovation—he inherited it from his father—but it was his downfall.

Among the holy men in the Jidur there sprang up one Hakkim Mehdad, a humourless and driven Ascetic, who regarded the sultan's womanizing and loose living as direct affronts to the Increate. Hakkim Mehdad preached a sermon so sharp you could trim your beard on it, and every day that he rose to his feet in the Jidur, his followers grew in number, until one day they stormed the palace and in an excess of homicidal devotion effected a regime change.

The sultan himself was beheaded, and his head mounted on a stake in the centre of the Jidur. Hakkim preached upon it, unable to resist such a potent illustration of the hollow, fleeting nature of earthly pleasures. Afterwards, inspired by his own eloquence, he ordered the sultan's wives and children similarly slaughtered, and their bodies burned upon a pyre.

The man charged with carrying out this order was one Ashraf, a fervent follower of Hakkim's now suddenly raised to the status of captain of the guard. There were no chinks in the armour of Ashraf's righteousness, and the atrocity caused him no pangs of conscience. Withal, he was something of a misogynist, and felt that the world would probably be a better place if the Increate had not put women in it in the first place.

But for all his faults he was punctilious and obedient, and also logical and methodical in his thinking. He did not stretch his brief into a wholesale slaughter of the royal household. The wives were to die, and the legitimate children: that was only sensible. The wives shared the husband's fate, as chattels wholly dependent upon him and wholly subsumed to his will. The children had to die because living heirs might someday challenge for the throne. The concubines, however, along with their bastard offspring, were outside Captain Ashraf's remit, and he told the men under his command to let them be.

Because of this forbearance, something happened which—though seemingly small—would have a profound effect on the lives of all the actors in this narrative. It was, veritably, the pebble that swells to avalanche; the feather that tips the scales; the fluttering wing of the butterfly that begets the mother of tempests.

Unlike the concubines, the wives were mostly of an age with the sultan himself: they had done their wifely duty long before, and the children they had borne the sultan, now grown to adulthood, had their own rooms spread throughout the palace. But there was one, Oosa, who was younger than the rest, and she had borne Jamal, the son of the sultan's old age. Jamal was but twelve years old, and since he had not been given rooms of his own, he lived alternately in his mother's chambers and in the seraglio with his illegitimate brothers and sisters.

On the day of the coup, when the sultan was dragged from his bed and beheaded, and armed men stationed themselves on all the stairwells and external gateways of the palace to prevent anyone from entering or leaving, Oosa saw which way the wind was blowing. She called her maid, Sharissia, to her, and with hot tears in her eyes, spoke thusly.

"I'm dead, Shari. We're all dead, and cannot be saved. But if I have been kind to you, and if you think of me as a friend as well as a mistress, take these jewels as a gift, and do me one final favour!"

Sharissia burst into tears in her turn. Through gulping breaths, she assured the queen (and perhaps herself) that nobody would die. Surely the new ruler would need queens! And servants! Why start from scratch, when you could inherit a whole household?

By this time the followers of Hakkim were already moving through the royal quarters, threshing their inhabitants with swords and knives. Screams ironically undercut Sharissia's words. She pressed her fist to her mouth and moaned. "Oh, the Increate preserve me!"

"And so he might, if you do as I say," Oosa said urgently. "My son, Jamal—take him to the seraglio, and give him to the Lady Gursoon. She's wise, and knows how to keep her own counsel. Let my son hide among the bastards. No one will look for him there, and I hope that no one will trouble to count corpses when this terrible day is over. Help me in this, Shari, that your own children may live long, and I will look down on you from Heaven and heap further blessings on you! In the meantime, this ruby alone is worth two hundred in gold, and here's a necklace, too. I think the white stones are diamonds. . . ."

Oosa thrust Jamal upon the maid as she spoke. That put four hands at her disposal, so to speak, and she piled absurd quantities of jewellery into the trembling grip of both Sharissia and her beloved son as they made their progress across the ransacked room. Finally she hustled them down a back staircase whose entrance on this floor was concealed by a tapestry (erotic scenes from the *Mufaddaliyat*—you don't want to know). Jamal's scream of "Mother!" echoed in her ears as she slammed the door closed.

As soon as the tapestry was tugged back into place, the queen turned to see a swordsman striding towards her, grim-faced and black-robed. It was that same Captain Ashraf mentioned earlier: he slew Oosa with a single horizontal stroke of the blade across her throat even as she opened her mouth to speak. The queen fell before the tapestry, pinning it in place with her body—but in any case, Ashraf gave the intertwined figures on the golden cloth only a single disgusted glance before turning away and striding off in search of new victims.

It's hard to pray with a slit throat, but in her heart Oosa thanked the All-Merciful that he had seen fit to save her child in this wise.

Sharissia ran to the seraglio, found the Lady Gursoon and gave her both the boy and the garbled explanation that pertained to him. Gursoon soothed the younger woman and reassured her, questioned her gently and patiently about the slaughter of the wives and legitimate princes and princesses, and considered what she and the other concubines should do next.

Some were in favour of fleeing, while flight was still an option—before the loathed Hakkim gave order for their deaths, too. Gursoon counselled against this. The seraglio was inside the palace walls, after all, and there was no entry or exit save through the main gates, which would be guarded. They were at the usurper's mercy, and could only hope that his thirst for blood would be sated by the atrocities already committed.

Knowing more than a little about how the minds of men work, Gursoon ordered the eunuchs to leave all doors unbarred and to retreat, themselves, into the inner rooms of the seraglio. Meanwhile, she asked those among the concubines who could play instruments to fetch them now, and to play gently in the great communal room where the women were wont to meet. In like wise, she burned sticks of sandalwood and oil of myrrh, and placed screens of coloured glass across the windows to diffuse and tint the sunlight that streamed in. Sharissia was mystified by these proceedings: she couldn't see how sweet perfume was going to hold back a sword. Her errand accomplished, she gave the prince Jamal one last tearful kiss, and fled.

When the men with reeking, dripping swords came loping across the doorsills of the seraglio, some four or five minutes later, they slowed to a halt, outfaced and stymied by the beauty and harmony they met there. The air was full of scents and sounds impossible to describe—a synaesthetic spiderweb that might be broken with a gesture and yet still held them fast. Women of inconceivable beauty offered them cool water from goblets of silver and pewter. The men drank, and realised too late how hard it is to disappoint someone who has offered you a courtesy. They were overstepping their orders in any case, carried here by the momentum of their own unleashed bloodlust. That tide abated now, and the killers retreated, checkmated by some dialogue between their hearts and this room that they hadn't consciously been party to.

Hakkim Mehdad took formal possession of the palace and its contents some hours later, and was publically proclaimed sultan of Bessa on the following morning. Captain Ashraf asked him, in the afternoon of that second day, what should be done with Bokhari Al-Bokhari's concubines.

Hakkim considered. The women were of no value in themselves, and certainly they could not remain in the palace: the idea was utterly repugnant to him. Killing them was a practical and economical solution. And yet . . .

Hakkim Mehdad was not a stupid man. He knew that a violent coup in Bessa would attract a certain degree of attention from the neighbouring cities and their respective potentates. They would wonder whether one city was the summit of Hakkim's aims—and all the more so because he was a religious zealot rather than a man motivated by the usual concerns of avarice and naked ambition.

He decided, therefore, to spare the seraglio and to send the women as a gift to the most Serene and Exalted Kephiz Bin Ezvahoun, Caliph of Perdondaris. Perdondaris was the most powerful among the cities of the plains, by a very long way, and such a gift would do no harm at all. Bin Ezvahoun might not need three-hundred-and-sixty-five beautiful young women, but he could always re-gift them to friends and family, and he would doubtless appreciate the gesture.

At the same time, he would read the deeper meaning contained within it. *Look upon me*, Hakkim was saying: *I cannot be bribed, and I am a stranger to the fleshly weaknesses that most men share. Provoke me, and you may find that you were better to have left me alone.*

The newly anointed sultan gave orders, and Captain Ashraf took the matter into his care. He arranged for camels and camel-drivers to be assembled, and chose thirty reliable soldiers to accompany the caravan. All that was needed then was a diplomat to present the gift and carry out whatever ceremonial niceties accompanied it. It didn't occur to the captain to inform the women themselves of their fate: they'd find out when the soldiers came to fetch them.

Finding a diplomat, though, turned out to be the most problematic part of the enterprise. There had been a great deal of looting and rioting on the day of the coup, and inevitably those of Bessa's citizens who had enjoyed the most lavish and opulent lifestyles had come in for the largest share of the Ascetics' crude score-settling. Diplomats as a class had been badly dented.

There was one man, though, who through the remoteness of his dwelling, the great height of his walls and the tenacity of his household soldiery had survived the cull. His name was En-Sadim, and he had several times served the late sultan Bokhari Al-Bokhari as a legate. Upon Ashraf's applying to him, En-Sadim declared that he would be more than happy to serve the new regime in the same capacity. Though not himself an Ascetic, being as fond of a glass of wine and an extramarital tumble as the next man, he believed that with a modicum of goodwill it was always possible to find common ground.

Captain Ashraf told him that his first official duty would be to take a consignment of concubines to the Caliph of Perdondaris.

En-Sadim said that he would be delighted to do so, and only raised an eyebrow at the number of concubines to be transported. "That must be almost the whole seraglio!" he exclaimed.

"It's all of them," Ashraf answered. "The Holy One has no use for female flesh."

For a moment, En-Sadim misunderstood. "Ah!" he began. "Yes, sometimes, indeed, one prefers for a change a good, hard . . ." The words died away in his mouth as he met the captain's gaze.

The silence persisted for a second or more.

"The Holy One is to be admired for his great virtue," En-Sadim concluded.

"Yes," said Ashraf coldly. "He is. You leave for Perdondaris tomorrow. Be ready."

You may imagine without my expanding on them the sorrows of the concubines, forced to depart so precipitately from the city of their birth; unable to say farewell to their families, or even in many cases to ascertain whether they still lived; thrown to the winds, and dependent now on the mercy of a stranger in a place so distant that for most of them it was only a word—a word that meant foreignness and power and white marble.

The children wept, and their mothers, weeping too, tried in vain to comfort them. "Well, well," the Lady Gursoon said, as she cradled the head of a woman less than half her age, and strove in some wise to still her tears, "from the dawn of time until now, a million cups have fallen, and wine has spilled across a million floors."

"So?" sobbed the other, entirely unconsoled. "What of that?"

"Sooner or later, my dear," Gursoon murmured, "one cup must finally land upright."

FIRESIDE STORY

For many of them, the worst thing was the desert itself. In the harem there was nowhere you could look without seeing a wall, even in the gardens. Now they moved across a huge emptiness with no shelter, nothing to cling to. Some of the smaller children, who had never seen the horizon, wailed and clung to mothers and older sisters, afraid they would be blown away, or sucked into the void of the sky.

Even for those who had lived outside, like Zeinab, whose parents were traders, there was something oppressive about the journey: the pitiless sun, and the stinging little whirlwinds of sand which could not be dodged. And above all, the heavy hands and voices of Hakkim Mehdad's soldiers, who herded them like cattle the whole day.

It was still night when they had first woken to find their sleeping-chambers filled with the black-shrouded men, who shouted at them to get up. In their old life, that alone would have been an outrage: the violation of their space by any man other than the sultan himself or the soft-voiced eunuchs. The soldiers threw sacks on the floor while their captain barked orders: pack clothes, and prepare to leave Bessa at once. "Take whatever you need," he commanded. "You won't be coming back."

In the courtyard some four hundred camels waited, their breath steaming in the cold air. Here the commander gave more orders. The concubines, as valuable commodities, were to ride, while the servants and children, all but the smallest, must walk.

There were protests from some of the mothers, but they were muted. The soldiers moved among them, enforcing their rule with kicks and shouted orders—but each man had a sword in his belt, and the women had seen over the last few days that they were prepared to use them. When one of the men hauled toothless old Efridah out of the saddle, and slapped the face of the concubine who had given the old servant her place, the women around them were cowed. Soraya, Zeinab's daughter, who had been perched on the saddle in front of her mother and hidden beneath her cloak, slipped quickly down to the ground before the men reached them.

The moon was still high when they were driven out of the palace gates, across the market place and out into the desert. There were many tears, and many backward glances, but the sobs were stifled, and the last glimpse of their home soon lost in darkness.

Soraya walked alongside her mother's camel until the plodding motion began to calm her. All around her trudged other children, her friends and rivals, most now subdued and silent. Little Dip, the cook's son, who had been adopted by the seraglio after his mother's death, cried quietly as he walked, his head bent so low that his tears fell on his knees.

It was cold enough to make them shiver, until the sun rose; then almost at once it became hot. That was when things got bad. The soldiers would allow no rest before the first waterhole, even when some of the smaller children began to stumble. Hayat tripped and grazed her arm on a stone; her big sister Huma, Soraya's friend, picked her up quickly and stilled her tears before any of the men noticed. But when the sun was almost directly overhead one of the boys, Zufir, fell full-length and lay as if stunned.

One of the soldiers came and stood over the boy, prodding him with his foot. "Get up," he ordered. Zufir moaned but did not move, and the man drew back his foot for a kick. It never landed. Prince Jamal, who had been walking with Zufir, had placed himself between the man and the boy.

Since the sultan's death, the children had been given strict instructions to treat Jamal as one of themselves. For his own safety, he was not to be a prince any longer. But Soraya saw with astonishment, and then with growing horror, that Jamal had forgotten: he was about to give the man an order.

"You, fellow . . ." he began—when someone barged into him. Aunt Gursoon, looking wider than usual in her travelling gear, had dismounted from her beast and swept down on them. She pushed Jamal aside, almost knocking him off his feet, as she bent over Zufir, tutting and scolding.

"The foolish boy's been walking with his head uncovered, and caught the sun," she said to the soldier. "He's recovering now, look."

She half-raised the boy as she spoke, then handed him to his mother, who had run up in her turn. As Umayma got her son to his feet, Gursoon addressed the soldier again, speaking with great deference, and not looking him in the face. "We'll make sure he gives you no more trouble, sir. If he might have a sip of water, he won't hold you up any longer. He's just not used to this sun."

The man scowled. "Stop your gabble, old woman," he said. "There'll be no more water till we reach the stopping-place. Just keep him moving."

He turned on his heel and left them. Only then did Soraya see that Jamal was standing close by Gursoon, his face white. She had his arm in a tight grip that looked as if it must hurt him, and she did not let go until the soldier was out of earshot.

"Not a word," she said to him then, as he rubbed his arm and glared at her. "You do not speak one word—to any of them." Remember your mother's wishes."

Jamal, still glowering, turned away in silence.

There was little talk after that, even among the children. Their mouths were dry and their feet sore, but there was no question of complaint. When the trees around the waterhole finally came into view, they were too tired to feel more than relief. Old Efridah sank to the ground, and two of the younger women found her a patch of shade, while others ran to arrange the filling of water-flasks, and those that knew how to put up tents showed the others how to do it. The soldiers showed no inclination to help them.

The camel-drivers took their cue from the taciturn soldiers and tended their beasts in silence—though Huma reported to Soraya that she had overheard two of them saying that they were bound for Perdondaris. The two girls shared a momentary excitement at the thought of seeing the great city, with its white towers, until the sound of a shouted order recalled their situation.

Once the sun had set, the desert was no longer infinite. The world shrank to the lit cones around their small fires, and the women did not feel the need any more to huddle together against the overwhelming space. Over on the flattest ground the soldiers who escorted them sat around a much larger fire. The legate, once his own elaborate tent had been raised by his servants, ordered a large wineskin brought to him and retired inside it. He had looked briefly among the women for a companion, but seeing most of the younger ones still disfigured by tears, or taken up with frightened children, he was discouraged and retired to drink in solitude, for that night at least.

The soldiers did not drink, or even loosen their heavy scarves. They sat upright, talking in loud, argumentative voices, with once or twice a burst of harsh laughter. But for the first time, they ignored their captives.

Away from the men's watchful eyes, there was a small lightening of tension. The women stretched out toward the warmth and talked of unimportant things: a good shawl; a cut hand; how long the raisins would last. The smallest of the children were already asleep, having long before worn out their sobs. Each now lay wrapped in rugs with their feet to the fire, squashed between the comforting legs of their aunties. The boy, Dip, still snuffling a little, crammed his thumb further into his mouth for comfort.

"What a baby," said Jamal, looking down at him with scorn.

"He's half your age, and missing his father," said Gursoon, who sat next to them. "Let him be."

"I've lost my father too," Jamal retorted. "And my mother and my brothers. But I won't cry, I'll go back and kill them for it."

The other children had joined in the discussion. "The sultan is everyone's father," said Zufir. "We've all lost him. I'm not crying either."

"That's because he didn't care about you!" Jamal said hotly. Zufir's mother nudged her son with her foot and sighed, "Don't squabble, boys."

"How about a story? Gursoon said.

Soraya and some of the other girls looked up at this. Aunt Gursoon was known for her stories: in fact Soraya had forsaken her own mother's side of the fire partly in the hope of hearing one. "The Fox and the Fisherman?" she said eagerly.

"We only just heard that one," objected Huma. "Let's have The Thief who Stole the Moon."

There was a chorus of protests and suggestions. Gursoon raised both her hands to fend them off. "I'll tell you a new story," she said, and waited for their silent attention before she began.

The Tale of the Dancing Girl

"There was once a girl whose family sold fish for a living. Her father laid his nets in the river, and she and her mother dried the catch and sold them two or three for a dirham in the village market. The river was narrow, and the village small, and the family was very poor. In that part of the country everyone was thin. But the girl's parents loved her and gave her the best of everything they had, so that she grew up fine and strong, with breasts like pomegranates, a slender waist and wide, swaying hips. But she was still a virgin, and had no lover."

"You wouldn't use such words in front of me if my mother was here!" complained Jamal. "Shall I stop, then?" Gursoon asked, and the nearest girls pinched Jamal until he yelled and shook his head.

"The girl went on carrying her father's fish to the village, alone now as often as not, for her mother's legs had stiffened. One day an old woman came up to her in the market.

"'I've been watching you, my girl,' she said. 'You're too pretty to waste your time here, smelling of fish. If you care to learn what I can teach, you could be a rich woman.'

"The girl was an innocent: she said yes at once and followed the old woman to her house."

"What's an innocent?" whispered Huma's sister Hayat.

"Ssh!" said Huma.

"The woman's house was no more than a one-room hut, like most in the village, but hanging on the wall was a thing the girl had never seen before: made of lacquered wood and shaped like a long-necked river turtle, with thin strings running down its back.

"'My tanbur,' the old woman said. 'Don't touch it.' She made the girl stand in the middle of the room and walk to and fro. She told her to step here, step there, lift her arms like so. Then she took down the tanbur and ran her hand over it. A rippling music came from it, higher and softer than the songs they played in the main square on festival days. 'Repeat the movements I showed you,' the old woman said. 'And now stay in time.'

"So the girl discovered dancing. She came often to the old woman's house in the next months, visiting her after she had sold her fish, and swayed and bowed to the shrill music from the tanbur. She learned the ten ways of holding her hips and belly, the sixty-six movements of hands, arms and shoulders, how to place the feet and angle the head. And she came to love the work, which felt more and more like freedom, like flying. She told her parents only that she had made a woman-friend in the village. The old woman took no payment for the lessons beyond a few dried fish, but insisted only that the girl must do exactly as she was told. She drilled her precisely in the movements, watching her with intent and glittering eyes and playing a little faster each day. And when the summer winds had come and gone, and the dust settled, she declared that the girl was ready.

"'I'll take you to someone who will see you dance,' she told her. 'If you do well, you'll never need to be hungry again.' She answered no more of the girl's questions, but instructed her to tell her parents she would stay with her friend in the village for two days. 'I'm visiting my daughter in the town while her husband is away,' the old woman said. 'You can tell them I need help preparing for the journey.'

"The girl's parents were doubtful—their daughter had never spent a night away from them—but they were old, and she was wilful. They begged her not to speak to any strangers, and let her go. She left her home before light the next day, and found her old teacher waiting for her.

"Outside the village they stood by the track until a trader came by with his cart; he seemed to know the old woman and agreed to let them ride for a half-dirham. The girl had never been so far from her home before. They travelled throughout the day, and when the shadows were

long the old woman told their driver to stop at a fork in the track and
climbed down, beckoning the girl to follow her. And before the sun had
dipped much further they came over a rise and saw distant shapes ahead
of them, which as they approached became high walls, houses and trees.

"By the time they reached the town walls, the girl was too excited to
remember her tiredness. She had never seen houses with upper floors
before, nor hangings as brightly coloured as the ones at their doors, nor
a tree much taller than a man. Beneath one of these trees they stopped,
out of sight of the walls, and filled their water pouch at a spring. Her
teacher made her wash her feet and face, and gave her dates and hard
bread to eat. Then she pulled from her pack a clean robe, light-coloured
and so thinly woven that a breath could blow it about. She shook out
something like a wisp of netting, holding it to her face in the manner of
a half-veil.

"'These are for you to wear,' she said.

"The girl knew that her teacher was not to be questioned, but as she
took the flimsy things with their glittering edges she could not hide her
wonder and doubt. But the old one simply looked at her." Gursoon fixed
Soraya and Huma with a glare to show them how the old one had looked.
"And she obeyed. Feeling half-naked, she stood in front of her teacher,
who pulled and prodded at her till she was satisfied. They waited for the
sun to set, and then the old one took her hand and led her through the
town's camel-gate. Though it was full night, the town was not dark: the
walls of the houses were pierced with holes, through which shone more
lamps and candles than the girl had ever seen in one place before. They
stopped at the tallest, brightest house, where the old woman pulled at a
silk rope that hung by the door. Then she turned to the girl.

"'I must leave you here,' she said. 'Obey the master of the house: do
whatever he tells you. I'll come for you in the morning.'

"A man came out from behind the heavy curtain. He was dressed in
grey, with a red sash. The girl shrank a little at the sight of him but he
merely glanced at her and nodded. He pulled a small leather bag from
his belt and handed it to the old woman, who turned away and left
without a word. The man motioned with his head for the girl to follow
him and darted back behind the curtain, leaving her alone in the dark.
Her teacher had already vanished. There was nowhere else to go, so she
breathed once and went inside.

"That old woman was wicked, to leave her so!" said Jamal. "And the girl was bad too, to go alone into a strange house. She should have run away."

Soraya thought Gursoon would glare at Jamal, or scold him for interrupting, but she did not. She gazed into the fire, as if for a moment she had forgotten them all.

"No," she said, at last. "There was no bad thought in her head. There was nothing there at all, in fact, only the wish to show off her skill to someone who might recognize it. She was stupid; no doubt about that. But some good came even of her foolishness, as you'll hear.

"Inside the room it was so bright that at first the girl couldn't see a thing. She heard the sound of men's voices, and laughter. There were lamps hanging from the walls, lamps on tables surrounded by meat-bones, cups and bowls. The men sat among the tables smoking water-pipes; all were old, and none of them seemed to notice her as she stood by the door.

"The house servant with the red sash spoke to one of them, a fat and bald man on a cushioned seat, and this man now raised his head to look at the girl. He nodded just as the servant had done, and clapped his hands. At this, a second servant appeared and began to push aside the little tables, while the first produced a tanbur. And now all the men were looking at the girl.

"For a moment she was afraid and could not move. But as the music began, she found her arms following in its train, and the movements she knew so well flowed through her. The serving man was a better musician than her old teacher: he played now loud, now soft, and her body swooped and dipped in answer. After the first dance he led her into a second and a third, running his fingers ever faster over the strings as if challenging her to keep up. She matched him step for step, note for note, and stood at the end triumphant, heated and laughing.

"The old men had put down their pipes. They struck their hands together and turned to each other, talking loudly and happily. They praised the girl for her beauty, grace and youth, and praised the fat man for providing her as entertainment. Then, one after another, they all stood up, thanked their host and left. The musician had gone too. The curtain closed behind the last of them, and she was alone with the fat man.

"He spoke to her then for the first time.

Gursoon's voice became low and oily to show how the fat man had spoken. Soraya and Huma shivered and moved closer together. "'That was well done, little pigeon,' he said. 'And now you'll dance just for me, eh?'

"For a moment the girl stared at him stupidly, not understanding. Then she recoiled and put up her hands in protest. So that when he reached out to grab her by the waist and tear off her veil, her hand was already raised. Her knuckles caught him across the mouth. She tore herself from his one-armed grip, leaving the rag of gauze in his hand, and ran through the door-curtain into the dark.

"She heard him howling for his servants, then coming after her. But he was old and very fat: before he was through the heavy curtain she had rounded the side of the house. There was nothing there but a long, low hut, clay-built and windowless. A strong smell of dung came from it, but she darted through the opening and found herself calf-deep in straw. She pulled the stuff over her and lay flat while the men thumped their way past. Someone looked in: the girl heard his heavy breathing and stopped breathing herself till his footsteps went away. She lay without moving for a long time.

"When the heavy feet had certainly gone, she moved the straw aside a little and peered out, wondering how she could find her way home. She had seen blood on the fat man's mouth before she ran: she could expect no mercy if he caught her. But as she stirred she heard a new sound: the clop of hooves outside, and then a man's voice. He drove the beast straight into the hut; she had to scramble away from its feet. It was not a camel. Its coat was sleek and as black as the night, its face long and gentle."

"It was just a horse, wasn't it?" said Hayat.

"It was, but the girl had never seen one before," Gursoon told her.

"Her wonder at the sight made her slow, and the man saw her as he came in. He filled the doorway so she could not run, a tall, broad man. But there was no threat in his face, only puzzlement.

"'Who are you?' he asked. His voice was accented like those of the nomad traders who came to the market sometimes with dates and palm wine. 'What are you doing here?'

"Since there was no escape, she answered him boldly. 'I'm a dancer. But the man in there thought I was something else, so I ran away.'

"The young man thought for a moment. 'I think you need to leave his house, then,' he said. 'Where do you live?'

"He sat her in front of him on the horse. She had never ridden any beast before and the motion was strange and uncomfortable, but the wind in her face was a joy as they sped away from the fat man's house. The young man had visited her village before and knew the way, he said, even by night. His name was Fouad. He belonged to a nomad tribe which caught and trained horses, but he had quarrelled with his brother and left to find work in the town. The horse they rode was the prized property of the fat man, and Fouad had been hired to tend and groom it. He described his human master as a skinflint, a glutton and a terrible horseman. 'Much worse than you,' he said. He made the girl laugh.

"They reached the village at first light and Fouad helped her to climb down. He had to return at once he said: his master would beat him for taking Belshazar out at night. His skin was very dark, and his hair curled tightly like a cluster of grapes. His eyes were long, slanted and green in colour. The girl had never seen such eyes, as pale as the slanting light along the horizon.

"'I would like to see you again,' the young man said, and the girl said, 'I'd like that too.'

"Her parents shouted and wept when they saw what she was wearing, but they did not beat her, nor ask many questions: they were afraid of the answers she might give. They forbade her to see her teacher again, which the girl was happy to promise. The next time the old woman saw her in the market she shook her fist at the girl, and cursed her as she walked away.

"When Fouad appeared to court her, her parents thought they understood what she had done that night, and scolded her again. But they were pleased that her suitor was such a strong young man, who looked well able to support her. They gave their consent.

"Strong and fine as he was, though, Fouad had no money, and the girl no dowry but dried fish. But each of them had a skill, and they trusted to their strength and luck to make their fortunes. Fouad left his skinflint master and returned to his tribe, working for a share in the next horse they sold. And one day he came to the girl in high excitement. The midsummer festival was coming, and the sultan of the city of Bessa had called for displays and festivities in the town square. They would pay well for skilled dancers, both men and women, to lead the celebrations.

"The girl's father was shocked: public dancing! But Fouad had seen such displays before, and assured him that there was no immodesty in them: ladies and children could watch them, he promised. He himself would accompany the girl as her brother, and he vowed on his life that no harm or insult would come to her. And the money would be enough to allow them to marry. He borrowed a mare from his tribe, giving them all his savings as security, and the two of them made the week-long journey to Bessa.

"There was a press of people outside the house of the master of ceremonies, but Fouad's horse made an easy path for them. The girl found herself among a crowd of women and girls, being ushered into a dusty courtyard where a fierce woman not unlike her old teacher made them stand in rows and follow her movements. The girl was the youngest there, and some of the others threw her sidelong glances of disapproval, but the old mistress nodded at her. She was chosen as one of the thirty women dancers, and Fouad, as her brother, was given a hundred dirham in payment. It was more than enough for a dowry.

"That week was the finest of the girl's life. Fouad had to leave her in the protection of the old mistress until the day of the festival, but she knew they would be together soon, and for good. Joy made her feet light. She laughed through the long sessions of practice while the other women moaned about their sore feet. She slept in the corner of the courtyard, dreaming of Fouad, and woke to dance again. The day came, and she whirled out with the others, surrounded by the great buildings of Bessa and feeling herself the centre of the world—for there at the edge of the square, Fouad was watching her from the mare's back, his face full of pride."

Gursoon paused, sighing.

"She never thought that others might be watching as well.

"When the festival ended, the two of them went back to the girl's village to celebrate their betrothal. Her parents were overjoyed: they began to plan the biggest wedding that a poor fishing village could provide. Then, three days later, a messenger came to the village from Bessa.

"He arrived with his own servants on four camels, and a crowd gathered around him at once, thinking him some great merchant. When he gave the name of the poor fisherman at the village's edge they were astounded, but they led him there. And so it was in the presence of half the village that the girl learned she was summoned to join the sultan's harem, chosen by the sultan himself, who had seen her dancing in the square and fallen in love.

"Her first word, when she could speak, was 'No.' But the messenger took it only as a sign of disbelief, and assured her that indeed, it was so. His master would not be denied. Her parents would be made rich for the rest of their lives—and he showed the bags of silver that he had brought to pay for her. At the sight her mother fainted, and her father, whose back had stiffened lately so he could hardly bend to his nets, let out a cry of joy. And Fouad, who was suddenly no more than her brother, stood still, his face as grey as the dry earth."

Gursoon's voice had become slower and heavier. She stopped now, and closed her eyes as if the story was over.

"Go on!" cried Soraya. "Did she go to Bessa? What did Fouad do?"

"What's to tell?" Gursoon sighed. "The sultan willed it. Next day the messenger placed the girl on one of the camels, and she said goodbye to her parents, who were still stunned with their loss and their good fortune. She could not see Fouad. Perhaps he was watching from a distance."

"And she never saw him again!" sighed Huma, her eyes misting.

Gursoon raised an eyebrow. "Did I say that?"

Soraya nudged Huma hard, and they closed their mouths.

"You know the palace. To a girl from the river, it was frightening. The size of it overwhelmed her. There were so many rooms! She could not tell the inside from the outside. But the other women were understanding: they explained things to her when she asked and left her alone when she cried. One of them took word to the sultan that the new girl was mourning for her family, and he allowed her two weeks before he called for her. And when he did . . . well, he was not so very old, nor fat. Not then. And he was not brutal . . . he had perfect manners, always.

"So the girl became a member of the harem. There was always enough to eat, and soft beds and beautiful gardens: luxuries that she had never dreamed of. In time she learned to live, not happily but in a kind of peace. The women around her gossiped and squabbled, sometimes, but most were kind, and they helped her to send a message to her mother and father, paying one of the sultan's scribes with a bracelet. Word came back that her parents were respected people now. They lived in the largest house in the town, with two servants. They said nothing of Fouad.

"The sultan sent for her nearly every night at first; then less often. She was one of his favourites still, but there were a hundred girls and women in the harem. And he had other affairs to trouble him: there was a land dispute with a neighbouring sultan and preparations for a war.

From behind the window-hangings, the younger girls of the seraglio would look out at the newly recruited men practising archery in the square. One day the girl saw Fouad among them.

"He did not see her. He was fitting an arrow to the string, scowling at the straw bales. She knew that look well: his frown of concentration when a task absorbed him.

"But he had come there only to find her. When she was taken from him he had ridden away into the desert, wanting to forget his life. But after some days or weeks of wandering his mare was bitten by a snake and lamed, and he knew he must return to his people. The horse recovered, but Fouad could no longer settle to his old ways.

When the tribe came next to the lands around Bessa, he learned that the sultan was paying young men to fight for him, and he volunteered, to the fury of his brother and uncles. He had been there for nearly a month when the girl saw him, training as a foot soldier. His tribe would not let him take one of their horses on such a wilful venture, and the sultan's captains would not trust a new recruit to ride, however skilled he was."

"But auntie," objected Soraya. "How did the girl know all that, about how Fouad was feeling, and what his uncles thought? Did he tell her?"

"Is this your story?" Gursoon said. "Wait and listen!"

"From that morning on, the girl found a way to watch the practice ground every day, from the tower at the top of the women's quarters, or through the branches of the orchard. On one of those days Fouad looked up, and her eyes met his. But she could never speak to him. And all too soon the men were marched off into the desert. She saw Fouad turn once and look up at the tower where the women were hidden. Then he went away with the others.

"Well, that was a bad time. But she started to see that she was not alone. Other girls in the harem were fretting as well, for brothers or cousins. And one or two, like her, never spoke a name, but sneaked up whenever they could to the tower window to look out across the desert. With these she became friends in sorrow, and as they talked, a hatred grew in the girl for the business of war.

"After many months the men began to return. It was nearly a year before Fouad came back. He was limping, and he had a great scar on his arm, but the girl's heart leapt to see him. She knew the ways of the harem well enough by now to be able to speak to him. He was no more use for fighting, he told her, but because of his faithful service he had been given work in the sultan's stables. And he stayed there. He had a rare skill with beasts, and the stable-master came to value him so much that he was given a home with the palace servants.

"So our girl's time of sorrow was past, but she could not rejoice. She had friends now, and some of them were grieving. None was as fortunate as her, able to see her beloved close by and know he was well. And their sultan was a man of fierce honour, as touchy as a cobra: he was always in dispute over land, and the merest breath of an insult could provoke him to war."

Soraya darted a look at Jamal. But he and Zufir had drifted away and were throwing stones into the fire.

"That was when a new purpose came to the girl's life," Gursoon continued. "She talked with the others, and found out what pastimes the sultan enjoyed, and what foods; what irritated him and what soothed him. And the next time he was visited by his neighbour sultan's emissary, and kicked the man out of the room and retired cursing to his study, the women were ready. They caught the messenger before he could leave, gave him a good meal and other hospitality, and sent him back to his master with a sweeter answer.

"The girl herself, meanwhile, visited the sultan with honeyed wine and gentle looks. In the days that followed she schooled herself to do whatever was pleasing to him: she danced for him, and learned to play chess. She listened when he cursed his grasping neighbours and his heavy responsibilities, and gave him soft answers. And in time, over many months, he came to trust her, and to call for her whenever he was troubled, knowing that she would listen to him.

"The whole household learned what to do. When their master was angry, he was offered the finest food and the sweetest music, and everyone gave way before him till he relented, feeling that here at least, he had the honour that was his due. Then the women suggested that their lord might show his greatness to his neighbours by inviting them to feasts rather than to battles. And when the other sultans round about came to the palace, they found such a welcome that they, too, were soothed. The sultan became famous for his great hospitality, and for many years there was peace between the kingdoms.

"So that is the story. That's how a poor village girl rose to be one of those who ruled the sultan."

The children considered this for a while. It was not the sort of ending they were used to hearing.

"Thank you, auntie," Soraya said at last. "That was a good story."

"But it's not finished!" Huma objected. "What happened to Fouad?"

"Fouad? He lived to be old. He rose to be stable-master in his turn, and never had to fight again."

"And did they really stop wars forever? Just by being nice to the sultan?"

"Did I say that? No, war always comes back. They kept peace for a time, that's all. Long enough for Fouad, not for his children."

"Fouad had children?" Soraya was shocked. "Did he marry someone else, then?"

"No," said Gursoon shortly. "He was true to his first love."

"But in that case," Huma protested, "where did the children—?"

Gursoon was Soraya's favourite among the aunties, for sure. But she had a scary way of looking at you sometimes, like the sultan's falcon when you got too close to it. She used that look on the girls now.

"The Increate provides," she said.

Soraya and Huma exchanged a quick glance and fell silent.

There was a small commotion beyond the fire. Zufir's mother dragged her son and Jamal back to their place, scolding in frightened whispers. They had thrown their stones too far. One of the men at the big fire was standing, looking around him and calling out angrily. Soraya clung to Gursoon's soft thigh; everyone was suddenly very still. Then another of the guards said something in a jeering tone, and all of them laughed. The standing man shrugged, and sat down again.

No one felt like talking any more. They watched the bulky shapes of the men through the flames, willing them not to turn round again. Finally Zufir broke the silence, in a voice as scratchy as a cricket's.

"What will those men do with us, auntie?"

"Nothing bad," Gursoon said firmly. "They're too afraid of their master to disobey him. They'll takes us to Perdondaris as they've been ordered, and we'll join a new household. There are rules for such things. The Caliph will respect those rules: he'll find us a place."

"He'll do more than that!" Jamal broke in. "When he hears who I am he'll reward all of you for saving me. And he'll help me get my revenge."

If Soraya had been sitting any closer to Jamal she'd have kicked him. Gursoon had turned her falcon-look full on him, but the fool boy seemed not to notice. "You've rescued a prince of the line of Al-Bokhari," he said.

"You can ask for whatever you like, I dare say."

When Gursoon spoke, her voice was harsher than Soraya had ever heard it. "We rescued a child," she said. "Nothing more." Jamal's jaw dropped, and Halima, one of the new aunties who was usually too shy to speak around Gursoon, ventured a protest. "Oh no, sister."

"Yes!" Gursoon said. "Hakkim Mehdad has just killed a sultan, in a well-defended city. And his wives, and his sons, and his bodyguards. He's sending us as a gift, but also to show what he can do to his enemies. And Caliph Kephiz Bin Ezvahoun has no reason to involve himself in another city's wars. Do you think he'd even take us in, if we came bringing that kind of trouble?" She glared full at Jamal. "You'll say nothing in Perdondaris, child—unless you're stupider than I ever thought you." To Halima she added, in a gentler tone, "That life is over, girl. Put it out of your mind."

The old aunt's eyes glittered: Soraya could not tell if it was with anger or tears. Over by the big fire some of the soldiers were getting up, casting glances in their direction. Gursoon rose too, and gestured towards their row of makeshift tents, set up as far away as they could manage from those of the men.

"And now it's time for you children to sleep," she said. "Take the tent nearest to the fire; I'll get you blankets. It will be a hard day tomorrow."

It was not wise to disobey Gursoon when she spoke like that. The girls said a hasty goodnight, and ran for the shelter of the tents.

And as the fireside conversations died, one by one, the desert night enfolded them into its silence.

THE CUP LANDS UPRIGHT, PART THE FIRST

As Bessa receded behind them, and the deep desert opened its arms to receive them, the fear and sorrow of the women and the children abated somewhat. They were not yet reconciled to what they'd lost, or to the new life that now awaited them, but they could at least contemplate both without absolute despair. The wisest among the women considered the fate of the sultan's wives and heirs, and reflected that things could be a lot worse.

Whenever anyone thinks "things could be a lot worse," the Increate seems to see that as a personal challenge.

In Bessa, the sultan's palace was still a ferment of mostly uncoordinated activity. Lists of those condemned to death as enemies of the new regime were drawn up by the hour, and then revised by the minute. A lot of actual executions took place, many of them *ad hoc* and based on quick answers to yes/no questions. Did you serve the old sultan? Did you live here in the palace? Are you loyal to the new regime? Do you drink or fornicate?

The nursemaid, Sharissia, kept her head down, did as she was told, and wherever she saw the men with the lists and the intent expressions walked the other way. Her position had effectively been terminated with the slaughter of Bokhari Al-Bokhari's wives and children. The memory of that horror was fresh in her mind, and she yearned to walk out of the palace gates and never look back. But the palace gates were guarded by grim-faced men in black robes with naked swords: Sharissia didn't want to have to pass them and potentially answer awkward questions about her former duties.

So she stayed put, and employed pretty much the same kind of camouflage that ostriches do.

On the third day after the coup, a harassed servant yelled an order to her as he ran by the door of a storeroom where she was pretending to count jars of olive oil. "Bring His Excellency a jug of water! Now!"

With a sinking heart, Sharissia obeyed. She filled a jug in the kitchen, put it on a tray with a pewter goblet, and took it to the throne room. The guards glanced at her once and stepped aside without challenging her. In a matter of seconds, long before she was mentally prepared for it, she was in the new sultan's presence.

In some respects, he was less terrifying than she'd imagined. He was less of a monster, certainly: slight of build and not overly tall. But the grim set of his features cowed her, all the same. Or perhaps it was just that in his black robes he looked like an executioner. In any case, her hands trembled as she set the jug down before him.

Hakkim Mehdad indicated with a curt nod that the girl should pour for him. She lifted the jug, but her hands betrayed her. Unable to keep them from shaking, she splashed water down the front of the sultan's robes.

Hakkim Mehdad clicked his tongue impatiently, and waved for the girl to leave him. Rooted to the spot with fear, she did nothing. A guard stepped forward to remove her. As his hand clamped down on Sharissia's shoulder she gave a great start and almost fell into a swoon.

Believing she was about to be killed, Sharissia began to beg and bargain for her life in a torrent of words, which spilled out just as uncontrollably as the water had. "I meant no harm! I'll do better! I was trained for the nursery, not the throne room! I have an elderly mother, and she can't survive without me!"

The guard was already dragging her towards the door, and as she thought, to execution. "I know where the crown prince Jamal is!" Sharissia shrieked.

Hakkim Mehdad looked at the girl for the first time. "Stop," he commanded the guard.

The guard released the girl, who fell on her knees before the sultan and performed a series of abject obeisances. Without even being asked, Sharissia blurted out her story: of how Oosa had come to her and given her the child, and bade her run with him to the seraglio; of how the Lady Gursoon had accepted him, and promised to hide him; of how the most merciful Hakkim, bless him, oh bless him, had been most indefensibly betrayed by odalisques and whores!

Hakkim listened to this spew of words calmly and silently, his brow set in a solemn frown. There was no need to have the girl tortured— the story was only too plausible, and beyond her wit to make up. He ordered the guards to take her away and put her in a cell; it was possible, although not likely, that he would have need of her again later. That done, he called for a scribe and a messenger.

The scribe being the first to arrive, Hakkim dictated to him a letter ordering the immediate execution of all the concubines, their children, and any servants who still attended on them. This was no time for half-measures.

The messenger arrived soon afterwards. He was a vain and self-important man, inordinately fond both of the perks that came with his job and of the sound of his own voice. He was one of the many who had joined the Ascetic movement when it became clear which way the wind was blowing, but had no instinctive sympathy with its goals. He began a speech summarising his good wishes for the new regime and his desire to serve it to the best of his ability until the breath died in his throat. Before he had got halfway through the first sentence, Hakkim Mehdad thrust the sealed letter into his hand. "Ride with all speed in the direction of Perdondaris," he instructed the slightly deflated emissary. "Find the caravan that set out two days ago, and give this to the legate, En-Sadim."

"As His Excellency wishes," the messenger murmured, bowing low.

As he retreated toward the door, bowing all the way, Hakkim fired further instructions at him. "Stay to see it done. And then bring word to me, here. At once. Day or night does not matter."

The urgency of the commission flattered the messenger's estimation of his own worth, which was already high. He positively beamed as he backed out of the throne room, parting the doors with his backside so that he could continue bowing until the last moment.

Then he went to the stables and demanded, with much ado, that the fastest horse should be brought to him forthwith.

In the deep desert, meanwhile, another event was taking place which would prove to be full of consequences.

The legate En-Sadim, who was as horny as a stoat, decided to dip his finger in the cookie jar.

He didn't put it to himself quite so baldly, of course. He was surrounded by beautiful women, he was far away from his own wife and hearth, and it seemed to him—chopping logic with his dick rather than his brain—that this was a victimless crime. In Bessa, the concubines had belonged to the sultan Hakkim. In Perdondaris, they would belong to the caliph Bin Ezvahoun. Here in the desert, though, they were his sole charge and his sole responsibility. Who could fault him if he carried out a little quality control testing? Surely it fell squarely within the bounds of his job description?

The woman who had brought En-Sadim to this Jesuitical crisis was named Zuleika. En-Sadim had noticed her on the first day, and had not failed to notice her as often as he could thereafter.

She was slender of figure—almost too slender, but with a wiry firmness of frame that suggested athletic possibilities in the bedroom department. Her breasts were small, but well defined. Her eyes were huge and dark, and her hair fell in black ringlets about her shoulders. There was in her face a contemplative calm that was more sultry than the sultriest of pouts. This woman would draw you into her stillness and show you her storms.

The legate indulged a fantasy in which he took Zuleika out from among the concubines and made her his servant: but sadly, it had to remain a fantasy. En-Sadim's wife would kill the both of them on the evidence of Zuleika's looks alone, and the caliph of Perdondaris almost certainly had scribes who knew how to count. No, it would not do.

But what happens in the deep desert, stays in the deep desert. On the journey, at least, En-Sadim could enjoy Zuleika's company and her person without reproof.

And so, when they ceased their march on the third day and stopped for the night at the oasis of Khuzaymah, En-Sadim called for the guard captain, a stolid and long-suffering man named Numair, and gave instructions for the girl to be brought to him.

Numair knew very well on which side his bread was buttered, and on which side it was laid with poisoned caltrops. Without a murmur or a hesitation, he saluted and went off to find the little number, armed with her name and a rough description.

A minute later, a slight, demure form was standing at the entrance to the legate's tent. Zuleika bowed to En-Sadim, not low but modestly.

"You sent for me, Excellency," she murmured. Her voice was deep, not musical but with a huskiness to it that was extremely arousing. En-Sadim nodded.

"Close the tent flaps," he said, "and come here."

The girl obeyed.

"You are Zuleika," En-Sadim said to her.

"Yes, Excellency."

"Do you play the buzuq, or the simsimiyya?"

"Excellency, no."

"Some other instrument, then?"

"I have no instrument, Excellency."

"Do you sing? Tell stories?"

"Neither."

"But there must be something you can do?"

She raised her head and stared into his eyes—provocatively, En-Sadim considered, but right then he'd have thought it a come-on if she sneezed.

"Many things," Zuleika said.

He touched her cheek. "Do the first of them," he suggested. "And continue down the list until I tell you to stop."

"Have you scented oils?" Zuleika asked.

Oils were duly brought, and she got down to business.

While the legate En-Sadim was being taken to the foothills of ecstasy, Captain Numair noticed a slender column of dust a few miles behind the caravan. To his practised eye, it suggested a single rider moving fast. The sun was still an hour from setting, and a single rider was more likely a messenger than a threat, but he deployed sentries and sent two men out to meet their uninvited guest.

They returned, some little while later, with Mehdad's messenger riding between them.

The messenger dismounted, and presented himself to Captain Numair. He did so with a certain degree of smugness, because he wore the sultan's colours on his sash, and the sultan's seal was very prominent on the letter he carried. Anyone could see even at a cursory glance that he was a serious man on a serious errand.

"Where is the legate En-Sadim?" he demanded. "I bear orders from the enlightened one."

"The most worthy En-Sadim is asleep in his tent," Numair

temporised. He knew that this was not the case: he had brought the beautiful young concubine to the legate's tent a scant half hour before, and he expected that it would be at least an hour or so before the business that was between them was concluded. But he did not wish to mention these matters. While the legate's sampling of the female merchandise was not expressly forbidden, it seemed unlikely that the new sultan would approve of it. At the very least, this was an awkward situation.

The messenger brushed the objection aside, making a great show of impatience.

"Wake him, then," he barked. "My business cannot wait."

Numair nodded reluctantly. "Very well," he said. "Wait here, and I'll bring him."

"Wait?" echoed the messenger. "I wasn't sent here to wait! Which is the legate's tent? Tell me!"

The captain knew better than to point, but his eyes answered the question involuntarily. The messenger followed the direction of Numair's gaze, toward the largest of the silk pavilions, and set off at a brisk stride in that direction. Abashed, Numair fell in alongside him.

"I'll tell the most worthy En-Sadim that you're here," he said, drawing slightly ahead.

"I'll announce myself," the messenger riposted.

Numair thrust forward strenuously. The messenger, refusing to be outdone, broke into a run. They bolted together past En-Sadim's startled bodyguards, who had retired to a discreet distance from the pavilion's entrance, and broke through the tent flap in a frantic squall of curtailed ceremony.

"The messenger of the enlightened Hakkim Mehdad!" Numair blurted.

"Forgive my unmannerly intrusion!" the messenger cried.

They both stopped dead at this point, staring at the scene before them. Zuleika was on her knees before the legate, naked to the waist, pleasuring him with her hands. Various pots and jars of sweet-smelling oils stood about, with which her glistening fingers had been anointed. The scented smoke of a small brazier drifted gently around them, making a teasing curtain which yet did not hide one single detail of the unfolding act. Captain Numair blanched. The messenger floundered, faced for once in his life with a situation which no protocol appeared to cover.

Zuleika was not outfaced to find herself performing in front of an audience. She ignored the newcomers as completely as if they were not there. En-Sadim did not. He frowned at them thunderously, and after a moment or two, caused Zuleika to pause in her ministrations by touching her lightly on the shoulder. She bowed her head, falling into decorous stillness.

"What is the meaning of this?" En-Sadim demanded, in a portentous tone.

The messenger realised at this point that he had overstepped the bounds of his office. "I bear a message," he said, his voice faltering, "from Hakkim Mehdad himself. He bade me not to wait, but to deliver it to you at once, by hand."

This last was pure invention, but the messenger thought it might allay the anger he read in En-Sadim's countenance. Belatedly he offered a bow of obeisance, the most ragged and unconvincing he had ever performed.

"A message?" growled En-Sadim. "You stride into my tent like a ruffian and offer me a message?"

"A most urgent message," the messenger qualified, trying to cling to some little shreds of dignity.

En-Sadim's eyes narrowed. "And what is the purport of this urgent message?" he asked.

The messenger looked at the scroll, then held it up for En-Sadim's inspection. "It is sealed," he pointed out.

"Then open it."

The messenger did so, with fingers that shook more than a little.

"Now read it to me. And if its urgency matches the enormity of your insolence, I'll spare you the flogging you've earned."

The messenger flinched at the word *flogging*. He glanced toward the tent flap, and for a moment it seemed that he might turn tail and flee, but Captain Numair stood squarely in his way, arms folded, and in any event he knew that while he was in En-Sadim's camp he was likewise in En-Sadim's power. There was no getting out of this.

"To the legate En-Sadim," he read, haplessly, "from His Excellency, the enlightened Hakkim Mehdad. There is in your charge, among the children of the seraglio, a legitimate prince of the bloodline of Bokhari al-Bokhari, formerly the ruler of Bessa, now execrated and not to be named . . ."

The messenger slowed, caught in a contradiction. Had he not just named the ex-sultan? And was that a sin? Surely not, since he was reading the words of the Enlightened One, which was a solid gold get-out-of-jail-free card.

The legate did not seem to have noticed the solecism. Behind him, though, and forgotten by all three men, Zuleika had raised her head and was listening intently.

"Continue," En-Sadim snapped.

The messenger took a moment to find his place again. "This . . . this prince," he read, "shall not be suffered to live. No more shall those who have sheltered him, in defiance of my edict. Kill the women of the harem forthwith, along with their children and maidservants. Let not one survive. Their bodies let the desert claim, and their names be fed to silence."

These were the last words on the scroll, but the messenger continued to stare at it as though more words might appear. The sultan Hakkim had not signed off in the manner demanded by protocol, which gave him no graceful exit from the horrendous sentence he had just pronounced.

He should not have worried. The legate En-Sadim had already moved his attention elsewhere. He turned to Captain Numair, who came immediately to attention and stepped forward, shouldering past the dithering messenger.

"Gather your men," En-Sadim said. His face and voice were grim, but he did not shrink from the commission: he was a career diplomat, and had seen and done worse things than this. "Give them their orders all at once, and in private, then have them divide the women and children into smaller groups, the better to ensure that . . ."

He stopped in mid-sentence, distracted by an unexpected occurrence. Zuleika, to the astonishment of all present, had chosen that moment to rise to her feet. En-Sadim turned to stare at her, perplexed.

"Resume your station," he said, with something of gentleness in his voice. "You at least will not die until you have finished the offices for which I called you here."

"Great sir," said Zuleika, in a low voice, "let me entreat some mercy for my sisters, and for the children. If you were to let us go free into the desert, we would not return, and the sultan would never know that his orders had not been followed to the letter."

En-Sadim looked stricken for a moment, then angry. "You must not speak before your betters," he said. "Kneel. I will return to you shortly."

"Great sir," Zuleika essayed again, "I beg you not to do this thing. It is a terrible crime, and will stain your soul into eternity."

The legate's face darkened. He strode two steps forward, which brought him directly before the concubine, and he drew back his hand to strike her across the face.

This action was not destined to be completed.

Zuleika leaned aside from the blow, her feet not moving at all but her upper body flexing like a coiled cobra. She caught the legate's hand in both of hers, and bending it behind his back, broke it quickly and expeditiously at the elbow. En-Sadim crashed to his knees, unmanned by pain.

Reaching behind her, Zuleika plucked the brazier from its stand, holding it in her bare hand without seeming to notice the fierce heat. The legate's mouth had opened by this time on what was presumably going to be a scream: the concubine emptied the red-hot coals and glowing ash directly between his parted lips and he spasmed in strangled silence, his head striking the ground as his spine folded forward.

The two other men responded to this astonishing event in very different ways. After one moment of stricken amazement, Captain Numair stepped in to save his master; the messenger, yielding to the same impulse that had almost possessed him earlier, turned to flee the tent and shout for help. Help might not be needed, since the captain would surely deal with this madwoman, but at least his own valuable person would be placed out of harm's reach.

Zuleika leaned down, drew the dagger from En-Sadim's belt, and threw it with whiplash swiftness. It was a ceremonial dagger, and poorly balanced. It struck the messenger in the back of the head, pommel-first, laying him out unconscious before he could reach the pavilion's entrance.

This allowed Captain Numair time to reach the concubine, but he had not thought to draw his sword along the way. He punched her instead, a solid blow to the jaw which he thought would fell her. Zuleika did not even appear to feel it. She jabbed her fingers, as straight as a ruled line, into the Captain's throat, and sudden agony spiked and splintered inside his gullet as though he had swallowed a draught of iron nails.

He opened his mouth on a bellow that would have brought the guards at a run, but no sound came from him. That first blow had ensured that the battle would be fought in silence.

The young concubine was upon him with such dizzying speed that she seemed to be three or four women occupying the same space, and only the Captain's armour saved him from an instant and ignominious defeat. Well, that and a lucky prescience that caused him to raise his forearms *en garde* in time to ward off the rain of slashing blows she aimed at his unprotected eyes.

Then she danced away before he could respond, so light on her feet she might have been a child's balloon, untethered from gravity. Numair did not think of retreating: this woman had assaulted his master, and it was his job to deal with her. Nor did he waste any further thought on the possibility of summoning help—he had no voice left to shout with, and he had seen what had happened to the luckless messenger when he had dared to turn his back on this termagant.

So he drew his sword and advanced, whirling the weapon before him in a wicked arabesque as he had been taught. Zuleika retreated, feinting left and right as if she wished to find a way past the whickering blade. Emboldened, Numair pressed her hard, his eyes only on her slender figure. She was in the corner of the tent now, with no more room to retreat.

The captain leaned forward to deliver the death thrust. Zuleika ducked under his blade and was for an instant on her knees before him. Then she came vertically upward. Her open palm caught Captain Numair under the chin and all the force of her rising body, her straightening arm, her flexing shoulders was somehow translated into a force that operated only at the base of her wrist. Numair's neck snapped with an audible crack, and he fell, bewildered and disbelieving as he died.

Zuleika took the captain's sword out of the air, as though the air had offered it to her, and cast her gaze downwards on En-Sadim. He was choking to death on the hot coals, his body wracked by terrible convulsions. Zuleika drove the blade into the legate's back and slid it along the runnel of his fourth rib to slice his heart in two. The angel of death is the angel of mercy, also.

The messenger recovered his senses to find the young woman kneeling over him, the bloodied sword still smoking in her hand. "I only delivered the letter!" he whimpered. "As I was charged to do! I bear no blame!"

"I offer you none," Zuleika assured him, and since he was watching the sword he did not see that in her other hand she had picked up the legate's dagger. A cold pricking in the messenger's chest made him gasp: looking down he saw that the hilt of the dagger now protruded from his flesh, where the blade was buried deep. The concubine leaned down as if to embrace him, and covered his mouth with her hand as he expired.

Nonetheless, the guards outside had heard some sound—the falling of the brazier, perhaps, or of one of the bodies, or the frenzied movements of En-Sadim as he was choking. Their footsteps approached the pavilion's entrance, uncertainty written in their halting cadence.

Zuleika gasped aloud, as if in the throes of violent orgasm. "Ah! Ah! Ah! Please! Yes! There!" The footsteps retreated again hastily.

Zuleika surveyed the carnage, her brow creased in calm but serious thought.

It is meet that we leave her there, for a moment or two, and speak about different but related things.

THE TALE OF THE GIRL,
HER FATHER, HER TWO SUITORS
AND THE KING OF ASSASSINS

Time out.

You may wonder—and I wouldn't blame you—how a concubine should come to be so very proficient in the business of fighting and killing. You may question the veracity of the tale, and suspect your narrator, with whom you've travelled so far and in such pleasant, companionable discourse, of being a lying daughter-of-a-whore with the morals of a professional card-sharp or a politician.

Be patient, as the Prophet says, and keep your mind open, that blessings may fall therein. And, please, cut me a little slack. This part of the story gets close to things that are close to me, and if I circle it like a wary trapper rather than marching right up to it like a brave soldier, well, that's my business. You can always go and read another story, with a more forthright style.

The woman named Zuleika was born in the city of Ibu Kim, and lived there until her fifteenth year. Ibu Kim lies to the south of Bessa, exactly as far as Perdondaris lies to its north; and if Perdondaris, with its palaces of marble and its roofs painted with gold, may be taken for Heaven, and Bessa for the middle ruck of common Earth, then Ibu Kim can surely stand for Hell.

Ibu Kim was a city of brigands, jackals and kiddie-fiddlers: a kleptocracy, a failed state, a gangsters' paradise and a rigged town. With few and insignificant farmlands, it relied on trade for its prosperity, but even its artisans were shiftless bums, happier to steal than to make, happier to fence than to steal. Whatever required the least effort was holiest gospel in Ibu Kim.

Within the streets of that town, the crime of rape did not exist. To despoil the wife or daughter of a wealthy citizen was, to be sure, asking for trouble, because wealthy citizens are chary of all their possessions. But a poor woman, without friends, had to stay off the streets at night or else fall victim to the first man she passed who had a mind to cope her. Nor could she call out for assistance, in such extremity: the city watch would either ignore her cries or, if it was a slow night, stroll up and wait their turn.

Zuleika, as I have said, survived to the age of fourteen in this horse-deficient shithole. She was sharp of mind and fleet of foot, and she took no heedless risks, but nonetheless, in that time, she had many narrow escapes.

Her father, Kishnothophur, known (to those who needed to refer to him at all) as Kish, was an innkeeper, at the sign of the Blue Wheel, and in his own small way a whoremonger, too. The profits he made from the twelve women in his employ were much greater than the profits he made from renting rooms, but in Ibu Kim, by a fine irony, for a woman to sell her sexual services was considered a crime—whereas for a man to take them by force was part of the ordinary rough-and-tumble of life. So the Blue Wheel was officially an inn, and a regular bribe of shiny silver coins prevented the city watch from inquiring into anything else that went on there.

Kish had taken a young wife and fathered one child on her before she died of a quartan fever brought on by drinking bad water (the wells of Ibu Kim were used by footpads as a convenient place to dump bodies, and so they were often unsafe to drink from). Thereafter, the girl fell from his thoughts: Zuleika was raised by whores, and much loved and doted on by them. They protected her from the myriad dangers of that highly dangerous place, which meant among other things that they kept her both out of her father's sight and out from under the feet of the clients.

Some of the whores came and then went, without fuss or notice; some, for reasons Zuleika was too young to appreciate, had more staying power. If the child had a favourite, it was Ehara, a woman of statuesque frame and generous nature. Ehara looked less like a prostitute than like a public building, but still inspired strong loyalty from her clientele.

Zuleika's duties at this time were many: buying food at the weekly market, drawing water, sweeping the floor of the inn, washing the wine cups and jars at the end of the evening and the bed linen twice a month, anointing the walls with white lime when they were soiled, and taking the weekly bung of ten silver dinars to the sergeant of the guard. Whenever she was not engaged in these pursuits, Zuleika would sit with the older woman and help her with her toilet—combing out her long hair, painting her toenails, or otherwise beautifying her various extremities.

Only on the nights when the moon was absent from the sky was Zuleika barred from Ehara's company. It was then that the inn received a clandestine but much valued visitor: Vurdik the Bald, the bandit chieftain of the Yashifia. Vurdik was legend in Ibu Kim; his men harried the caravans of every neighbouring city from sunrise to sunset, and though his industry was much admired, he was still a proscribed criminal with a price (which varied according to the season and the vagaries of government) upon his head.

But in the Blue Wheel, Vurdik was a paying customer. He went by a different pseudonym each month, lived lavishly, and was rewarded with every luxury the house had to offer. One of those luxuries was exclusive access, whenever he stayed, to Ehara's body.

After one of Vurdik's visits, Ehara was unable to work for three days because of a beating the bandit chief gave her when he was in his cups. Zuleika tended to her friend's injuries through those days. Her father decided not to summon a doctor, both because of the expense and because of the awkward questions that might be asked about the identity of Ehara's assailant.

Still a child, untutored in the world's ways, Zuleika was moved to rage and tears at how Ehara had been hurt—and then to horror at Ehara's own reaction. "Oh, Vurdik isn't so bad, my love," the older woman told the girl, through thickened lips. "I could do without the beatings, but the beatings are nothing compared to what he'd do to me if I ever tried to leave. And with a man who's just a thug, if you're quick, you can always dodge the worst of it. It's the clever ones you want to watch. They've got worse ways to hurt you, and you don't always see them coming."

I mention this anecdote because of its wisdom and wide applicability—and because it stayed in Zuleika's mind and ultimately formed the foundation of a more advanced social theory. Different people menaced you in different ways, it seemed, and you needed to have a suitable answer for all of them. It was a long-term project for Zuleika, but it started on that day.

Meanwhile there were other things going on in the young girl's life, and some of them presented with a lot more urgency. She was coming into her change, now, and men were starting to notice her. One of them was her father, whom she caught watching her on a number of occasions with a thoughtful expression. She knew Kish well enough to discount the possibility that he wanted to bed her himself—he was hugely uninterested in sex, except as a commercial proposition. He did, however, know what virginity was worth, and how best to package and retail it.

Another man who showed a definite interest was the saddler (if he had a name, he kept it to himself) who lived and worked directly opposite the inn, in the Courtyard of the Trades. This gentleman watched Zuleika stumble-step towards puberty, and he conceived a lust for her. In Ibu Kim, a woman's first bleeding is taken to be a gentle reminder from the Increate that she should by now have been married or sold. The saddler saw this moment coming, from a considerable distance, and (as it were) decided to stake a prior claim.

On Zuleika's fourteenth birthday, he made Kish a gift of a silver-inlaid saddle, with a brushed silver saddle horn, and complimented him on his daughter's great beauty. "She'll make someone a fine wife," he hinted, over a jar of wine (the cheap stuff) which Kish had cracked open for the occasion.

Kish agreed that Zuleika promised well.

"A woman is like a camel," the saddler opined. "If a man cares for her, she will carry him in comfort through the longest journey."

Kish allowed that this was so. Further, he argued, it was so even of a camel that another man has already ridden.

The saddler looked up from his drink, and a complicated discourse of raised and lowered eyebrows ensued.

"The two cases are not comparable," the saddler said. "A camel that's already been broken in becomes more valuable as a result. A woman, substantially less."

"But if it were a choice," Kish mused, "between an unbroken wife and no dowry at all, and a broken wife with silver in her train, a man's very reasonable expectations might be tempered by a certain judicious pragmatism."

"Broken once?" the saddler asked bluntly. "Or broken many times?"

"Once," said Kish.

"And how much silver?"

"Twenty pieces."

"Ah."

"At least twenty."

"Ah, well."

"Possibly thirty."

"Ah, well, now."

Zuleika witnessed all this camel-trading in solemn silence, even when the saddler smiled and winked at her—as though his blunt bargaining for her body were some sort of compliment or tribute to her beauty. He was a huge man, as big and shapeless as a pile of flour sacks, and radiated a stench of sweat so strong and searing that even in the open air it made the eyes of those passing by blur with sudden tears. The dyes he used in turning raw leather into finished saddles had stayed on his skin in places, giving it a hectic, parboiled appearance.

Zuleika did not love him. This is not a matter of size or smell or dappled pigment: it is a mystery, as all must agree. She could not give to him the part of her soul that was relevant to the matter. As to her body, she knew she could trust the two men to come to a mutually agreeable arrangement.

In the end, it was decided that Zuleika should stay in her father's house until she was fifteen. At that time, she would be inducted into the profession of prostitute and then cashiered out of it again in the same night: she would entertain a single client, chosen and vetted by Kish himself, and on the very next day she would be married to the saddler. "Whoever lies with her, he must be clean!" the saddler insisted, many times. But of course he would be clean; he would, after all, be rich, and the one presupposes the other.

So Zuleika had a year to wait before she was given over to this unwelcome destiny: a bare year, and she had no plan. There were few options, in that city and at that time, for a girl who wished to be more than a beast of burden. In Bessa, it was said, women could sell goods at market, run inns and brothels, work in stable yards and mills. Bessa was three days' journey for a camel, nine or ten if you had to rely on your own feet.

In the spring of that fifteenth year, Zuleika packed a few clothes into a bag, stashed the bag under her bed where it would be ready to hand, and waited for a night of thick cloud.

It duly came. Zuleika stole down the stairs in her bare feet, carrying her sandals in one hand, the rest of her meagre possessions in the other.

Her father was waiting for her in the yard. He dragged her back inside the house by her hair and beat her black and blue.

In spite of his stolid demeanour, Kish was no fool. He had noticed the resolve growing in his daughter and had decided that the best way to head it off would be to allow it to grow to fruition and then to come down hard. He didn't see this as cruelty, only as good husbandry, of the same order as beating a dog to teach it not to foul the floor.

Ehara wept for the girl, and washed her bruises with wine vinegar. Zuleika didn't weep for herself. She thought about her mistake, and promised herself that she would never misclassify a man again—you couldn't base good decisions on bad taxonomy.

But she was still a child, and she still saw the world—or parts of it, at least—in ways that were romantic and simplified. There was a boy four years older than her, Sasim, into whose orbit she fell, slowly and thrillingly, in the weeks after she recovered from the beating.

She met the boy for the first time when she was walking to market with a basket in each hand and a sack tied to her back for vegetables. She met him again, the next time she carried the weekly bribe to Rhuk, the sergeant of the guard—and then a third time, when she went to the well for water. Eventually, it occurred to her that the tall, dark-eyed lad who loitered at the corner of the street close to the inn yard and greeted her so civilly when she passed was not there by chance. She began to slow down when she passed him, and exchange a few words: remarks about the weather; jokes about how many bags and baskets one girl could carry; finally, with a prickle of forbidden pleasure, given names.

Their courtship was an astonishing thing to Zuleika: she had already come to associate men with danger, and now here was one whose company, whose voice, whose gaze, brought dizzying pleasure. She was cautious; she had learned that much, at least. But when he told her that he loved her, and offered himself as the solution to all her problems, she did not know how to resist. They could run away together. He could protect her from her enemies, take her out of their reach, marry her so that her father's claim on her lapsed.

Zuleika didn't see the contradictions or the logical lacunas in these promises; she just accepted them, as a starving man might accept a landmine if you painted it so it looked like a loaf. She told Sasim which room, in the three-storied edifice of the Blue Wheel, was her own, and she pointed out to him the cracks in the stonework by which an agile climber might reach her tiny window. She told him the window would be unlocked. She put herself in his hands.

He came to her that night, and they made love in reverent silence. The creaking of the bedframes in the rooms of the whores provided more than enough camouflage, so Zuleika could have abandoned herself to loud and indiscreet yells with no real risk, but her father's room was close, and she was fearful. Also, the whole thing was over so quickly that they seemed to move directly from the anticipation to the aftermath.

"When will we leave?" Zuleika asked Sasim, as they lay in each other's arms.

The question seemed to throw him. "When will we what?"

"When will we leave, Sasim? When will you take me away, and marry me?"

The boy was silent for a few heartbeats.

"It's not a good idea to rush into something like that," he told Zuleika at last. "I'll have to make arrangements, first. Find a house for us to live in, and explain to my father. And clothes. You'll need clothes."

"I've got clothes."

"I mean decent clothes. Suitable for a wife. What you wear makes you look like a whore."

Zuleika felt a shiver of presentiment. Her best friends were whores, and she saw no shame in what they did. In her opinion, formed by the daily experience of life in a brothel, only the men who first used whores and then spoke the word with such vehemence were to be despised. But how do you say that to a lover, with the blood of your own virginity drying on your thigh?

Zuleika knew she had taken an irrevocable step. She had given away for free something which figured very largely in her father's short-term profit forecasts, and when he found out, the shit would hit the fan so hard, the fan would probably be damaged beyond repair. She had to make good her escape before that happened, and Sasim was her only hope. She kissed him and embraced him and welcomed him into her a second time. Then, with many protestations of love, he exited via the window.

He came to her often in the weeks that followed, climbing in through the open window with unconscious grace, sliding into her bed and into her body as smoothly as an otter slides into a river. Their ardour was undiminished, their lovemaking hectic and joyous, but the small talk afterwards began to take an alarming turn. Was it true, Sasim asked, that Zuleika's father had a fortune salted away? Where did he keep it? Did the door of the inn open with a key alone, or was it secured from the inside by deadbolts or chains?

Zuleika actually knew the answers to all these questions; they were, respectively: a moderate fortune, under a loose stone in the kitchen floor which was too heavy for her to lift, and two deadbolts and a bar. But unnerved by Sasim's predatory fascination, she feigned ignorance. Sasim shifted tack. Perhaps, he said, Zuleika could make him a map of the inn's interior, showing the location of her father's room and of any storerooms she knew about. Perhaps, also, she could ask among the whores. Kish was certainly sampling his own wares, after all, and he might in the throes of drink or passion have let something slip.

Zuleika listened to these musings with a heavy heart. When the dark of the moon came next, bringing with it Vurdik the Bald and Ehara's regularly scheduled ordeal, she acknowledged what in her heart she already knew; that men are mostly shits, and that any hopes she harboured from Sasim were reeds already broken. Worse, she knew that if they carried on rutting like rabbits in the springtime, sooner or later the odds would catch up with her. If she got pregnant, she was truly dead.

From now on, she decided gloomily, she would bolt her window shutters and take a different route to market.

At this point, two things happened. The first was that Zuleika realised that she had to save herself by her own efforts. The second was that a *deus ex machina* popped up right inside her guard.

The *deus ex machina* was, embarrassingly enough, another man— as though Zuleika didn't already have a superfluity of those in her life. But this was no suitor, potential or actual—he came to stay at the inn of the Blue Wheel, a paying guest, and Zuleika, who was waiting tables when he walked into the room, knew from the sudden silence that this was a man of some importance.

She would not have known as much from the man's build or bearing, or anything else about him. He was of unremarkable height, had a bland and forgettable face which looked as though it had been sanded smooth, and wore a drab tan djelaba that had known better decades.

But her father's deference to the man was very marked. He was offered wine without ordering it, and the wine was the good stuff from one of the jars with a black line painted around its base. When he asked for a room, he was given the sky chamber, which faced the east on the inn's top floor and was the best and largest room the Blue Wheel could boast of.

Plucking up her courage, Zuleika asked one of the other patrons who the stranger was.

The man looked at her in surprise, as though she'd asked what day of the week it was, or the name of the city in which she lived.

"That's Imad-Basur."

The name was enough, without any qualification or description. Imad-Basur, the Caliph of Assassins, the black-apparelled teacher, was known everywhere, and commanded through fear a level of respect as great as any real caliph had ever enjoyed. Indeed, he numbered caliphs among his victims. He was feared by the rich and powerful, but also extensively employed by them, his immunity from harassment guaranteed by the secrets he held and by the vast resources of the shadowy organisation he commanded. Nobody knew how many assassins had studied under him, or where they went once they graduated from his tutelage; nobody wanted to find out in a way that involved knives, poison or strangling cords.

Zuleika's mind, when she heard that name, went into overdrive. Obviously, Imad-Basur had come to Ibu Kim to kill someone: and it must be a prestigious commission, or else he would have sent an underling. The Increate had dropped a priceless opportunity in her lap, and despite the dangers involved it would be madness for her to ignore it.

When everyone in the inn had retired for the night—even the whores clocked off at last when the moon rose—Zuleika knocked on the door of the sky chamber, and the stranger's voice, from the other side of the door, bade her enter.

She walked in, carrying a tray on which was a jug of wine and a bowl of candied fruit. "Compliments of the house," she said.

Imad-Basur was sitting in the window seat reading from a slender scroll. He appraised the girl for a few moments with a cool, neutral eye, before finally pointing to a table beside the bed. "Thank you," he said. "Set it down there."

Zuleika did, then she stood back and waited, arms at her sides, trembling slightly.

Imad-Basur stared at the small pile of coins that the girl had put down next to the tray, and then at the girl herself.

"What's this?" he asked her, a slight edge of irritation or perhaps of warning in his voice.

"I'd like to hire you!" Zuleika blurted. That was all she could manage to get out.

The assassin king stood. His movements were slow and measured, as though in everything he did he was enacting a pre-existing ritual. He walked across the room, picked up the coins and counted them. He weighed them in his hand. Meagre as they were, they represented the sum total of what Zuleika had been able to squirrel away over the past year.

"Seventeen coppers," Imad-Basur said, his voice like a knife in a sheath. He stared at the girl again. "You think a man's life is to be bought with such an amount?"

"Two men," Zuleika said. "I need two men killed."

There was a moment of strained silence, but then Imad-Basur laughed—a near-silent heave of chuckles that shook his frame, and went on and on until Zuleika almost screamed. This wasn't an answer! This wasn't anything!

"Two men," Imad-Basur agreed. "Of course. So long as the intended targets live close together, cut rates can usually be arranged. Who are they, if I may be permitted to ask?"

"My father," Zuleika said, relieved that they were getting down to specifics now. "He's the innkeeper here. And the saddler who lives across the yard."

"And what have they done to deserve death?" Imad-Basur pursued.

"My father wants to whore me out, and the saddler wants to

marry me."

"Contradictory goals," said the assassin.

"No. They've sealed the bargain already."

Imad-Basur crossed to the girl, took her hand and pressed the coins into it. "Go to bed, child," he said. "This will be our secret. I think it might go hard with you if your father found out you had spoken to me in this wise. But he won't. Go to bed. Sleep. Tomorrow is another day."

Zuleika stayed where she was. This was a blow, but she was not ready to admit defeat.

"So you won't take the commission?" she asked the assassin.

Imad-Basur chuckled again, his face no longer blank and bland but creased with amusement. "No. I won't take the commission."

"But you train assassins, too, don't you?"

"I've trained many."

"Then would this money be enough to buy a lesson?"

The smile slowly left Imad-Basur's face: he looked at the young girl with a sort of puzzlement. "No," he said. "But even if it were, I didn't come here to teach. And the first lesson wouldn't help you. Nor the second."

"Then give me the third lesson," Zuleika suggested.

Imad-Basur slowly shook his head. "No."

Zuleika opened her mouth to speak again, but the assassin king raised his hand in a forbidding gesture. "No more words," he said. "I have to meditate, and then I have to work—and after that, I intend to sleep. There's nothing I can do for you tonight."

Defeated, patronised, shamed, Zuleika strove to keep at least a little of her dignity. She nodded, bowed, and turned to the door.

When her hand was on the latch, Imad-Basur called out to her. "Wait."

Zuleika waited, her gaze still on the floor.

"Kill them yourself," Imad-Basur said. "Both of them. In different ways."

"And then?" Zuleika asked, her heart in her mouth.

"Then come to me, at my school in the mountains north of Perdondaris, and tell me how you achieved it. If the story pleases me . . ."

"Yes?"

"Then I may teach you some of the rudiments of the craft, although being a girl, you couldn't formally enrol as a student."

Zuleika looked up, and met the assassin's gaze one last time. "Thank you," she said.

"You're welcome."

The footing of their relationship seemed to have changed, in a way that defied definition. Zuleika struggled with various formulas of farewell.

"I pray the Increate smiles on your business here," she said at last.

Imad-Basur bowed to her. "And on yours," he said gravely.

Retiring to her room, Zuleika immediately set her mind to the task before her. She spared not a moment of compassion or doubt for her father. Her years of unpaid servitude quit any debt she owed him for her birth, and his coldblooded bartering over her body, as though it housed no soul, sealed his fate. For the saddler, she had some slight qualm, but it passed when she remembered his leering wink. Fuck him, and the dog that had sired him—this was about survival.

It was about a lot of other things, too, though, and the more Zuleika looked at the problem, the more intractable it seemed. She believed she could cut a throat, if she were brought to it, but to carry out two murders by two different methods was a problem of a different order. She knew, of course, why Imad-Basur had made that stipulation; it would be proof that she could approach the task of killing with the proper professional detachment. Anyone could kill in hot blood, without reasoned thought. But reasoned thought was what the assassin king insisted on.

Reason told Zuleika that she was unlikely to succeed in two assaults against men much bigger and stronger than she was.

So she lengthened the odds, and went for four.

She began with Sasim. The next night, for the first time in a week, she left the shutter of her window unbolted. She thought it might take more than that, but it was like putting out a bowl of jam to attract honey bees: Sasim hauled himself over her sill a little after midnight and stood looking down at her with a mixture of wariness and arrogance.

Zuleika beckoned him to her, and gave him what he'd come for. Then, when they lay spent in each other's arms, she told him about the saddler across the yard. "He wants to marry me, and he was boasting that I wouldn't need a dowry because he has so much wealth already. Sasim, he showed me a bag bigger than his belly—too heavy for me to lift, although a strong man like you could lift it. He said it was full of gold!"

Sasim was very excited at this news, and begged Zuleika to tell him where in the saddler's house the bag was hidden. "He didn't let me see where he took it from," she told him. "But I thought I'd go to him and ask to see the bag again—and this time, I'll spy on him when he goes to fetch it. And I'll make absolutely sure it's full of gold. Would that be a good thing to do?"

"An excellent thing!" Sasim assured her, and he embraced her warmly.

Got you, you avaricious little rodent, Zuleika thought—but she was overwhelmed by a sense of loss and longing when she thought of how she'd loved him and believed in him. Of the four, his death was the saddest for her to contemplate.

All that remained now was to wait. On the day before the moon's dark, Zuleika's father gave her the weekly bribe for sergeant Rhuk. She put the purse in her pocket and went to see, not the sergeant, but the saddler. He was hard at work in his shop, tanning hides in a vat as big around as a millwheel. He was astonished to see her, and even more astonished when she confessed to him, shyly and with many comely blushes, that she could not wait until the year was out. She had to be with him.

The saddler was both flattered and delighted—but saw the downside of this suggestion at once. "What about your father, though?" he grunted. "He'll be furious if you lose your maidenhead, and there'll be no dowry."

Zuleika reminded him that a woman and a man, if they are so minded, can disport themselves in many ways that offer no harm to a hymen. The saddler's mind filled at once with incandescent, carnal visions.

Zuleika said that she would slip away—alas, not that night, because she had too much work to do at the Blue Wheel; but the next night, for certain. She told him to leave his door unlocked at midnight, and to expect her soon after—and before she left, she made him show her how to find her way, in the dark, from the door to his bed. The saddler was minded to put the bed to good use right there and then, but Zuleika slipped out of his grasp. "I'm still a maiden," she reminded him, demurely but firmly. "I'd blush to take off my dress and stand naked in a full light. Put a candle by the street door tomorrow night, beloved, but make sure there's no lamp in your chamber!" Then she took to her heels.

From the saddler Zuleika went again to Sasim, whom she found loitering in one of his usual haunts. She put on a sad and chagrined face, and let him see that she was cast down. When he asked her what ailed her, she shook her head and blinked away imaginary tears.

"I've been a fool, Sasim," she said. "I went back to the saddler, and I told him I didn't believe his boasting. And he went to his workshop and reached into the biggest of the three vats there. That's where the bag was. But it wasn't full of gold."

She waited out his reaction, the sudden draining of hope from his face. Then she took his hand and pressed five of her father's ten dinars into it. "It was only silver," she said.

Sasim's face was a marvel to behold: he stared at the dinars with incredulous joy. "A bag full of silver!" he exclaimed, his voice trembling. "You did well, Zuleika. You did very well. It's not gold, but still . . . a whole bag full of silver! A man could live like a king!"

Sasim's delight abated a little when Zuleika told him that the layout of the saddler's house was very complicated. But when she offered to come along on the raid herself, and lead him to the right place, his doubts vanished and he embraced her with as much fervour as he ever had in her narrow bed.

"But tomorrow night is best," she told him. "It will be dark of the moon, and we won't be seen."

It took a little more persuasion—Sasim's impatience was hard to curb—but finally he accepted Zuleika's argument as good sense and agreed to wait a day. "Bring a knife," she told him as they parted. "If the saddler wakes, we'll have to kill him." Sasim assured her that he would come armed and ready.

Now, at last, Zuleika went to the guard station for her weekly encounter with Rhuk. Normally this was brief and straightforward: she handed over the silver, he counted it, gave her a curt nod, and she left.

This time, she handed over an empty purse. Rhuk held it upside down and shook it, as though the missing dinars might somehow have lodged in its lining. "What's this?" he growled.

"My father has decided he can get better protection from the watch post by the Eastern Gate," Zuleika said. "He won't pay you any more."

Rhuk gave her a look of glum ferocity. "Is he mad?" he asked her. "I know damn well he runs a gaggle of whores in that flea-pit. I can have him in chains before sunup if he tries to stiff me!"

Zuleika shrugged. "For whoremongering, he'd get a fine of five dinars. He thinks that's preferable to paying you ten a week."

Rhuk sighed, stood, and reached for his sword belt, which spent far more time hanging on a nail next to the door than it ever did around his waist. It clearly pained him to have to go to such wearisome lengths in order to administer justice.

"If you kill the cow," Zuleika said quickly, "you can't milk it afterwards. I know a way you could turn this to much better advantage, and profit both of us."

Rhuk sat down again, with an even bigger sigh. "I'm listening," he said.

Zuleika spoke with the captain for some several minutes, and left him well pleased with the intelligence she had provided. Returning to the inn, she went to Ehara—her final port of call—and asked her for a favour. She even told her a little about what she was planning, but omitted some salient details. Ehara was worried for the young girl, but agreed to fall in with her scheme for the sake of the friendship that had long existed between them. "But you need to watch yourself, sugar lump," she warned her. "If this goes bad on you, you'll have nowhere to run."

If it goes bad, Zuleika thought, *I won't live to see another morning.* It was all or nothing, and she felt that she could accept either of those extreme outcomes. It was the broad spectrum in between that terrified her.

That night she couldn't get to sleep at all. She thought of all the ways in which she could fail: of how flimsy her plan was, in the end, and how much it depended on her understanding of these men whose downfall she plotted. What if she was wrong about one or more of them? What if her system of classification still had some bumps and holes in it?

But she was in the hands of the Increate now—it was already much too late for doubts or second thoughts. She endured the night, and the day that followed, with all the stoicism a fourteen-year-old can muster. The sun rose and fell again; the moon absented herself. The night was a quilt as thick as wool.

Sasim was the first link in the chain, and Zuleika knew him, at least, very well indeed. So much so, that when he arrived at the back door of the inn a little after midnight, and confessed to her that he had forgotten to bring a knife, she handed him, without a word, a seven-inch carver from her father's kitchen on which she had put an edge that could have parted a flea's leg hairs. She also had a wooden mallet with iron bands wrapped around the head to weight it—a weapon her father kept stowed behind the bar for use on rowdy drunks. This she retained herself.

They went together to the saddler's house. Sasim was ready to pick the lock, but Zuleika tried the latch and the door opened at once. "Look," she said. "The fool has left his door unlocked!" She stood aside deferentially to let Sasim enter first, as was only right and proper, then once inside she led the way, not to the saddler's workshop, but to his bedroom. The door stood ajar: again, Zuleika opened it wide, and stood aside meekly to let Sasim precede her.

He stepped inside, and found himself in pitch darkness. He stumbled on a sandal that was lying on the floor, and the saddler, lying awake in an erotic fever, sat bolt upright at the sound.

"Sweetest of blossoms!" he cried. "Come to me!"

Sasim, when that huge bulk rose up before him in the dark, was almost petrified with fear. But he had a knife in his hand, and instinct took over. He ran at the saddler and stabbed him through the heart. The saddler fell back onto the bed, with a sound like a broken bellows.

Sasim had never killed a man before, and in the aftermath of the act he was rooted, for a moment, to the spot. In that moment Zuleika struck, hitting him a stunning blow on the head with the iron-chased mallet. Sasim collapsed in a heap on the blood-slicked floor.

Zuleika ran to the saddler's workshop and threw the five dinars she still had (the remainder of Rhuk's diverted bribe) down on the floor beside the big vat. This detained her only a second, but she could already hear Sasim stumbling and cursing behind her; she had only dazed him with the blow, not knocked him unconscious. She threw the window bolt and slipped out into the night.

Sasim had a shrewd suspicion that he had been betrayed, but he was still sold on the idea of the bag of silver in the saddler's shop. Lighting the lamp with trembling fingers, he found the largest vat demonstrably empty, but a scatter of silver dinars lying on the ground beside it.

These few coins told a clear story. Zuleika had been there before him, and had stolen the bag of silver!

Enraged beyond reason at this duplicity, Sasim found his way back to the door, staggered across the courtyard and rounded the façade of the inn until he stood below Zuleika's room. The shutters were ajar, and a lamp burned within. So the little double-crosser thought she was safe, did she? She was going to find out how wrong she was!

Sasim had made this climb a dozen times or more. Woozy though he was from the knock on the head, he made it again now, scaling the rough stones with the kitchen carver clenched in his teeth like a bandit in an old story.

He slammed the shutters wide and jumped over the threshold, transferring the knife to his hand so he could bellow out the words that boiled in his chest. "I'm going to slice you thinner than paper, you filthy little traitor!"

Vurdik the Bald did not enjoy being interrupted in the act of love, and it was considered prudent in the circles in which he moved to keep a sword or a dagger ready to hand even in the quietest moments. He was already rolling off Ehara's voluptuous body and reaching for the blade he'd left under the bed before Sasim had taken three steps into the room.

On the fourth step, as Sasim was slowing down in the realisation that he was not addressing Zuleika after all, the bandit's scimitar came up and knocked the carver from his hand with a ringing clash of steel.

There was no fifth step. The bandit's blade swept across Sasim's throat on the repass, and so keen was its edge that it all but decapitated him. The boy sank to his knees, his mouth opening and closing on voiceless protests and reproaches, and then fell face forward on the floor.

"Why did he call me a traitor?" Vurdik wondered, belatedly. "I don't even know him."

Down below, in the inn's kitchen, abandoned at this hour, Zuleika lit a lamp and waved it three times out of the window—left to right, right to left, left to right. Watching for her signal, Sergeant Rhuk ordered his men to move from hiding and surround the inn. The door of the Blue Wheel was knocked down with a wooden ram, and watch officers poured into the building.

In vain, Kishnothophur the innkeeper protested and remonstrated, pleading both that he was innocent and that he was up to date with his bribes. Rhuk ordered a search of the inn's many rooms, and although it yielded no whores (the whores having been warned by Zuleika to leave quietly on the midnight hour, except for Ehara who Zuleika swore to the officers was her mother), it did produce one bandit chieftain, just as Rhuk had been promised. Vurdik injured three officers before he was subdued, but finally a thrown club laid him low. He was arrested for multiple thefts and murders, and Kish for harbouring a known desperado.

The double execution was held on a market day, and was therefore very well attended. Seeing his daughter in the crowd, Kish cursed her with sobs for her treacherous heart and her whore's lies. Zuleika took out an apple and ate it slowly, in his sight, until the trapdoor fell open and the last breath caught in his throat.

The stone under the kitchen floor that was too heavy for Zuleika to lift offered no problem to a dozen determined women. Ehara counted Kish's hoard carefully, in full sight of the other whores, and then divided it into twelve equal portions. She wanted to give Zuleika a share, too, the more so because Zuleika had given her father's inn, in perpetuity, to Ehara to own: but sergeant Rhuk had been as good as his word, and passed on to the girl a full quarter of the reward he won for the capture of Vurdik. Zuleika already had all the money she needed, and a little over.

The time had come to part. Ehara asked Zuleika, not for the first time, to stay with her and be her daughter. Zuleika embraced the older woman fervently, and thanked her for all her many acts of kindness, but she had no intention of staying in Ibu Kim. Through many tears on both sides, she promised to return and visit often.

The next morning, on a fine camel bought with her share of the reward money, she left the city alone and took the direction of distant Perdondaris. Many things can befall a woman alone in the deep desert: Zuleika feared none of them so much as she feared dying in the city where she had been born.

Imad-Basur was surprised to see her, but listened with rapt attention to her story. He admitted, when it was done, that Zuleika had certainly succeeded in the challenge he had set her. Two men hanged, and two others dead by the blade: it was a tally that few of his students could claim for a single night's work.

"Then will you teach me?" Zuleika asked him, bluntly.

The caliph of assassins thought long before replying. To train up a woman in the arts of death! Such a thing defied all convention, all propriety. But clearly this was a most unconventional woman—and Imad-Basur had never thought propriety worth a turd.

"I will teach you," he told her. "And I believe you will make me proud."

The Cup Lands Upright, Part the Second

Zuleika surveyed the carnage in the legate's tent with a frown. An onlooker might have thought—assuming he lived long enough to think anything—that she was mourning the dead. She wasn't; she was only considering what had to be done next, and how best to do it.

If the legate's body was discovered, the situation would quickly become impossible. Not only would she herself be killed for what she had done, but the other concubines and their children would soon fall victim to sultan Hakkim's edict. Other people besides the guard captain must have seen the messenger arrive; they would either return to Bessa or send a rider there to know the sultan's pleasure. That must not be allowed to happen. And if it was to be prevented, Zuleika had to carry out a lot more killings in very short order. Doing so was going to present a serious logistical challenge.

There were some thirty guards in the caravan, and they were widely scattered along its length. Some had presumably been posted as sentries, a good way out from the camp. They all had to be dealt with, and in such a way that none of them were forewarned by seeing or hearing the deaths of the others. Zuleika was good, but she wasn't that good. *Nobody* was that good. However the feat was to be accomplished, she was going to need help: and she knew in what quarter it must be found.

Having reasoned the thing through to this point, Zuleika forgot all doubts and equivocations and got down to business. She dragged the bodies of the guard captain and the messenger into a corner of the tent, out of any line of sight from the entrance. The legate's corpse she propped up in a chair, with his back to any incoming traffic.

Next, she repaired her own appearance. She used what was left of the massage oils to remove En-Sadim's heart's blood from her hands and face, her bare breasts and belly, very thankful that she had disrobed before she began to go to work on him. Wiping her hands dry on the messenger's cloak, she dressed quickly. Though there were some dark red stains on her leather sandals that she could not remove, she was confident that she could pass a casual inspection.

She retrieved the sultan's letter from where it had fallen. Zuleika had never learned to read, and the import of this fell heavily on her now. If En-Sadim had not insisted on hearing the letter read aloud, all of this would have transpired very differently.

She tucked the scroll into her bodice and stepped boldly out of the tent. Letting the flap fall to behind her, she stood there, framed against the pure white of its fabric, as the guards outside turned to look at her.

Zuleika was breathing heavily, and her face glistened with sweat. She might have disguised these things, but instead she exaggerated them: under the circumstances, they would be seen as signs of passion rather than clues to murder. She looked like a woman who had just surfaced from the most abandoned and extreme throes of love. She met the gaze of each guard in turn, without shame, before finally and belatedly bowing her head—the wanton, reassuming the demure look of a respectable woman. She shuddered as though the cooling evening air, hitting her super-heated flesh, caused an involuntary chain reaction.

"They are discussing," Zuleika said, her voice thick, "things. Important things. They don't want to be disturbed."

She held the pose a moment longer. Her hands smoothed the fabric of her dress, as though unaware that in doing so they emphasised the curve of waist and thigh.

She walked away, swaying her hips in age-old and unambiguous provocation. Every eye was on her, and every thought was "lucky bastard!"

So much for the circus. It would hold for a while, but not for long. Sooner or later, some situation would arise that compelled one or other of the guards to seek his captain's approval for something, or to take orders from the legate, or consult his wishes in some trifle. Zuleika had to be done before any of those things happened.

She went to Gursoon, who was talking to the children at the

campfire—telling them another story, perhaps. There was really no other choice. Perhaps there were other women in the harem who were Gursoon's equal in intelligence, but there were none who carried so much authority. Only Gursoon could make the other women act within the narrow window that they had.

The older woman saw Zuleika approaching, and moved up a little to make room for her at the fire, but Zuleika did not sit. She handed Gursoon the letter. "I think you should read this," she said.

Gursoon unwound the scroll and read it in silence. Zuleika waited.

It was impossible to tell, from the woman's face, how she felt about the letter's contents. She remained impassive; her expression and her breathing did not change. When she had reached the bottom, she read it again, the second time more quickly with her eyes flicking from line to line.

Finally she rolled the letter up again and tapped it against her knee.

"Yes," she said. "Thank you for showing me, Zuleika. That's interesting news indeed. Soraya, it's time for bed now. Take the younger children to their tents and see them settled in."

Zuleika could never tell the children apart, but the young girl Gursoon was addressing identified herself by being the first to protest. "But you didn't finish the story, auntie! And the sun is still up!"

"The sun will go down soon enough," Gursoon said, grimly. "Do as you're told, dear. Now. And tomorrow . . . well, tomorrow we'll see how it all came out."

The children were gathered up and led away. All but one—a skinny whippet of a boy with a face of almost feminine beauty, who was staring at the two women with naked suspicion in his eyes.

"What's happening?" he demanded.

"Nothing," said Zuleika. "Go away, boy."

The brat stayed where he was.

"Jamal," Gursoon said, a little more gently, "go and look after the little ones. They're still afraid, and it will comfort them to see you watching over them."

The boy hesitated a few moments longer, his gaze flicking from one of the women to the other, and Zuleika pondered the wisdom of sending him running with a smack around the head. But he left of his own accord at last, and she turned her attention back to Gursoon.

"Where did you get this?" Gursoon asked her, holding up the letter.

"From En-Sadim," Zuleika said, "who had just received it from the sultan's messenger. I killed them both—along with the guard captain. As things stand right now, nobody but you and me knows what's in that letter."

Gursoon nodded slowly, her brow creased in thought. "If the bodies are found . . ." she said.

". . . then we're all lost. Yes. We can't go on, and we can't go back. Only death waits in either direction. The guards have to die, and we have to leave. To go where they can't find us."

Gursoon was silent for a few moments longer. Zuleika also said nothing, allowing the older woman time to check her logic.

"You're right," Gursoon said at last. She shot Zuleika a shrewd glance. "A question, dear, before we begin. How does a young woman kill three armed men?"

"Clean living and regular exercise, auntie. Also, five years of training in the arts of murder."

Gursoon smiled thinly, mulling over the holes in this answer. "And can you kill the rest of them?" she asked at last.

Zuleika didn't bother to boast or dissemble. "Only if they have no idea what's happening. These are trained soldiers, and some of them have bows and slings as well as swords. The last one has to fall before the first knows what's happening. That's the only way."

Gursoon immediately rattled off some names. "Nafisah. Rihan. Firdoos. Dalal. Umayma. Zeinab. These women will be the most useful to you. But I don't know whether they'd be able to do any of the killing themselves. What we need, I think, is a stratagem which allows you to kill one man at a time, while keeping the others in ignorance of his fate." A thought occurred to her, and she looked up at the setting sun. "There's no way that this can be done until darkness falls," she said. "That gives us half an hour. Come. Let's spread the news and build our trap."

Each of the named women, and three more besides, was approached and recruited. All were distraught and terrified when they heard the news—Rihan fainted, and Umayma vomited out of pure shock and terror—but all declared their willingness to help. Gursoon was no fool, and had factored into her choice the fact that all these women had children in the caravan. She knew they'd fight to the death, if necessary.

Sitting a little aside from the fire, with En-Sadim's tent directly in their view, they discussed various plans before settling on the simplest.

The sun sank slowly behind the horizon as they talked, and Zuleika stared with unblinking eyes at the entrance to the legate's pavilion, knowing full well that if any man entered, all bets were off—in that case she would leap up, kill the nearest guard and take his sword. What happened after that would be whatever the Increate willed, but it would certainly involve widespread slaughter.

Briefed and prepared, the women went to their places.

The guards who were actually on duty, and therefore stood alone at their stations, were targeted first. Each was approached by one of the women and told a tearful story about a snake in one of the tents which might or might not be venomous. Happy to take the role of rescuer, and to show off in front of these beautiful but inaccessible ladies, the man would usually need little persuasion to leave his post for a moment or two and step into the nearby tent—where Zuleika, standing inside the door with dark-adjusted eyes, drew a sword across his throat. Two or three of the women then helped her to hold the man immobile and silent while he died, and two or three more added the corpse to the growing pile at the back of the tent. Some of the women wept after the first and second killings, but by the third they were inured to the work and put their backs into it quietly and efficiently.

There were now two groups of enemies to consider: the knot of a dozen or so off-duty soldiers who were talking and dicing around their own fire, and the sentries who had previously been despatched by Captain Numair to remoter distances from the camp's perimeter.

The sentries had to come first, Zuleika decided. They would certainly see and hear any disturbance in the camp, and would have far too many options as to how to react; whether they took flight to Bessa, came riding in to attack or simply fired on the women from the dark, all Hell would be out for noon.

Zuleika was hampered by not knowing how many sentries there were, but she had a very good memory and made a rough guess based on the faces that were missing from around the fire. She armed her assistants with swords and daggers, but instructed them to keep the weapons well hidden. They should only be used if the relaxing guards ventured into En-Sadim's tent, discovered its grisly contents and came armed against them. She hoped that she would return before that could happen.

Walking quickly through the deepening dark, Zuleika headed out from the camp and then circled it at a half-mile's distance. She had tried, while the sun was still up, to locate by sight the best places for sentries to be posted, and she headed for these first. She was lucky three times, finding her quarry each time before he found her, and despatching him quickly. A prolonged search failed to find a fourth. She returned to camp, carrying with her three bows and three quivers of arrows.

The silent combat now entered its final stage. She handed two of the bows to two of her assistants. The rest were already armed with bows taken from the men who had been despatched in the tent. The last bow Zuleika kept for herself.

The women dispersed and took up their positions in the darkness around the guards' campfire, fifty yards or so away from it in all directions. Zuleika counted the men still seated around the fire: there were fourteen, tightly grouped. She drew back the bowstring, took careful aim, and fired.

Her first arrow took a luckless soldier through the throat. She nocked a second immediately and fired again, but the first death was the signal and now arrows were whistling in on the men from all sides. Most went wide, but that didn't matter—the important thing was to let the guards know that they were surrounded, so that they'd kick out the fire and take up defensive positions. This would have been indubitably the right thing to do if they were indeed facing a hostile host sitting out in the dark of the desert, but Zuleika, firing from right on their doorstep, killed three more while they were doing it.

The extinguishing of the fire was the second signal. The waiting women raised a fearful noise, filling the air with high-pitched battle cries. The soldiers, embattled and terrified, returned fire with bows and slings, though they could see no enemy. Zuleika, meanwhile, drew sword and dagger and walked among them.

The dark was almost absolute. The women's fire, a little way off, was still lit, but nobody had been tending it and it had died down to a red glow. The desert night was moonless, and the stars hoarded their glimmer for themselves. Zuleika's blades flicked at throats and poked at hearts: man after man fell, seeing her only when it was too late.

The last three fights were the hardest. The men's eyes had accommodated to the dark by this time, and they'd realised that they were facing a single opponent close to hand as opposed to an army firing from a distance. The three men threw themselves on Zuleika at once, and she was so busy defending herself against their flashing blades that she could make no headway against them. She saw an opening, leaped in and stabbed one of the three through the throat, but a sword hilt smacked her in the side of the head and she fell. The body of the man she had just killed fell across her, pinning her.

She saw the sword reversed in its owner's hand and raised above her, ready to plunge into her chest.

Something shot out of the night, like a darker line drawn across the darkness: the soldier fell, with a small grunt of surprise.

The sole surviving guard might still have pressed his attack and slain her, but finding himself alone he turned and ran. Zuleika's dagger took him low in the back.

Climbing to her feet, still a little groggy from the blow to her temples, she examined the corpse of the man who had almost killed her. In a deep wound in his forehead she found the slingshot stone, still embedded in the hole it had made in his skull.

The boy Jamal stepped out of the darkness, his sling in his hand, and stared down at his handiwork. Triumph fought with sick horror in his face.

"You have my thanks," said Zuleika quietly.

"You should have told me," the boy said, his tone cold. "They're all traitors and jackals. I wish I could have killed more of them."

Then he burst into tears.

When the other women ventured to approach at last and view the outcome of the skirmish, they found Zuleika cradling the wildly weeping boy to her breast, her face—for the first time in all of this—betraying something like alarm.

THE TALE OF THE LIBRARIAN OF BESSA

There was once a young woman who—having a deep and strong affinity for the written word—disguised herself as a boy and petitioned the chief librarian of the city of Bessa for paid employment.

The work that was available was menial at best, consisting mainly of the sweeping of floors and the refilling of ink wells in the Library's scriptorium, but the woman was more than satisfied with this. She was of a solitary nature, and often uncomfortable or embarrassed around other people. This natural reticence was made worse by the fact that she had been blessed with the gift of foreknowledge, the sight. She could not remain long in peoples' company without her senses being assailed by the tangled webs of their past, and the myriad branching roads of their possible futures.

In the company of books, by contrast, she felt a serenity which she could hardly describe: as though all the contradictory forces which she experienced when she was forced to interact with those around her reached a perfect and timeless equilibrium.

She had come to the city of Bessa along with her mother, who had since died, leaving the young woman not quite destitute but certainly with few and straitened resources. So the work at the Library was in many ways

No, this won't do at all. It doesn't feel right.

It's so much harder to tell this story than the others. That's ridiculous,

I know it is, but the sense of solidity, of purpose and direction that I find in other people's lives is gone in an instant when I contemplate my own. It feels as though I'm describing patterns of light in water, that change a hundred times in the space of a heartbeat.

But let me draw breath, for a moment or two, and try again.

THE TALE OF THE LIBRARIAN OF BESSA

The Library sometimes reminded Rem of a city deep underground. It was cool, hushed, lit by far distant skylights: a city of labyrinthine streets through which she moved in reverential silence, the sole human citizen, a city of towering shelves thronged with scrolls which leaned over her as she walked, watching her progress with infinite, aged patience.

Now, she strode swiftly beneath their comforting gaze. Her gait, the way she carried herself, had changed since she first came to the Library. She had arrived awkward and shuffling, dressed in the shabby grey garments of a sweeper boy. It was ten years since that day; now, Rem wore the red sash and cap of the Third Librarian, and walked with an unassuming pride.

She reached the end of a long avenue of shelves, turned right, and instantly came upon a prone figure on the floor. She had grown used to encountering the Second Librarian, Warid, stretched out and semi-comatose after a night of heavy drinking, in odd places in the Library's corridors and reading rooms. In earlier days, she used to trip over him, earning an easily dodged swipe and a string of curses for her carelessness. She had soon learnt, however, to check the path before her for his presence. Now she stepped neatly round him, giving him as wide a berth as she could manage. He gave a gentle groan as she walked past, and rolled over.

He was a decent man really, aside from his gambling and drinking, and although he did no good to the Library ostensibly under his care, at least he could not be said to do it any harm. On the whole, Rem had grown rather fond of him—he was a rare human companion in her world of parchment and stone and, more importantly, a wonderfully quiet one, making few demands on her conversational skills.

And his incompetence was a blessing to her. Every duty in which he failed was one where she could succeed in his stead, every task he neglected one which she could fulfil. His complete lack of professional pride had delivered the entire Library into her care. She was its custodian. Sometimes, even now, the joy of that thought would well up in her so strongly, she had to fight back the urge to laugh. Rem was a Librarian, and the title fitted her perfectly, the knowledge of it becoming as intimate to her as her own name, her own skin.

She continued past the Second Librarian, walking on until she came to a small, ornately carved wooden door. Here she gave a respectful knock, then entered without waiting for an answer—it was always a long time coming. The First Librarian hadn't even noticed that she had come in. He was bent over his rare scrolls as usual, attempting to conquer his trembling hands long enough to patch their torn parchment. Rem coughed politely as she approached, and he looked up at her with his watery eyes folded in wrinkled skin. "Ah, Rem." He paused, as if collecting his thoughts, but then slowly bent his head back to his work, seeming to forget her presence entirely.

Rem coughed again, gently. "Sir," she said, "I see you have finished repairing the embossed and illuminated scrolls which arrived last month from Ard-al-Raqib. I've come for the key to the Rare Texts room, to replace them there."

The First Librarian appeared to consider this pronouncement. "Mmmmm . . . You know, Rem, the Third Librarian is not supposed to have access to the Rare Texts room. That sort of responsibility is a little above your station yet, I think . . . good initiative, lad, very good. But I think this task falls to my son, rather than you. Still, still . . . I am glad you reminded me. You just run along and ask him to sort it out now, yes?"

"Sir," Rem replied promptly, "it is your son who has just sent me to you with the order that I should retrieve the key and give it to him. He is at the market currently, considering the purchase of some new inks reputed to be uncommonly resistant to fading, but he would like to start moving the scrolls immediately on his return. You know," she added after a short hesitation, wondering if this was not going too far, "how dutiful the Second Librarian is in his work, and the pains he takes to complete everything in a timely fashion."

"Ah! Very well, very well. That's commendable . . . splendid. Here is the key . . ."

The old man reached hesitantly for a drawer in the front of his desk, and drew out a thin copper key with shaking fingers. Rem took it smoothly from his hands and, bowing slightly, turned and marched out.

This kind of deception came naturally to her now; nothing would ever get done without it. It was the same when she travelled to Perdondaris and Gharia in search of new texts, acquisitive missions supposedly reserved for the Second Librarian alone.

In other respects she lied by omission—neither of the other Librarians were aware that she was slowly putting the scrolls into alphabetical order by section. Nor did they know that many of her own stories and poetry now had a place in the Library, their bright new parchment glowing conspicuously amongst the swathes of ancient, yellowed scrolls.

They certainly did not know that Rem slept in the Library every night. She had done this for the first time one night a few months after her mother died. She placed her bedroll at the end of a small cul-de-sac of shelves devoted to sacred texts. They surrounded her as she slept, a sensation she found oddly comforting.

It was after this that it occurred to her that the Library was a city, and she felt herself for the first time to be one of its true inhabitants. Scholars came and went. The First and Second Librarians arrived in the morning and departed in the evening to the small house they shared on the edge of Bessa. Only Rem wandered the Library's passageways at night, when the stillness was alive with the whispers of the scrolls as they rustled soft messages to one another in the dark.

She stopped paying the rent on the room she used to share with her mother. She never slept there again. Increasingly, she began to notice that after a trip to the market or the Jidur, where she went sometimes to listen to the debates, a subtle change would come over her on returning to the Library. Her shoulders would relax, almost imperceptibly. She would release a breath she did not know she held, or feel a lightening in her step. She did not recognize this change at first; she had not experienced it since she was very young. Later on, much later, it came to her that it was a homecoming she felt, as she pushed open the great doors and slipped into the cool and quiet of the Library once more. She felt as if she was coming back to a place where she absolutely, unquestioningly belonged.

Lately, however, her homecomings had an urgency to them, each one heralded by a sweet and desperate relief. Returning to the Library now, Rem felt that it was a sanctuary as well as a home, suddenly wonderful not only for itself, but for the protection it seemed to offer from the world outside it. That world was changing in rapid and sinister ways.

It had all begun a few months before, with the appearance of a new speaker in the Jidur. His name was Hakkim Mehdad. The doctrine of Asceticism which he preached had never been particularly welcome in Bessa before, its inhabitants being too fond of their brothels and drinking houses to embrace any philosophy of abstinence. Bessan preachers tended to focus their attention on more exciting religions, ones that would be likely to draw a large following. The listeners in the Garden of Voices, however, would never embrace a creed on its own merits alone, valuing a convincing performance above all moralising and painstaking argument. The teachings declaimed in the Jidur soared and fell on the voices of their speakers. And, though it had never happened before, the odious doctrine of Asceticism was now placed in the mouth of one whose voice could kindle it into beauty.

The evening she first saw Hakkim in the flesh, Rem was walking through the crowds of people gathered in the square on her way back to the Library. She noticed as she passed a group of men dressed in long black robes, an unusual sight in Bessa at any time, and especially in the oppressive heat of summer. They were clustered around a tall, wiry man, also cloaked in black, who had just mounted the podium. They seemed to be his disciples, and were watching him with rapt attention. Those standing near them were eyeing the dark figures a little uneasily. At first, Rem barely registered any of this, perceiving Hakkim as merely another actor in the street theatre of the debates. Then he began to speak.

"Consider the desert *Nihareem*," he said. "These evil sprites confuse the weary traveller, turning him from his path with their bright lights at night. Deceived into thinking he has found a town or caravanserai, he strikes out towards these lights, only to lose himself utterly in the vast desert, to die of thirst or founder in quicksand."

The man's voice rang out across the square. Although he did not shout, his words cut through the noise of the Jidur, making the sounds of both crowd and debaters alike appear a dull murmur by comparison. People started to pool around him, drifting away from the other speakers towards this compelling new presence.

The unlucky preachers glared at Hakkim for depriving them of their audience, yet even they listened to him. They were drawn in by his utter conviction, bent around the blunt steel of his certainty, in spite of themselves. Words of refutation or attack died on their lips. Rem, too, was arrested by some indefinable quality in his tone. Passion was in his words like oil in a wick, saturating them with dormant fire.

"These lights are beautiful. They are full of promise. Yet it is their very beauty which reveals their deception. It is their very promise which warns the wise to shun and fear them. So is it with the pleasures of this world. Wine, gambling, naked flesh, these are base desires, the lesser lights which blind us to our proper path. They are snares! Only by turning from their poisoned glow may we perceive unhindered the safe and uncorrupted path!"

His voice dropped to a whisper. Heads craned towards him as he went on, "For there is another light, my friends. A greater, brighter, purer light, a hundred times lovelier than those lesser lights which entrap us. This is the light of the One Truth. This, and only this, is the light which will guide us to safety through the desert, the light which illuminates our proper way. So why, you may ask me, have you not seen this light? Why have you had no glimpse of its beauty? Why have you not basked in its transcending beam?"

Now his eyes flashed sparks, and the flame caught. The fire sleeping in his voice woke to a roar.

"Because you are lost in the desert! Because you are deceived by the *Nihareem*! Abandon your drinking, leave your gambling halls, conquer your licentiousness and your lust! You are only turning aside from death. You are only spurning the temptations of demons! And when you have forsaken these things, think, only think, what you will gain in return . . ."

Hakkim's voice sank to an ecstatic murmur as he described the joys of his One Truth, and Rem glanced at the faces around her. Not everyone in the crowd, transfixed as they were, was reacting well to his words. She could see several people muttering uncertainly to one another, and not a few smirks and grimaces at the notion of conquering licentiousness and lust. It was nearing midday, the time when life in the hot city slowed to a crawl, and the square was shimmering in the summer heat. The sun stewed in the sky. It was one of those days when the heat boils and thickens in the air, begging to be lanced by a storm. It sapped people's spirits, making them weak and tired and angry. To Rem's right, a plain looking man with sweat patches under his arms shouted, "Why not leave off eating and drinking as well, and have an end to it? Won't be any future for humanity anyway, since we're forbidden to procreate."

The audience had swelled by this time to such a size that when it happened, the people standing at the front had no idea. Insulated by a growing cushion of onlookers, they were aware of nothing more than a slight stir in the crowd, an intensification in the background noise which always filled the Jidur.

Hakkim's voice ran on, sinuous and smooth, now a sensuous whisper, now a bright clarion call, as his disciples oozed like tar through the crowd, congealed around the man at Rem's side—not quick enough to startle him—and then closed in. The whole thing seemed melted by the heat into a warped dream: their movement, a viscous fluidity, the man's face waking into slow surprise, the grunts of his pain.

Rem watched them beating him, too horrified to cry out. A sickening sense of helplessness overwhelmed her. She stood shackled to the spot until the dark figures turned and stalked off, leaving the bloodied man curled in a broken ball on the ground. People around her began to shout and point; some men started to give chase, but checked themselves and hung back, or went instead to fetch a doctor for the man, who had begun to groan and stir. The Ascetics left the Jidur unchallenged, in the same silence in which they had conducted their attack. And through it all, like music, Hakkim's voice flowed. His tone now was one of profound and terrible pity, as if he would wrap his listeners in his arms.

"Oh, my brothers! Oh, my friends! How I wish that you could see the light of the Truth as I have seen it! It would transform you!" Rem ran from the square in disgust.

She wanted to forget it, to dismiss the entire incident from her mind as an aberration, never to be repeated. But something had broken, that day in the Jidur. Not the hoped-for storm, come to lance the boil of summer, but some foul, rotten thing, grown fat on darkness and secrecy. Its belly had been slit, and now the contagion was pouring out. At first she saw the black-robed figures only with the inner eye of foresight, but soon they were seeping through the streets of Bessa like ink spilled across parchment.

They were mostly young men, the sons of butchers and weavers who had always felt destined for greater things than a career in their father's shop. They drank Hakkim's words, sneaked to the Jidur against their parents' wishes, and began refusing wine at dinner, rising long before the rest of their household to sit in silent meditation.

A little oddness in a growing boy was to be expected. Youth came with confusion and frustration—such things were natural, and would find an outlet, sometimes in a drunken brawl, sometimes in a little religious eccentricity. But Hakkim was a prophet. He looked at a thousand separate wellsprings of uncertainty and rage and saw a river in potentia. All it lacked was a direction in which to flow. Asceticism had no God, yet in its name he performed miracles, bringing a new nation out of the midst of another nation: a young nation, dressed in black, united by a single purpose.

The purpose was blood. The Ascetics shunned the pleasures of the world, but hounded those who lived by them. Gambling halls were torched and inns attacked, their customers pelted with stones. Dancing girls were followed on their way home from work. Soon, no woman dared to walk alone after nightfall with her arms and head uncovered. It was said that Bokhari Al-Bokhari had intensified the security around his own harem. A publican was found hanged from the sign outside his establishment. Men and women who lay with others of their own sex were also targeted. The Ascetics practised strict abstinence, and considered all sexual practices apart from those conducted between husband and wife to be sinful and abhorrent.

When the attacks began, groups of women would congregate on their way to the market, gossiping in hushed, fearful tones about the latest atrocity. Then the Ascetics began to patrol the city by day, walking in groups of three or four and pausing to listen in to conversations. Suddenly, no one talked in the streets any more.

They were not loutish; the violence of the Ascetics was silent and whisper-swift, begun with the noise of soft footsteps at the top of some narrow street, and ended with the discreet swish of a blade wiped clean on a fold of dark cloth. It was this silence, this imperturbable silence, that Rem found most chilling about them. She had lived with silence for most of her life, but this was different. Her silence, the silence she loved, hummed with mute voices; it was the silence at the end of a song, the silence of lovers in the moments just before and just after coupling. The Ascetics were silent in the way of dead things, and Rem felt this and recoiled from it in dread.

The fear that filled Bessa had even permeated the thick stone walls of her Library, usually so reassuringly cut off from the city and its problems. The First Librarian came out more and more often from his office and tottered around anxiously at odd moments, looking for his son. Several times now Rem had been forced to drag the Second Librarian into the Rare Texts room to hide him from his father, meeting the First Librarian with an excuse about a purchase at the market, or an unexpected meeting with one of the sultan's legates. The First Librarian was well-wadded with delusions, but even he was not quite so oblivious that he had no inkling of the real reasons behind Warid's long absences from the Library, and the fact that Rem did most of his work.

Deep down, in some dark, shameful little chamber of his mind such as is reserved by cuckolds for the knowledge of their wives' exploits, he knew that Warid had a certain reputation. He had managed to ignore it up until now, but suddenly, a certain reputation was a dangerous thing to have in Bessa, and the consciousness of encroaching threat had woken him to panicked activity. Every week now brought some story of an inveterate gambler beaten and left to bleed in the street, or a collapsed drunk gutted in his sleep, gashed throat gaping as if in terror at some dream from which he would never awake. So the First Librarian would search for his son, accept Rem's lies with nervous acquiescence and, on those few occasions when he found Warid sober enough to talk, clasp him in trembling arms, tears leaking from the folds of skin around his eyes, and quaver vaguely, "You will be careful, won't you, my boy? These are dangerous times, you know . . . dangerous times. . . ."

The Second Librarian would brush him off in an embarrassed fashion, breaking out of his embrace with a cough and a muttered, "Yes, yes, of course, father. Don't fuss so." His behaviour did not alter in the least. He continued, reckless and unrepentant as ever, in spite of the First Librarian's fears. Rem watched these repeated scenes between father and son with disapproval and apprehension. As the Ascetics' violence escalated, the number of people frequenting Bessa's drinking houses and gambling halls was falling rapidly, and men like Warid were starting to stand out. Her more pointed warnings were met with a similar rebuttal.

"Oh calm down," he would say. "Can't put everything on hold for a few hooligans. Stop nagging. I'm not afraid of them."

The Second Librarian was not afraid for himself, but he had cause to be. Nor was he the only one at risk. Rem began to insist that he come into the Library through the side entrance rather than the main doors, and took to hiding him more carefully when he was passed out drunk, far from the eyes of any scholars who might happen to be passing. The Library had become the eye of some inconceivable storm, and she clung to it even harder than before, stalking its corridors and guarding the fragile equilibrium of its peace with a ferocious intensity.

And then one evening the storm shifted its ground, as she had always known it would.

Rem was sitting outside on the Library's imposing marble steps like a sentry on duty, soaking up the last vestiges of heat from the stone. Inside, the First and Second Librarians were asleep. It was long past closing time, and she should have woken them hours ago so that they could go home. But instead, she had left the Second Librarian where he lay on the floor, and let his father doze off in front of his desk, his evening cup of hibiscus tea untouched at his side.

She sat gazing at the stars with an expression of intense concentration such as is often worn by people lost in thought, so that afterwards, an observer, had anyone been around to see, would have said that she seemed to be watching for the faint plume of smoke that curled in an elegant cursive towards the darkening bowl of the sky. As it was, the only sign she gave of having noticed the fire at all was a slight stiffening in her posture, perhaps merely a reaction to the growing cold.

After a few minutes, she rose from where she had been sitting and walked deliberately over to the well in the square in front of her, where a few women had gathered to draw water for the evening.

"Look at that smoke," she said as she approached them, pointing in the direction of the plume. The women glanced up with worried faces. "Must be another attack," one said quietly. "That's the fifth this week!"

"It could easily catch, especially in this dry weather," Rem said. "I'm going to see what I can do to help." A couple of the women went with Rem, while others ran to fetch husbands and neighbours. As they hurried through the city, they were joined by more and more people, flocking towards the source of the smoke. Some carried jugs of water, running with care to avoid spilling any.

Rem began to see confusion on the faces around her: the smoke was coming from the outskirts of Bessa, not the pleasure district. The western edge of the city was a respectable residential area, a neighbourhood of lower-order dignitaries and the better class of merchant. The frightened murmuring of the crowd increased.

"They're targeting people's *homes* now?"

"But this is a good area. What could they want with anyone here?"

"Oh, we all know *that*," a large woman dressed in orange interrupted loudly. "We all know what they're doing *here*." She glanced around to make sure that she had people's interest, but did not continue, only raising her eyebrows significantly.

The street was becoming thick with smoke, forcing many to turn back, coughing and choking. With the fire this far advanced, there would not be much left to save.

Rem pressed onwards, following the white tendrils which threaded with lazy menace around her feet, as if to trip her. Speculation was growing in the crowd. Whose house could it be? Were they at home when the fire started? Were they still alive?

For her own part, Rem already knew the answers to these questions. She had seen this fire in her mind's eye long before she noticed the smoke in the sky. The houses around her were already starting to look familiar, resolving into forms which she passed frequently enough that their new shroud of smoke rendered them uncanny, like the faces of friends seen under water.

She rounded the last corner to see the First Librarian's house ablaze, flames leering from its windows. A circle of people had gathered at a safe distance, shielding their eyes and monitoring the progress of the fire. No one wanted their own house to catch a stray spark. Rem could hear Warid's name being muttered, in tones ranging from pity to malicious satisfaction. The orange woman nudged her arm.

"I only pity his poor father," she said. "That reprobate son of his knew what he was letting himself in for, but what did his father do to deserve it? The poor old man had no idea. Where is he going to go now? It's a mercy they weren't at home—no question where the son is, that drunken lecher. Now I'm not saying he deserved it, but . . ."

The woman carried on speaking, but Rem no longer heard her. She was staring at the burning house, the mesmerising flicker of the flames, but her gaze passed through it, penetrating the crumbling walls to scrutinise their own past, and the hearts and minds of those who had burned them. She winced as the full horror of what she was seeing came clear to her.

"They didn't come for Warid," she whispered. Then, louder, cutting the woman beside her off in mid-squawk. "You're wrong. You're all wrong. They didn't come for Warid. They came for his father. They came for the First Librarian."

The people around Rem stared at her as if she was mad, but she didn't notice. She was running over all she knew about the Ascetics in her head, hoping desperately that she was wrong. They scorned the pleasures of the world. They worshipped a single truth, against which all other truths were counted deceit, and what they counted deceit, they burned. No, she wasn't wrong. In fact, she had been a fool not to see it before.

By this point she had turned away from the burning house, was already shoving through the crowd, running back the way she had come. She had thought the Ascetics would target Warid, had even expected them to, but she had been mistaken. They had come for his father. His father, the head of the Library, the archivist of ten thousand different truths, all clamouring at once. The Library in Bessa was a paradise; it had more voices within its walls than the Jidur. But as she ran home, Rem could see it for the first time as it must appear to Hakkim: a desert of dry parchment, filled with *Nihareem*.

Her first priority, obviously, was to save the scrolls. How exactly this was to be done was a difficult question. Back in the Library, Rem fought tears as she gazed at the crowded shelves, knowing beyond certainty that she must empty them, and as quickly as possible.

There was no point in going to the sultan for protection. Al-Bokhari was as worried as anyone by the Ascetics' violence, but the strength of his armed guard was focused on keeping peace in the streets and maintaining the security of his palace. Besides, he was too concerned about his own position to spare much thought for the health of civic institutions. In the Jidur, Hakkim's speeches had taken a turn deeply disquieting to Bessa's ruler. His general condemnation of excess and pleasure was becoming more pointed and personal in import, containing dark references to a certain great man's fondness for drink, or his wild feasting, his revelries which lasted for days on end. He had recently delivered an attack on the evils of Bessa's brothels in which he singled out for special mention Al-Bokhari's own seraglio, with its decadent cohort of three hundred and sixty five concubines.

All this was bordering on the treasonous, but Hakkim's invectives were unsurprisingly popular with an audience of poor shopkeepers and artisans. Al-Bokhari had many faults, not least the free sway he gave to his appetites, but he was no fool, and he knew full well that the last thing the Ascetic cause needed was martyrs. So Hakkim and his followers were left, for the time being, to continue their activities largely unhindered.

And so was Rem.

She had decided from the start that it would be better not to confide her decision to the First and Second Librarians. Though they were unlikely to oppose her, the prospect that they might provide useful support for her efforts was still more remote.

The chances of them discovering her actions unaided, moreover, verged on impossibility. The First Librarian had taken the loss of his house badly. Most of his dead wife's possessions had been inside when it burned down, reduced to ash along with his clothes and a large portion of his savings. Rem had made up a bed for him in his office, and now he rarely ventured outside. The Second Librarian mooched around as he had always done, but drank less frequently and with greater secrecy. He guiltily avoided his father's presence, and, Rem noted, made a conscious effort to stay sober when making enquiries about renting a new house. She had taken to spreading a blanket over him when she found him sleeping in between the shelves, feeling both resentful and strangely tender towards these new inhabitants of the city once reserved for her alone. The First and Second Librarians weren't much of a family, but Rem began to feel protective towards them all the same.

The Library had turned into a sort of crisis centre, filled with the dispossessed and afraid, and it was under her care. During the still nights, hearing the other Librarians' distant snores and feeling the comforting presence of the scrolls around her, nestling like ancient birds in the darkness, it was easy for Rem to slip back into the sense of peace she had felt in earlier days, to forget the terrible warning that the sight of the burning house had awakened in her mind. But her visions were filled with burning scrolls and crumbling masonry: she knew beyond a doubt that the Library was no longer the sanctuary it appeared, and none of those who sheltered within it could do so for long.

It was not difficult for Rem to borrow the key to the Rare Texts room again from the First Librarian, and even easier to get a copy cut in the market for her personal use. Although their existence was not put about widely in Bessa, for fear of unwelcome attention, some of the scrolls in this room were of great value, if one knew where to sell them. After a decade of service, Rem knew. She also knew that these would be the easiest ones to rehouse, the ones that were coveted by the world at large for their beautiful illustrations and exquisitely illuminated characters, their wooden rollers inlaid with jewels and their gold leaf. It was the others, the hundreds of thousands of plain scrolls written on simple parchment, that would present the challenge. They had no market. No one, aside from herself and a few penniless scholars, had any interest in them at all.

It was here that Rem moved into the next phase of what she privately termed her evacuation plan. Selling the contents of the Rare Texts room raised less money than she had hoped, but still enough for the purchase of a disused bakery in Bessa's merchant district. Its previous owner no doubt felt that he had thoroughly cheated her, could not believe his luck when his eccentric buyer seemed unconcerned at the sight of the rotting door hanging from its hinges, picked her way through the piles of rubbish and dead rats inside without comment, and smiled with satisfaction as she pronounced the place perfect.

She had found what she wanted as soon as she entered the room, gleaming dimly in the far corner: the heavy metal ring of a trapdoor. Bakers in desert cities like Bessa had a simple method for stopping their produce from spoiling. They built their storerooms underground, where the air was cooler. Coincidentally, this also made them ideal for storing scrolls, the lower temperatures protecting the parchment from heat damage, degeneration and the risk of fire.

Rem cleaned out the traces of mouldy bread and flour from the cavernous room, and moved a steady stream of scrolls into it over the course of the next month. If either of the other Librarians noticed the slowly emptying shelves in the Library, they did not think it important enough to comment on.

When she had filled the storeroom almost to its ceiling, she began the long-term loans. This was not an easy decision to make; putting the scrolls in hiding was one thing, but sending them into exile, into other peoples' homes, where she would in all probability never see them again, hurt Rem deeply. But Hakkim had started burning the sacred texts of other preachers in the Jidur, and it was a mark of the fear he commanded that none of them had tried to stop him, or even protested. If the threat he posed to the Library had seemed at all distant or unreal to Rem before, it was ever-present now.

So she steeled herself, and decided to work by section, starting with the scientific and medical treatises. This area always had a steady trickle of visitors, mostly student apprentices working for Bessa's doctors, surgeons and apothecaries. The Library was large, however, and it was never difficult to find a reader who was standing alone, or at least far enough from the next person that there was no risk of their conversation being overheard. Once she had spotted a potential candidate, Rem would wander to their side and cough politely, waiting until they looked up from the scroll in their hands.

"Are you finding it interesting?" she would ask softly, "Do its ideas please you? Then take it home with you. Read it, share it with your friends. All I ask is that you keep it safe."

A huge advantage of dealing with scholars is that they are not stupid. They had all been to the Jidur on occasion, had all heard Hakkim speak, and they understood what she wanted almost immediately. Most accepted a scroll without question. Some even offered to take a few more. No one asked why: the only really surprising thing to those who had paused to think about it was that the Ascetics had not attacked the Library already. Many were confused when Rem waved away their offers to return the scrolls after the trouble had died down. It seemed only logical to them that it would die down, that Hakkim's hold on Bessa would be broken any day now, that Al-Bokhari would move against him, and the Ascetics would dissipate, as if they had never been. After all, the violence had been escalating for months: surely someone would do something about it soon?

That each day which passed without change signalled more clearly than the last that no one would do anything, did not seem to have occurred to them. But the people of Bessa could not be blamed for their lack of foresight. The city was hiding its eyes behind its hands like a little child, waiting to be told that everything was alright now, that it was safe to look, that the worst was over. One peek and the city would dissolve into abject terror; a lack of clear vision was the only thing keeping it going. By the very nature of her gift, Rem did not have that luxury.

It was a slow process, but gradually the Library was emptying out. Considerable sections of the shelves were empty now, like patches on an ornate rug worn through to the bare weave. Yet there were still thousands of scrolls left; the Library was vast, and Rem knew that it would take more than the scattered efforts of some well-meaning scholars to save it all.

She increased her efforts nonetheless, trawling the corridors ceaselessly for likely looking candidates. Soon, she was speaking to everyone she came across, even if they seemed uninterested or slow-witted. She abandoned her efforts with the medical texts when there were so few of them left that students no longer came to the Library to read them, and moved on to the poetry scrolls.

It was here that she met Nabeeb. She came across him by chance one day when she was patrolling the long avenues of shelves. He was a slight man, dressed in black, though in a different style to the Ascetics. Where they wore thick cloaks, his garments were less voluminous: a simple black shirt and a pair of trousers. Looking at him carefully, Rem realised that he was a regular visitor to the Library. She had seen him many times before, wandering between the rows of texts with a measured pace and an earnest expression. She came closer to him and looked at the scroll he was reading. He glanced at her with mild grey eyes.

"Can I help you?" he asked.

"You come here quite often," Rem replied, "you must find many things that you like. I am Rem, the Third Librarian here, and I would be honoured if you would take some of these scrolls away with you, that you may read them at your leisure. I only ask that you keep them safe."

The man put his head on one side, appeared to be considering.

"I'm Nabeeb," he said. "I know what you're asking. I've seen you talking to others before. It won't work, you know."

"What?" Rem was startled into abruptness, and there was an edge to her voice.

"I only meant," he answered, holding up a hand in placation, "that it will take you a very long time. Individuals, a few scrolls at a time. It's no way to clear a library this size."

Rem leaned closer to him, eyes brightening with interest. "Do you have a better idea?"

"Corpses," he answered promptly, and then, in a shy rush, "I am an undertaker by trade. All corpses must be buried outside the city's walls. So, I prepare them for burial, then drive them outside Bessa's gates. The funerals themselves take place within city limits: when I actually bury the bodies, I am alone. I never get any trouble, from the Palace Guard or the Ascetics. People are put off by the idea of searching a hearse—it seems disrespectful, somehow. So if I were to carry some scrolls out with me the next time I make a burial trip, I could get them outside the city in complete safety. We could wrap them in winding sheets, and no one would ever think to check them."

"What would happen then?" Rem asked. "They will be hardly any safer in the middle of the desert than they are here."

"I have some friends in Perdondaris who have similar interests to myself. I can write to them now, ask them if they will take the scrolls back to their city. I know it's a long way," he said anxiously, noticing how Rem's face fell, "but at least they will be in good hands, amongst those who will value them."

With the prospect of success suddenly so near, the thought that she might really be able to save the entire Library from destruction, Rem was unexpectedly engulfed by a feeling of desolation. The thought of the endless avenues of her city bereft of scrolls, the echoing emptiness that would replace the living silence she loved, hurt like a fist to the stomach. She embraced Nabeeb a little harder than she had intended, thanking him profusely for his kindness. He blushed, insisted that no thanks were necessary. "I'm doing this for love, like you," he mumbled, suddenly embarrassed.

Given that the mail service between Bessa and Perdondaris was comprised of a single recalcitrant camel, the reply from Nabeeb's friends was a long time coming. He visited the Library every day, and every day he met Rem's eyes with a slight shake of his head, disappointment in the set of his shoulders. Meanwhile, Rem continued with the long-term loans, though at Nabeeb's insistence she made her enquiries more subtle. "Stealing from the sultan's Library is still a treasonable offence, Rem, whatever the circumstances," he reminded her. "You need to tread carefully."

"Oh, there's no cause to worry about Al-Bokhari," Rem scoffed. "He wouldn't notice if we harnessed the entire Library to a team of elephants, drove it across the square and crashed it into the palace. His mind is on other things."

The image made Nabeeb laugh because there was a lot of truth in it. Bokhari Al-Bokhari had never been the most observant ruler, but now, all his attention was claimed by the Ascetics, and bands of street urchins could piss against the palace walls without the least fear of consequences. Increasingly, the entire palace guard was sent out to patrol the streets, to guard Bessa's largely abandoned pleasure district and to police the Jidur. It did no good: the Ascetics picked their fights, and large groups of guards were left to their work unchallenged through the heat of the day.

But at night, when nervous watchmen patrolled alone, that was the time when a black shadow would detach itself from the lighter shadows all around, and start to follow them. The flash of a blade, a muffled cry, a dull thump—it was over in seconds, and when the next patrol came around, all that was left was a body.

The worst thing about it all was that there were no suspects. Hakkim himself was maddeningly peaceable, only emerging from his humble lodgings to preach in the Jidur. Every other Ascetic was just a figure in a black robe, able at any moment to turn a corner, shed their disguise, and don once again the anonymity of a common citizen.

The spreading poison of their presence seemed impossible to remedy. Al-Bokhari's counsellors had tried to bribe Hakkim, who would not even speak to accept or refuse the offer. His spies had searched for some piece of information with which to blackmail Hakkim, but none could be found. As far as the covert agents of the sultanate could ascertain, the Ascetics had no lieutenants, no headquarters, no hierarchy. Kill one, and another would take his place. They were a river of black, and a river has no angles, no weak spots, nothing to grapple with and nothing to attack. They had been mobilised by words and cunning argument, but Al-Bokhari had no such weapons at his disposal. Military force is a blunt instrument at the best of times, and in the face of the Ascetics it seemed worse than useless. So the sultan waited in indecision, orders hovering on his lips. And the city held its breath.

The day that Al-Bokhari made up his mind to act was the day Nabeeb received his reply from Perdondaris. There was a crowd in front of the Library that morning when Nabeeb arrived, clutching the long-awaited letter. He was pushing through them without a glance, eager to greet Rem with the good news, when he felt a hand on his arm and saw her standing at his side, a grim expression on her face. "Come and see this," she said, pulling him along.

The crowd were not facing the Library at all, but the palace on the opposite side of the square, staring at something suspended from the palace gates. As they moved closer, Nabeeb could see that it was a man. Hefam Shafiq was a vizier of unremarkable talents, known in court, if he was known at all, for his reliably dull counsel. He was a fat man of solid opinions, a sure bet for a lifelong career as a royal advisor. His life was entirely banal. His death, however, was a declaration of war.

Rem and Nabeeb stared up at the pathetic figure, his face showing wan and ghastly above the sign hung around his neck: *I was the servant of corruption*. Wordlessly, they looked at one another, turned and headed towards the Library.

"We have to move the scrolls tonight," Rem said, as soon as they were inside.

"What, all of them?" Nabeeb protested. "Surely that's not necessary? It will be safer if we move them out in stages."

"The time for that has passed," Rem shot back, "Al-Bokhari will begin arresting the Ascetics immediately. They've forced his hand, but he isn't strong enough for a show of power, and the weakness of his retaliation will expose him. Everything is coming to a head. We must move the scrolls tonight!"

"I'll go and fetch my hearse," Nabeeb said. If he was puzzled by her certainty, he did not show it.

They spent the day wrapping scrolls in winding sheets and piling them up by the side entrance, waiting for the cover of night to move them to the hearse which Nabeeb had parked in the alleyway at the side of the Library, far from the main square. Rem had barred the great wooden doors to prevent visitors, but there would be no scholars in the Library today. Once the Palace Guard started pouring into the streets, they had emptied, most people fleeing to their homes, locking their doors and covering up their windows in preparation to wait out whatever storm was coming.

For a while, the only sounds in the city were the tramp of feet and the bellow of orders as troops of guards ran past. In the afternoon, they heard the fighting begin. It intensified as evening came on, and a great roar of voices started up in the square outside. Nabeeb went out to investigate, returning with the news that the remaining Ascetics had congregated outside the palace gates.

"Rumours are running wild out there," he told her. "They're saying that Al-Bokhari's guard rounded up most of the Ascetics and put them in the keep, but they're breaking out. People are saying they're throwing themselves against the door, again and again. Beating themselves bloody. And it's working! The guards are falling back!"

"Then we need to hurry," Rem replied.

In the surreal, hushed urgency of the falling night, Rem and Nabeeb made a series of journeys which came in time to seem like one unending journey: from the Library to the waiting hearse to the Library again, holding winding sheets filled with scrolls in their arms like limp bodies.

Time was a naked flame in a high wind, sometimes flaring with sudden life, sometimes sinking to a creeping shimmer. At first, Rem had found it easy to carry the scrolls. In the aeons of time and space spent running between hearse and Library and hearse, they began to feel like boulders.

She and Nabeeb took it in turns to run round to the mouth of the alley and peek into the main square, to see how the situation was progressing. When Rem saw that the sultan's standard was on fire, she knew their time was up. "They've breached the palace," she said, rounding the corner and helping Nabeeb load his bundle into the hearse. "We don't have time to take any more, but I would appreciate it if you could do one last favour for me."

Convincing the First and Second Librarians that their lives were in danger was fairly easy. Fear was rife in Bessa, and the sight of the hordes of black-cloaked figures swarming round the palace gates made Warid's lips go white, and his father tremble.

"Nabeeb here is taking some of our scrolls out of the city to Perdondaris," Rem told the two men. "I would strongly advise that you go with him." She turned to Nabeeb, her voice dropping into a swift murmur. "If you go now, you will be able to make it before the Ascetics take the city gates. The sultan's men have fled, so there will be no one guarding them at the moment. Hurry, and go in safety."

Nabeeb stared at her. "Aren't you coming too?"

"I can't. The Library is not yet empty." He opened his mouth to speak, but she saw the intention as he formed it, and firmly shook her head. "No. You need to drive the hearse. They"—jerking her head at the First and Second Librarians—"don't know the way to Perdondaris. They wouldn't even make it out of the city. You need to go."

"But they'll catch you if you stay! Why won't you come with me?" Nabeeb's eyes were glistening. Rem knew, with the knowledge that was her gift, what was in his mind. She could taste all the flavours her words had for him: confusion, grief, and beneath these the bitter tang of spurned affection. Nabeeb had thought throughout that Rem was a young man, and wished to flee with him to a place where they could both read and love without the fear of oppression.

"Nabeeb," she said, as gently as she could, "I must stay with the friends I cannot save."

He saw her resolve and nodded, began to turn away. Rem caught his hand and kissed him, just once, on the cheek. Let him make of that what he wanted; she could give him no more.

She waited until she was sure they were gone before she allowed the tears to come. When they flowed at last, they left dark tracks down her face like smudged kohl, staining her pristine uniform with dark patches. Tears of black ink. Her second dubious gift, and the reason why she never cried in public. When she was younger, Rem had sometimes imagined herself as a scroll, with all her words securely wrapped inside her. They must be very sombre words, if they only escaped when she cried.

Behind her, the Library's heavy wooden doors shuddered in their frame, rocked by the impact of some heavy object. The Ascetics were charging them with a battering ram, but they were sturdy, and would hold for the time being. Rem wiped her tears away hastily with the hem of her shirt: another distinctive thing about them was that, once dry, they would not fade. She had about an hour, she guessed, and a good third of the Library was still full. She had put up a good fight, but there really was nothing more to be done. Well, there was one thing. Rem headed for the First Librarian's office, to prepare for her last stand.

When the great doors finally shattered, and the Ascetics poured inside, the first man to step across the Library's threshold was greeted by a silver stylus in his chest. He staggered backwards, the men to either side of him starting in surprise. They were confronted by the sight of a naked woman, her body covered in curling, cursive script, the ink jet black. Some of the words they did not understand—they appeared to have been written in a language they could not decipher, though the characters belonged to their own tongue. *The distances of space and time were one, and swans far off were swans to come* ran snakingly up the length of the woman's left arm, but none of the Ascetics had ever seen a swan, or even knew what it was.

"I am a scroll," the woman said, her fierce eyes gleaming at them, a pointed stylus in each hand. "Burn me!"

Even as they overcame her, bound her hands behind her back and dragged her down the front steps; even they carried her towards the palace, while still more of them swarmed into the Library, Rem was laughing. What more could the bastards do?

Hakkim waited until the morning of the following day to pass sentence. The night had been taken up with other things. Rem was not the only one in Bessa who had angered him, and in the immediate aftermath of the coup there had been those whose sentences were in more pressing need of execution. Now, he stood on the Library steps, surveying the crowd gathered in the main square, and spoke with a tone of dire warning. "The light of the One Truth burns with a baleful fire. Where does its anger fall? It falls upon those who will not feed its flames. It falls upon those who follow lesser lights, who glut themselves on deceit!"

He held up a scroll. Rem, held behind him on the steps by two strong guards, her hands and feet bound, strained and struggled. He was standing by a pile of them, stacked on the ground in front of him. There was something wrong with them. They glistened as if wet, though there had been no rain.

"Yes, deceit, deceit such as is contained in this scroll," he spat the word, "that I hold up before you now. This scroll of lies claims that the pleasures of the world are not to be abhorred. It holds the love of woman to be a *sacred* love, it cries that the lust for food and wine are *healthy* desires. It is a polluted thing. You see before you the woman who tried to protect this lie, and others like it. She would use it to corrupt us all. Yet she shall not succeed!"

Rem felt dizzy with his shouting and the closeness of the crowd, and something else, some foul smell in the air, sharp and metallic. Suddenly, she felt outside herself, looking out on the scene with a sickening helplessness as Hakkim flung the scroll back onto the pile at his feet.

"She shall not succeed," he roared again, and now he was taking something from a fold in his robes, a dull grey box, and a piece of flint.

"All that oppose the fire of the One Truth will be consumed by it!" He was raising the box now, and Rem knew what he was about to do and tried to start forward, but she was too far away, and the guards were too strong, and the frenzied shouting of the crowd too loud, and it all blended into a solid wall of sound and spit and hatred as Hakkim struck the flint against the tinder box, the spark leapt, and the scrolls ignited, their oil-soaked parchment catching light immediately, irrevocably.

Rem was overcome by a wave of nausea. She vomited, again and again. The flames in front of her eyes began to turn black. She was losing consciousness, the awful smell sapping her of any energy. The last thing she felt before she collapsed was the guards lifting her onto their shoulders, the cold steel of Hakkim's voice as he pronounced her sentence. "She lived for this hubbub of lies. Now, she will die for it."

How Hakkim Found His Enemy

In the kingdom of Bessa, thirty years after the death of the prophet Al-Mutassin, there lived a scholar by the name of Hakkim Mehdad.

Hakkim was not in the first instance a scholar by his own choosing, but he seemed predestined by nature to pursue such a calling—he puzzled and alarmed his parents, an elderly shoemaker and his much younger wife, by refusing to speak until his fifth birthday, and even thereafter could seldom be coaxed into uttering more than two or three words together; but it was clear even to the casual observer that Hakkim's silence was not the silence of vacancy. On the contrary, he would spend hours in silent reverie, or tracing abstract figures in the dust by the door lintel with the end of a stick.

This thoughtful demeanour was accompanied by a singular aversion to action. When his older siblings bullied or berated him, which was often, Hakkim would stand with head bowed and face grimly set, as if he hoped by extreme stillness to merge into his surroundings and be forgotten. His retaliations, such as they were, would come later, when a favourite tunic, or doll, or stick-and-ball, belonging to one of his tormentors would be found mangled and broken, the subject of some sublimated assault.

Hakkim's father was only a humble cobbler, and so had never had the opportunity to pursue learning for its own sweet sake. He took these signs for what they were, evidence that his son lived far more in the fastnesses of his own mind than in the everyday ruck of two over-crowded rooms over a narrow shop in the narrowest of Bessa's teeming streets. It must also be said that young Hakkim showed no skill in his father's trade, and could not be used in the workshop even in relatively simple tasks such as waxing leather or punching eyelets. Any pair of shoes he touched was unlikely to survive the acquaintance, no matter where in the process of manufacture their paths crossed.

Over his wife's tearful protests, Hakkim's father therefore determined to place his youngest son in service with a local holy man, the bargain being that Hakkim would tend house, cook and clean, fetch and carry, and would in return be granted both ineffable wisdom and a daily meal of bread and beans.

A suitable holy man was duly found. His name was Rasoul, and he was an Inviate, which is to say a cryptotheist: the core of his belief was that the Most Holy deliberately obscures His path so that humankind may not sully His greatness by approaching near it with their lowly understanding. Alone among the sects, then, the Inviates do not pray for enlightenment; they pray to reassure God that they're not going through his trash (that is to say, the created cosmos) in order to find out what he's up to.

Hakkim's soul was fervent, primed for belief. He progressed quickly in his studies, and astonished his master with the retentiveness of his memory. By the age of ten, he could recite all the three-hundred-thirty-and-three Inviate prayers (most of which are variations on "we're not peeking") without a pause or a stammer, accompanying each with its prescribed repertoire of hand movements and postural shifts.

For most of his eleventh year, too, young Hakkim continued to take pleasure and pride in these accomplishments. Such feats of will and memory were a playground for his intellect, which hitherto (like his skinny, wiry body) had lived within the straitest of bounds. Then, gradually and inexorably and very much to his own surprise, that delight began first to lessen and then to be seasoned with irritation. Probing the tender place, the young adept found that there were passages in the Inviate scriptures on which his mind, though not his facile tongue, faltered.

In particular, he questioned the Inviate stance towards the supreme being. Why show such exaggerated respect for God, Hakkim wondered in the privacy of his heart, when so much about His programme and His motives had to be taken on trust? It seemed to him both craven and sycophantic to thank the deity for undoubted benefits—sentience and reason—whose use was then so hedged about with prohibitions that they might just as well not have been bestowed in the first place. It was as if the Almighty had given him a sword, perfectly balanced and ecstatically sharp, and bid him in recompense to keep it in its sheath at all times.

When Hakkim tasked his master with these troubling thoughts, the pious old man was ready with a cogent and unanswerable argument: he beat his errant disciple with a switch made from supplest cedar wood, until the lad could scarcely walk.

"Your questions are heresies both in and of themselves, Hakkim," he pointed out gently, when his aching muscles finally compelled him to lay down the cane. "You must cleanse yourself of them. Come, and I will show you how."

He went out into the courtyard behind his house, with Hakkim limping respectfully along three paces behind him. There was a well out there, with a stone coping, and a small mound of loose stones left over from the making of the well. Most of the stones were negligible in size, but one was a dull grey boulder as big and broad about as a festival loaf.

"This," said Rasoul, pointing to the grey stone, "is the burden of negative thought. Carry it across the courtyard, and set it down beside the gate."

Hakkim obeyed, with great difficulty. The wounds of his beating had not yet begun to scab over, and his blood made the heavy stone slick, so that it was hard to hold onto as he hefted its considerable weight and staggered across the dusty courtyard to its further end.

"Now bring it back again to the well," Rasoul commanded.

Again, the lad did as he was told, though his sinews cracked and his heart fluttered like a pennant in a gale.

"One hundred times must you bear your burden thither," the holy man told his novice, "and one hundred times bear it hither again. And when you are done, this burden will pass from you. Go to it, my child."

Verily, this was an ordeal. It would have been a big ask even if the boy had been hale; stiff and sore as he was from the beating, it was an endless labyrinth of torment. He could have walked away from it, perhaps, if he had been a different boy. But he was who he was, and so he obeyed.

Through the watches of the night, he bore the stone hither and thither. The first ten journeys he was able to count, and the ten after that still had some separate and definable existence. After that, and with surprising abruptness, they merged into a terrifying totality. Possibly the beating he had received made him feverish—possibly the hidden God sniped at him from cover, petty and implacable. He had always carried the stone, and always would. He could no longer remember picking it up, and could not imagine putting it down. It seemed a part of him: the anchor to which he clung, the spine that kept him upright, the whirling planet in whose soil his feet were rooted. When he realised that he had lost count, he started again from one.

Some time toward morning, the fever broke; or else God relented and withdrew. Hakkim came slowly back to himself, slumped over the stone, his breath sounding in his chest like a dying rat thrashing inside a paper lantern, his cold, waxen skin running sweat in the way a half-scalded cheese runs with whey.

It was a terrible irony that Hakkim's punishment should become his vision, and therefore the foundation of his spiritual life. He clung to the stone, and the stone welcomed his embrace.

It was the burden of negative thought, Rasoul had said. It did not seem a burden now.

As the first cocks began to crow in the neighbouring yards, Hakkim took the stone into his master's chamber and brought it to his master's bed. He stood there in the dawn light, the burden of negative thought cradled in his hands like an infant. He spoke his master's name, calmly but commandingly.

Rasoul opened bleary eyes, half-seeing, half-rising from the shallow, milky well of the dreams that come after the dawn.

"Quietly," he mumbled. "The birds—"

Hakkim let go of the stone, which in falling crushed Rasoul's head to a pink, bone-seeded pulp. Then he went through the house to his own room, packed his meagre belongings, a skin of water, some bread. He left while the muezzins were still singing the faithful of a thousand churches to a thousand devotions: he held none of those holies in his heart, and he saw, with the clarity of youth and sickness, how strong that made him.

Hakkim's second master, Drihud Ben Din, was an Ascetic, a denier of pleasure. The boy sought him out by reputation, and auditioned him rigorously while seeming to submit himself to the master's interrogation. The questions Ben Din asked him about his habits both of thought and of life pleased him—they implied an austere and self-denying lifestyle, in which negative thought, so far from being eschewed and punished, was elevated to its proper status. Through negatives, through denial, we come at last to the truth: without them we labour forever in the *qu'aha sul jidani*, the labyrinth of masks.

In the Ascetic's house, Hakkim flourished—although he would not have used that word, with its overtones of vegetable excess. He grew straight and upright, toward the light, never deviating to any direction that might be marked on a compass, never falling for the snares that the world sets in the path of the righteous.

Ascetic: a barbarous word, of Occidental provenance. It comes from the *askesis*, the emptying out, of the appetites, the intellect, the habits both of thought and action. Hakkim experienced now the transcendent consequences of that emptying: his soul filled up with itself, balancing the pressure of the world and holding him in perfect, dynamic equipoise.

Drihud Ben Din was most impressed with his disciple. He had never before encountered such self-abnegation, such steadfast will, in a boy so young. He tutored Hakkim well in the tenets of his new faith, until the day came when Hakkim began to add to those tenets himself and to expound their wisdom to his master more eloquently than the older man could express them himself. "You are ready now," Ben Din said approvingly, "to test yourself in the Jidur."

The Jidur, the Garden of Voices, was a place unique to Bessa. It was a large public square, paved with pink stone, where it was the right of any marabout to bid against other holy men and visionaries for the souls of passers-by, using as coin his eloquence and his sanctity. To the Jidur, then, Hakkim set forth, early enough in the day that the sky was the same colour as the stones beneath his feet. He was the first to arrive, and he picked the choicest spot, at the centre of the square where four wooden benches had been set underneath an old and wide-spreading lemon tree, to allow weary travellers a momentary respite from the heat. A fat and oleaginous adept of the Tsevre school, arriving some minutes later, argued without much conviction that this highly desirable pitch belonged by rights to him, but Hakkim was not to be cajoled or browbeaten. He held his ground, as the other spaces around the square began to fill up, and the Tsevretist retired at length with bad grace to stand out in the heat of the day.

When the sun was as high as the upper branches of the lemon tree, the first curious souls began to wander in from the adjacent streets to see what flavours of enlightenment were on offer that day. Hakkim was ready to receive them; or at least he thought he was, until the moment when he opened his mouth.

"The pursuit of pleasure is as hollow and futile as the pursuit of a beautiful woman," he opened. His voice sounded a little weak and quavering even to himself, but it was the first proposition he had ever offered up in public, and he was confident that his delivery would improve. Unfortunately, in the moment of hesitation that these thoughts occasioned, a Durukhar marabout who was stationed to Hakkim's left, and who had not yet begun his own sermon, spoke up.

"That's an unfortunate simile," he said. "They might be one and the same thing. When a man pursues a beautiful woman, surely pleasure is exactly what he promises himself."

"And that promise," Hakkim agreed, only mildly outfaced by the objection, "is deceitful, for the pleasure that woman brings is fleeting, like all—"

"Have you ever experienced the pleasure that woman brings?" asked a sceptic sitting comfortably with his back to the base of the lemon tree. "You look a little young."

"All pleasures," said Hakkim sententiously, "are alike in that they divert the flesh at the expense of the mind and soul. For everywhere in life, we find—"

"Wait, wait, wait," said the Durukhar, who was evidently of a pedantic turn of mind. "All pleasures divert the flesh? What about solving a rebus or a riddle? That's a pleasure that diverts the mind."

Hakkim was momentarily gravelled by this, but he dived into the breach as best he could. "The mind is of the flesh," he pointed out, stammering a little now. "The brain is the seat of intellect, and the brain is a bodily organ. Therefore all pleasures of the intellect are pleasures of the flesh."

"That's ridiculous," a third man piped up. He was cradling a lemon in his hand, but it was not apparent whether he intended to eat it or throw it—both pursuits were allowed in the Jidur. "So there's no difference between fucking and arguing?"

"Certainly my wife can do both at once," the man sitting under the tree observed, and the sally was approved with loud guffaws all round.

The pestilential Durukhar perceived now that he was in a position to drive off the opposition. "And it were as much nourishment to think about eating a sherbet as actually to taste it—since the pleasure in each case is comparable."

"Comparable in kind," Hakkim corrected his rival angrily. "Not in degree. My point is—"

"So what, wise master, is the rate of exchange?" asked the Durukhar, with feigned politeness. "How many times must one think about a sherbet before one has attained the same amount of pleasure as could be had by tasting it?" The crowd laughed, encouraging the Durukhar to further efforts. "And would you advise the same approach with your beautiful woman? You could think many times about enjoying her, instead of essaying her once."

"He's thinking about her now," jeered the man with the lemon, seeing Hakkim's furious blush. There was more laughter, and a number of vulgar exhortations.

It might, even then, have been possible to regain the attention of the crowd and build again from some more propitious foundation; but the Durukhar, inspired by the reception of his previous jest, now embarked upon a pantomime in which Hakkim approached an imagined lady, kissed and caressed her invisible body with great enthusiasm, and then was beaten away by her invisible fists. The crowd were ecstatic, their yells of delight and coarse catcalls quite drowning out Hakkim's attempts to address them again. When he raised his voice to be heard above the uproar, the man with the lemon let fly—the fruit smacked hard against the side of Hakkim's face, leaving a red welt. The Durukhar opined that Hakkim's mysterious woman had left some of her rouge on his cheek when she kissed him goodbye.

Beaten to the wide, Hakkim slunk away. He spent the rest of the day hiding in an olive grove, replaying the debacle in his mind with many different outcomes, all of them much more favourable to himself. In the evening he went back to his master's house and told him that the day had gone well.

That night, Hakkim was visited by an unsettling dream; or rather by the absence of a dream, since on waking he could not remember exactly what it was that had troubled his sleep. He only knew that he had been fleeing from some terrible thing, as black as pitch, without shape or substance, which hated him and pursued him with deadly, ferocious intent. It seemed to come from below, to rise about him like a maw, open to swallow him down, until he wrenched himself desperately into wakefulness at the last moment before he was consumed. Lying in his straw cot in the pre-dawn dark, he pressed both hands against his narrow chest to keep his heart from leaping out of its bounds. The fear that gripped him was more terrible than anything he had ever felt.

If the first day of Hakkim's career as a marabout had been unsuccessful, the second was an unqualified disaster. The Durukhar was back in the same spot, and was delighted to see Hakkim arrive. Hakkim tried to avoid him, but the Durukhar swapped pitches to be next to him again when he spoke. It was clear that he saw Hakkim very much in the light of a straight man; more distressingly, Hakkim realised, it was very easy to cast him in such a mould. His earnest statements could be misinterpreted in a great variety of ways, and his over-complex metaphors could be made to fall in upon themselves at a single touch.

Hakkim fought back with all the weapons at his disposal: reason and truth, precept and example, parable and exhortation. They were useless. The Durukhar's words ran over and about him like rats, evaded his grasp, withdrew before him and then bit and clawed him from covert. Even silence couldn't help him—if he said nothing, the Durukhar supplied his half of the dialogue, too, to hilarious and crowd-pleasing effect. Once more, Hakkim retired without a single convert, and the Durukhar as he left switched from comic to didactic mode without so much as a pause.

Every day for fourteen days, Hakkim went to the Jidur. Fourteen times he broke against the same rock. Every night for fourteen nights he woke with screams rising in his throat as the hateful, night-black tide of his dreaming rose to swallow him whole.

Just before the dawn of the fifteenth day, after the latest of these nocturnal ordeals, Hakkim prayed at the peculiar shrine he kept in the corner of his room. The shrine was a squat, grey boulder: the boulder of negative thought, which he had brought with him from his former master's house. Its surface now was smeared with bloody fingerprints and flecked here and there with some small morsel of cerebral matter, but it was otherwise unchanged. Its solidity, its mass, its blunt, asymmetrical shape: these things were reassuring to the boy, and in due course, negative thought brought enlightenment, just as he had known it would.

On the fifteenth day, he did not preach, but waited in a dusky corner of the Jidur and watched the Durukhar perform without a straight man. He was still good, it had to be said: glib of tongue, expressive of countenance, and alert to the responses of his audience. He had reduced the four virtues of the Durukhar faith to a four-line poem, which he chanted at regular intervals as a mnemonic. By the time the sun fell below the city walls, his voice was hoarse and his alms-bowl was full.

Hakkim followed the Durukhar to his lodgings, a single upstairs room above the Fountain Court. He waited a few minutes after the man had gone inside, and then followed him in. The Durukhar was surprised to see the young adept, but only for a moment. After that, his attention was entirely taken up with the knife that Hakkim had plunged into his chest.

This second killing pleased Hakkim in a way that the first hadn't. Then, he had been delirious and wild; now, clear-headed and full of reasoned calm. He was therefore able to see how well the act of murder meshed with his chosen and avowed principles. It thinned out the clutter of the world, stilled a distracting voice; the voice, moreover, of an unbeliever, who was standing between others and the light of truth. In every way, it was a devotional act and a thing of beauty.

The Durukhar's corpse, by contrast, was vile and unpleasant to contemplate: Hakkim cleaned his knife on the man's sleeve, and withdrew.

This murder proved to be a turning point for the young adept. In the years that followed, Hakkim found the confidence as a public speaker that had formerly eluded him. He preached passionately in the Jidur, and drew large crowds. If some of his hearers remembered the awkward boy who had been the butt of the Durukhar's jokes, they did not recognize him in the fire-eyed marabout who hectored them now.

Hakkim preached emptiness, *askesis*, the joy of silence and absence and the restraint of desire. In denying mind and body the diversions which they craved, he promised, any man could find within himself the face of God, stripped of all masks; the peace which hides at the heart of *qu'aha sul jidani*.

He believed in that peace, despite the blind, black well of hatred into which his dreams still plunged him more nights than not. Others believed too, and the Ascetics of Bessa became a cult with Hakkim Mehdad as their priest and prophet.

Hakkim's stern message brought him into conflict with many; he did not flinch from it. Rather, he rejoiced now in the ferocious clash of truth on falsehood, and engaged in hundreds of debates that lasted from sunup to sundown and turned the Jidur into an arena. Mostly he won these duels, and left his opponents lessened. Occasionally he lost, returned after dark, and left them dead.

In his thirtieth year, he took a serious injury in one of these nighttime encounters, when a slick-tongued Re'Ibam prelate fought back somewhat harder than most and turned Hakkim's knife blade into his own shoulder. This was what decided him to seek, as it were, advanced training in the particular branch of theology which he had made his own.

He took the money he had saved, and the money he had inherited when his master Drihud Ben Din died (of insufficient piety), and he enrolled in the school of assassins.

The assassin school was not in Bessa itself, because Bessa's caliph, Bokhari Al-Bokhari, didn't approve of freelance killers (while being wholly comfortable with the idea of killers in his own employ). In fact it was a private fiefdom in the mountains beyond the city of Perdondaris. It was owned and run by the so-called Caliph of Assassins, the legendary Imad-Basur, who personally vetted all potential students. Entry was by fee (strictly non-returnable) and audition (oftentimes fatal).

While he was waiting his turn to be interviewed and tested by the great master, Hakkim was permitted to wander within the grounds of the school and take in something of its atmosphere. Most of what he saw there pleased him: the students were hugely and relentlessly focused on their learning, and lived the frugal life that befitted such serious aspirations.

One thing, however, disturbed him. In a courtyard toward the rear of the building, a slender young woman, dark of hair and of eye, was sharpening a blade against a whetstone. Five or six other knives of varying sizes were lying at her feet, neatly arrayed, ready to be whetted in their turn.

All the students Hakkim had seen were—of course—male: he assumed that the servants would be, too. Such was the norm in schools, as in monastic retreats. He could not understand the woman's presence. He asked a passing attendant who she was.

"A cousin of Imad-Basur," he was told. "Zuleika. She lodges here."

"But she has no converse with the students?"

The attendant was mildly scandalised. "Certainly not!"

Hakkim thanked the man, who scurried on his way. He watched the woman for a while longer, somewhat impressed despite himself at the diligence with which she stropped the knife, forward for twenty strokes, backward for twenty strokes, forward again. Though he abhorred the bodies, minds and speech of women, he found her dedication to the task pleasing.

Hakkim passed his audition with flying colours and was accepted as a student.

He stayed with the assassins only for two years, which meant that he did not finish out his studies and his name was never written in black ink upon a black scroll. But he took from them what he needed, and he parted with them on the best of terms—so much so, in fact, that before he left, he was summoned into the presence of Imad-Basur himself. The Caliph of Assassins asked Hakkim why he did not wish to graduate and then to remain at the school as an assassin plenipotentiary, taking such commissions as the elder masters chose for him and sharing in the wealth these bespoke murders brought in.

Hakkim explained that his was a religious vocation, to which murder, as such, was only an adjunct. Imad-Basur showed a flattering interest. The two men talked at length about asceticism; it was a discipline which had a certain appeal to the Assassin King, and he was impressed by his young charge's passion and conviction.

For whatever reason, he felt moved to make Hakkim a gift. He asked the younger man whether—despite his contempt for earthly pleasures—there was any particular thing he craved.

Hakkim thought of the dreams which had troubled him in his childhood, and which still recurred even now, of the dark tide that hated him and rose to whelm him while he slept.

"I would like to see the face of my worst enemy," he said. "I believe there is one who hates me, and will cog and cumber me wherever he can—though it may be that we have yet to meet."

Imad-Basur nodded thoughtfully at this short, blunt speech. He knew that there were many ways, both good and bad, in which souls could be twinned. He also knew that there were pharmacons and magics that could help in identifying such invisible entwinings long before they became apparent. However, he wanted to be sure that he had understood his pupil aright.

"In any life," the Assassin King said, picking his words with care, "there is a striving toward a desired or destined end. That striving calls forth its opposite, or else is called forth by it. Is it your wish to discern the shape of your opposite? Of the man or force or idea against which you must strive and over which you must triumph, if your life is to have meaning?"

Hakkim nodded fervently. "That is exactly what I desire!" he agreed.

Imad-Basur crossed to a chest of oak chased in iron, unlocked it by means that Hakkim couldn't see, and took from it a pouch of soft leather. He took it back to Hakkim and handed it to him. Hakkim opened the pouch and saw within a quantity of powder the colour and texture of fine ash.

"It's called *siket arilar*," Imad-Basur told him. In the tongue of the Heshomet, which Hakkim vaguely knew, the phrase meant "the light shining from the knife blade."

"Take it at midnight," Imad-Basur instructed his student, "in a completely darkened room. The visions that come to you then will show you your opposite, your nemesis, though there may be veils of illusion and metaphor that you have to pierce first."

Hakkim thanked the great assassin, for this gift as well as for the less tangible gifts he had received at the school, and so departed. But he experienced a certain ambivalence about the powder, and for a long time after he returned to Bessa he did not touch it. He knew of marabouts who used chemical compounds to achieve visions, and he had the utmost contempt for them. It seemed to him that in most cases their transcendence was illusory, and their quest for it concealed a hunger of a baser and more material kind.

On the other hand, to know the face of one's enemy was a great good. Hakkim thought about the black tide that persecuted him in his dreams. He considered his own strength of will, and the probability that—should the pharmacon prove to be addictive—he could conquer his body's cravings.

The cult he led was a considerable power in Bessa now, numbering more than two thousand adherents. Hakkim chose the four strongest and most zealous from these and ordered them to guard the door of his chamber, permitting entrance to no one. Then he went inside and closed the door.

Imad-Basur had instructed him to take the smallest possible amount of the powder on the tip of his finger and touch it to his tongue. He did so now, and for a moment was convinced that it had had no effect on him; then, looking up, he perceived that the walls and ceiling of his room had melted away. He was standing in a forest glade, under the light of a sickle moon.

It was something of a relief. Hakkim had been sure in his heart that the dream of darkness would come again, rising like a flood tide around him and seeking to devour him in one peristaltic heave. At the same time, however, he felt himself at a disadvantage: if his enemy were watching, he presented a very easy target standing there in the openness of the glade. Crouching low, and careful to make no sound, he moved swiftly through the long grass and merged with the shadows under the trees. There he waited for a long while in perfect stillness and silence, but nobody appeared.

Emboldened, Hakkim searched the environs. If anything living was within that wood, he felt sure that he would find it—the assassins had taught him how to move so silently and swiftly that his passage would not stir a single leaf upon a tree, nor make a tear even in the fabric of the wind.

There was nobody in the glade, or in the trees around it. Hakkim ventured further afield, and saw, now, a watering hole nearby. He circled it carefully from a great way off, approached it with exquisite care, and found it deserted.

From the waterhole, however, he saw a cliff with many caves set into its face. He found a path that led to it, and searched the caves one by one. A million bats had made the caves their home, but nothing else lived there.

What is time within a dream? Hakkim Mehdad journeyed far and wide, for what seemed like months and years, across trackless plains, up and down mountains, along dry river beds and through meadows lush with dew-soaked grass. Nowhere in his journeying did he catch a glimpse even of his enemy's shadow, let alone his face.

Wearied by the quest, and by the solitude, and by the sense of a mystery he could not solve, he sat down at last on a rock beside the shore of a black and silent ocean. He pondered there, in this forbidding place, wondering why the powder had not seen fit to bestow its wisdom on him. Perhaps it had no revelations to give in the first place.

Gradually, though, as the waters of the black sea rolled around his feet, a conviction stole over Hakkim. He knew this place. He studied the contours of the beach, the dunes, the cliffs that overhung on all sides. None of them were at all familiar: none of them explained the sense of homecoming he felt.

It was only when he looked beneath him that he realised what it was that he was sitting on: though it was much larger, its shape was unmistakeable. It was the boulder of negative thought, which he had brought with him from the house of his first master, Rasoul, and which he still kept in a curtained closet within his private chambers.

With that realisation, and from that vantage point, the scene before him took on a different aspect. Revelation came to him, and enlightenment opened its beneficent inner eye within him. He knew now that he need seek no further—that the vision was indeed showing him what had erewhile been promised.

His enemy was nowhere to be found in the world, because his enemy was the world: *qu'aha sul jidani,* the labyrinth of masks, which postures before man's eyes like the gaudiest and most hollow-hearted of whores, and betrays him from the path of righteousness with blasphemous display. Hakkim's mission was to turn men's eyes inwards to the truth; to make them shun the beauties and the pleasures of life as the lethal snares they were.

The scale of the task both dizzied and elated him. In order to succeed in it, he would need to become the marabout of marabouts, the caliph of caliphs: he would need to extend his rule not just over the whole of Bessa, but over the whole of the east—and then, after that, over the barbarous nations of the west, where men ate excrement and talked in barks and whines like dogs.

Hakkim rose to his feet, his arms outstretched as if to receive an embrace. "I am ready," he whispered.

The landscape faded from around him as the powder's efficacy waned. Daylight and consciousness resumed their mundane duties, and Hakkim Mehdad, thenceforth and forever after the scholar with the strangling cord, went forth from his chambers to sing the dawn prayer. In his heart there was a louder singing, and in his mind the beginnings of a plan so insane in its ambition that the gods must either bless it or bow down to it.

The disciples marvelled, not just at the unwonted ferocity with which their master prayed, but also at his feet. For though he had washed them before retiring the night before, as was most proper, they were dirty and dripping now—not with mud, but with the blackest ink.

Hakkim Mehdad had found his enemy. But his eyes were on loftier things, and he did not see.

The Youth Staked Out
in the Desert

Issi the chief camel-driver woke from a restless sleep to find someone pressing on him. It was not unheard of; his assistants often huddled together on cold nights, when the fire had died down and the only warmth was the nearest body. This, though, was altogether too much— he was being crowded on both sides. Irritable and only half-awake, he made to cuff one of them.

"Get off me, you son of a donkey . . ." he began—and realised that he had not moved. His arm was pinned to the ground; both arms. And his legs. A hand was laid over his mouth.

"Don't move. Don't try to shout," said a woman's voice.

Issi's eyes shot open. It was still the pit of night, but he recognized the woman leaning over him as one of the concubines, the tall fierce-looking one that the Legate had taken. There were other women kneeling around him, one holding his left arm, and someone else pinning down his legs.

"We need some camels made ready," the tall woman said. "Also the litters. If I uncover your mouth, will you answer softly? There's no need for your men to see you like this."

She was—astonishingly—stronger than he was. Issi struggled but could not move a limb. The woman waited calmly until he nodded, then took away her hand.

"Let me go!" Issi demanded in a furious whisper. He had seen that En-Sadim was a man of effete appetites, unlike most of the new sultan's followers—but what sort of perversion required a litter, and forcible holding-down by women? "What can the Legate want with me? I'm an honest working man."

"The Legate is dead," the tall woman said. "I killed him, and all his soldiers. It may be that I don't have to kill you. Will you help us, or must I think again?"

Something cold was pressed against his throat. This was clearly a madwoman. Issi fought to hide his terror. "I'll help you," he croaked.

"Good," the woman said. In the darkness he could not read her expression, but she took the knife away from his neck and summoned one of the others to help him to his feet. Issi's legs gave way beneath him, and the two women half-carried him to the makeshift enclosure where the camels were penned.

Another group of women were waiting there, and to his inexpressible relief Issi recognized one: Lady Gursoon, a senior concubine whom he had sometimes met at the stables. She had always treated him civilly, and had once brought him water with her own hands. A woman like her could surely be trusted to keep her head. He broke away from his two guards and ran to her. They did not follow him, but still, he kept his voice low, not wanting to antagonise the madwoman.

"Lady, you must go and wake the Legate at once! That lady there" (he gestured with his eyes, afraid to move his head) "is sun-struck. She's seeing visions of murder—and she has a knife."

Lady Gursoon did not move. He tried again: "Lady—we must get help now!" But he saw with disbelief that she was shaking her head.

"Zuleika told you the truth," the old lady said. "She did kill the Legate, and we helped her to kill the others. It was to save our own lives. But you and your men are safe." She moved away from Issi, settled herself heavily onto one of the rocks that bordered the enclosure and patted the place beside her. "Here. Sit down, and I'll tell you what happened."

They had to use seven camels, and all the litters that Issi kept for travellers laid low by the sun. He helped the women to load the dead men four or five to a litter, trying not to look at the gaping wounds and the staring eyes. Then he and six of the women—they would not let him wake any of his own assistants—led the camels out toward the eastern dunes, while other women walked alongside the litters to make sure their runners did not catch on rocks, and to prevent their grisly burdens from slipping off. There was no light but the stars, and their progress was slow. When they reached the dunes they scraped a shallow trench in the ground and laid the men in it, side by side, covering them with sand. Issi knew they would be uncovered again in a day or so, to be stripped by the birds and jackals, but by then the women and their children would be long gone.

By the time they returned, the sky was beginning to lighten. They built up one of the fires from its embers and burned those clothes that had been fouled by blood. Then most of them slumped on the ground staring into the flames, unwilling to talk and trying not to think. Last night, Issi would have refused even to sit in such a way, the only man among women. Now, his mind dulled with horror and tiredness, it hardly seemed to matter. He did avert his eyes, though, when a few of the younger women pulled up their robes and stretched out bare legs to the fire. He looked instead at Lady Gursoon, marvelling at her air of composure despite her scratched hands and the straggles of grey hair now hanging around her face. She had accompanied the burial party, leading a camel, and closing the dead men's eyes as they were laid in the ground. Now she sat and gazed into the fire, her face thoughtful.

"Where will you go now?" Issi asked her.

He suddenly noticed how still she was sitting, and it came to him that she had expected the question. "That depends," she said slowly. "Will you come with us?"

Issi was taken aback. "Come with you! How can we? Hakkim Mehdad will be wanting his camels back."

"Yes he will. And if you return them he may forgive you for being among the men who allowed us to escape; and for failing to prevent the deaths of his soldiers. . . . But if you and your camels return to Bessa, there's no hope for us. The children won't be able to walk much further. Perdondaris is too far to reach now, even if we were wanted there. We might get to Agorath, but it's too small a city to disappear in. And sultan Mahmoud won't protect us from Hakkim; now he's seen what the man can do, he won't seek a war with him."

"But you have children with you!" Issi protested. "The children of his old friend. There are obligations."

"The old friend is dead," she said. "And his killer is very powerful. I met Mahmoud several times, Issi, and he never struck me as a man of sentiment. Prudence, rather."

Issi hesitated as long as he could before replying. Gursoon waited calmly, her hands folded in her lap. He had no choice, he realised.

"I'll come with you," he said heavily. "And the boys too. I'll explain it to them. So, lady: now that you have my help, where will you go?"

She wasted no time on thanks.

"South," she said at once. "Hakkim is less likely to follow us there. Our sister Zeinab used to go on trading journeys to the mountains with her father, and knows where the oases lie. But we'll need to find a place where the camels can feed when we arrive. Do you know of one?

"Only beyond the mountains! There's good grassland below the northern slopes—but the pass is far too narrow for such numbers. We could take a string of twenty beasts or so, no more."

"We'll have to do it twenty times, then," the Lady Gursoon said. "I think you should rest now."

She gestured to someone behind her, and a woman came to her side: the tall, frightening one who had first attacked him. Issi was on his feet in a moment.

"I've given you my word," he said with what dignity he could muster. "But I'm not going anywhere with her!"

The tall woman only gave him an indifferent look, as if a small dog had barked at her. Gursoon stood up in her turn, forestalling any further discussion.

"Keep an eye on the fire for me, Zuleika," she said. "Our friend must renew his strength for an hour or so, if he's to help us tomorrow. I'll find him a bed."

Issi was glad to follow her: he was suddenly overwhelmed with the need to sleep. But as Gursoon showed him into an empty tent, he turned back. The question would not let him rest.

"Your . . . sister there. She would have killed us, wouldn't she? All of the men."

Gursoon looked at him for a moment, then inclined her head in the smallest possible nod. "She had that thought."

"And you said no?"

She nodded again.

"But if I hadn't agreed to help you, would you have killed us then?" This time she made no move, and Issi was suddenly angry. "What made you so sure I'd agree?"

"If you had refused, I would have let you go," Gursoon said. "You have no weapons, and you don't wish us any harm. But we needed the beasts. And I think we have a better chance of surviving with your help. Do you remember the stables, back in Bessa? You worked there sometimes with the head groom."

Issi was mystified. "Yes, Fouad," he agreed. "A good man. What of him?"

"Oh, nothing. Only he once said the same thing about you."

The camp woke in fits and starts next morning. Imtisar, senior courtesan, thought at first that it was mere inefficiency in the men who were guarding them, when Zeinab came to wake her at first light, drawing her past tents where the children were still sleeping. From one of them, she could swear she heard snores that could only come from a full-grown man!

"Three days we've been gone," she murmured to herself, "and already there are no standards."

Zeinab took her to the edge of the camp, where most of the older women were already gathered. It was Gursoon who had called the meeting, Imtisar saw with displeasure. Of course, she was the oldest of them now—several years older than Imtisar—and so was entitled to respect, but it could not be denied that the dumpy little woman cut an unimpressive figure. And yet she would persist in running things. And she had called together an odd assortment of women, now Imtisar came to look at them: there were a couple of the servants, and that hard-faced new girl, Zuleika, with several others who had no seniority.

These thoughts vanished, however, when Gursoon began to speak. Imtisar was shocked beyond measure to hear of the events of the night. She was more horrified still when they began to talk of their current prospects. Of course, they could not now go to Perdondaris. Imtisar had no illusions that the powerful Kephiz Bin Ezvahoun would take in four hundred women and children who had belonged to someone else, if there was nothing in it for him but trouble. Besides, it was too far, without any protection but a few camel-drivers. But there were other, closer cities where they might have more of a claim. Sultan Mahmoud of Agorath, for instance, had been vocal—and frequently tactile—in his appreciation of the harem on his visits to Bessa. Mahmoud was a vulgar and ill-mannered man, to be sure. But if the alternative was to live in the hills, eating stewed goat and sleeping on rocks!

"That's absurd," Imtisar said. "We should go to Agorath, and ask Mahmoud for his protection. Or to Ishar, where I have a cousin. Many of us have family in the closer cities."

"Zeinab," Gursoon said. "How many days' travel is it from here to Agorath?"

"Six days at best, Auntie," the girl answered respectfully. "At the speed we've been going, I'd say closer to eight or nine."

"And there's our problem," Gursoon said. "Agorath is the closest of the cities, so it'll be where Hakkim Mehdad first looks for us. And make no mistake, he will look. At this moment, he believes his men are burying us at the dunes. In a day, maybe two at most, he'll expect their return, and then he'll send more men out to find them. When their bodies are discovered, I imagine he'll be searching for us with some eagerness. He has horses at his disposal, and skilled archers. How hard do you think we'll be to find, four hundred of us, on the road to a city?"

"But the mountains!" Imtisar protested. "There's nothing there! Rocks, and snakes, and bandits! Nothing!"

"No roads leading there, either," Gursoon said complacently. "And our most urgent need is to disappear. Where better?"

They had a story ready to tell the children and the camel-hands. In the night, a messenger had come from Hakkim Mehdad summoning the Legate and all his men back to Bessa. They had gone at once, leaving their charges to their fate in the desert. One or two of the camel-hands wanted to follow the soldiers, despite Issi's orders, but faced with the piteous wailing of some of the younger women, they all agreed to help the unfortunates to find a place of safety first. Fernoush and Halima wiped their eyes and thanked the young men prettily, while Zeinab, who was helping to water the camels, watched with amazement. Despite Fernoush's assurances, she had not expected the men to be so easily swayed.

Having agreed to take on the role of saviours, the men were ready enough to leave at once, though a little puzzled by the women's urgency. They were more than puzzled when they learned their intended destination.

"The mountains! How can you go there?" the skinny, moustached one asked Zeinab. They had finished the watering and were now tightening saddles. "Why not one of the cities?"

The women had agreed in advance how much of the truth could be allowed. "It's because they left us so suddenly, without any instructions," she told him, eyes lowered. "We think Hakkim must want us to die in the desert. So the aunties decided it might be best for us to disappear, at least for a while."

"But there's nothing in the mountains!" The man looked unexpectedly concerned. "How will you live?"

"There are goats, and other animals," Zeinab said. She looked up at him. "And you and your brothers must be skilful hunters."

"That's true," he said, teeth flashing through the moustache. Suddenly animated, he began to tell her about the big gazelle buck he had brought down last month. *Fernoush was right*, she thought, *they can be swayed. Maybe we can make this work after all.*

They were packed and ready to go before the sun was fully over the dunes, the children tumbled out of bed at the last minute and onto the backs of camels. No one would walk today, except for the drivers. The smaller children rode two or three together, with their mothers or elder siblings. If the camel-drivers noticed that there were suddenly more beasts to go around, no one mentioned it in the flurry of departure. Every waterskin was filled, and thirty of the women had each concealed an extra one among their baggage. Neither Zeinab nor Issi knew of another oasis closer than two days away to the south. They would have to make haste for more than one reason.

They left by the road to the north, leaving a thousand footprints in the soft ground near the waterhole for Hakkim's men to follow. When the ground hardened and the shifting sand began to drift over their path, they abandoned the road and turned southwest. Zuleika stayed behind with half a dozen other women to cover their tracks at this point, sweeping over the ground with bundles of sacking tied to poles. Zeinab was one of the group. She had not slept all night, but for now she felt as if she could never be still again. She worked side by side with Umayma; the two did not speak, but now and then exchanged glances of complicity. The other women who had taken part in the night's grim work were riding with their children, holding them close and reminding themselves at every step of what the killing had been for. But her daughter Soraya was old enough to ride with one of her friends, and Umayma's son was the chosen companion of Prince Jamal.

When the work was done to Zuleika's satisfaction, they mounted their camels and rode after the caravan. Zeinab would be needed later on in the journey as a guide, but for now she was glad to stay at the back, out of sight.

She glanced at Umayma, riding beside her, and saw that she was smiling, as if at a pleasant memory. The sight filled Zeinab with unease. "Are you well, Umi?" she asked cautiously.

Umayma seemed to consider this.

"Yes. Yes I am," she said. "My son is alive, and so am I." They rode in silence for a while. Then Umayma said abruptly, "Did I ever tell you, my father sold me?"

"No," said Zeinab, confused. In fact, she thought she had heard this before, but it was the experience of several of her sister concubines. And Umayma seemed to want to talk.

"He sold me to a merchant he had dealings with. I was glad to leave the house at first, even though he was a very ugly man. But he didn't want me for a wife—he took me in his baggage train, as entertainment on the long journeys. He told people I was his daughter. When he came to Bessa, the sultan asked him for me. I think he got some sort of trade agreement in exchange. He said he was sorry to part with me. I was relieved. I hated the desert, or I thought I did. Of course, what I really hated was the merchant. It looks so different now, seeing it as a free woman."

Zeinab had not viewed their situation in this light before. Freedom?

"You may be right," she temporised. "But before we can live free, don't forget that we have to find the next waterhole . . ."

"You'll find it," said Umayma with absolute certainty.

"And then we have to get through the mountains. We don't even know how we'll find food and shelter. It's not going to be easy."

"We have Zuleika," Umayma said. "She can hunt, and we'll learn from her. Nothing will stand in her way."

Her confidence both impressed and daunted Zeinab. She too had seen Zuleika in action: it was an-awe-inspiring sight, and one that Zeinab planned to forget if she could. But Umayma's face was alight with the energy of the convert. "She'll teach us how to live out here," she said.

Their luck held, at least for the time being. The plain was not entirely featureless; before the sun reached its height Issi recognized a certain tall rock that had a depression at its base large enough to shade the children through the worst of the day's heat. The rest of them put up the largest of the tents for shelter. They had made fair time, Issi reckoned, and Gursoon allowed them two full turns of the glass to rest. Zeinab called her daughter Soraya into the tent with her and embraced her fiercely, to the girl's surprise. Lying beside her daughter, she fell at once into sleep so deep that she only wakened when the dressmaker Farhat came round to shake the laggards two hours later.

The old servant had brought her a cup of water, which she sipped gratefully. Her mouth was painfully dry, but she knew, none better, how strictly the water must be rationed now. She gave half the cupful to Soraya, and saw with approval how carefully her daughter drank, not gulping, making it last. Perhaps we can learn to live in the hills, she thought. If I can lead us to the next water. She tried again to remember every detail of those two journeys, nearly eighteen years ago, and her throat tightened.

Farhat came out with the cup, and nodded to Gursoon. "She's awake," she said. "Her daughter is with her."

"Good," Gursoon said. "That'll help to calm her. She's a good girl, but last night was hard on her. And we need her to get us to that water. Issi says he knows the way, but he's an old man. I don't entirely trust his memory."

Farhat didn't point out that the camel-leader was about the same age as Gursoon. The two women had been friends for many years; it was chiefly this friendship that had led her to come with the seraglio into the desert, though she could have stayed with her dead husband's family in Bessa. "Who else still needs waking?" she said instead.

"Just Adiya and Imtisar, I think. The younger ones are all ready." Gursoon pulled a face. "I'll do Imtisar, shall I? She gets bad-tempered when she's woken."

Farhat grimaced too. "You mean when she's awake," she said, and both women laughed.

The camel-drivers made up for the lost time by driving the beasts into a lumbering trot whenever they were sure of their bearings, slowing only when the desert stretched emptily around them and Issi and Zeinab cast about for new landmarks. Before nightfall they found the ring of stones that they had been seeking, set up by earlier travellers to mark the route.

The oasis would be another day's journey directly to the south.

"I remember it took us longer, though," Zeinab said. "We had to travel through the night."

"I wouldn't risk that," said Issi. "We should camp here; we can't risk losing the way now."

Their luck changed on the following day. Finding the stones had raised everyone's spirits, but it seemed that no more markers had been left. They trudged across empty sand with only the sun and the fading line of their footprints behind to give them direction. The heat grew; some of the water-flasks were already empty, and no hills were yet in sight, but no one dared to think of stopping to rest.

A little after noon an argument broke out between Zeinab and Issi when they spotted something in the sand a fair way to the east, a darkish smudge low down to the ground.

"It can't be a marker," Issi insisted. "It'll lead us off the route. I'm telling you, our way is directly north."

"But how long ago were either of us here?" Zeinab said. "Whatever that is, it doesn't look natural. Someone left it there, and it could help to guide us."

"If it's not a waterhole, I don't care what it is," the camel-leader growled. But there was no point quarrelling. They had passed no other landmark for an hour or more; even Issi was less certain of his way than he liked to show. Besides, the children were beginning to cry with thirst and tiredness. They agreed to put up tents, for no more than an hour, while a small group went to investigate.

It was not a marker. Zeinab had gone ahead of the group, peering through the heat haze and the dry flurries of sand stirred up by the wind. They were almost at the thing when she stopped, staring. She said nothing as the others caught up with her.

"So?" Gursoon demanded, puffing slightly at the back. "What is . . . Oh."

In times past, some of the more traditionalist sultans had done this, as a punishment for treachery, perhaps, or for some insult deemed unforgivable. Now, Gursoon would have said it was too barbaric for any but the worst of brigands.

"But he's just a boy!" someone muttered. "Look at him!"

A young man—very young, it seemed, from his slight build—had been laid out in the sand, his outstretched hands and feet tied with ropes which were attached to four stout wooden stakes. His clothes were ripped; his bare face scorched by the sun to a mask of black and red. His eyes were closed, but he moved his head a little as they approached, and let out a faint sound that might have been a groan.

"What do we do?" Fernoush whispered.

"Do?" said Gursoon. "Cut him loose! He's alive!"

"No." Zuleika laid a hand on her arm. "Think first, auntie. We have next to no water as it is, and the journey's more than uncertain. We can't afford to delay. And the boy is all but dead."

"Then he'll die in what comfort we can give him," Gursoon said. Her tone allowed no argument. Zuleika stared at her for a moment, then nodded once, and strode over to the prone figure.

"This isn't a boy," she said. "It's a woman."

Zeinab and Gursoon were already cutting the ropes that held her feet and hands. The young woman gave a single hoarse scream as her arms were released, than fell silent. Her eyes had opened, black-on-black in her burned face, but it seemed she had no more voice.

Zuleika took the woman's shoulders and Fernoush and Zeinab held a leg apiece. They carried her as gently as they could, but her face still twisted in pain from time to time, and her breathing hitched into ragged gasps with any unevenness of the ground.

"Was it a marker?" demanded Issi as soon as they reached the camp. His face fell when he saw what they carried. But he offered no criticism, and set up one of the litters to pull the sick woman when they set off. They laid her down and gave her a little of the precious water, dribbling it into her mouth a drop at a time.

"We should wait an hour longer," said Gursoon, looking down at the woman's ravaged face. "Her breathing's a little easier. I think she may live, if she can rest in the shade awhile."

Both Issi and Zuleika started to protest. But it was the sick woman herself who answered. She stirred on her makeshift bed and murmured something.

"What was that, child?" Gursoon bent closer. The voice was fainter than a whisper.

"No . . . You go now."

"What's that?" said Gursoon, startled. The young woman's black gaze was fixed on her.

"You set off now," she croaked, her voice a hoarse whisper like the whisper of dust against stone. "At once. And when the mountains come in sight you turn a little to the west, as Issi remembers. Keep going. You find the water an hour after sunset."

Gursoon rocked back on her heels and stared down at her. After a moment, she said, "How can you know that?"

The young woman's mouth twitched in a fleeting grimace. "I know. Believe me."

"Who are you, girl?" Gursoon asked.

Her eyes were closing as if she had exhausted herself, but the old woman caught one word in answer.

"Rem."

THE FATE OF THOSE
WHO SEARCH FOR TRUTH

In many ways my life has been far longer than its actual span. The visions that beset me come from both before and after my time—and what I see is not always my own life. This has caused me much anxiety in the past. Often I can't tell whose fate it is that I'm viewing, or even whether that fate is in the past or still to come. Only by focusing all my attention on a single situation or individual can I ever get what might be called a prediction—and those are partial, conditional and usually unwelcome. For reasons that may be apparent, I don't tend to seek them out.

So while I'm aware it sets me apart, my sight is no better as a guide to everyday living than anyone's day-to-day experience: frequently unclear, and best made sense of with hindsight. Despite the promise made to me, I can't see everything, or not in a way that does me any good. The two events that have most shaped my life were both unforeseen—or as near unforeseen as makes no difference—and both beyond my power to control. When I recall either of them, as I do often, it's in a perpetual present. They will never leave me, never grow any less sharp in my mind.

The first begins as a story. Some of it I remember only as a tale, told to a child before she slept. It was told with tears, as befits a tale of guilt and sorrow, but for all that it was the one I most often demanded, and I would not permit a word to be changed. As I repeat it now, my mother's voice sounds in my head, by turns fierce with grief and tremulous with wonder.

There was a woman named Rahdi, who had grown to mistrust her husband. She had married him for love, defying her parents to go with him—but once she had no home but his, she felt his fiery heart cool and his thoughts turn away from her. He became like any husband, eyeing other women in the market and sulking when his dinner was late. Even their little daughter failed to rouse his interest, once he had ascertained that the child was not a boy. And as time went on Rahdi became certain that he had taken a lover.

She could prove nothing. Many husbands came home late; many left the house in their finest clothes and stayed out drinking with their friends. Alone with her sleeping child, Rahdi stared at the walls and remembered her father's bitter words when she left his house, four years before: *You think you know what you're doing, girl. But no one knows all that's to come. No one!* She brooded on this, and when her husband came home silent and sulky, and turned from her in the night, she resolved that she would know, would know this one thing at least.

On the day that her daughter turned four, Rahdi waited for her husband to leave the house. She took a great waterskin on her back and took the child by the hand, and went with her out of the town, into the desert. Years before, when she herself was a child, her grandmother had told her of a certain cave, within the desert hills some two days' walk to the east. In that cave, her grandmother said, lived the djinni, who could grant gifts to those reckless enough to seek them. One who gained their favour might be rewarded with knowledge of hidden things, or of things to come. Of course, the old woman had added, they might curse you instead for your presumption; even kill you. Who knows the ways of the djinni?

The little girl's legs were short, and the journey took fully three days. The child never complained: she had not yet learned to speak in her four years, and she said nothing now. But Rahdi breathed a silent prayer of thanks when the hills loomed above them in the heat of the third day, and she saw the rock with its standing stones as her grandmother had described it to her, and heard the sound of water. She fed herself and the child, and filled their waterskin at the tiny spring. Then she followed the old woman's directions to the djinni's cave.

The djinni were there. They came out at the dark opening to meet her: three of them, or four, or maybe more: their shapes flickered so that it was not easy to tell. One of them was like a tall woman with a light behind her veil instead of a face; another like a naked man with the head of a bull. Another was beaked, with white feathers pouring from its head, and another—or maybe it was one of these three—had eyes too large to belong to the face of man or beast, as flat and round as cooking-stones. The sight of them filled Rahdi with terror; she thrust the child behind her and fell on her face. But no fire fell from heaven to blast her; there was no sound at all, and after a moment she raised her head to see the creatures still shimmering before her, while her daughter stared at them with dark, unblinking eyes.

Summoning her courage, she spoke to them, her voice sounding thin and faltering in her own ears.

"May I find favour in your eyes, great ones. I have come here to beg for knowledge."

Nothing changed in the flickering faces, but one of the djinni now stood before the others and addressed Rahdi. Its form shifted as it spoke, so that the speaker was now the woman, now the bull-man, now the bird-thing, now some other, even less possible to describe, while the figures behind it took on others of the fleeting shapes.

"The knowledge you seek will do you no good." Its voice was many voices, harsh and sweet jarring together.

Rahdi looked it in the face then, staring into the stony eyes. "And yet I ask it," she said, and heard her voice grow stronger. "I cannot bear to live as I live now. I must know."

A sound like the cry of birds came from the djinni: Rahdi thought it might be laughter. The speaker opened a great curved beak.

"Know?" it repeated. "Know what?"

"Everything," Rahdi said.

The speaker of the djinni turned its head—now horned and black-pelted—to where the child stood silently watching. "What is her name?" it said.

Rahdi was taken aback. She reached out to pull the child closer to her; but one did not refuse a djinn. "Rem," she answered.

The speaker nodded once, and the shadowy figures behind it nodded. "Good," it said.

And the child's black eyes grew wider. For an instant her face writhed like the faces of the creatures before her. Then she threw back her head and howled.

From that moment it is no longer a story: this is where memory begins.

How can I describe it? I could say that all the words of the world rushed in on me at once. That happened, but more than that. There were voices too, a mad cacophony of them, and images. I saw a great army marching in the desert, and the sand at their feet red with blood. I saw the sultan's palace, the servants with cups and heaped trays, the newest concubine weeping in a corner. And I saw houses taller than any house could be, palaces like monstrous stone tablets. A room filled wall-to-wall with books . . . a beggar woman shouting and waving a crutch in anger . . . a bearded man called Hakkim Mehdad, plotting war. Children gazing entranced at a box, which painted their faces with flickering light. My father, embracing a strange woman . . . The market near our home, with its stalls on fire and the merchants running in terror. All this in an instant, and at the same time the words pattering around me, telling, explaining. All the words. I had not known most of them even existed. Now they were mine.

There was so much, and I could not put it away. At first I howled because I did not understand. Then I howled because I did.

I scarcely felt my mother's arms around me. She knelt with her face pressed against mine, shaking me with her cries which I could not hear. After a time she took my shoulders and stared appalled into my weeping eyes. Black. Black tears. Her own face was streaked with them.

"What have you done?" she screamed at the djinni.

"We have granted your wish," the speaker said. "But we did not give the gift to you."

Rahdi shrieked curses at the shadowy figures, forgetting all her awe and terror. The speaker seemed to ignore them.

"She will see," it said, and now its form and voice were that of the veiled woman, calm and withdrawing. "She will understand, and remember, and record."

It turned its head to me, the white light shining for an instant through the veil and into my eyes. Was there pity in its voice, for that one instant?

"All things will unveil themselves to her," it said. "Except those which touch her most nearly."

And it was gone, all of them were gone. My mother and I faced a blank rock wall. We held each other in silence, as her shaking subsided and the black tears dried on our faces.

And then? I had been marked, but there was no great destiny to take up; the world went on as before. Only my mother and I were changed. She talked to me as we journeyed back, and I replied. A few nights later we left my faithless father, taking with us his cashbox and all my clothes, and walked back to the town where my mother was born. Her own mother had died, but we stayed for a while with my grandfather; long enough for me to understand that my new gift was best viewed as an affliction, and to learn some of the skills of concealment. When he died, we travelled to Bessa, where my mother found a job at a pastry cook's shop and I spent my days in the market, and discovered the written word. And so embarked on the path that would lead me here, into the desert.

Was it all preordained? I can't believe that. I foresaw this end, of course, but only as one of a hundred outcomes. Not all of them could happen to me: some, I think, will never happen because others took their place. In any case, once I learned some measure of control over my visions, I would never dwell on the uglier ones, preferring, like most people, to be soothed rather than disturbed. And how could I recognize that splayed, ravaged figure in the sand as myself?

At the end of my trial Hakkim Mehdad had given me one look in which contempt was mixed with a kind of horror, before he turned away. "Let her die slowly," he had said, his back turned. And so they led me out into the desert. We travelled for two days, away from the beaten tracks, Captain Ashraf of the Ascetic cult and two of his men. I went with them quietly—what else was there to do? The three men rode, and I walked behind Ashraf, roped to his camel. It was the rule of the Cult to acknowledge no obstacle that was merely physical in nature, so we travelled through the heat of the day, halting only briefly when the sun was at its height. To give Ashraf his due, he rode slowly enough to save me from stumbling, and allowed me water and would not allow his men to rape me when we stopped for the night.

None of them would speak to me, but I was able to distract myself as I walked with memories and imaginings. The books I had hidden were safe, I thought, and the others might yet be rescued. As for myself, I don't think I really believed I would die then. There was so much else I had seen: my sense of a future was still strong. But that changed when the men stopped at the end of the second day, in the middle of a plain that had no end in any direction.

"Here," Ashraf said, and the men dismounted and took down wooden stakes and mallets from the backs of their two camels. At the sight, the terror I had kept back flooded over me like the bursting of a dam. I suppose my face whitened, and I began to shake. The men saw and laughed, but Ashraf's face never moved. He directed his men to drive the stakes into the sand. When they threw me down I was too weak with fear to resist, and only tried to curl up on the ground like a child. They tied me hand and foot, I remember Ashraf's look of distaste as he seized my legs to pull them out straight. One of the men tore off my scarf. The other ripped my robe with his sword and made to strip me, but the captain stopped him with a motion.

"Leave her!" he said. He looked down on me with the same blend of contempt and horror that I had seen on the face of Hakkim Mehdad; then like his master, he turned away.

I could not see them as they mounted and rode off. I don't know if any of them looked back.

The first pain is only from the ropes which cut into my wrists and ankles. I struggle, try to loosen them, but they hold me fast. Then the sun is directly in my eyes and I must close them, seeing the pulsing redness through my eyelids. The cramps begin then, first aching, then agonizing. It can't get worse than this, I keep thinking, but it does. At some point I know that I am screaming. It's dark now, the darkness pressing on me and no one to hear. The voices in my head are silent, for the first time in fifteen years; I can't even call up the sense of them. Later the pain goes somewhere further off, my legs and shoulders are numb, and my mind too. It's cold now, I begin to shiver, and then to shudder so violently that I think I will pull the stakes out of the ground, but they hold still. When the shuddering stops, for a while I don't feel anything at all.

I wake to see grey light, and feel something brushing my face. An instant later there's a stabbing pain in my cheek—a black bird, its beady eye glaring into mine. My scream makes him recoil, and I find that the night's dew has given some slack to the ropes: I can thrash my arms enough to scare him away. I do this for a long time, while he and his companions gather around me, making exploratory stabs until I manage to hit one directly on the beak and they all take off with harsh cries. I have a moment of idiotic triumph, before I remember where I am. And then the sun rises, and the air starts to burn.

Maybe memory becomes less sharp now, or at least less defined. There is a torture of thirst, and the skin baking and splitting on my face and exposed arms and legs. The ropes tighten again, pulling my body apart, and I cry out until I have no more voice. I can't weep. My eyelids are squeezed shut, and I have a fear that they will shrivel in the heat, turn to ash and leave my eyes exposed to the merciless light. I hear again the harsh cries overhead, and think not of the carrion birds but of the djinni and their birdlike laughter. And see them again, as clearly as I did in childhood, when they gave me the gift that has doomed me. For the first time I wonder: what was it for? I saved the books, was that it? Did they take and shape a woman's life, just so that she could preserve the words of others, not to make any stories of her own? And I remember my mother's words: who can understand the ways of the djinni? The waste of it fills me, not with rage, but with a vast and empty sadness.

When the ground begins to shake beneath me, I take it for an illusion. I have borne enough sun to strike me mad a dozen times over. The shaking intensifies, comes closer, and now I hear voices, outside my head. They are women, and they seem to be arguing. This is so unlikely that perhaps it strikes me even then. But I'm beyond wonder. I keep my eyes shut. I listen to the voices.

Part of my gift is to understand words, all words, in whatever language. But try as I may, I can't recall one word of what they say. I hear the voices: pity, astonishment, warning. And then a shadow comes between my eyelids and the punishing sun, and I feel hands on mine, cutting the ropes that bind me. And I open my eyes, and see her.

In the Mountains
of the North

It took another eight days of travel for them to reach the foothills of the mountains. They did not attempt to negotiate the pass, which as Issi had said, was barely wide enough to take two camels abreast. Instead, Zeinab led them to a spring a few hours further away, not large but well-hidden, among so many rocks that it was hard to find any greenery. It was the farthest her parents had ever taken her.

"Even coming this far was a risk, twenty years ago," Issi said. "The hills were full of bandits in those days. I hear it was better after Vurdik the Bald was caught, but by then most of us had found different routes."

"And how safe is it now?" demanded Imtisar. "Have we come this far to be murdered in our beds? Not that we can call them beds."

"There's much less traffic through the pass these days, and none this far west," Issi assured her. "We'll be safe enough now."

The rocks provided more shade than they had seen for days. The camels huddled discontentedly on the sand while the children, and then the women and men, scrambled over the stones to drink. The sun was near the horizon before all had drunk their fill, but even after the beasts were watered, the little spring still bubbled up clearly. Gursoon looked at it in satisfaction.

"This is a good place," she said to Farhat. "Zeinab and Issi did well. We'll stay here for a few days while we decide what to do next."

They brought water to the sick woman, Rem, whom Farhat had adopted as her personal charge. The girl was improving day by day, though her face was still so burned and blistered that it was hard to make out her features. For the first two days she had been too weak to eat, and even now that she was gaining strength she moved slowly and painfully, and spoke little. But she stirred when she saw Farhat, pulled herself upright on the litter and took the drinking cup in her own hands, wincing only a little. She murmured her thanks, and sank back as if the effort had exhausted her.

"She's a strange one," Gursoon said as the two women withdrew. "Did I tell you, Farhat, that she knew we'd find water, that first day we found her? She told me we had to leave at once, and walk on after dark. She was right."

"She has the sight," Farhat said. "I've heard of such a gift before, but never seen it. But yes, I believe the girl knows things." She stopped, looking around to check that no one could overhear. "Mistress Gursoon . . . There was something she told me that's been weighing on me. But I don't want to offend you."

Gursoon was taken aback. "How long have we known each other, Farhat? Am I so easily offended? Come now, we're friends."

"I hope so." The seamstress's face was still uneasy. "Yesterday, then, while I was feeding her. She spoke to me, called me by name, though I hadn't told it to her."

"That's strange," Gursoon agreed. "But not alarming, surely."

"I don't know. Some of what she said was plainly wild talk; she's not over the sunstroke yet. She spoke as if she knew me, and said she admired my work, as if I were some kind of artist. I told her the only work I did was with the needle, and she just nodded." Farhat laughed. "She said I was a master of my craft. So I told her again she was mistaken, I was just a servant. Then she seemed to realise what she'd been saying:—she looked confused, and begged my pardon. But as I left, she said something else, something that has stayed with me. I wasn't sure I'd heard her right, she speaks so softly. But I think she said, 'You're not servants now.'"

Farhat darted a look at her mistress. Gursoon had dropped her hands to her lap, a sign of attention, but she did not seem shocked. "She said that to you?"

"Maybe to all of us. And I think she's right. Look at where we are, how we'll all have to live from now on. I'm not a servant here. None of us are."

There was a silence between the two women. Around them, the

women of the seraglio were making camp for the night. Most of the serving girls were helping to fasten tents or chivvying the children. Imtisar was scolding one of them for slowness. Nearby, Najla and Jumanah giggled together while two maids brushed out their hair, for all the world as if they were sitting on divans back in the palace, rather than on a barely shaded rock. For a moment they all seemed to Gursoon like children: little girls playing a game, as if they could raise the sultan's palace in the desert by pretending they were still there.

"You're right," the older woman said at last. "Yes—we all have to change now. There'll be arguments, of course. Probably screaming." She looked out again over the busy camp. Maybe it was only a game, but it was a calm and orderly one, at least. For now, each woman had a role to play, and seemed content to play it.

"Farhat," she said, "do you think we could keep this from the others for a day or two? Just till we can work out where we're going."

Gursoon spent an hour in conversation with Zeinab and Issi, questioning each of them closely on what they knew of the mountains and the land beyond. Issi had traded sometimes in the northern lands, and found them rocky and inhospitable, with few settlements and cold winters. Zeinab knew only that fear of brigands had kept her father from ever venturing north of here.

"Well," Gursoon said, "even brigands must have needed food and shelter. If they've gone now, maybe we can find where they lived."

"But what if they're still here?" demanded Zeinab.

"In that case," Gursoon conceded, "we'll have to plan more carefully."

She went to find Zuleika, and told her some of what she had in mind.

"It seems to me," she finished, "that a woman of your abilities could be useful to us in this situation. But there are one or two things I need to know first."

"You need to know whether the bandits still live here," Zuleika said, "and their numbers and strength. Was there something else?"

"Yes. It concerns you."

Zuleika's face was impassive. She tilted her head, inviting Gursoon to continue.

"In the next few days, we have to decide our own fate. Whatever we do, lives will be at risk. And if I'm to trust you in this task, I need to know who you are—what you are."

"A few days ago, I saved the life of everyone here," Zuleika said quietly. "Does that not lead you to trust me?"

"No. One day, if we live, we'll all honour you for what you did then. But no, it doesn't make me trust you. How long have you lived with us, Zuleika: three years? In all that time, you never quite seemed to belong. You'd walk into a room as if there was an enemy there. You could sit for an hour, quite still, as though you were waiting for something. And whenever you spoke to one of the guards, you looked him in the eye. No other woman would do that, not even me. I used to wonder about it sometimes. Now it seems I know why."

"It's true, I wasn't bred to your life," Zuleika said. "But what of it? Did I not do everything that was required of me?"

"That's not what I mean and you know it," Gursoon said coldly. "Five years studying the art of murder, Zuleika? Were you telling me you were some kind of assassin?"

"Yes. That's what I was."

"Then, in the name of the Increate, what were you doing in a seraglio?"

"You can't trust me unless you know this?"

"No."

Zuleika sighed.

"If I tell you, I'll be false to my oath. But I suppose it was already broken. Well then: I came to the seraglio to kill someone. And I stayed because I changed my mind."

She waited for an answer, but Gursoon was suddenly silent, staring at her as if something she had long dreaded had at last come to pass. Zuleika sighed again.

"Sit down here," she said. "I'll tell you everything that happened."

The Tale of the Assassin
Who Became a Concubine

There was once a woman who was trained as an assassin. She lived quietly and alone, in a small house on the edge of the town, and was known to her landlord and her neighbours as the widow of a prosperous merchant. This was a lie, but the neighbours believed it for two reasons. Firstly, she asked for neither work nor charity from the women of the town, and therefore must have a legacy. And secondly, though she was still young and beautiful, she kept herself as strictly veiled as any old widow, and discouraged her inevitable suitors so effectively that none ever came to her door more than once.

The way the woman lived was this.

Within the town, at some distance from her home, was a school where assassins were trained and from where they might be hired. It was an extraordinary establishment, created and ruled by an extraordinary man, the so-called Caliph of Assassins, Imad-Basur.

A steady trickle of men came to the door of the school at night, seeking the removal of insults, business obstacles or otherwise intractable problems. Imad-Basur offered a discreet and efficient service, and further assured his clients that no assignment was too large for his skilled staff. (Given the scale of their charges, the question of a job being too small had never arisen; the assassins took lives, but not lightly.)

On occasion, however, a commission might arise that required particular discretion: where the target was hard to approach, say, or unusually suspicious. On such occasions, a messenger would be dispatched from the school to the home of the woman at the edge of the town. Over several years she had built up a reputation for reliability, and in recognition of this, and of her status outside the school's official auspices, she was allowed to keep three-quarters of the payment for her work.

At that time, the desert kingdoms were wont to war among themselves for power and prestige. Every year or so, an army of hot-blooded young men would be sent out against some city, to avenge some or other insult. They would return in tatters, or else tear a hole through the city's army and return with booty. The following year, the defeated city would retaliate. In this way the treasure of the various cities was kept in circulation, and the population of hot-blooded young men kept within manageable limits.

One sultan, however, had for many years avoided war, thus keeping his treasure to himself and his army relatively strong. This man, Bokhari Al-Bokhari of Bessa, had moreover extended his influence over the neighbouring cities through the judicious use of bribes, and through regular and lavish hospitality. The power he had thus acquired in the region had, of course, earned him several rivals, who found to their dismay that he was not to be provoked into fighting. With the traditional means of conquest denied to them, it was only a matter of time before one such rival approached the Brotherhood of Assassins.

Here an immediate problem arose. The sultan was old and cautious: he kept himself surrounded by bodyguards at all times, and only relaxed his guard in the company of his family, or among his concubines. Accordingly, the master of the assassins sent a messenger to the woman at the edge of the city, who agreed to meet the client. His proposal was for her to enter the sultan's seraglio, from where she would be able to fulfil the commission without interference.

The woman did not immediately accept the assignment. Her hesitation had nothing to do with the eminence of the intended victim— the assassins made no distinctions of rank, except in their scale of charges—nor with any concern about difficulty. It was simply that she had not been among women for a long time, and had forgotten how to act in their company. Also, her client behaved toward her with more than customary arrogance, brushing aside her questions about the palace with a curt order to be quiet and follow instructions. But she reflected that her calling required flexibility—and besides, a girl had to live.

She demanded a hefty retainer, counted it out to the last dirham, and consented to be brought to the palace by a silversmith in the client's pay, posing as his cousin from Yrtsus. She was skilled in dealing with men— the sultan was charmed, and immediately entered into negotiations to acquire her.

So the assassin entered the seraglio.

She was unmoved by the perfumed rooms, the silk hangings, the gardens of fig and apricot trees, and the surpassing beauty of the inmates, any of which would have overwhelmed most interlopers. But she was not prepared for the life of the women's court, nor for her treatment there. She found a perpetual quiet hubbub: women arguing, gossiping, swapping hair-combs, pins and stories, while children played freely around their feet. And she was accepted at once as one of them.

Since her fifteenth year the assassin had lived among men and, since she entered her training, with little human contact of any kind. It pleased her now to be spoken to as an equal, and to feel herself, for a while, part of a community. And since she felt no great sense of urgency about her allotted task, she resolved to delay its commission for a day or two.

That night the sultan sent for her to visit him in his chamber. Her plan had been to break his neck at his moment of ecstasy or smother him as he slept afterwards, and make her escape the same night. She did neither. Instead she bore the man's attentions patiently, and returned next day to the women's quarters.

Over the days that followed the assassin became accustomed to life in the harem. She spoke with the other women, questioning them about how each had come to this place. All of them had been sold to the sultan by their families or guardians, and some wept as they told of betrothals forcibly broken, or of beloved friends and sisters never seen again. But most seemed content enough with their lot. This puzzled the assassin.

"You were bought and sold like slaves," she said. "Turned over for life to a man who can give you no pleasure."

"True," agreed the woman she spoke to. She was one of the oldest members of the harem, and the most respected by the others; she had taken an interest in the newcomer and spent part of every day in her company, teaching her the rules of her new life. "That was our misfortune," she said, "and yours too, now. But we've built ourselves a life here. We're free from want, and our children grow up in safety. And we do have a measure of power." She smiled at the other's expression of disbelief. "We know the sultan's moods, and his weaknesses," she explained, "the means by which he can be guided. He's a man of whim, quick to take offence. In his younger days he would start a war for an imagined insult. But treated with care, he can be calmed and diverted. For twenty years now we have kept him peaceable, and in that time the city has flourished."

This was certainly true: in fact it was the reason for the assassin's presence there. But she could not speak of that.

The same night, she was summoned once more to the sultan's chamber, and once more spared his life. The next day she spoke again to the woman who had befriended her.

"What would happen to you," she asked, "if the sultan should die?"

The older woman frowned. "It's true that we fear his loss," she said. "The crown prince is as hot-tempered as his father was twenty years ago, and far more foolhardy. He'd send all us older women away, of course, and his wives are empty-headed creatures. Those of us that were left would have to begin the work all over again."

The assassin was thoughtful for some time after this conversation. The sultan's death would certainly lead to an invasion, and even if his sons won the resulting war, the city would return to the old cycle of battles and preparation for battles from which the women had rescued it. And either way, her new friend and many others with her would be cast out. She knew what this would mean for them. She had seen at first hand the fate of women who were owned and used by men, when they were no longer wanted. And it came to her that this was unjust, and not to be borne. The old concubine was both more honest and more intelligent than either the sultan or his enemy; furthermore, she reminded the assassin of one who had shown her kindness in her youth. She said to herself that these women deserved her protection, even at the cost of breaking her code.

If an assassin refused a commission after taking payment, he was barred from the Assassins' Brotherhood forever. Because of her sex, the woman had never been admitted to the Brotherhood in the first place; still, she had sworn an oath, and accepted the protection and patronage of the master. These she now renounced.

She made enquiries and found a messenger whom the women of the harem sometimes entrusted with gifts of money and valuables to their families. She satisfied herself of his reliability by her own means, and sent him with a package to a private house in the city. The house belonged to Imad-Basur, and the package contained the bag of silver that she had taken as her retainer, together with a gold bracelet that would more than cover the cost of any down payment her client might have made to the master himself. The woman had never learned to write, and so could send no message, but the master assassin was an intelligent man: he would understand from the gift both her refusal of the commission and her acknowledgement of some remaining obligation to him.

So the assassin became a concubine. Her duties were not arduous; the sultan's love-making was irksome, but her profession had inured her to necessary discomforts. Most of her energies were given to the task she now set herself: the protection of the man she had sworn to kill, and through him, of the women of her new community.

As she had expected, the sultan's next feast was attended by her rejected client, who risked both his own life and hers by arranging a private meeting with her. She was able to convince him swiftly, and without leaving any mark upon his skin, that he could not compel her to do his bidding. She could not persuade him, however, to abandon his designs against the sultan. Over the next year or two she was fully occupied in spotting and thwarting the fresh assassins he sent. They showed varying degrees of skill, and had all, she assumed, been warned about her, but not one of them took the warning seriously until it was too late.

And so she lived, protecting an unworthy man for worthy reasons. Until finally an enemy arose that she could not overcome despite all her vigilance, and with his army destroyed the sultan and all his family. On that day she accompanied the women—now her sisters—into exile in the desert, all of them concubines no longer. And what she would become next, this tale does not tell.

Zuleika finished her story, and fell silent. She had used far fewer words than are given here, but still, Gursoon had never heard her speak at such length. And she had seldom felt less ready with an answer.

At length she said, "So the envoy from Arakh—the one who died of apoplexy at the feast—that was you?"

Zuleika nodded. "I switched their glasses."

"And the guests two summers ago? The ones who killed each other in a duel in the palace grounds?"

"It wasn't a duel. He'd sent two men in the hope that I would miss one of them. That was harder to arrange."

"But . . . there were others?"

"Five other attempts. The earlier ones came in as servants, or merchants."

Gursoon looked at her sharply. "I don't remember five other deaths."

"I only had to kill one other," Zuleika said. "I made the sultan's guards believe that one of the princes had stabbed the man while drunk; they buried him secretly. All the rest I persuaded to run away. It seemed best to avoid too high a body count."

"It seemed best to avoid . . . ?" Gursoon began. She stopped. She began to chuckle, looking at Zuleika's calm face, then leaned back against her rock and laughed for a long time.

"You've done well, Zuleika," she said at last. "We're all in your debt, far more than I had realised. And yes, I trust you. Will you take our lives in your hands for a third time?"

Before first light the next day, Zeinab and Zuleika crouched among the rocks on a ridge high above the oasis, squinting into the dim shapes of the other side. Each of them wore a makeshift grey cloak and hood, sewn hurriedly together from sacks.

"When can we go down?" asked Zeinab for the second time.

"Maybe not at all," Zuleika said. "For now, we watch. If there's someone there, they won't stir before sunrise."

Zeinab stared unhappily down into the valley, where new humps and hollows were emerging in the first grey light. She sighed and shifted her knees to a new position on the stony ground, then started.

"Keep still, girl; how many times?" Zuleika began. But her companion was staring at one spot far below them, her eyes suddenly wide.

A slender shape in the greyness moved, walked and revealed itself to be human. It moved towards them across the valley, to the foot of the rise where they were concealed. Both women froze.

The figure stood beneath them, and seemed to be reaching for something in its clothes. At that moment the first light of the sun shot through a gap in the hills ahead, nearly blinding them, and, below, reflecting gold off a bright arc of piss.

"At least a dozen men," Zuleika reported to Gursoon that evening. "We saw no more than a few at a time, but they were cooking for as many as that when we left. Maybe twenty, though I'd say less."

They had stayed for most of a day, moving from cover to cover, and watching the men as they laid their traps for mountain hares and fetched water from a hidden pool. It seemed, as Issi had said, that there were few pickings for bandits these days: only one traveller had come over the pass all day, an old man who looked even scrawnier than his malnourished donkey. Three of the brigands had waylaid him, relieved him of his purse and let him go without even troubling to check his pack.

"They're not very thorough," said Zeinab. "Any trader coming this way would have a second purse hidden somewhere."

"They've grown careless, maybe," Zuleika said. "But be assured, if they saw a prize worth fighting for, they'd fight. We don't know what weapons they may have. And we're a group of women travelling alone, and richly dressed. If they see us like this, there will have to be killing."

"Then we must make sure they don't see us like this," said Gursoon.

TALES WHOSE APPLICATION
IS MOSTLY TACTICAL: BETHI

The bandits lived in a tiny valley, surrounded on all sides by walls of sheer rock. On one side of this valley, opposite the ridge from which Zuleika and Zeinab had spied on them, the large cave where they slept opened out of the mountains at its back, a great yawning mouth with its roof overhanging the sand like a drooping upper lip.

The cave smelled foul, and the thieves' residency had not improved the valley much either. However, it was blessedly cool, there was a grove of wild dates and salt bushes which provided them with food even when traffic through the mountain pass was slow, and, better still, the same water which fed the little spring to which Zeinab had brought the seraglio gushed between the rocks at the base of the ridge into a much larger pool.

It was here that the twelve bandits washed and drank. In earlier days they had pissed there too, until one of their number, Anwar Das, had educated them in the finer points of basic hygiene. Anwar Das was a man of multitudinous talents, and in many respects almost as clever as he thought he was. He had tried to educate the bandits about a lot of things since he first joined their ranks, with varying degrees of success. Now, he addressed his companions as they lay on the ground or tossed pebbles idly at the cave wall, and patiently explained for the fourth time an idea that he had suggested earlier that day.

"But brothers, if we picked a base that *overlooked* a valley, rather than sitting at the bottom of one, we would be in a much better position.

Anyone could ambush us here! Perhaps if we just *tried* a new site? For a day or two?"

"Shut up, Das." Yusuf Razim, the head of the bandits, flicked a pebble in his direction. Das ducked it adroitly.

"I could go and search for a suitable spot myself. You wouldn't even have to stir from your place! I'm sure if we—"

"Shut *up*, Das. Here I've been cutting the way for thirty years, and you come along, a bare scraping of a boy, trying to tell me my own business."

Das, who was five-and-twenty, sighed inwardly and decided to change tack.

"Surrounded by walls like this, someone could be overlooking us at this minute, and we would never know of it until the guard arrived to arrest us all," he said.

"That's the whole point, you little piece of camel shite! Surrounded by walls like this, no one can see us in the first place. You can't overlook something you can't see." Yusuf rolled his eyes at Das with withering contempt.

At that moment, as if underscoring Yusuf's words, the bandits' attention was arrested by the distinct sound of a woman weeping. The noise cut through the air from the sheer wall to their left, so close that each man felt his skin prickle as if the woman was standing directly by his side. Shattering the desert silence, her voice was a high, ethereal keening that made their hearts leap and their hair stand on end. In an instant, the chief bandit's face had transformed from swaggering triumph into terror.

"A ghost maiden," he breathed.

Das imagined banging Yusuf's head repeatedly into the cave wall, in the vain hope that some good sense might trickle in through a crack.

"Fortunate for us if it is," he muttered through gritted teeth. "Right now, brothers, the graver possibility is that it is in fact an actual woman, the wife of some merchant who has lost his way and whose armed entourage might discover our whereabouts, *as I warned you*. If that were the case, we would have to choose between killing the woman out of hand or abandoning our base with precipitate haste."

"Or keeping her as a doxy," suggested one of the others.

Eleven men reflected cheerfully on the prospect. Anwar Das shook his head in mute despair.

"May I suggest that we go and investigate?" he muttered. "And that we take our weapons?"

There was a general rush for the back of the cave, where the swords and daggers were stashed. There followed a few moments of physical comedy as they picked up each other's favourite implements, then fought and scuffled until they had all swapped back. Sometimes, Das wondered that these interludes produced so few actual casualties.

As it turned out, the woman was not the wife of a merchant, though she did not seem to be a ghost maiden either. She was kneeling in the sand not five feet away from the concealed entrance to the valley, completely alone. She turned a tearstained face towards the bandits as they rushed upon her, her expression suddenly becoming panicked.

"Don't come any closer!" She was sobbing hysterically in her fear. "Please! For the love of the Increate, stay away from me!"

The bandits looked at one another uncertainly. The woman was clearly no ghost, but how could she have got out here, into the middle of the desert, when they saw no others near, nor any camels that could have carried her? They could not expend much thought on the mysterious lady, however, so transfixed were they by the pile of gold that lay at her side. Gold bangles, gold necklaces, gold earrings, all tangled together in a shimmering mound. Yusuf was just stepping towards it greedily, when Anwar Das made a swiping motion with his arm, bringing him up short.

"You idiot! What are you—" the bandit exploded at him.

"Look," Das raised his arm, directing the bandits' gaze away from the gold that had been holding their attention as if they were a flock of magpies.

The woman was surrounded by the carcasses of desert jackals: five big, furry bodies, teeth drawn back from their rigid lips in a voiceless snarl. Though they looked and looked, the thieves could identify no wound on their bodies to suggest how the beasts had met their end. They radiated out from the girl in a perfect circle, and at the edge of that circle the bandits stopped, eyeing her warily and brandishing their swords.

"Who are you, lady? What do you want here?" Yusuf growled, trying his best to sound intimidating.

The woman answered him with another burst of frantic tears. "It's too terrible! Too terrible to tell!"

The brigands were nonplussed. This woman was alone—she had clearly brought down five jackals by herself, and yet she cried like a little child. Mustering the sum total of his persuasive skills, Yusuf grimaced at her in an approximation of a friendly smile.

"There, there," he grunted. "We're not going to hurt you. Just tell us what you're about here, and we'll let you be on your way." He avoided mentioning that when she left, he and his brothers would be in possession of her gold jewellery. By this point, the men were more intrigued than uneasy, and were readying themselves for an interesting account.

"All right," the woman sniffed, "I'll tell you. Only don't come too close!" She gestured helplessly at the dead jackals at her feet, her face crumpling as if she was about to cry again, "I don't know what would happen!"

With those words, she raised her head and began:

THE TALE OF
THE POISONED TOUCH

"I hail from the distant city of Izz-ud-Din. Doubtless you have never heard of it; it is far, far from here. Indeed, I have wandered for many years to escape it.

"The sultan in Izz-ud-Din, in the days of my youth, was my own father, Ibtsaheem Ramid, and he was mad. His madness was like a poison poured in at the mouth of the city. Under his rule, Izz-ud-Din, once so fair, so prosperous, rotted and fell into poverty and decay. My father imposed such heavy taxes upon his people, that very soon they had nothing left to give him, not even the cloth they wrapped their corpses in. But what did he care for that? The old man had only one concern in this life, and that was gold.

"He prized gold above his very position and his kingdom. Certainly he prized it far above his daughter, and her sickly mother, dead long years ago from the grief of a cold bed and a cold husband. He hoarded vast piles of it, a glittering ocean of metal, in the caverns beneath his palace, and loved nothing better than to sit gazing at it for hours or even days on end, turning it over in his hands. Fondling it, lavishing it with kisses too precious to be spent on his pale daughter, who pined in the shadows for the dead mother whose arms had held her too briefly, and the mad father, whose arms had never held her at all.

"You may think that with his reason so far overthrown, the people of Izz-ud-Din might easily have risen against my father, and cast him from his throne. Indeed, even his own guards hated the man for his miserly ways and cruel temper (though none felt the sting of his hand or his stick more than I).

But when still a young man, the sultan had made the arduous journey to the cave of the seven djinni, and they had blessed him with the power to bestow curses on whosoever he chose. Because of this he was immeasurably powerful and his people could not, for all their anger, raise so much as a finger against him. His cook once brought him bad meat, so he conjured mad dogs to tear the man apart and consume him alive. If he disliked a vizier for whatever reason, he would root him to the spot and cause scorpions to crawl upon him until he was stung to death. So he continued his corrupt rule in the city, and none dared risk his ire."

By now, the thieves were fully absorbed in the tale. Over the course of the woman's narrative, most of them had lowered themselves to the floor and were sat clustered at her feet, though they still maintained a safe distance. They shuddered at her description of her father the sultan's terrible powers, and even Anwar Das was listening to her with a guarded attention.

"And if his people lived in fear of him, then think how much worse it was for me! His daughter, his only child, who in his madness he loathed and despised. In his rages he would kick and beat me. Worst of all, though, were his words. He called me an ugly whore. He said that no man would ever want me, because his gold, my dowry, would remain forever in the palace, jealously hoarded.

"As if to grind my face in this pain, he would command me to spend my days in the cavernous gold vaults underneath the palace, endlessly polishing his many treasures. There were more in those vaults than I could count. What you see here is only a thousandth part of it.

"One day, my father called me into his throne room, his manner even wilder than usual. He had taken it into his head that all his gold should be melted down, and made into a giant statue to his eternal glory. The work was to begin immediately. Nothing would dissuade him from it. Though his own people had no bread, though their children were starving in the streets, he would have his golden statue, parading his wealth over his city's crushing poverty.

"He called for giant smelting fires to be lit, and day and night he commanded his unwilling workers to carry his gold to the fires and melt it down. He oversaw their progress himself from the palace balcony, and any man that he caught stealing, or even working at a slower pace than he liked, would be punished with the most grievous torments.

"He forced me to work too. I suppose he saw it as the ultimate humiliation, and he was right. Seeing my dowry and my inheritance thrown away to flatter this madman turned my stomach. It turned my mind, too. Slowly, my shame and sorrow hardened into rage. The sight of my father once cowed and frightened me. Now, I spat at the mention of his name. A determination grew in me that his tyranny could endure no longer. He had ruined my life for long enough. And what better punishment, I reflected, than one which fitted the crime? What end more fitting than the one he had wrought upon himself years ago?

"It was not difficult to slip a little molten gold into a lead bowl while I was at my work. I ran to him in his bedchamber, and, finding him asleep, tipped the sluggish liquid down his throat. You will think me an unnatural daughter, and so I am, perhaps, but what of that? The pain I had suffered would needs have its utterance.

"I had planned to run then; I turned, and made a step towards the door. But the gold in my father's mouth scalded him as it slid down his airways. He awoke, coughing on the already congealing metal, choking on gold and blood as the burning liquid ate him from the inside out. As vicious and ironic as one of his own curses; a suitable end for a miser.

"At the sound of his awaking I turned, and that was my mistake. For I saw him curse me with his eyes. I staggered forward, and his strong hand grasped hold of my wrist. His touch seared my skin, as if the boiling gold had spread out to the very tips of his fingers. Screaming, I broke away, but not before his hand had branded me where he had clutched me. See the mark I bear there still!"

The woman slid back her sleeve and showed the awestruck bandits the mark of a man's hand, blazoned in bright gold on the duller brown of her forearm. As one man, they drew in their breath.

"I ran from the room," she continued, "in horror at what I had done and at the dire promise I saw in my father's dying look. I reached the palace gates, and the two guards on duty there stepped forward, intending, perhaps, to enquire as to my business at this late hour. In my wild desire to flee, I shoved them roughly from me and continued on.

"It was the thud the first body made as it fell that froze me in my tracks.

"I turned, filled with a creeping dread, to see the first soldier I had touched lying on the palace steps, livid in death. His comrade was undergoing a sickening transformation. Before my terrified eyes, his armour where I had touched him was turning to gold, the bright colour spreading swiftly through it like a fever. It flowed over his corselet, up to his helmet, down to the very point of his sword, until he gleamed all over. At the selfsame moment, his body became rigid, his skin deathly pale, and he fixed upon me a gaze filled with hatred, that thickened the blood in my veins and burned my heart with grief.

"I left the two men where they fell, and ran sobbing from the city. I have wandered the desert ever since, shunning human company these many years for fear of my strange powers and the horrors they might work.

"And that is the tale of how my father gave me a curse for my dowry, as I suppose I deserved. He punished me as I punished him, with a torment befitting my misdeed. I murdered him with gold, and now I am tainted with a touch that brings both great riches and ineluctable death. All that is metal, the slightest contact with my skin will turn to purest gold—and all that is living, that same touch will slay at a stroke.

"My hands are bloodied with the lives of three men, and my contrition is vaster than this desert. Yet I might turn it to an ocean with my sobbing, and not turn back the glass of time. All things pass, as the Increate wills, *baraha barahinei*, and I cannot undo the things that I have done. That too, is my curse, one that I must bear alone. And I am so, so lonely!"

The woman ended her tale as she had begun it, with an explosion of violent tears. One of the bandits moved to pat her on the back, then recoiled as he remembered what would become of him were he to try it. They were all completely astonished. Any who might have doubted her tale were incontrovertibly convinced by the dead jackals and the pile of gold.

Some had begun stripping off their swords and daggers before the woman had even finished speaking, and had laid them in a little pile by her side. Now, they gazed at her with a strange amalgam of compassion and eagerness as Yusuf Razim stepped forward, bowing respectfully.

"Your tale is deeply moving, my lady. My brothers and I are truly sorry for all that you have suffered."

The woman sniffed mournfully. "Thank you," she said. Yusuf coughed once or twice, awe and pity fighting a losing battle in his mind against the greed and concupiscence that made up most of his comfort zone. He continued with as much courtesy as he could manage: even bandits have some pride.

"Meaning no offence, my lady, I don't suppose you might oblige us by bestowing the benefits of your powers upon my brothers and myself?"

"Nothing would give me greater pleasure. You have been so kind to me!"

Anwar Das looked uneasy, and laid a restraining hand on Yusuf's arm.

"Brother, I'm not sure that's a good—"

"Shut *up*, Das."

"At least let one of us keep hold of his sword, in case she's lying."

"How dare you impugn her good faith! Besides, are you insane? That way we get less gold!" With an impatient movement, Yusuf Razim tugged Anwar Das's sword from his resisting grasp and tossed it onto the pile at the woman's feet.

Immediately, her face lit up, all traces of tears vanishing.

"It worked, everyone!" she called.

Eleven of the bandits looked confused. Das looked horrified. He dived for his sword at the same moment that what looked like an army of women erupted from the surrounding rocks and ran down upon them from all sides.

"It's a tra—" he started to yell. Then a fist or a cudgel slammed into the back of his head, and for a while at least he was untroubled by worldly matters.

The women flooded into the thieves' valley, chattering excitedly. They were elated from their success, and cheered Bethi, the servant girl who had pulled off the stunning deception. She grinned back at them, using the edge of her robe to wipe from her arm the hand mark that Farhat had drawn there in *kehal* paint.

When Zuleika had suggested that they kill some jackals to add weight to the story, the other women had thought it impossible. But the assassin had a tiny vial of clear liquid in a lace pouch at the bottom of her pack, and once they had added a few drops to five raw camel steaks, they were soon rewarded with five jackal carcasses with not a mark on them, quite plausible victims of Bethi's death touch. Issi and Zeinab had protested a little at the prospect of killing a camel, but with almost four hundred of them in the train, they agreed that one could be spared.

Now that they had assumed control of the valley, the women and the camel-drivers took it in turns to wash in the pool, letting out little cries of relief and pleasure as they did so. Then they filled their water skins from the spring as it flowed over the rounded stones. After sniffing doubtfully at the dank air inside the cave, they pitched their tents as near as possible to its opening and, leaving a small group to guard the thieves, ventured inside.

It turned out on exploration to be not one cave but a whole network, running under the mountains for what could have been many miles. The braver girls ran in with whoops of excitement, calling out to see how their voices echoed. At the cave mouth, Jamal and his friends had begun a game of hide and seek, with the older women looking sternly on to make sure that they did not stray too far.

Apart from the group of bound men under armed guard in a small room off from the main cave, the scene seemed almost like an afternoon of leisure back home in the seraglio. Laughter and conversation, such as had not been heard since they were first sent into the desert, began to drift through the air.

"You know we're going to have to do something about them." Zuleika said to Gursoon, as they collected wood for the fire. She jerked her head in the direction of the bandits.

"I know," Gursoon sighed, "but look at everyone now. It will sadden them greatly when we tell them. They're good girls, Zuleika, and brave too, but it's not in their natures to be violent. Let's give them this evening, at least, to celebrate—and leave the killing, if killing there must be, until tomorrow."

TALES WHOSE APPLICATION IS MOSTLY TACTICAL: ANWAR DAS

Now there was among the thieves one Anwar Das, who had this much of virtue in him: he wasn't very keen on killing, and had sometimes dissuaded his colleagues from unnecessary massacres by resorting to the pragmatic argument that it drove away repeat business.

Anwar Das was used to winning arguments. He had a keen mind, and a smooth tongue—the latter cultivated in Ibu Kim, where in the course of a woefully misspent youth he had plied the trade of a professional gambler. It was a tribute to his eloquence, his persuasiveness and his charm that he had come out alive; in Ibu Kim, let's not forget, disappointed gamers who feel themselves cheated will often lop a limb from the suspected trickster so they'll know him the next time they see him.

During the day after their defeat and capture by the women, Anwar Das pondered his likely fate—and, to a much lesser extent, that of his comrades. He wanted to live to see another dawn, but it was clear to him that the women were renegades of some kind, trying to evade pursuit. In such a situation, he had to admit, it made solid sense for them to kill the men outright, and thereby avoid any possibility that their precarious refuge might be compromised.

He tried to think of some stratagem that might save him, but inspiration didn't come. In the meantime, while the other thieves muttered sullenly to each other about what they'd do to these whores if they once got the upper hand, Anwar Das chatted to their guards—who were changed frequently—about their origin, their adventures and their reason for being in this remote mountain fastness.

Most of the women were only too willing to talk. Anwar Das was handsome, as well as eloquent, and when he put himself to it could charm the pants off anyone. He had blond hair, a rarity in that region then as now, fine features, and eyes like wells in which a woman saw herself reflected ten times more beautiful than she was. In some ways, charm and subtlety were his stock in trade, and it had felt like a comedown for him when he finally made Ibu Kim too hot to hold him and had to join the bandits, whose idea of subtlety was to say "look behind you" before they whacked you on the head with a club.

So the women poured out their hearts, or at any rate their recent histories, and Anwar Das listened with very flattering attention, occasionally throwing in an interjection of the "how you must have suffered" variety. He was not proud of himself for doing this: the women were still disoriented from the recent collapse of their entire lives, and full of fear to boot. Their guard was down.

Only the tall, wiry one with the hooded eyes refused to rise to Anwar Das's bait, and had no words to give him. Not even her name, although he learned from the other women that she was Zuleika. She would be the one, he thought—the one who finally gave the order to cut throats, or more likely got stuck in and did the job herself. She had the look, somehow: the stare that takes cold count of all it sees, and does not shrink from the tally no matter how it comes out.

So how to win clemency from the women, when their very existence depended, for the moment, on ruthless pragmatism?

He considered a verbal seduction: one of the guards might be persuaded by sweet words and proffers of love to cut his bonds and set him free. But he'd still have to get out of the caves, through many chambers no doubt filled now with women. There would be other guards on duty elsewhere in the tunnels—since this Zuleika, at least, was no fool—and it was likely they'd make short work of him.

A mass escape, then? Get his own hands untied, then free his comrades and try to fight a way out? But they were too heavily outnumbered, and in any case the bloodshed, once started, would play out by its own logic. Even if they escaped, they'd escape with blood on their hands, and they would be pursued, brought down, slaughtered like dogs.

The tricks by which Anwar Das had made his living, back in Ibu Kim, mostly depended on making the mark see something that wasn't actually happening, or making him fail to see something that was obvious. He had to do the same thing here, in a sense, but without the benefit of any props. He had to do his heypass-repass with words alone.

At sunset, the guards came for them and brought them out from the supply hole into the larger chamber where, in happier times, they had been wont to enjoy their supper. The chamber was cool, even on the hottest of days, and it had a large smoke-hole through which, if one lay awake at night, one could watch the stars wheel across the sky.

The bandits were made to kneel, and the tall woman walked along their ranks. Many other women lined the walls of the room, staring at them from all sides. Anwar Das could sense their tension. He noticed one in particular—older than most of the others, and with a kind of authority in her bearing. When she raised her hand, all conversation in the room died away.

"Whatever we decide," Zuleika said into the silence, "we decide it now, without debate. It's not mercy to let these men linger with their fate in the balance, tormented by hope as much as despair. Vote now, and let it be done. If the vote is for death, I'll do it myself—and I'll give these thieves the same mercy I've shown to kings and noblemen. I'll kill each of them quickly and cleanly, with a single stroke. When it's done, I'll need a detail of twenty to help bury them.

"If for life, bear in mind that if even one of these wretches escapes, he'll go straight to the nearest town and tell the story of what happened here. A chain of whispers will start then, and in the space of days or weeks it will reach Hakkim's ears. From that moment on, we are as slaughtered cows, their throats already cut, that yet stand and believe themselves alive."

The stark image caused dismay across the room, and Anwar Das saw in the faces that surrounded him a few dozen votes for clemency summarily torpedoed.

The older woman frowned. "I don't like to pay for our freedom in the coin of atrocities," she said.

"Why not?" Zuleika asked, bluntly. "Trust me, Gursoon, it's the currency most commonly used."

"Then why did we go to such lengths to take the men alive?"

"To spare our own numbers," Zuleika said. "For no other reason."

They held each other's gaze for the space of some three heartbeats.

"A vote, then," the older woman said, at last. "Life, or death. But you will not take this on yourself, Zuleika. All who vote should be ready to bloody their own hands, rather than another's. We'll draw lots. Twenty throats, twenty hands to cut them. So each of us has an equal chance of coming out of this a murderer."

Zuleika acquiesced with a curt nod. "I vote for death," she said. "All those who agree with me . . ."

"I wish to speak!" Anwar Das called out, in a ringing voice. All eyes turned to him, and he went on without a pause. "Esteemed ladies, I beg you to let me speak. I have words in my breast to which I must needs give utterance. And since, if I tactfully wait out your deliberations, I might be somewhat handicapped by having my throat cut, this present moment seems opportune."

"Shut up," Zuleika told him sternly.

"No let him speak," Gursoon countered, and there was a murmur of agreement from around the room. Anwar Das was pleased to discover that his day's schmoozing had not been wasted. "What is it you want to say to us?"

Anwar Das climbed to his feet. With his hands tied behind his back, it wasn't easy, but he felt he cut a better figure upright than on his knees. It was clear from the wistful looks he saw on many faces that he was not alone in that opinion. But they were wistful glances, not merely admiring ones; the women thought this was a waste, which meant they were resigned to his destruction.

"He just wants to beg for his life," Zuleika said impatiently. "Any man will make any promise, when death's hanging over him, and then break it after. Don't listen."

"A confession," Anwar Das said, to the room at large. "I've done terrible things, and now, as I leave this life, I yearn to unburden my conscience. Let me do so, ladies, and I'll die with a light heart. I don't plead for life. Far from it! I've deserved death no fewer than three times, and only wish to tell you how."

Gursoon looked around the room. Most of the women were nodding or murmuring assent. It seemed a reasonable request, from a young man of such fine features and attractive build, whose time on this Earth was about to be so tragically cut short.

"Go to it," Gursoon told him. "But be brief."

"I ask that my hands should be untied," Anwar Das said. "I give you my word, I won't try to run or offer violence to anyone here."

He was speaking to Gursoon, and Gursoon nodded. Zuleika rolled her eyes, but came around behind Anwar Das and cut the rope that bound his hands.

"If you offer violence," she murmured to him, "you make this quicker and easier. You'll be dead before you draw two breaths."

"Thank you, lady," Anwar Das said, massaging his swollen wrists. "Your candour is appreciated."

He struck a stance, and began his story.

THE TALE OF THE MAN WHO DESERVED DEATH NO FEWER THAN THREE TIMES

"There was once a young man," Anwar Das said, "of noble birth, good family, honest character and astonishingly attractive features, who nonetheless had been marked by unkind fate for vicious and unexpected reverses."

There was a shifting and shuffling among the concubines. Several sat down, crossed their legs and rested their chins upon their fists.

"Stick to the point," Zuleika suggested tersely, but this injunction was met with reproachful glances from many quarters, and Anwar Das felt sufficiently encouraged to continue.

"This young man," he said, "was the son of a great merchant in the city of Yrtsus. And when I say a great merchant, I don't just mean a wealthy one. Isulmir Das had a generous heart, and was always mindful of those less fortunate than himself. He held this opinion: that the holy duty of *zakaad*, the giving of alms, is the most important of the commandments laid upon us by the Increate. He never passed a beggar's bowl without blessing it with silver. Never cheated a trader. Never made a bargain by lying to or tricking those he dealt with. Why, once I saw him give back to a wine merchant a barrel of brandy that had been sent to him by mistake, when he had ordered small beer. Your mistake, he told the man, shall not be my exultation, nor your loss my profit."

Zenabia, whose father was a wine merchant, nodded vigorous agreement with this sentiment.

"But alas!" sighed Anwar Das. "Virtue must be rewarded in Heaven, for on Earth it is trodden underfoot every day by triumphant vice. My father—I'm sorry, I mean the merchant, of course—was murdered by an unscrupulous courtier, the Most Upraised Nilaf Brozoud, who hated his goodness and had a covetous eye on his properties. Worse! The innocent son was falsely accused of the father's murder. So not only had he lost a parent, but he stood guilty in the world's eyes of the foulest crime there is—patricide! He fled into the desert with nothing but the clothes he stood up in, a bare inch ahead of the baying mob, who pursued him with swords and cudgels and, if they had caught him, would have deprived him summarily of his life."

The concubines were agog. Zuleika tutted and fingered her dagger. Gursoon looked wryly amused, but did not intervene as the camel thief got fairly into his stride.

"Pity him!" he cried. "This noble youth, brave but untried, barely old enough yet to wear a beard. Thrown to the mercies of the world, he was. Every man's hand raised against him, and every door closed in his face. He wandered long over the dunes, in the heat of the day, his tongue parched, the tears of filial grief evaporating unfallen from his eyes."

Zuleika could not withhold a profane oath at this point, but Anwar Das rode right on over it, his glance flicking from one of the women to another, always holding each one's gaze until he received some hint of a response. "For days and nights he staggered on. Lost, alone, closer and closer to death. And at last he fell among thieves, who roamed wild in the deserts of the west and considered all who came there to be their rightful prey.

"They would have killed the young man. He had no means to defend himself, and his clothes, though ragged and dusty now, were of rich cloth. That would have been enough to damn him in their eyes, and indeed the leader—the infamous Vurdik the Bald—raised his sword over the young man's head and made to bring it down.

"But the Increate watches over all things, *baraha barahinei*, and in that moment he sent a shaft of light into the bandit chief's soul, so that he was struck with unwonted compassion. Instead of cutting the young man into four pieces, he took his own waterskin from his belt and gave him to drink from it."

"A good way of picking up all sorts of unsavoury diseases," Zuleika growled. The women furthest from her line of sight shushed indignantly,

171

but fell silent when she turned to look in their direction.

"They made him one of their own," Anwar Das said. "And though by nature he recoiled from the terrible acts by which these ruffians earned their daily living, still he owed them his life, and he paid that debt by participating in their depredations."

"This is starting to sound like a plea for the defence," Gursoon said sternly.

"By no means, lady," Anwar Das protested. "It is, as I said, my confession—and here we have already come to the first mortal sin. The young man had been raised to value life and respect property, and now he became a bandit, a canker, a depraved and reckless thief, practising on the goods and livelihoods of his neighbours and fattening on their misfortunes. Is this not terrible? And yet, what choice did he have, since to defy the miscreants who'd found him meant certain death at their hands?

"And moreover, a hope grew in his breast that if he could survive, he could obtain justice—could go back to the city that birthed him and face down the most execrable moneylender, Nilaf Brozoud, who had murdered his blameless father."

"You said Nilaf Brozoud was a courtier," Zuleika pointed out.

Anwar Das nodded. "So he was. But he also lent money at interest. That was the source of much of his wealth. Also . . ." he tried to remember what he had learned from his conversations with the women ". . . he hobbled horses, in order to lay complaints against guiltless ostlers, and raised a tax on cloth that bankrupted the seamstresses of Yrtsus and caused terrible suffering to their innocent families."

Gasps of outrage and muttered execrations from those women whose background included stables or sewing.

"The young man longed to face this man—this ignoble monster, rather—and throw his villainy in his teeth. And so one day, when he had been with the bandits a year, he bade them farewell and set off across the mountains to Yrtsus, determined at last to requite the death of his excellent father. The bandits offered to accompany the young man, and make his fight their own, but he thanked them and said that he would not have them come into danger for his sake.

"But in the mountains, even if one has a map, it's fatally easy to become lost. The young man strayed from the path, and was soon confused by the myriad peaks and valleys, all alike, with which these hills abound. When night fell he was alone and without shelter, and a sandstorm greater than any witnessed on the Earth until then had descended out of the north, driving him—all unknowing—even further from his way.

"Stung and blinded by the sand, all but dead from exhaustion and thirst, the young man sank at last to his knees, and then fell prostrate. In that moment, he succumbed to despair—thereby, sweet ladies, deserving death a second time, since in despair we turn our backs to the Increate's mercy and assume, always falsely, that he has no plan for us. The young man cursed his fate, and so proved himself unworthy of rescue or redemption.

"But though he abandoned the Increate, the Increate did not abandon him. The tips of his fingers, as he lay there on the face of the desert like a child upon his mother's breast, touched something cold and hard. Drawing it forth from the sand, he discovered that it was a bottle.

"The young man was, as I have said before, almost dying from thirst. So he pulled the stopper from the bottle, thinking that it might contain water, and to his astonishment, out from those crystal confines came—"

"A djinn!" Zuleika grunted, in disgust. "He's telling us a story with a djinn in it. The kind that lives in a bottle and grants wishes. Please let me kill him now!"

"It was no djinn," Anwar Das said with dignity, although it had been about to be exactly that. "Please, lady, no interruptions. Out from those crystal confines, I say, poured an army of infinitesimally tiny men. Men the size of ants, whose voices were so small and so shrill that the astonished young man could make out nothing of what they said. And yet, by cleverly arranging themselves into the shapes of letters and words, they contrived to speak with him."

It was the best that Anwar Das could do on the fly, having been deflected from his djinn, but the women seemed interested in this implausible development, and prepared to roll with it for a while at least.

"The tiny myrmidons told the young man that they were the lost legions of Jugul Inshah, who had been sent against the mages of Treis in the days when the world was just created and the Increate's touch was fresh upon it, so that everything dripped magic as the trees drip water after a storm.

They had fought, and they had lost, and the mages of Treis had trapped them in a bottle, cursing them with the doubled curse of infinitesimal size and eternal life. The only way they could be restored to their former stature and live once again the life of normal men was to win the blessing of the king of Treis himself. But Treis had passed from the Earth ten thousand years before, and none knew now even where it had stood, so their plight was a parlous one.

"The young man told the diminutive army his own story in turn, and they commiserated with him on the perfidy of the evil merchant—"

"Courtier," Zuleika muttered.

"—courtier, with mercantile interests, Nilaf Brozoud. Indeed, such was their pity and fellow feeling for the young man, whose person was so fine and whose morals were so upright, that they swore themselves into his service and offered to go with him into Yrtsus.

"The young man was loath to accept their assistance, since his purpose was so terrible and the risk so great, but they importuned him until he agreed. He went on with the bottle in his pack, and soon found the right way again. He was in Yrtsus before nightfall, and found an inn, the Seven Stars, wherein he could spend the night."

"My father's inn at Saruqiy was called the Seven Stars!" one of the women exclaimed.

Anwar Das knew this already, from an earlier conversation, but reacted with polite surprise. "Perhaps," he suggested, "this inn was named for your father's, for who has not heard of the Seven Stars of Saruqiy, its legendary hospitality, the sweetness of its wines, and its entirely reasonable prices?"

The woman nodded happily, and Anwar Das mentally moved one vote from the nays to the ayes.

"The innkeeper," he went on, "a worthy man of advanced age, gave the young man news that saddened his heart. The grand vizier of Yrtsus had died only a week before, and Nilaf Brozoud had been appointed to that most honoured and impregnable of positions. He was now second only to the sultan himself, who placed absolute trust in him and loved him like a brother. The feasting and celebrations at the palace were still going on, and were set to continue until the first day of the month following.

"The young man's heart was heavy. He had hoped to challenge a private citizen—wealthy, and powerful, but with no special protection under the law. Instead, he was setting himself up against the rule of the sultan himself, so that even if he succeeded in his quest he would likely still be treated as an enemy of the state and brought to the block or the scaffold."

"Aren't we owed a third mortal sin round about now?" Zuleika demanded.

"It's coming soon," Anwar Das assured her. "The young man gained entry to the royal palace, and . . ."

"How?"

"The gates were unlocked, and unguarded because of the feasting."

"That's ridiculous!" Zuleika exploded. And Anwar Das had to admit that it did sound weak.

"I misremembered," he said. "The gates of the palace were indeed unguarded, because the guards had been given permission to attend the celebrations. But the gates were stout and heavy, made of oak seven inches thick, and locked with seven locks. Moreover, the walls were as high as twenty men, and as smooth as glass. When the young man came to the gates, he could see that it would be no easy task to gain ingress.

"But he took from his pack the bottle containing the miniature army, removed the stopper and set it on the ground. The tiny soldiers poured out once again, and stood awaiting the young man's command. He told them about the gates with their seven locks, which stood now between him and his enemy.

"The minute legions once again flowed like sand to spell out their answer with their own bodies. 'Once,' they said, 'we would have knocked down these gates with a battering ram, or levelled them with stones flung from mighty siege engines. Now, we have no such resources. But we will see what can be done.'

"They swarmed upon the gates like termites, these diminished heroes. The wood that seemed so smooth to me—I mean, of course, to the young man—offered to their small hands any number of shelves and escarpments and conveniently placed rugosities.

"They marched into the locks and set their shoulders to the wards, pushing them one by one into the neutral position. They hauled the tangs out of the recesses in the wall, and pushed them back into their housings in the locks themselves, until finally the young man had only to push upon the gates, and they fell open of their own accord on their well-oiled hinges.

"With the bottled army once more in his pack, the young man strode on into the palace. It was by then three hours after midnight, and though some were still at their revels for the most part they lay asleep where they had fallen, overwhelmed by drink and other pleasures to the point where their bodies had finally surrendered.

"The young man knew of old where the former grand vizier had had his chambers, adjacent to those of the sultan and in a tower less lofty by the merest inch. He went there now, and walking past the swinishly dozing sentinels presented himself, with no announcement or fanfare, before Nilaf Brozoud himself.

"He said not a word, and the mischievous courtier stared at him for a long moment, first mystified by his presence there and then fiercely indignant. 'Begone from this place!' he commanded. 'Or I'll have you whipped until there isn't an inch of unbroken skin left on your body.'

"The young man only smiled, and said 'Will you so, Nilaf Brozoud? With my father you were able to work it so, because he was old, and had no strength left in his limbs. But I am not Isulmir Das. Take such a high hand with me, and you will rue the day you tried it.'

"Then the wicked vizier recognized the young man, and saw in his eyes on what business he came. He fell, then, to his knees, and begged with heartfelt sobs to be spared. 'I have led a life of depravity!' he wailed. 'And surely if I die now, the Increate will set spirits of malevolence and pain to torment me! Oh let me live, that I might repent. Please, Anwar Das! Only let me live, and I swear I shall repent!' And here, ladies, we come to the third sin."

"About time!" Zuleika observed sourly.

"Anwar Das was a dutiful son, and he had sworn to avenge his father's death. The Increate, who disapproves of murder, nonetheless smiles upon filial piety, and also upon the fulfilment of sworn oaths. Yet the young man, hearing the sobs and moans and whimpers of the wretched Brozoud, was moved to compassion, and deflected from his noble purpose. A father murdered, and yet he stayed his hand! Thus did he deserve his death a third time over.

"And now he turned, and walked back to the open door. But foul Brozoud, whose tears had been but feigned, rushed on him with a dagger and drove it to the hilt into his back."

Anwar Das touched a spot low down on his left side, and Zuleika shook her head in scornful despite. "If he'd stabbed you in the kidneys," she said, "you wouldn't have walked out of that room."

Anwar Das unfastened the knot at the neck of his shirt and let it fall from him. He turned so that all could see the ugly scar above his hip. There was a communal gasp, and then a communal silence. In truth, the scar that Anwar Das was displaying had been earned in a less than creditable enterprise, when the husband of a lady with whom he was enjoying some intimate converse returned home unexpectedly, but it served him well now as proof of probity.

"The young man," he went on calmly, "felt a terrible, tearing pain in his side. But he did not fall at once; rather, the fury he felt at receiving such a cowardly blow empowered him, so that he turned on his enemy, wrested the dagger from his hand and slit his mischievous throat with it."

"Good thing too!" cried Farhat. Then she blushed and fell silent again.

"But the act took the last of his strength," Anwar Das concluded. "He fell into a swoon, and was found there, beside the vizier's slain body. The fury of the sultan was immense. He gave order that the young man should be executed on the morrow morn. And until that time, he should be thrown into the dankest cell in the city's oubliette, whose fairest apartments are famed for their dankness.

"That night was the longest the young man had ever endured. He wept for his fate, but rejoiced that he had at last kept the oath he made to his father's ghost. He mourned that his life would be cut short, but contented himself that he had ended the career of a poisonous reptile who would have wrought even worse evil had he lived. And in such contrary extremes of emotion, without sleep to relieve them, the dark hours at last were passed.

"When dawn came, the young man was taken out to the royal square, where a platform had been erected for his execution. His sentence was read out before a huge crowd, all of them come to see the man who had slain the grand vizier. The executioner asked his victim's pardon, as was the custom, and the young man gave it freely—the more so since he himself had taken a life a scant few hours before. He knelt at last and laid his head upon the block, and the headsman hefted his blade.

"But at the last moment, the young man bethought him of the miniature army in the bottle, which he still carried in his pack. He owed them much, and did not wish them to be buried with him, and lie in the dark throughout the future ages of the Earth. He begged the headsman to grant him another minute of life, which the headsman vouchsafed to do, thinking that the young man wished to utter a last prayer for forgiveness.

"The young man took the bottle from his pack and set it down at the edge of the platform, opening the stopper so that the soldiers could leave it when they chose. He thanked them for the help they had already rendered, praised their courage and ingenuity, and blessed them for all the many kindnesses they had shown him.

"In that moment, a sound like a fearsome thunderclap filled the air, and a light like the shining of a thousand suns flared upon the scaffold. When the light faded, the whole of the royal square was filled with armed and armoured men, who quickly overpowered the sultan's guards.

"I leave you to imagine the young man's astonishment. He had not known until that point that he was of the royal lineage of ancient Treis, and that therefore his blessing would be potent enough to end the immemorial curse upon the bottled army. Now, as they freed him and lifted him on their shoulders in triumph, he realised that this must be the case, and he thanked the Increate in his heart for engineering such a miracle.

"The soldiers would have made the young man sultan, but he had no interest in power or politics. He embraced them all—it took several hours—and took his leave of them with many touching displays of affection. Then he went back to the thieves, who had been his first saviours when he wandered in the wilderness, and towards whom he still felt a great debt of gratitude. Perhaps, ladies, that is a fourth sin—that he was determined to cleave to these rogues, although he knew that what they did was wrong. That he was loyal, even to wicked and lawless men.

"But I leave the final count, and of course my fate—the fate of all these men who kneel here—to you. *Baraha barahinei*. And may your days on Earth be strewn with blessings as thick as blossoms in spring."

A smattering of applause broke out among the women, and voices could be heard returning Anwar Das's blessing. Discomfited, Zuleika fell back to confer with Gursoon.

"I'm going to lose this vote, aren't I?" she muttered.

"I think it's very likely," Gursoon said. "And you could argue that he's paid us back in our own coin. We took them in with a story—and here he's done the same thing to us."

"It's only because he's good looking! I should have let one of the ugly ones speak."

"It's partly because of that, but also because of his ready tongue."

"Yes," Zuleika agreed gloomily. "I'm sure many of them are thinking of his ready tongue."

"He could be an asset to us," Gursoon pointed out.

"He could be a pain in the arse," Zuleika countered.

They both had many weighty matters on their mind right then, and might have come to other conclusions if they had had the leisure to think longer on the matter. But they were both right.

Reading Lessons,
Part the First

In the evening of the same day, the seraglio had its first meeting. An outcrop of flat rock outside what had previously been the bandits' cave formed a natural stage, and when the air cooled, the concubines, the serving women, all twelve bandits, and Issi and his team all congregated in front of it, sitting on the sand, which was still warm from the sun's heat. Gursoon climbed heavily onto the rocky platform and addressed them all in a voice that remained loud and carrying, despite her age.

"We have come far today," she said. "This morning, we had nothing but our thirst. Now, we have a home, or at least something that will serve as one for the time being, and"—and here she gave Anwar Das and the brigands a meaningful stare—"some new allies, who have promised us their aid."

A few of the girls blushed and giggled at Gursoon's words. The thieves had already attracted considerable attention, and Anwar Das, with his charming smile and winning manners, was proving particularly popular. Standing together towards the back of the group, the brigands were beginning to reconsider their earlier reluctance to surrender to a bunch of women, and swelled a little at getting a mention in the lady's speech. Some of them were returning the interested glances of the women around them with what they optimistically hoped was a smouldering animal magnetism.

Gursoon, as far away as she was, noted this with a wry smile. The closer the group became, the easier it would be to prevent friction and schisms when the difficulties of their new life began to bite. She continued, however, in a stern tone. "Let me be clear about our situation, and what it means: we are in the middle of the desert. The very nearest village is many days' journey away. Out here, those of us who were in the sultan's seraglio are no longer concubines. The term has no meaning any more.

"But that is not the only thing which has no meaning. Farhat, Bethi, Thana." The serving women stirred in surprise as they heard some of their number mentioned. "If I am no longer a courtesan, then you are no longer servants. We all of us served the same master, in our different ways, but he is dead, and the man who killed him would have killed all of us, too. His rules do not apply to us here, and neither do the hierarchies he created for us. In order to survive, we are all going to have to work until our fingernails bleed, and if the hundreds of us who were concubines sit around waiting for the few of us who were servants to do all the work, whining at them to brush our hair and put up our tents, then we're lost before we start!"

Gursoon's voice had risen towards the end of her speech. Some of the girls, she noticed, had bowed their heads in shame at the sharpness of her rebuke. "From this point on," she concluded, speaking more gently, "we are all equals. Now, we must decide what we are going to do next."

"And I suppose you're the one to tell us, are you?" Imtisar's voice cut viciously through the crowd. She had been seething throughout Gursoon's speech, first at the way Gursoon had swept in and taken control, then at the personal insult she had felt implied in her comments. Imtisar remembered all too vividly how she had told Bethi off for waking her roughly that morning, and then shouted at Thana for drinking from the spring before she herself had had her turn. What was more, she felt that she had every right to act in this way, and bitterly resented Gursoon's interference. What could a dancing girl know of the correct way to treat servants?

"Actually, I was going to suggest that Zuleika give her counsel," Gursoon replied mildly. "Without her presence of mind, we would be in a shallow grave right now. She has protected us this far, and I think she will have more idea than I of how we should proceed."

Zuleika needed no further encouragement. "We need to find a new city," she said, striding to the front and mounting the stage as she spoke. "A city which will take us in, and which is far enough from Bessa that we will not be sought there." This was met with a general murmur of assent, though there were those who looked a little disappointed. Umayma's face fell at the thought that she was so soon to relinquish her newfound freedom, but she held her peace in deference to Zuleika's wisdom. Zuleika noticed Zeinab getting hesitantly to her feet.

"Zeinab?" She motioned for the girl to speak.

"If we need to find a city that's far from Bessa, then our best chance of success is Yrtsus," she said shyly. "It's a good six months' journey to the east. Even my father has only been there once."

Her announcement caused consternation. The murmurs of agreement turned into alarm, and several people stood up at once to speak. Imtisar was first.

"Yrtsus? Are you sun-struck? That's leagues away, you stupid girl!"

"We can't go all the way there," Layla wailed. "We would die on the journey!"

"If we don't try it, we'll die here!" Zuleika silenced the group with a motion of her hand. "What do you think will happen if we go to Perdondaris or Agorath? Do you really think that Hakkim will stop looking for us? We have with us an heir to the throne!"

Jamal glanced up in sudden interest from where he was sitting by the cave mouth, surrounded by a small circle of other children. The meeting had already moved on, however, so he returned to impressing them with tales of his father's power.

"Zuleika is right." Gursoon spoke from where she sat, on the edge of the stage. "Agorath has always had strong diplomatic relations with our city, while Perdondaris cares for nothing save its own security. If we looked for sanctuary in either, they would send us straight back to Hakkim. But Yrtsus has hardly any dealings with Bessa. In all the time I spent at Al-Bokhari's side, listening to the reports of his envoys and watching him receive foreign visitors, I never met anyone from there, or even heard the place mentioned. It's a small city, forgotten by most."

"Then it's perfect for our purposes," Zuleika continued, "But such a long journey will be extremely arduous. We must prepare carefully. We need enough food and water to get us fairly on our way. Buying that many provisions will be costly."

Zeinab stood up again. "I know how to drive a bargain. My father was a tradesman. Let me sell some of our camels in the market at Agorath.

We have a few more than we need, now," she said, though she shuddered slightly as she thought of the men who had once rode those spare camels, and their grim fate. "If we sell them off we can use the money to—"

Issi stood up hastily. "Zei, those camels are not yours to sell," he interrupted. He had already admitted to his men what had really happened on the night the guards disappeared, and to his surprise, their reactions had contained more anger at the sultan's cruelty than at him for lying to them earlier. A few of them had been chosen by the women of the seraglio as their companions, and other bonds had grown up between them over the few weeks they had been travelling.

Issi himself, notwithstanding his antipathy to Zuleika, found many of the women very good company. Bethi the serving girl made him laugh with her dirty songs, and he often gossiped with her about the scandals and secrets of the servants they had left behind them in Bessa. For Zeinab he had an almost fatherly affection. She had a remarkable memory for the routes she had taken with her father on his trading journeys, and Issi had started to teach her the markers and layouts of the other trading routes he was familiar with, as well as the trails to Galal-Amin and Jawahir along which he used to drive his camels as a younger man. She listened to his recollections with real interest, asking lots of questions and making him sketch out the paths he described in the sand whenever they stopped to rest. Privately, Issi thought she had more potential as a camel-driver than any of his own boys. Her daughter Soraya had started coming to him and begging for piggybacks. All things considered, his loyalties, and those of his men, lay more with those who were now their travelling companions than with the new ruler they had left behind. Still, he felt he must speak up.

"My men and I have families back in Bessa," he pointed out, "and the camels you speak of belong to the sultan. If we return home with fewer than we started out with, what are we going to tell him when he asks what has become of his livestock?"

"You forget, Issi, you are travelling with murderers and fugitives now." Umayma, who sat at Issi's side, flashed him a slightly frightening smile. "We dispatched Hakkim Mehdad's soldiers; I doubt he'll have trouble believing that we stole a few of his camels into the bargain."

That silenced Issi, though it left him wondering anew that such beautiful women could be so perverse and unnatural in their behaviour.

"Even if we sold all of them," Zuleika said, "they wouldn't fetch enough. We need something else."

There was silence at that. Then, a bandit stood up and eyed the group awkwardly, going red under Zuleika's quizzical gaze. "Well, it probably hasn't occurred to ladies of your pedigree, but me and the lads have some—well—we have some less—umm—legitimate ways of making money."

The suggestion was met with howls of outrage. He sat down again hurriedly.

"We appreciate the offer," Gursoon addressed him with stony dignity, "but the crimes we have committed were forced upon us. We're dealing now with choices, and I doubt that any of us would choose to save ourselves by attacking and despoiling others."

Sitting beside the humiliated bandit, Anwar Das put his head in his hands.

"Increate preserve us, Rahid," he muttered, "now is not the time to be reminding everyone of why we're not to be trusted. We need to direct their attention elsewhere." Suddenly, his eyes lit up. He considered a moment, head on one side, and leapt to his feet.

"How many of you know how to weave?" he asked. There were confused looks, then all of the servants and most of the concubines raised their hands.

"Good! Then I think I see something you can do. Both Zeinab and Zuleika have spoken with wisdom. Selling a camel or two would raise you some money, but not enough to buy all the provisions you need. The thing about money is that it is shy and skittish, like a jerboa. It won't come of its own accord; it must be coaxed from its hiding places, and it is rarely at ease unless it is surrounded by more of its kind. You shouldn't squander what little you can make from the camels on provisions, you should use it to lure more money in. If you spend it on a few reels of thread, some weaving tablets, and a loom, then you can make tapestries, woven belts and bracelets, and sell them in Agorath. The money from the camels will vanish as soon as it is spent, but you can keep weaving until you have enough to fund a journey to the ends of the earth!"

Anwar Das had hit upon an ideal plan, and the group rippled with approving murmurs and nods as he spoke. When he finished, there was a flurry of voices. Warudu, one of the older women in the Seraglio, exclaimed with some excitement, "Why stop at weaving? I can whittle some of those little wooden animals that I make sometimes for my sons.

They're not much, I know, but they would probably fetch a few dirhams."

Maysoon got up next. "My father is a potter," she said, in her quiet, accented voice. "If we buy some clay, I can make bowls and jugs as well, and I'd be happy to teach others the craft."

Farhat listened to the chorus of eager voices uneasily. She was thinking of her mysterious conversation with the sick woman, Rem, when she was raving from the heat. It felt presumptuous to offer her services as an embroiderer, yet she did have a certain talent—all the women said so. She rose uncertainly to her feet, her face heating under the force of the gazes that turned upon it.

"For what it's worth, I do a little needlework in my spare time," she mumbled. Gursoon smiled at her old friend encouragingly.

"I would say more than a little, Farhat. Your skills are admired by us all, and they would be a welcome addition to our efforts".

In the general hubbub, at first no one noticed the slight figure approaching from the cave mouth. Farhat had left Rem to sleep, judging her too weak still for much exertion. The noise of the group had woken her, however, and she knew already the subject of their discussion. Now she walked slowly, still dizzy from sleep, to the stage.

"Rem!" Gursoon hesitated, then helped the girl up. "Do you have something to say?"

"Yes, lady. It won't take long, I promise." Rem turned to face the group, who had quieted in anticipation of her words.

"Most of you don't yet know me, but believe me when I say that I know all of you better than I know the lines on my own hand. My name is Rem. I give you all my grateful thanks for allowing me to accompany you. Without your kindness I would have died. There isn't much I can offer you in return, but I heard you all talking about your crafts, and thought of one thing that I might contribute. I'm afraid that it will not make you any money, but I think it valuable nonetheless. I have no skill at weaving or embroidery, but back in Bessa I worked in the library disguised as a boy, and I know how to read and write. I would like to teach any of you who are interested, to make myself useful, if you will permit me."

There was a buzz of excitement. Few women in Bessa knew how to read, and most of the concubines had simply never thought of it before. With the offer laid before them, however, there came memories of brothers poring over scrolls or sent off to learn under an older scholar, fathers who read aloud in the evenings, older cousins speaking with offhand arrogance about their latest visit to Bessa's magnificent library. Most had not the faintest idea of how one even went about reading, but suddenly it had all the savour of a forbidden thing.

Zuleika frowned; in her opinion, anything which did not generate money would only serve to distract them all from their immediate and pressing business. But Rem's idea had stirred a thought in her own mind. She remembered the messenger arriving in the tent, the scroll he read out, the news it contained. If he had not decided to read that scroll aloud, things would have turned out very differently. It discomfited her, even offended her sense of her own professional competences, to think how close they had all come to death. So she answered Rem with a curt nod, rather than the dismissive refusal she had originally intended. "Yes, being able to read might prove useful," she agreed.

"Then let us carry it so," Gursoon said, cutting off further discussion. "For now, though, the night is far advanced, and we must rest. Issi, Zeinab, you two should start for Agorath tomorrow at first light to sell the camels and buy everything we need. Keep your heads down, and Zeinab, wear a veil to avoid being recognized. It's an outside chance, I know, but still possible. Anyone who wants something bought, speak to these two before they leave tomorrow!"

With that, the group dispersed.

The selling of the camels was accomplished without drama or incident, but it was a full week before Issi and Zeinab returned, hot and exhausted but triumphant. They had retained two of the beasts, which were loaded down with the goods they had purchased.

During their absence, Warudu had already cut down one of the stunted wild acacias which grew by the side of the pool next to the cave, and was busy instructing a large group of women in the techniques of carving. A couple of bandits were loitering nearby, trying to overhear as much of her advice as they could without appearing too interested. On the other side of the small valley, Rem was deep in her reading lessons. Anwar Das, Zuleika, and a cluster of others sat in front of her, while she scratched characters in the sand with a sharp stick borrowed from Warudu's tree. Issi's men had cut down some more acacias, and were constructing some sort of rough framework of wooden stakes.

"It's for drying strips of meat," the chief camel-driver explained to

Zeinab when the workers came into view. "They want to go out and hunt oryx tomorrow. Their meat doesn't taste too bad, and their horns sell like white gold to the ivory traders."

An air of intense concentration hung over the small groups as they worked, talking quietly amongst themselves. To Rem, it felt as if the silence which had always saturated her library had risen from out the gutted building like a spirit sent forth from a corpse, drifted over the desert till it had found her, and settled where she was.

When she saw Issi and Zeinab approaching, she gestured to her students, and went over with them to unload the camels. Sounds of movement came from the caves as the women sleeping inside woke up and came to help. They emerged stretching into the pleasant evening air, running across the sand with eager voices to greet their friends and ask what success they had had. Through a mixture of Zeinab's wily haggling and Issi's stubbornness, the two had managed to return with six reels of thread, a bag of weaving tablets, a block of clay, and some fabric for embroidery, as well as grain to eat. Gursoon grinned at the sight of their haul piled up outside the cave mouth.

"This is impressive! I know camels can go for a high price, but you two have really outdone yourselves. It looks like you brought the entire market home with you!"

It was decided that work would begin in earnest the next day at dawn. Warudu already had her group of carvers, and Issi and his men were going hunting. Umayma declared that she would go with them, causing them to murmur and shift their feet a little uneasily.

"I'm not sure that a hunt is a safe place for a lady—" one of the camel-drivers began. She shot him a fierce glare and he subsided into uncertain mumbling. Then she brandished a long wooden spear in his face, its point wickedly sharp.

"I made it," she told him smugly, "from the tree Warudu chopped down". She was immediately surrounded by a small crowd of interested men, examining the spear and nodding approvingly, or offering opinions as to its sharpness and heft.

Maysoon volunteered to teach another group how to shape clay, while Farhat offered to instruct others in the skill of embroidery. Everyone who found that these crafts were not to their liking was laid to the charge of Rihan, the most experienced of the weavers in the seraglio, who agreed to oversee the creation of woven bracelets, belts and tapestries. Gursoon looked on the five groups of assorted women and camel-drivers with satisfaction, then glanced at the bandits, who still loitered sulkily at the edge of the crowd.

"Get over here," she said sharply. "If you can't weave, you won't hunt, and you refuse to try your hands at anything else, then I am sure you can at least cook."

Anwar Das gave her a lopsided smile. "Nothing could be easier, lady. I feel I should warn you now, however, that when you taste our cooking you will have only yourself to blame."

For most of the concubines, the days that followed were some of the hardest of their lives. Their tender skin burned, unused to the searing heat. Their hands and feet, soft from lives of comfort and ease, blistered from the strain of endless work: chopping down the scraggly trees around the oasis to get wood for the evening fire and Warudu's carvings, moving heavy bags of provisions into the cave, butchering the oryxes Issi's men brought home in the evenings. The weavers' arms ached from twining thread, and the whittlers cut their fingers when their knives slipped.

The food was dull almost beyond endurance. Tough, chewy oryx meat or maize porridge, more often overcooked than not, and seasoned only with a few wild dates or the bitter, fleshy saltbush leaves that made them all wince with their sharpness.

The days were long. They woke when it was still dark, and their work occupied them until there was no light left in the sky. The heat was terrible during the day, the water strictly rationed, and at night all the warmth seemed to drain out of the air, leaving them freezing cold.

When Farhat had said that there would be no more servants in the desert, Gursoon had envisaged arguments and screaming. In fact, the baking sun wrought a reversal of roles on its own, and with no need for persuasion on her part. The servants had always had to work long hours in the sun; their skin was tanned and their hands tough from it. They were used to toil, so they were the ones who coped best with the unceasing work, the pitiless extremes of heat and cold. Several of the courtesans, as they struggled to carry bags of grain or recoiled at the prospect of cutting up a dead antelope, felt shamed when their own serving maids took up the work without complaint, and completed it more expeditiously.

Where before they had been meek and obedient, now it fell to Bethi, Farhat, Thana and the others to boss and direct, scold and comfort. For the first few days, many of the younger concubines were sure that they were going to die. Fernoush got heatstroke, then Halima, then several others. It began with a pulsing headache behind their eyes, a pain that was both sharp and dull at once, then weakness, numbness, vomiting. The others laid them all in the shade of the cave, looking on with terror while they groaned and thrashed about, weeping piteously.

Anwar Das and Yusuf Razim watched all this for a while, exchanged a few quiet words, then walked over to the oasis. They returned with a handful of wild dates, some salt bush leaves, and a skin of water, and proceeded to mix them together into a concoction that tasted so hideous, many of the girls could hardly bring themselves to swallow it. They all did, however, whereupon Das told them to rest for a few hours, promising that they would soon feel better.

Zuleika gave Das a sceptical look as he passed her on his way to prepare some more of the disgusting mixture. He returned the look with a cheerful grin. "Not so useless as you thought, are we, lady?" he said to her. "We may not be good for much, but one thing every desert bandit knows is how to survive heatstroke. We wouldn't have lasted long out here, otherwise." The sun-dazed girls recovered, and Zuleika was glad for the first time that she had spared these troublesome brigands' lives, even if Anwar Das's cooking did not taste much better than his medicine.

Things became easier by degrees, almost without them realising it. Sunburn peeled off, and the concubines' skin baked to a deep brown. The blisters on their hands healed, leaving them strong and calloused.

Issi and Zeinab took the first lot of bracelets, tapestries, pots and statues to the markets of Agorath and returned smiling, with food for the month and a generous purse of coins to spare.

Umayma brought down her first fully grown oryx. The men carried her into the camp on their shoulders, cheering and slapping her on the back as if they had never had doubts about her presence in the hunting party.

Life in the camp began to settle into a rhythm: long mornings of work, a break at midday to escape the worst of the heat, meetings in the evenings. At first Zeinab and Issi made the trip to Agorath once a month. Soon, however, the seraglio was producing so many goods that these journeys became weekly, and a rotating shift of people was set up to make them.

There was no shortage of volunteers. Everyone loved going from the silent desert into the bustle and noise of a great city, and they always came back full of gossip, relating details of the latest fashions and the other wares on sale in the market to crowds of fascinated listeners. Even Anwar Das wanted to try his hand at haggling. When he suggested it, however, Zuleika gave a snort of derision.

"Entrust our business affairs to a criminal? You presume too much on our good nature, camel thief," she growled.

The other reason that everyone was so eager to go to Agorath was because of the news they heard there about Bessa. None of this was good. It was Zeinab and Issi who first discovered that Al-Bokhari and his wives had been executed, from a couple of women gossiping at a nearby stall. All the women had expected that, but it was still painful to hear of it. Other reports were even more disquieting. Men publicly flogged for loving other men, women forbidden to go out in public without a male escort. And executions, dozens of them, in front of the royal palace every week. Zuleika, however, cautioned them all carefully against pressing the people they heard for too much information about the state of affairs in their home city.

"We don't want to draw attention to ourselves," she reminded them. "In Agorath, no one knows where we're from. We're just merchants, we don't have a story."

She was right, and they held their tongues, but nothing could prevent them from worrying about the parents, brothers and sisters they had left behind. Though there were days when the women who went to the market came back excited and laughing, on other occasions they returned with their faces shadowed by worry.

Zuleika was recognized by everyone now as the unofficial leader of the group, and the others spoke to her with a new deference and respect. It was not just her unshakable assurance; her judgements were sound and, as Gursoon had pointed out, she had saved their lives when Hakkim's soldiers would have slaughtered them. At the evening meetings, her opinion on any matter was always eagerly anticipated, and it was usually she or Gursoon who had the last word.

Another respected presence in the camp was Rem, although when she was not teaching she seldom spoke. The women of the seraglio had grown used to her long silences, which they knew now were a part of her nature, and did not stem from any coldness or hostility. When she did speak, people paid attention. Rumours about her mystical sight had spread through the camp; she commanded awe, and would perhaps have inspired a little fear, were it not for the fact that her silence was companionable, and her manner friendly. In spite of her gift, she put people at their ease.

Whenever anyone had a spare moment, at breaks in their work, or at the close of the day before the evening meal, or in the early mornings before work began, they would spend it at Rem's reading lessons. These she ran constantly: there was always someone free who wanted to be taught. Even some of the bandits were wont to attend.

The different groups of craftswomen began to stagger their breaks, so that everyone could have their time with Rem without flooding her with too large an audience at once. Even so, attendance at the lessons was so high that she was constantly having to recruit her more advanced students as assistants to help teach the others. The adults were too busy to do this; however useful reading was as a skill, earning money for the journey to Yrtsus still had to be their main priority. So the task fell to the children, who took a delicious pleasure in instructing their elders.

Work in the camp was progressing well, and little by little the seraglio was accumulating a store of money. This fund grew slowly, however. What they made in the market could not all be spent on provisions for their journey, and besides the cost of buying more thread and clay, mere daily necessities such as food ate up a significant proportion of their profit. In the time it took them to amass enough money for a month's worth of provisions for the proposed exodus, almost everyone in the seraglio had at least basic reading skills, and most could write a little as well.

Two students stood out from the rest. One of these was Anwar Das, who picked things up almost faster than Rem could teach them. The other was Zuleika, who was quite astonishingly bad, mastering even the simplest concepts only with great difficulty, and quickly becoming sullen when the point of an exercise was not immediately apparent to her.

As Zuleika watched the truncated curves of the words she formed in the sand with a puzzled scowl, Rem watched Zuleika. The assassin was at once inexpressibly graceful and strangely awkward in her movements with the stylus, bending the whole of her sinuous body into the new skill, her hesitant arm and delicate fingers as yet unfamiliar with the motions she tasked them with.

Rem looked at her face, intent on its work, her lashes lowered as she concentrated on the sand at her feet. Even then, she reflected, when she seemed so utterly caught up in what she was doing, there was something constantly alert about Zuleika. Her body was drawn back like a bowstring, taut with a barely perceptible tension, tensed in perpetual readiness to embrace or to strike. Rem found herself contemplating, with a strange fascination, both of those extremes. To meet Zuleika in the profoundest depths of some passion, whether of murder or of lust: it was a prospect that thrilled her, and afterwards left her flustered and ashamed.

With the exception of Anwar Das, none of the thieves showed any particular talent for reading or writing. They sat alongside the women sheepishly, each chewing his wooden stylus with an expression of consternation and slight alarm. Yet they still attended every session that they could, as did everyone else, regardless of their aptitude.

It has to be said that this was only partly for the interest of learning. It was also for the stories. Rem's stories were incandescent. She had begun them one day as a way of rewarding the seraglio children when they worked hard and listened attentively. She thought, besides, that experiencing some of the pleasures to be found in the written word would encourage them in their application and enthusiasm.

But a story from Rem lifted the floodgates between all stories, so that they roared from out their confines, mingling their rushing waters together. Her words had the music of many voices in them; she wove her narratives into a tapestry on the living air, one that seemed to shine in peoples' minds long after it was finished, like the after-glow of a bright light. She told the women, the children and the men of bright cities, filled with huge beetles with metal carapaces. She told them about far off lands where the deserts were made of ice, and argosies that sailed the skies as now they did the sea. Sometimes her tales were peppered with questions, and she could barely get through a sentence without a cluster of voices piping up from the crowd gathered at her feet. This was the way with the very first one she told.

"Would you like to hear a story?" She addressed the question to a group of children, though their mothers immediately drew closer, relishing the chance for some entertainment.

But the story baffled them.

"What's a whale?" a boy asked.

"It's like a big fish."

"And the man with one leg hated the fish," one of the mothers broke in. "Why was that?"

"Because it took away his other leg."

"But the fish was just an animal. How stupid to hate an animal! Starbuck should have told him it was nonsense!"

Other times her subjects were more easily grasped. Rem told the camp all the old stories from the scrolls in the library, and many more besides. She told them the folktales of their own childhoods, and even Zuleika listened to the half-remembered things with a half-smile curving across her lips.

Soon, this entertainment was a regular feature of the evenings, when the daily meeting was done. Rem was not the only gifted storyteller amongst the concubines, though her tales were doubtless the strangest. Bethi and Anwar Das, of course, entranced everyone with their convoluted tales, delivered in dramatic tones and accompanied by frequent re-enactments. The story of how the seraglio fooled the thieves they performed as a two-hander; it was fast becoming a favourite with the children. Fernoush knew some ballads, which she sang in her high sweet voice to great acclaim, and some tears. Gursoon had always regaled the concubines and the children with her stories—romance for the little ones and smut for their parents—and it was seldom hard to persuade her to treat them to a tale or two when the firelight dipped low. One of the bandits once started to relate a joke about an old camel and somebody's mother-in-law. Luckily Gursoon had heard it before, and reminded him sharply that there were children present. Other people delivered accounts of great battles or conniving murders, of daring escapades and foul brigands—though Anwar Das protested against these last, as being prejudicial to himself and his comrades.

Nor did the stories end when the fire died. They wove their own way through the camp, conjuring songs to people's lips and thoughts to their heads. Warudu and her apprentices carved new and beautiful shapes, and soon Rem had a whole host of wooden figures to accompany her tales: a platoon of tiny soldiers, a menagerie filled with leaping antelopes and soaring birds. Scenes of great battles and magnificent pageants worked their way into Rihan's tapestries. Farhat embroidered a frieze devoted to the tale of how the seraglio was cast out into the desert.

One day, a tale Rem told about a man with a beautifully coloured robe made Taliyah's eyes light up. The girl had been brooding and silent for some time now, and all but her mother and siblings had kept their distance from her, knowing that she sorrowed. A daughter of the seraglio, she had loved a dyer in Bessa, and planned to marry him. The young man was respectable and fairly prosperous, and everyone had expected the sultan to approve the match any day. Then the Ascetics took the city, and Bokhari Al-Bokhari was no longer in a position to approve anything. Taliyah was sent into the desert, along with all the other concubines. She had hardly spoken to anyone since.

But that evening, Taliyah began chipping bits of rock from an outcrop near the base of the cave wall. She ground them up, heated the powder in a shallow stone bowl over the fire until it turned red, then mixed it with gum from a little box around her neck. In a few days' time, after grinding up many different rocks and plants, Taliyah had a small collection of paints and dyes, and the seraglio another shanty trade to swell its income.

When Taliyah suggested to Maysoon and Warudu that she decorate their handiwork, they agreed readily. She was a bright girl, and had learnt much from her lover about the skill of crafting colours. Her lush greens, brazen reds and cool, delicious yellows not only fetched a high price at the market by themselves—when she painted Maysoon's pots and Warudu's statues, they almost doubled in value. Gradually, she began to talk again, chatting quietly to the other women as she worked.

She grew especially close to Warudu. The two had never known each other that well when they lived in the seraglio, but Taliyah became fond of the older woman's forthright manner, and respected the pains she took over her statues. For her part, Warudu had known Taliyah's mother. It had saddened her to see her friend's daughter, once a happy and excitable girl, turn pale and withdrawn, and she was glad that she seemed so much improved.

Taliyah did feel better. She liked the peaceful life of the camp, with its large community and constant, reassuring hum of voices. Her art brought her joy, and she was pleased with the respect her skills earned her. However it was still a source of astonishment to her that the other women in the camp were so perennially cheerful. Hadn't they all left people behind? Yet Zeinab and Issi joked and laughed as if they were back in Bessa, and Warudu sang as she carved, pausing now and then to look out over the camp with a broad smile on her lips.

Even Jamal, who had been delivered to the women screaming and crying, clutching at his mother's robes, seemed at times to have forgotten her existence entirely. He was a somewhat troubled child, to be sure: he often sat apart from the group, deep in troubled thought, but then, noticing the other boys engaged in some game, he would run off to play with them, rolling with them in a laughing, shouting heap. Taliyah could not understand how everyone but her could shake off their sorrow so easily; hers felt like a weight she could not shift, the very thought of shedding it a betrayal.

"You seem happy here, aunty," she remarked to Warudu one day, as they sat side by side, Warudu whittling, Taliyah painting the finished figures.

"Yes, I am," Warudu agreed. She sneaked a sideways glance at the girl's frowning face and laughed. "Come on, Tali! I have good cause to be. You don't really think that the sultan would have taken me in, if we had gone to Perdondaris as planned? No, I am past forty, child, and he owes me nothing. Bin Ezvahoun would have cast me out into the street, and my two sons with me, to beg or to starve. Most of the older women had the same fears. When Zuleika killed the soldiers, she granted us a reprieve in more ways than one.

"And life out here isn't so bad," she continued, passing Taliyah a tiny wooden oryx, ears pricked and head raised at an unknown sound. "It's not many women who can earn their own bread, and fewer still who can do it through a craft they love. Besides, the attention is becoming quite flattering, don't you find?"

Warudu had a point: at the market in Agorath, a queue had begun to form in front of the concubines' pitch each week, and there were disappointed looks at the end of the day when the last of the stock had gone. Along with the usual crowds browsing the stalls, customers far grander in their manner and attire had several times now graced the blanket on which the women of the seraglio laid out their wares. Once, when it was Fernoush and Halima's turn at the market, one of the sultan's legates came by specifically looking for one of their woven bracelets for his wife. Another asked if he could commission some of Warudu's wooden statues for his young son. The camp beamed with pride at each fresh report. Only Zuleika looked grim.

"I fear the attention we are drawing to ourselves," she confided to Gursoon, the evening they heard the news about the legate. "Gratifying though our success is, the very purpose of this endeavour was to disappear, and on that score at least, I think it's safe to say we're failing."

"At least we're bringing money in," Gursoon said. "It won't be long now before we have enough to buy the provisions and leave." But her face as she said this was not serene.

A few weeks later, Bethi and Nasreen returned from the market whey-faced and shaking.

"I made a mistake," Nasreen stared at her feet in shame as she explained to Zuleika what had happened. "A woman came to buy a shawl, and while she was looking for one that suited her, we started talking. She said that she didn't recognize my accent, and asked me which city I was from. I told her the truth before I had thought to check myself!"

Zuleika could see the girl's distress, and tried to temper her reply. "It was a foolish mistake, Nasreen, but not a disastrous one. Many traders in the market come from Bessa."

"You haven't heard the worst part," Nasreen wailed. "After I'd told her where I was from, she looked at me so strangely, and told me that I must have had a lucky escape. 'I haven't seen a woman from Bessa for weeks,' she said to me. 'I hear they're not allowed outside any more.' It's getting worse over there, Zuleika. My sisters must be so afraid!" Nasreen began to cry, sharp, gasping sobs. Fat tears rolled down her face and fell to the ground, making little craters in the sand at her feet.

Zuleika reassured the woman, but absently. Nasreen's words were ringing in her mind. A thousand merchants came to trade in Agorath. That some of these came from Bessa was almost certain, the two cities being so close. But clearly, they were the only women. It narrowed things down.

There was a new atmosphere, tense and apprehensive, as the concubines gathered for their daily meeting that evening. Everyone knew by now what Bethi and Nasreen had heard at the market, and their thoughts were back home with their mothers, sisters and daughters. Meetings usually began with Farhat, Maysoon, Warudu or Rihan giving a report on the day's progress, but today, it was Zuleika who stood up first. It was clear at once, from her bearing and expression, that what she was about to say was of serious import.

"We've all done well here," she began. "However, our efforts will be wasted if our presence in Agorath is discovered. It's been a long time now, and we have put by a fair amount of money—more than sufficient, I think, for the journey to Yrtsus. And we are starting to draw attention to ourselves. What Bethi and Nasreen discovered today has changed things. It is clear that Hakkim Mehdad is ruthless in the exercise of his power, and if we ever had doubts that he would seek us out, I think they are gone now. We have dwelt here long enough. We ought to buy what we need and set off before the end of the week."

Although this had been the plan from the start, Zuleika's words were met with a groan of dismay. Taliyah's face crumpled as she set down her mortar and pestle, which Zeinab had bought her only that week to make the work of grinding pigments go more quickly. The powder she had been pounding spilled out into the sand. Warudu tutted. Umayma set her mouth in a hard line and stalked off towards the cave.

It had been the plan all along, the goal they had all been working towards, yet few of them, now that they were brought up against it, could quite stomach the prospect of leaving.

Even the bandits looked downcast. Each of them, it should be noted in passing, had had more—and more varied—sex in the past month than in the three years that preceded it. Several times they had discussed escaping from the termagant women, but it had become clearer and clearer that their hearts weren't really in it.

Gursoon looked around her at the disappointment on every face, and felt an answering sadness in her own breast. They had been free in this place to do as they chose, free to earn and to spend and to look men in the eye, as they had never been in Bessa. She bowed her head, reminding herself of the necessity of their swift departure.

Zuleika looked around the group in surprise. "We can't live in the desert forever," she pointed out bluntly. "It's no place for us."

"Your own experience belies that every day." The voice was quiet, but charged with passion. The Seraglio looked around to see Rem walking towards the outcrop of rock on which Zuleika stood, just as she had done on the night of their arrival, after they had overcome the thieves.

"We are happy here," she said, "and we're thriving. The work goes well."

Zuleika waved a hand dismissively. "The work isn't important. It was only ever a means of making enough money for the journey to Yrtsus, and return to a life like the one we knew. We make money, we buy provisions, we leave—that was the plan."

"Why?" Rem countered.

Zuleika stared at her in consternation. "I've just told you why."

"No, I mean why would we want our old lives back? If we go to Yrtsus, we go back to servitude and impotence."

"We go to save our lives—"

"What are our lives worth, if we have to live them in hiding?" Rem demanded, suddenly impassioned. "How can we slink into a city that is not our own, and leave all this behind?" She gestured at the valley around them. It was sunset, and the sky was a dream of pink and orange silk, shot through with golden light. It fell upon the hand looms clustered together like big-boned women, Warudu's workshop strewn with wood shavings, a line of clay pots drying in the cooling day. The light touched every face in the watching crowd, and coloured it with splendour.

"Yes, we thought at first only about surviving. And look—we've survived. It's just that we've done so much more! Made so much more. We've become a city here, in the desert, which sets its face against cities. And now you want to go back to a world where women are bought and sold as the works of your hands have been bought and sold? To a world where the whim of a mad and pitiless man can decree a hecatomb of women, and other men will not raise their voices against him but will hurry to do his bidding? The plan was wise, but the plan is past. The present is this thing that we have wrought."

Zuleika saw the truth of what Rem said blazing from her eyes. She felt it too; she had been happier in the desert than she had been in a long time. But she hardened her heart, and spoke coldly when she replied.

"Howso that might be, unless we want to live in fear of Hakkim's vengeance every day, Yrtsus is our only option. Unless you have a better idea?"

She had meant it as a closing argument. But Rem was soaring now, and did not need to search for her answer. It had always been there, a dimly shining vision at the back of her mind since the moment when the sight had first come upon her. Suddenly, through all the strands of what was and what would be, it sharpened into dazzling focus.

"When Hakkim took Bessa, he made a pyre of its laughter and its art. He killed the joy in the city; now it is like a shell. But us he cast out, and in the desert we became a city of our own. That is what we do. We take the city back into the city. We parade the city that should be through the streets of the city that was, and we make it our own once again." in her jubilation, she had moved very close to Zuleika, and though her voice was loud enough for everyone to hear, yet in a sense she spoke to her alone. "That is what we do. We take back Bessa."

For a moment, Zuleika remained utterly motionless, her mouth open in mute astonishment. Rem's words hung over the seraglio, a tidal wave suspended before the moment of impact. Then time began to move again. The wave crashed down in a roar as everyone began to cheer. And Zuleika, borne forward on the surge, feeling her anger loosed into a sort of fierce joy, took Rem in her arms and kissed her, hard, on the mouth.

THE COUNCIL OF WAR

A record of the meeting of the Council of Women, formerly the Seraglio of sultan Bokhari Al-Bokhari, late of the City of Bessa.

This meeting is called to decide our future course of action. In attendance are all four hundred and thirteen Bessan citizens in exile, including our allies Issi and his eight apprentices, and also the twelve men of fortune led by Yusuf Razim, currently inhabiting the caves of the northern Hills.

The meeting was called by Imtisar, Gursoon, Zuleika, Farhat and Zeinab. By their joint agreement, the discussion was begun by Gursoon.

Notes of the meeting to be taken by Rem the Archivist.

GURSOON: I hope all of you can hear me. Many of us have been arguing about what to do next. This meeting is to let the whole community hear what each of us has to say, and then decide together which course of action to follow.

[Many women begin to talk at once.]

But if we are all to be heard, it seems sensible to allow one of us to be the gateway, and determine who speaks at any time. Is it your will that I take this role?

UMAYMA: It should be Zuleika. She's the one who saved us.

GURSOON: Zuleika, then.

ZULEIKA: I would not do it well. Gursoon speaks better.

SEVERAL VOICES: Gursoon!

GURSOON: Anyone else?

Very well. I will explain our situation as it appears to me; then anyone who wishes may speak, to suggest how she thinks we should proceed. I know that Zuleika, Imtisar and Farhat each have a proposal to make. Who else wishes to speak now?

[There is a silence.]

Then with your agreement, we will begin by hearing those three. Then anyone who wants to comment should raise her hand. We will try to hear everyone who has something to say.

IMTISAR: All four hundred of us! That's absurd. We'll never reach a decision!

GURSOON: We've been through this, Imtisar. This concerns the lives of every one of us. We must work together to survive. And we work together by consent.

IMTISAR: But every single person? The children? The babes in arms? And don't forget that most of these men are thieves!

GURSOON: Everyone. The mothers have a voice, if the babes do not. And these men have shared their food and their shelter with us. Now can we get on?

Thank you. Sisters, we have received many blessings here. We've avoided our enemy for three years, we've kept our children safe, and with the help of our hosts here, and Issi and his men, we've even prospered. But we have always known it could not last forever. This place was never made to support so many. We must ration water in summer and fuel in winter. We would all like better food.

[A general murmur of agreement.]

And now it seems that our very success, the sale of our goods in the markets, which brings us so many of the things we need, has put us in danger. We are attracting too much attention. We know that our enemy, Hakkim Mehdad, is single-minded and pitiless. If it should come to his ears that a group of women from Bessa are abroad in the world, he'll renew his search for us. And though he's mad, I fear he is also intelligent: it would not take him too long to find us.

It's clear then, that we cannot continue as we have done. Our first thought was to travel as far away from here as we could; maybe to Yrtsus. Since then, two different plans have been put forward. Others may come out of this debate. But at the end, I think we must vote for one course of action, and decide quickly how best to achieve it. Do you all agree?

MANY VOICES: Yes!

GURSOON: Then, with your consent, I'll give the voice first to

Imtisar.

IMTISAR: There should not even be any reason for debate. We've lived here safely enough for a while. But now this monster, this murderer is about to find us, the best thing to do is leave at once. And what will he be looking for? A mass of women, four hundred of us huddled together. Wherever we go, so large a number will attract attention. So we should separate—go in small groups to different destinations: maybe a dozen to Saruqiy, twenty or so to Perdondaris, and so on. We'll be less noticed, and we can go immediately.

Some have said that if we can get as far as Yrtsus, we'll be safe from pursuit. But how can we be sure? The one thing we know is that it would still take weeks of preparation before we could leave—and our danger is now.

There are twenty towns and villages within a journey of a few weeks or even days from here. And some of us have families in these places, who might receive us with joy. We can spend the winter with roofs over our heads, as we should.

That's my counsel, and the wisest course.

FARHAT: May I speak now?

GURSOON: Yes, Farhat.

FARHAT: Imtisar is right about one thing: we're not yet prepared for a journey to Yrtsus. We need firewood, more blankets, and a score of other things. Getting them will be harder, now that we dare not return to Agorath—but there are other markets. Issi and Zeinab can pick up most of what we need in a week or two. We could be ready to set off very quickly. And we have so much to gain by staying together! We've built a community, these three years. That's too valuable to throw away.

I know there's a danger we'll be found. But I don't want to give up all we've created just because we're threatened now. So I say we hold out for a few more weeks, and then for the time it takes to get to Yrtsus, or even beyond it, to safety. Maybe there we can find a way to live more comfortably—I'd like that too. But the important thing is . . . when we work together, we rule ourselves. We can make beautiful things, we can teach all our children. We'll lose all that if we split up. We'll just go back to being somebody's wife, somebody's servant, when we've been free.

GURSOON: Zuleika. You also wanted to speak.

ZULEIKA: Both of those plans involve running away. I think we should retake Bessa, and live there.

[There is a silence.]

BETHI: Is that it?

ZULEIKA: You all heard, yesterday, what Rem said. I've nothing to add to that.

GURSOON: If that's all you wish to say, we'll move on. But the other two have given their own arguments, and told us how their plans might be achieved.

ZULEIKA: Very well.

What Farhat said just now is right, we ought to stay together. And what Rem said before her was right as well. We've built a city here, a good one, and we should fight to keep it. But it would be a better city in Bessa. And Bessa is ours, it's our home. Mine too, since I chose to stay there. When Rem said all this I knew it was true, but I thought then it could not be achieved. Hakkim has a standing army, and weapons; we have none. So at first I wouldn't consider the idea, believing it was a dream and nothing more.

But then I started to think about how we might actually do it, retake Bessa. And it is possible. It will require most of you to fight. We will have to buy swords, and train with them: turn ourselves into an army. We cannot match their numbers or their experience, but we have some advantages. We know the city well, and we will have allies within it if we can reach them. Hakkim has weaknesses we can exploit. If you are willing to learn what I teach, we can succeed.

That's all I have to say. Rem has the sight, and she believes we should take Bessa back. And I think we can do it.

GURSOON: Well. You've heard three choices. Does anyone wish to add to them? Or to ask a question?

JAMAL: We should attack Bessa! Kill Hakkim and avenge my father!

ZUFIR: Yeah!

SORAYA: You boys just want to fight. Have some sense!

[Many people speak together.]

GURSOON: Be quiet, all of you!

If you want to talk, raise your hand. I'll point to the one who is to speak next.

[There is a silence.]

You, Halima.

HALIMA: Auntie, I don't think I can give my vote for any of these plans. I want with all my heart to go back to Bessa, and see my mother and my little brother again. I can't bear the thought of going far away, or parting from all my sisters and aunties here. But I can't fight! I know I'm a coward, but I don't think I could ever kill anyone. Is there no other way?

BETHI: Don't cry, girl! Halima speaks for me too. For most of us, I'd guess. If she's a coward, so are we all. But I don't want to run off to the edge of the world, either. Or to split up our company and leave my friends. None of us does. So what's to be done?

MAYSOON: None of the choices is good, but I think Yrtsus is the least bad of the three. It gives us our best chance of safety. And I think we need to stay together. If we separate, we lose each other's support, and we lose the chance to carry out the trades we've learned. And what do we have then?

NAJLA: But Farhat says we'd have to prepare for weeks before we could start that journey. We could all be murdered in our beds before we even set off!

FARHAT: If the vote is for Yrtsus, Zeinab and Issi can go at once for supplies.

ZEINAB: We could leave at dawn tomorrow. I think we can get all we need at Beyt Kirim, and be back in less than a month.

FARHAT: And if Hakkim is looking for us, it's surely safer to stay here for that month than go travelling in groups to all the cities around Bessa.

UMAYMA: Like chickens running from the hawk! No: we should take the fight to him. Attack Bessa and regain it. We've shown we can do it.

MAYSOON: I come from Ashurai. When I was young, we had three new rulers in five years, and the city burned each time. If you'd seen that, you wouldn't be so ready to call for war.

UMAYMA: But Bessa is ours, not Hakkim's. Isn't it worth a fight to get our home back?

ZEINAB: I don't know. Before, when we fought, we had no choice. This is different.

UMAYMA: Before, I fought for my life and my son's life. I'll fight again for our freedom. Zeinab, what else can we do? If we run, if we go anywhere but Bessa, we'll be in hiding every day we live. And even if Hakkim never comes after us, what can most of us hope for but slavery in some man's household? We've built better than that!

[There is a silence.]

ZEINAB: Then I have a question for Zuleika.

We know we can fight: some of us at least. And yes, I'll fight again to get Bessa back, to give my daughter a life there. But you said you'd make us into an army. We've seen what an army does. Hakkim Mehdad's soldiers killed old men without weapons. They burned houses with people inside. They killed women and children, without thinking, because their leader told them to. I think that's what soldiers do, they follow orders blindly, and I won't do that. I don't think any of us will.

[Many voices speak in agreement.]

So that's my question, Zuleika. If the others feel like me, if we are your army, do you still believe we can take back Bessa?

[There is a silence.]

ZULEIKA: Yes.

It will be harder, and more dangerous. But you're right, Zeinab. I can't ask any of you to be what you're not. A good general works with the materials he has. There are ways in which we can turn your limitations into strengths.

[Many voices speak in protest.]

MAYSOON: Sparing the innocent! That's not a limitation!

ZULEIKA: But then I have a question for you in return. If we're to avoid wholesale killing, we'll have to use other means. Subterfuge, and spies. It will take time, and it will increase the risk for all of us. Are you prepared for that?

RIHAN: To risk our own lives, yes. Not our children's.

JAMAL: Why can't the children fight? It was my father they murdered. And it's our city. Anyone who stands in our way deserves to get killed. Why are you having all this argument?

GURSOON: Jamal, if you speak again without raising your hand, I'll send you out of the meeting.

IMTISAR: The boy's no more foolish than anyone else here. Are you telling us in all seriousness that we must pretend to be soldiers?

ZULEIKA: Become soldiers.

DALAL: Not you, Auntie. You won't have to fight.

IMTISAR: But you want to make your sisters into murderers!

DALAL: No.

UMAYMA: Yes. We'll have to kill people. And some of us may die. But we're all at risk right now: there's no safe course here.

ZEINAB: That's true. And if we can make a safe place for ourselves at the end, it would be worth it. Zuleika, I'll take your training. But I won't kill old men or children.

[There is a silence.]

GURSOON: Does anyone else wish to speak?

ISSI: Pardon me, lady, but my men and I need to know. Do we have a vote in this?

GURSOON: Certainly. Bessa was your home too. You have the same voice as us.

ISSI: In that case, I must tell you that we all want to go back there, but we're not too keen on killing either. We don't want to be called on to cut the throats of men we've worked side-by-side with in better days. But we'll help you any way short of that. And if you decide to go to one of those other places, we'll help you on your way as best we can. We'll lend you the beasts, and we'll go as far as Yrtsus with you if we must. But when you're safely arrived, those of us with family in Bessa, we have to go back there. As long as that's understood.

MAHMUD: The ones without family, we might stay, though, if we're wanted.

[Several of the camel-men speak together. Gursoon holds up a hand to still them.]

GURSOON: You are all free agents. And thank you, all of you, for your honesty now and for your past help to us, when we would have died without it.

Now, if everyone has said all they need . . .

ANWAR DAS: One moment, lady, I beg you.

I know we have no vote in this momentous debate, but our chief has something he needs to tell you before you decide. Go on, Yusuf.

YUSUF RAZIM: It's just that, well, we've got used to having you ladies around the place, and we all agreed . . .

TARIQ: Says who?

YUSUF RAZIM: We *all* agreed that we'll help out too, if you want it. And we're not so picky about cutting throats, either. And if you manage to go back to your own city, maybe you and us could still, what's the word?

ANWAR DAS: Remain allies, lady. It would sadden us beyond measure to break our newfound friendship—especially now, when every path before you seems fraught with danger. As the most excellent Issi has just said, who but a worm, a man without feeling, would abandon you in such circumstances?

YUSUF RAZIM: That's right. And then, once we've won, maybe this city of yours would have a space for a few good men, if you know what I mean? Get off, Das!

GURSOON: Our thanks to you too, Yusuf Razim, and to your lieutenant. Be assured that once we have made our decision we will be grateful for any help you are able to give us. And now, does anyone have any other suggestions to make?

Then we have three choices before us. We must decide on one, and agree to carry it out. We can separate and go in small groups to the nearer towns, starting at once. Or we can stay together, and travel to Yrtsus in a month's time. Or we can resolve to fight, to retake Bessa for ourselves.

But before we vote, there's something I must add. If a majority of us vote for Imtisar's plan, we can put it into action at once. If not, we will need to take measures to keep ourselves safe here for at least the next month, in case Hakkim Mehdad comes looking for us. We will have to keep watch, and arrange a means to escape or to hide ourselves: those arrangements must be made at the same time as our wider plans.

And one more thing. If the vote is for Zuleika's course, everyone who has chosen it will begin training with her tomorrow. Please be clear: if you vote for us to reclaim Bessa, you are volunteering for the army that will attempt it.

And now I hope we are ready.

[The vote took place like this:

Farhat, Imtisar and Zuleika stood each to one side of the great rock, and the women, children and men were directed to stand with the one whose plan they supported. Anwar Das, who had no vote, offered to marshal the count, which he did by asking those who voted to arrange themselves in rows ten abreast. Some refused to choose at all, but most went to one or other of the three advocates. A solid square formed next to Zuleika; smaller blocks by the other two women. When Zuleika's count topped two hundred and fifty, it was evident that the choice was made: for Bessa, and for war.]

GURSOON: The vote is clear: we stay together, and use all our power to reclaim Bessa for ourselves. Imtisar, Farhat, will you abide by this decision?

FARHAT: Yes, but with many misgivings. I don't wish for anyone to be killed in my name.

IMTISAR: I cannot consent. But I'm an old woman—you'll decide this without me.

GURSOON: I'm sorry, then, Imtisar. You can at least stay away from the fighting yourself.

I'll ask Zuleika to speak to you now, since she is the one who can best lead us in this undertaking. When she's spoken, I'll declare the meeting over. Anyone who has a question or complaint can bring it to me afterwards.

ZULEIKA: Everyone who is prepared to fight will begin training tomorrow. I'll also need several groups of volunteers to go to Bessa. This will be the most dangerous of our tasks. They will be required to disguise themselves, and to lie well.

As Gursoon has said, the next priority is our safety while we train and formulate our plan. We must post guards at the pass and further down in the hills, to watch for riders from the direction of Bessa. And we must prepare some of the deep caves, so that everyone here can hide for several days if the need arises.

IMTISAR: I have something to say. This whole scheme is crazy, and I will take no part in it.

ZULEIKA: I've just said that you don't have to. Only volunteers will go . . .

IMTISAR: Nor do I mean to spend my days in a cave, waiting to hear that my idiot sisters have got themselves killed in Bessa. Gursoon, I have sixty women here who wish only to leave this place and seek a new life in another city. Zuleika has just said she has no need for us. Let us go! We'll split into caravans of ten or twelve to avoid notice; maybe two or three groups can travel separately to Perdondaris and the rest to Heqa'a or Diwani. Issi can lend us the camels and men for the journeys, and bring them back afterwards.

ZULEIKA: No.

GURSOON: Zuleika, there's been no discussion.

ZULEIKA: No. Don't underestimate our enemy, Gursoon. If Hakkim hears that some of us have been seen, he will try to hunt us down. Do you think he'd miss a caravan of ten women, on the road to Perdondaris? Still less half a dozen caravans, all on the roads at the same time? One group at least would be captured. If that happens, he will discover our plan and we will fail.

IMTISAR: We would never tell him anything.

ZULEIKA: I spent some time studying the assassin's trade. One thing I learned is that there are ways of forcing a man to reveal even matters he's sworn to keep secret; they would work just as well on a woman.

IMTISAR: But you can't imprison us here!

ZULEIKA: I can. Try to leave these caves, and see how far you get.

GURSOON: Stop this.

Imtisar, I'm sorry, but I think Zuleika is right: it's not safe to travel openly now. You have a right to take that risk for yourself, but not to endanger all of us. If you still wish to go, then leave on the day of our attack; then if we succeed you'll be safe to go where you will. And if we fail, at least Hakkim will be distracted for some days afterwards.

IMTISAR: And you talk of safety! Listen to yourself, Gursoon! This woman wants to lead us against an army. We're women. We don't even have weapons! What will you do, march up and storm the city walls? They have archers. They have hundreds of armed men.

ZULEIKA: Gursoon, we should end this meeting.

GURSOON: We can't end it now.

NAJLA: I agree with Imtisar. How can we defeat an army? It sounds like madness.

[There is a chorus of voices from the women with Imtisar, sounding agreement.]

BETHI: Maybe we can get help from outside. Zuleika, you told us you learned about fighting in a school. So you'll have friends there, yes? Let's go there and ask them to fight with us. We can pay them. And they'll have weapons, too.

ZULEIKA: No. My bond with the school ended when I joined the seraglio. They would not help us.

IMTISAR: Oh, this is all stupidity. We might just as well go for help to the seven djinni!

[There is a silence.]

BETHI: Well, why not?

JUMANAH: All the stories tell of people who visited the djinni before a great undertaking. They could tell us how best to succeed. Or at least let us know how much chance we have.

NAJLA: They could help us. But they could strike us down as well.

BETHI: They can't be more dangerous than what we're planning anyway! I think we should try it.

FERNOUSH: What, all of us?

JUMANAH: Just a few representatives. And we have to plan very carefully what to say to them. . . .

ZULEIKA: Wait. You mean all this seriously?

MANY VOICES: Yes!

Why not?

They're powerful. What other help do we have?

ZULEIKA: We have knowledge of the enemy, our resolution, our own hands and minds. We can make our own plan. We don't need help!

IMTISAR: And can you foresee the future, Zuleika? The women have spoken. We should visit the djinni: perhaps you might listen to them.

ZULEIKA: Gursoon. This is foolishness, and we don't have time for it.

GURSOON: I agree. But I think we will have to do it. Look at them!

SOMEONE: Who will go? Who will talk to the djinni?

SOMEONE: Has anyone here seen them before?

END OF THE RECORD.

Postscript, by the hand of Gursoon:

At this point in the discussion our scribe, Rem, became ill, and the record was interrupted. Only a dozen more people spoke before the meeting ended. It was agreed that I, Zuleika, Imtisar and one or two others would make the journey to the cave of the djinni, and if we could find those beings, ask their counsel. In accordance with tradition, we will leave tomorrow at sunset. The extra day will allow us to set up the safety measures that Zuleika has advised for the whole community, and to agree on the final number who will be in our party. Issi may accompany us to represent the men: we go on foot, of course, but he could be invaluable to us in finding our way back here after the meeting. By choice we would bring Rem, as the only one among us who has met the djinni before, but she has no wish to see them again.

REM:

I never saw it. Not even when I spoke the words that led to this. How did that not warn me? Every action has consequences, and I see them. When someone makes a choice, when I make one myself, a dozen futures will be there that were not there before, immediate and potential, both trivial and momentous. I once almost lost my mother her job by running off with a cake she was about to sell, because I saw a child choking. When I decided to disguise myself and work in the library I was overwhelmed with new visions for days, so many that I could not steer a path between them.

But I said: "We take back Bessa!" I said it to Zuleika, for whom decision is action, and to all the women of the community, who would support her. And I never saw a thing. I was so swept away by my own enthusiasm that I didn't even notice. I never considered what that blindness could mean.

The djinni are jealous and secretive—the gifts they give do not include power over themselves. And now we've put the final decision in their hands, and I cannot see even a glimpse: not of them or what they might say. And not of the future that will come from their words.

The thought of them makes me sick to my heart. How could I bear to go back there?

But how can I bear it, not knowing?

GIVERS OF GIFTS

They set off, as agreed, at sunset the next day. The party was in some ways an oddly assorted one: Zuleika, as leader of the disputed campaign; Imtisar, as her chief opponent, and Gursoon, to keep the peace between them; also Issi the chief camel-man, who had agreed to come for reasons not entirely clear, but whose expertise would be valued as a pathfinder. Lastly, there was the foundling, Rem, who had not wanted to come at all.

"Look at her," whispered Bethi to Thana, as the slight figure followed the others into the setting sun, her head bowed. "I heard she's been there before—she even has the sight herself—but she looks like she's being sold off in marriage."

"To a fat man of eighty," Thana agreed.

"With bad breath."

They giggled, but Thana quickly sobered. "If she has the sight," she said, "that long face of hers is a bad sign. What's she so frightened of? There are some bad stories told about the djinni."

Most of the women watched the pilgrims' departure in silence. Many shared Thana's fears—word had spread that Rem, alone of all of them, had once met the djinni, and the girl's reluctance to go there again gave them no great hopes for what the venture could achieve. A few of the children, more curious or adventurous than the others, looked on with envy. Jamal scowled and swiftly turned away to throw pebbles against a rock. But most felt only anxiety for the fate of the travellers, mixed with a wordless sentiment that translated roughly as: *Sooner them than me.*

It was Farhat who dispelled the mood, turning from the others to spot a pile of sacks and blankets still stacked in the middle of their camp.

"Zeinab!" she cried. "We need to get all the foodstuffs stored in the lower cave. Can we organise a team to carry the rest down? It's almost dark. And Umayma, does everyone know who's on the guard rota for tomorrow?"

The women turned from their watch, some sighing, some grumbling, to resume their evening tasks. Small fires were lit in their usual hollow, and Thana and Halima brought out the dried meat and saltbush leaves for supper, helped by the bigger children. The youngest ones were fed and chivvied into bed. Any woman or man not immediately engaged in work was rounded up by Farhat and Zeinab to carry the last of their supplies underground, to the hideout that Zuleika had ordered in case of attack from Bessa.

Unobserved now, the tiny pilgrim group plodded on its way, already lost in the shadows. There was no need to stop with darkness: the way to the djinni is not to be found by landmarks. They would walk straight ahead until their legs tired, then next day set off again with the rising sun behind them.

They did not speak, maybe from a sense of tradition, or fear, or simply from the pressure of the darkness all around them, which seemed to muffle sound. None of them heard the light tread of the one who followed behind.

On the first day the mountains accompanied them as a dark line to the north. Early on the second day they were still visible as a fading shadow over their shoulders. After that there was nothing but level sand and empty sky. The sun set in their faces, and the after-images flashed before their eyes as darkness gathered around them.

Late on the third day a shadow appeared ahead of them, growing as they approached it to become a line of slender rocks.

"Is this the place?" Gursoon said to Rem. The girl stared ahead wordlessly, seeming not to hear.

"It had better be," said Imtisar. "We can't go on for another day."

"It's too soon to tell," Issi said. "Land as flat as this, it could be leagues away."

But the rocks drew steadily closer, resolving themselves into four narrow spars and a single stub.

"This is the place," said Zuleika. Beside her, Rem was shivering.

They had talked about what they would say to the djinni. They had agreed that Zuleika would speak of their plans, and ask for guidance and strategy. Imtisar would ask about the dangers they would face, and test her belief that the venture was doomed to fail. But as they passed the Hill of the Hand and entered the valley, all thoughts fell away.

The sun hung low and red between spikes of stone on each side, making it impossible to see what lay ahead. Rem stumbled and came to a halt, staring into the sun as if blind. Zuleika took hold of her arm to draw her forward, then started. The girl was silently crying, and her tears were black. Her eyes welled as if with ink. Dark streaks barred her face and dripped onto her clothes and hands. Gursoon, ahead of the group, turned to urge them on, and exclaimed in horror. But there was no time to delay. The old woman turned back and took Rem's other arm. The girl stood passively for a moment, then seemed to pull away from them.

"Not this!" she whispered.

"You could wait here . . ." Gursoon began. But Rem was reaching for the dagger in Zuleika's belt. Suppliants to the djinni do not go armed.

Zuleika nodded and loosed the dagger. After a moment's thought she drew a smaller knife from her shoe, and laid the two blades together on the path. Then they went on together, supporting Rem between them and signalling to the two behind to keep close.

After a few more steps the spires of rock on each side began to curve down and inwards, the tips pointing towards them. A little farther, and the stones gave way to a wall of rock, at its heart a jagged black hole. The red light was all about them now, but the sun was nowhere.

In its place were the djinni.

Gursoon did not know them at first. There were bulges in the stone, outcrops that could perhaps, from a certain angle, be taken for carved figures. Yes: statues of men and women, or rearing beasts, crude and stylised and melting into each other at the edges. Silently and all together, the figures stepped away from the wall, towards her. And opened their eyes, all dark as the smoke of a forge, and with the same heat behind them.

Gursoon recoiled, and found that she could not move. She turned to Zuleika, but her companion had vanished. Even Rem, who had been leaning on her arm, must have loosed it without her noticing. She was alone with the djinni.

They waited. She had meant to say nothing, to leave it all to the taciturn Zuleika, who would not be tempted to speak a word off the purpose. But Zuleika was gone, and the figures before her demanded acknowledgement.

Gursoon's skin crawled. She spoke the only words she could find, and they hung in front of her like breath in cold air.

"We want no gifts, no changes. We only ask for your words. If you deny us those, we have no request to make."

There was a movement in the figures before her, a ripple. The stone faces had no mouths; they answered in voices she felt rather than heard.

But you must have gifts, if you are to succeed.

Gursoon choked down panic. Better to have nothing than too much, she told herself. "We're not asking you for gifts," she repeated.

Her voice wavered in the air before her. The answer came before it faded.

Then how else are you to get them?

The djinni appeared as soon as Zuleika reached the rock wall. They were armed and armoured, as she had half-expected: men and women, by their bodies, all helmeted and in ceaseless motion. By their absence of wounds they must be training, not fighting, yet the slashes and blows she saw were as furious as any she had known in battle. They lunged and feinted, turning around and against each other with the grace of dancers. And even as they fought, each helmeted head turned immovably in her direction.

Zuleika ignored the racing of her heart and spoke loudly the words she had prepared.

"Great djinni. We are women. We plan to take the city of Bessa for ourselves, by guile and by arms. I want to know if we can succeed, and how best to achieve it."

An urge came over her to beg for strength, for wisdom or for weapons that might outweigh Hakkim's forces. She bit it down and said nothing more.

The whirling combat did not falter, nor did their attention on her. Zuleika stood and bore it. At length, a cry came from all of them at once, like a battle shout.

What you need, you must take from each other!

It was only reasonable, of course, that the djinni should take the form of great caliphs and queens—they emerged in procession out of the dark hole, and the splendour of their jewels, their clothes, lit up the dry and barren place like little fires.

But something about them was not right. The slender lady with the emeralds: her face was beautiful, but the skin had an odd shimmer, as if clad in scales. The man with the golden beard smiled to reveal a suspicion of tusks, or fangs. And the lord in the velvet robe, so magnificently tall: was that a tail flicking beneath the purple hem?

They fixed their royal gazes on Imtisar and on her alone. And at once all the fine words she had rehearsed flew out of her head, and she was left barely able to catch a breath. But she had to say something.

"What do we do?" she stammered. They looked down at her gravely, not answering. And for an instant she saw that flick of a tail again; the horns not quite concealed by a jewelled turban; the queen stroking the edge of her robe with a taloned claw. They were mocking her, she thought, with a flash of anger, and this time the words came without thought.

"Is that it? Must we follow this lunatic plan? All I want is our safety. For all of us. To live free of fear and poverty. Is that too much to ask?"

They smiled, then. The faces were more than ever those of boar, lion and snake, but the same smile was on every one. The tall man with the tail spoke for all.

There is no safety, he told her. *You may have freedom, if you choose it. But you must give something, and take something in return.*

Issi could never remember later how the djinni came to him, nor quite what they looked like, nor how they sounded. A gust of sand blew up around him as he entered the valley, stinging his face so that he had to bend his head and squint at the path. Imtisar, just ahead of him, seemed not to notice. But the wind rose. In a moment he was surrounded by a dust storm, cutting out sight and sound.

Issi had encountered enough desert storms to know what to do; he threw his cloak over his head and stood still, only throwing out an arm to brace himself against the rock wall. But the wall was not there: all his groping failed to discover it; and at the same moment the noise of the storm vanished. He was blind and deaf, with no point of contact to the world.

In a sudden panic he threw off the cloak. The storm still whirled all around, but no stinging grains hit him. The noise had receded to a distant buzzing. There was nothing else to hear; nothing to see. But as he peered through the dust cloud for any sign of his companions, he could make out shapes. They might have been angels: winged giants, so far off he could barely see them through the storm. In another moment they seemed as small as insects, buzzing almost around his head. *They are the djinni*, he thought.

There seemed no way he could make them hear him, but he had to know the answer. He cupped his hand and shouted through the churning motes. His voice came back to him as less than a whisper.

"My wife and sons: are they well? Will I see them again?"

And miraculously, an answer came, buzzing in his ears with the storm:

They are alive, and remember you.

"Please," Issi begged the insect voices. "How can I get back to them?"

This time his own voice sounded so faint he thought the djinni would not hear. But their reply came stronger than before.

Make exchange with the boy behind you.

The storm stopped as suddenly as if it had never been. Crouched behind him, wide-eyed and trembling, was Jamal.

It had not been a whim, to follow them. When it became clear that he was not to be included in the party, he had already filled the largest water-skin he could find and hidden it with a blanket under rocks at the western edge of the camp. He had taken a bag for food, too, but had not been able to fill it: just the morning's bread, and a double handful of dried fruit hurriedly snatched from the stores, for which he risked humiliating punishment if caught. There was no time to get more. He watched them leave just before sunset and waited for his opportunity. When everyone around him was busy with Farhat's chores, it was easy enough to slip into the darkness.

For almost as long as he could remember Jamal had longed to be older, had fretted about his small size and lack of strength, so that they all ignored him and treated him as a child. But now, moving unseen behind the chosen five, matching their footsteps with his own, keeping just within earshot, he revelled in his own lightness and speed. When they finally stopped to sleep he moved a little further away and dug himself a hollow in the warm sand, feeling, as he wrapped himself in his blanket, that he could have gone on for much longer.

He woke chilled and stiff in the darkness to the sound of their voices, and scrambled to his feet: they were moving on already. He trudged after them as the sun rose at their backs. When the sun reached its height he regretted that he had not brought a scarf for his head, or any kind of tent. The adults, his quarry, made a shelter of three of Issi's light wood poles and a thin cloth to hide from the worst hour of the heat. Jamal had to huddle beneath his heavy blanket, holding it away from his face with his knees and trying not to move.

Many times during the next two days he thought about calling out; running to Zuleika and the others and announcing that he was joining them. They had come too far already to turn back, and too far to send him back alone. But something always prevented him: pride, perhaps. At other times he wondered why no one had simply turned around and seen him. But not one of the five looked back, or if they did it was in blindness. All their attention was fixed on what lay ahead; Jamal's too.

By noon on the third day his water was gone. It came to him that he might die now if he did not call to the five ahead, but he kept on in silence, and they did not turn. As the day wore on he realised he had no more voice to call.

Towards evening he passed a rock that he thought must be the Hill of the Hand. In some of the tales, pilgrims had found water there, and he thought he could hear it trickling. But he had fallen too far behind and the sun was nearly down: there was no time to waste in searching. *Afterwards*, he thought, and went on into the ravine.

He saw his father there, fighting with Hakkim Mehdad. Just past the stone spikes at the entrance they stood, locked together and swaying, their hands around each other's throats. The sultan was dressed as Jamal had last seen him, in his silk chamber-robe: his bald head gleamed beneath the setting sun. Hakkim Mehdad was all in black, his head swathed in a black scarf. Jamal had never seen the man's face; all that was visible of him now was his eyes, which glowed like those of a wolf at night.

His father turned his head and nodded to Jamal, then went back to throttling his enemy. With a cry that caught in his throat, Jamal ran to help him.

His way was blocked. Where his father had been there was now an army: countless stern-faced men, their spears all pointing at his heart. They did not attack, but stood waiting for him to speak. So this was the moment; but Jamal had no voice. Nevertheless, he made his demands, shaped with his lips and hurled towards them with all the breath he had, though his throat made no sound but a hoarse gasp.

"I want my kingdom back. And I want to avenge my mother and my father. Help me take back my rightful place!"

They heard him. At least, they seemed to answer. A voice came to him; he could not tell if it was one or many.

Some of your desires you will gain, it told him. *But you must offer something. Now.*

The last word was like a thunderclap. It wiped out the army, the spears and banners, like mist in the sun. Jamal was kneeling on bare sand, looking at bare rock. And beside him, gazing down with horror and amazement, was Issi.

NOW, the djinni said, heavy as a great book closing, and vanished. The six gazed at each other in the empty ravine, in the last light.

"Jamal!" Gursoon exclaimed. How . . . ?"

"Not now," Zuleika cut in. "What did you hear? What did they tell you?"

"That we need gifts . . ." Gursoon's voice was doubtful.

"They told me I must give something," Imtisar said. "And take something."

"Make exchange . . ." Issi said. "But what does it mean?

"It means the gifts come from us."

It was Rem who spoke. She had been sitting hunched, pressing herself against the rock wall furthest from the cave, and her voice was muffled. "I think . . . we have to give gifts to each other. Now, before the sun sets."

"What gifts?" Zuleika seemed almost indignant. "We have nothing here!"

"Maybe when we get back . . ." Gursoon began.

"No!" Rem was suddenly on her feet, and shouting with desperate urgency. They turned to her in amazement. Her face was paper-white, the black tears marking it like bars.

"No. It has to be now. That's how they work . . . Whatever you have, whatever you have with you, give it to someone. I don't know why. But we must do it, before it gets dark." She felt inside her tunic, pulled out a reed pen and pressed it into Zuleika's hands. "Like this. Here. This is for you."

Gursoon nodded, and pulled a ring from her finger, holding it out to Imtisar. The other woman, after some hesitation, reached up to take a comb from her hair. But as she took Gursoon's ring she started and tried to give it back.

"I can't take this! This is Bokhari's ruby. It's worth a fortune! Give me something less . . . that little silver ring you have . . ."

"This is what I'm giving you," Gursoon said firmly. Take it, Imtisar, with my blessing." She turned away. Imtisar gazed at the ring with appalled delight.

Issi had been patting down his clothes, finding nothing detachable. At length, with visible reluctance, he took something on a string from around his neck.

"It's the key to the sultan's stable yard," he said to Jamal. "Just don't lose it." Jamal had nothing to hand him in return but an empty waterskin, which Issi took a little sourly.

Rem turned to Zuleika, who had not moved since she had accepted the little pen. It still lay in her hand, narrower than her smallest finger. She looked down at it as if uncertain what to do with it.

"I have nothing to give you," she said. "There were only my knives, and I left them on the ground, back there. Shall I go now and get them?"

"No!" Rem was adamant. "It must be here and now."

They held each other's gaze for several heartbeats Then Rem looked down at the pen in the other woman's hand.

"The lessons I gave you," she said. "Do you remember them?

Zuleika made a movement of irritation, suppressed it, nodded.

"Then give me a word."

Rem blinked fiercely, and the black tears welled again. She reached to take the pen from Zuleika's hand, dabbed the point into the black stream beneath one eye, and returned it. She held out her right arm, turning it to expose the white skin below the elbow.

"Just here. Write a token for me."

It seemed to take them a long time. Zuleika, so sure and graceful with all the tools and motions of her chosen trade, was clumsy with the little slip of wood, handling it as if she were afraid of causing damage. She wrote her name in large, spiky script, separating each letter. The last one ended in a round blot. They stood together, Zuleika still holding

Rem's arm, and watched the word dry.

"Is it enough?" Zuleika asked at length.

Rem nodded, still gazing down at her arm with its new mark.

"So what do we do now?" Zuleika said.

Rem looked up. Her face was still white, but the black tears no longer welled from her eyes. For the first time in days, she smiled.

"It's done," she said. "Now we can go home."

READING LESSONS, PART THE SECOND

Let's back up a little.

After I spoke those words, "We take back Bessa," everything began to move in double-time. The council of war, the visit to the djinni: the flood of revolution engulfed us with such astonishing speed that most of us never paused to consider the precise nature of the current that swept us along. But it is part of my gift, and my burden, always to consider the current, and I would neglect the responsibilities of both if I avoided it now.

When I spoke to the women of the seraglio about retaking the city, I planted an idea in their minds. It was an idea of freedom and beauty and power, of women leaving the bedchamber and entering the throne room. It was the embryo of a political ideology at least six centuries before its time, but that does not even begin to explain its potency. It was not the newness of the concept, but its familiarity which moved them. They had all seen the rights to their own flesh passed from one man's hand to another, and all had felt keenly their own powerlessness in those exchanges. In such situations, a version of the same concept has formed many times in many people's thoughts, and most of the time fear, or reason, or a sense of overwhelming odds, has stifled it before it can be uttered. A thousand stillborn revolutions are buried a thousand times over for every day that the world has endured. It is very seldom indeed that one is delivered alive.

For an idea of the general effect my words produced, imagine a bomb going off in four hundred minds at once. And if the story I am about to tell now seems as strange and unbelievable to you as it does to me, then I can only say that the fallout from such arcane explosions is never the same twice, and most likely is beyond the power of human minds to anticipate.

At first, the party who had visited the djinni spoke little on the return journey. Their memories, not only of the djinni's words, but of their own and each other's speech and actions, differed in such fundamental respects that for the first two days after their departure all their conversations foundered into uneasy silence. More than this, for many leagues, each one of them was haunted by the sneaking conviction that the djinni watched them still, and though none dared voice the suspicion, all could feel that tightening sensation at the base of the skull which suggests the gaze of unseen eyes. It was not until a little before noon on the third day, when they reached the flat rock which lay a half-day's journey from the bandits' cave, that they began tentatively to discuss the djinni's mysterious instructions, and the gifts they had been asked to exchange.

"Well, that was a waste of six days," Imtisar proclaimed. The others shushed her hurriedly, even Jamal looking alarmed at this blatant disrespect.

"Please, lady, do not insult them," Issi hissed, glancing behind him as if he expected a djinn to rise up from the sand at his back.

"Why not? We're far from them now. Besides, I'm only speaking the truth. Why they decided not to help us is beyond me, but whatever their reasons, they have given us nothing we didn't have already. All this trip has achieved is the redistribution of our own belongings."

"Perhaps the djinni have enchanted them, so that they will help us in the battle," Issi suggested. Imtisar shot him a disdainful look.

Gursoon was of the opinion that the function of the gifts was symbolic; perhaps they were meant as clues to how the seraglio should proceed, or warnings of the dangers they would face along their way. Imtisar seemed more convinced by this argument, but still eyed the objects sceptically.

"They don't look symbolic to me," she said. For the hundredth time, her gaze fell on the ruby Gursoon had given her, and lingered there with pleasure.

"Take this stone for example," she pursued, her tone dubious. "Granted, it's very beautiful, and one of the biggest I've seen, but what could it possibly signify?"

To her surprise, Gursoon laughed. "I can answer that, after a fashion. That ruby has a very specific significance, though only to me, it must be said. It was given to me by Bokhari Al-Bokhari, who had received it from a visiting legate of the city of Sakhradin. It was during his fractious phase, when he used to make war with every city-state within a hundred leagues, and the gift of the ring threw him into a monumental rage. As you have doubtless noticed, its centre is scored with a thousand cracks. Bokhari declared that such a flawed stone was an insult to his dignity: none but a perfect gem was a worthy gift for the sultan of Bessa.

"Well, the night the legate left, Bokhari called me to him, and learning the source of his anger, I decided to do what I could to avert a disaster. After I had called for a bowl of Mahalabiyyah to soothe his temper, I asked if I could see the trinket which had provoked his most righteous and entirely justifiable ire. He flung it onto the bed, whereupon I immediately made my eyes go round with awe. After a few moments, he glanced up to see my reaction and noticed my pose of exaggerated astonishment. 'What is it?' he asked petulantly.

"'Oh, majesty, this is a rare thing,' I replied, my tone reverent. I told him that in my town, we called such rubies the stones of diplomacy, as their internal fault lines, rather than causing the whole gem to shatter, instead produced beautiful displays of coloured light. I demonstrated this fact with the lamp on his dressing table, and the stone duly filled the dim room with kaleidoscopic points of brightness. To the wise, I explained, these stones taught that the best among us must always view a cause of strife and difficulty from many different angles; in this way, we may come to find that it is actually a source of bountiful opportunity. The metaphor was well chosen. Sakhradin is famed for its jewel mines, and after a few days of thought and sulking, Bokhari abandoned hostilities with the city in favour of trade negotiations. He gave the ring to one of the sultanas to wear the next time the legate came to stay, and when she did not want to keep it, he gave it to me."

Imtisar sniffed, but she was looking at Gursoon curiously. "That's a meaning that you attached to the ruby yourself," she pointed out.

"Well, the djinni are supposed to be able to see all things," Gursoon replied. "Maybe they knew the story of this ring, and wished to remind us all of the uses of diplomacy. Certainly we will have need of it if we succeed in taking the city."

For a while, Imtisar walked along in silence. She appeared to be thinking, and the delight in her eyes when she looked at the gem was mixed with a sharper note of interest. Eventually she spoke up again, in the same disgruntled tone as before.

"Well, whatever its meaning, it's a far finer gift than the one I gave you," she said, glancing bitterly at the wooden comb in Gursoon's hair. "Ever since we went into this blessed desert, my hair has been so full of sand and grit that whenever I even attempt to comb it, it only throws up great clouds of dust. That thing is no use to anyone out here, unless they wanted to choke themselves with it."

Zuleika left the rest of the group to their conversation, striding ahead until she walked on her own. She was locked in deep thought, and had been, intermittently, since before they departed for the djinni's cave. It took a lot to rouse strong feeling in Zuleika. She was laconic by nature, and having chilled her blood, after long practice, to the requisite temperature for reasoned murder, she found but few things of sufficient moment to warm it again. She understood the evils and vicissitudes of life in the same way that she understood the twelve different ways of breaking a man's neck, and it had been a long time since either point of knowledge had inspired her with any emotion deeper than indifference.

Since Rem's speech, however, a change had come over the assassin. Like a spark, the prospect of liberating Bessa caught in some shadowed corner of her mind, flaring up into a desire which burned with an uncharacteristic intensity. Her thoughts had been filled with training schedules, the procurement of weapons, intricate tactics and stratagems, even before the council voted for war.

And then there was Rem herself. Zuleika had a new admiration for the slight librarian, whose eloquence had touched her with that thrill of recognition born from seeing the shapeless mists of our own impulses bodied forth in the words of another. It was that elation which had moved her to kiss Rem when she first suggested retaking the city, a loss of control that slightly unnerved her whenever she thought of it. Rem puzzled her. She was reserved almost to the point of silence, but when she did speak her words were wonderful and strange, with an electric charge to them which made Zuleika's skin prickle.

Rem was one of the matters which occupied her mind now. The atmosphere of numinous unreality which had permeated her encounter with the djinni still filled Zuleika; though she had not been in favour of the visit, she could not now deny the djinni's power, nor did she feel that she could afford to ignore their advice.

She had spent the entire journey considering the gifts that she and Rem had exchanged, but still she could see no way in which they might help them to take back the city. A pen and a word: they were not weapons, and they had no story attached to them as did Gursoon's ruby.

The more Zuleika thought about it, the more convinced she became that their significance was not to the battle ahead, but to its aftermath. A knowledge of reading and writing, after all, was essential to the rulers of a city. If they gained control of Bessa, treaties would need to be drawn up, new laws recorded, and correspondence exchanged with neighbouring sultanates. Bokhari had been engaged in such matters all the time. But in this area Zuleika felt herself to be on uncertain ground. The swirling characters that the other women seemed able to discern so easily all looked alike to her, and her progress in Rem's lessons had been slow. Asking for favours did not sit well with her, yet the gift of the pen, and her own reason, persuaded her that in this case she must. She quickened her pace.

Rem had not said a word to anyone since asking Gursoon for a rag to wipe the tears from her face, and had walked far ahead of the others for the whole journey, lost in miserable reflection. She had seen before the effect her tears could have, when she stayed at her grandfather's house as a child, and she was still very young when she had learned how to stifle them. Now, everyone had seen the black rivulets flowing from her eyes. Zuleika had seen them. She only hoped that, if they did not see her cry again, the women would think the tears a temporary affliction, sent by the djinni for some unguessable purpose of their own.

She was jolted from these thoughts as Zuleika fell into pace beside her, bringing with her that tightening in Rem's chest, composed in equal parts of pleasure and apprehension, which always accompanied her presence. She straightened a little and smiled. Zuleika did not notice. As often happens when we are forced to rely against our inclination on the goodwill of others, she approached Rem expecting to be refused, and so put her request in the form of an order.

"Now that we are to prepare for an attack on Bessa, your lessons will have to stop. Our time will be taken up with other things." The assassin spoke with more than her usual bluntness.

"Oh, that's alright." Rem seemed unperturbed. "Most of the women and children have learnt all that I can teach them, for the time being at least. There's not much more I can do without actual scrolls."

Zuleika was rather discomfited by this response. She had spoken in the anticipation of hostility or at least dissent, and Rem had not only agreed with her, but substantiated her agreement with all of the arguments Zuleika had secretly intended on using to beat her down. Thrown from her expected course, she paused for a few moments before replying.

"You say that most of us have learnt all we can."

"For the moment, yes."

Zuleika gritted her teeth. "I am an exception. You probably have not noticed—I am one among many—but I am finding it more difficult than most to master what you teach."

Rem, who had noticed everything, from the first flicker of consternation in Zuleika's dark eyes to the latest furrow in her brow, feigned surprise.

"I think it important that I become more proficient," Zuleika continued, a note of belligerence creeping into her tone. "In preparing to take the city, my talents are necessary, but the gifts we exchanged seem to indicate that yours, too, will be called for. So while there will be no longer be time for you to teach everyone—"

Rem's eyes widened. Suddenly seeing where this was heading, she cut Zuleika off. "You wish me to give you private lessons," she finished.

Zuleika misread the incredulous delight written on Rem's face as indignation at this request for special treatment.

"I need to learn," she snapped. "In the early days, many of the women will be looking to me to—"

"Of course, the others will expect you to play a leading role—"

"The governance of a city requires—"

"—good literacy skills. Yes, I—"

"I cannot acquire such skills without your instruction," Zuleika interrupted.

"Well, exactly."

The voices of the two women had risen to the point where the rest of the group could easily overhear their conversation, and were starting to glance in their direction.

"So. You won't do it," Zuleika growled.

Rem stared at her in dismay. "But I've just said that I will," she blurted.

There was a brief pause, during which they both noticed the four curious stares directed towards them. Rem blushed furiously.

"Oh," Zuleika muttered. "Fine, then."

"Shall we start tonight?" Rem asked.

"I would appreciate it."

Seeing that the argument, if it had been an argument, was at an end, the others resumed their conversation. Rem turned her attention back to Zuleika, and continued in a more even tone, "I can teach you every evening if you want, or in the middle of the day, when it becomes too hot to train. The others won't miss out. Most know enough now to continue practising themselves, and those who don't can learn from those who do. Anyway, I can restart the regular lessons once we've taken Bessa."

Zuleika raised an eyebrow. "You seem confident that we will take Bessa," she commented.

"I'm not. But if we don't, then reading lessons will not be our most pressing concern."

Zuleika laughed. Quietly, companionably. "Very true. If we do, though, you will likely find many others who wish to learn from you."

"Yes, I've been thinking about that. We'll need to build a few schools. Houses of learning," she added, seeing Zuleika's expression.

The two women conversed in this wise for a full turn of the glass before Zuleika moved off to ask Issi whether he had spotted the next marker yet. Rem watched her retreating back, the delicate arch of her neck and curve of her hips, waiting until she was quite sure that she would not turn around. She hugged her joy to herself, afraid to give it utterance.

The evening that they returned to the camp, there was a meeting of the seraglio. After Gursoon had briefly related what transpired during their visit to the djinni, Zuleika stepped forward to explain their future course.

An attack on Bessa would require extensive preparation and training; Zuleika estimated that a year would be sufficient for this. During this time, the seraglio would remain at the bandits' caves, where Zuleika would train them in the arts of war and develop a more detailed plan of attack.

The production of goods for sale would cease: though not everyone would have to fight, all the women and men of the seraglio would be needed for the war effort, and there would be no more leisure for other activities. This would not bring them to hardship and deprivation, however. During the now abandoned preparations for the journey to Yrtsus, they had amassed sufficient savings to support them for almost a year.

At many points while she spoke, Zuleika was interrupted by raised voices, their tones ranging from fear to indignation. Many among the seraglio pointed out that the vote for war had been precipitated by the threat of discovery, yet Zuleika's plan left them no less vulnerable to that danger than they had been before.

Zuleika allowed that this was so, but repeated what she had said in the council about preparing the deep caves to hide in, and positioning scouts a day's ride to the south and east, so that any movement towards them from the direction of Bessa would be detected. To this she added the further precaution that they should stop trading for food and supplies in Agorath, moving instead to Jawahir, which they would visit for brief periods only, and with their faces heavily veiled. Enough people were satisfied by these assurances that the discussion was able to move on to other matters, and before long the meeting drew to an end. Before the women dispersed, Zuleika spoke once more.

"When the vote was cast for war, you chose me as your general," she said, "but although I can teach you how to fight, I cannot plan this attack alone. I am not a native of Bessa, and have seen very little of the city outside of the seraglio compound. But many of you grew up there. You know its squares and buildings, the layout of its streets and the location of its gates, and we will need all of that knowledge if we are to succeed in capturing it. I need to know these things. So I want to form a council to discuss them, and ultimately to decide on the means by which we should take the city." She paused, as it occurred to her that some of the women might misinterpret this brief. "Its role will be advisory only," she said firmly. "Battles cannot be waged by committee, and the final decision on the tactics we adopt must rest with me. However, I would value advice, and anyone who feels they can provide it should come forward at the end of this meeting."

It was a diverse and unusual collection of people who volunteered for the war council. There was Gursoon, of course, as well as four of the nine who had helped Zuleika to defeat the guards, Umayma, Dalal, Nafisah and Zeinab. Rem offered to act as a scribe, and Issi and Bethi also placed their knowledge at Zuleika's disposal. Unlike the women of the seraglio, their work had taken them all over the palace compound: Issi knew the grounds and stable block like the back of his rough hands, while Bethi had been everywhere in the palace itself, from the royal chambers of Bokhari's wives to the servants' quarters. Jamal argued that he, too, should be included.

"I am of the lineage of Al-Bokhari," he proclaimed, drawing himself up to his full child's height. "Military strategy runs in my veins."

The women, who well remembered Bokhari's love for military strategy, laughed at Jamal's pomposity. Still, he had been present at the cave of the djinni, so perhaps he was entitled to a voice. In the end he, too, was admitted to the council.

The last, and by far the most surprising of those who volunteered was Imtisar. Zuleika narrowed her eyes as she saw the older woman approach the group, which had clustered at the side of the cave mouth.

"When last we spoke on this theme, you said that you could not abide by the decision to go to war," Gursoon said sharply.

"I know," Imtisar replied. "That makes it even more important that I have some say in these proceedings."

"If you are coming to try and change our minds," Zuleika began in a warning tone, "then we have voted and it's clear—"

The courtesan cut her off. "Of course not. I won't interfere with the decision of the group. But nor will I leave all the decision making to the warmongers. No, if I am forced to stay, then I will help to lead this campaign. Not because you want my opinion, you've made that clear enough, but because you dearly need it. I'm the only one on this council with enough good sense to save us all from suicide."

So saying she stalked off, casting a last contemptuous look over her shoulder at the group of women, who watched her leave in stunned silence.

"Not her," Zuleika said, in something like horror. "We'll never get anything done!"

"You did make an open appeal," Gursoon reminded her. "Besides, it's an improvement on her former position."

Zuleika scowled at the woman's retreating back, but Gursoon's expression was more circumspect. She had noticed that Imtisar was wearing the flawed ruby on her finger.

"I have a feeling that organising this war is going to be like herding camels," Zuleika remarked that night, as she and Rem sat in her tent. They had decided to hold the reading lessons in the evening, the cool air being more conducive to mental application. Rem nodded her agreement, smiling wryly.

"Gursoon was right though. It's better that Imtisar should join the council than refuse to recognize it." She glanced down at the sloping sentence that Zuleika had scratched out tentatively on the parchment in front of her.

"That's a good start."

"It's wrong, isn't it?"

"It's not wrong. You've only misspelled a couple of words. Look, I'll show you."

As Rem took the parchment from her, Zuleika shifted her position, peering over Rem's shoulder while she worked. Rem could feel the other woman's skin pressed lightly against her back, her breath brushing her cheek. She felt her thoughts begin to disintegrate. A minute passed, then another.

"Rem?" Zuleika frowned. "You haven't written anything down."

"Sorry, I'm a little tired."

"Should we continue tomorrow?"

"Oh, no, I'm fine."

In fact, Rem was almost overwhelmed by the sense of Zuleika's presence. It filled the tent like thick incense, muddling her thoughts and clouding her mind. Zuleika was pregnant with significance, so permeated with the residue of future emotions that she seemed to blur as she moved, leaving a trail of after-images wherever she went. As in every case concerning her own life, Rem's sight did nothing but confuse her on the subject of Zuleika. Raw feelings, shorn of context and chronology, assaulted her whenever she so much as thought of the beautiful assassin. She could not see her as she was through the intoxicating haze of what she would be; each version obscured the other, so that Rem could not say what Zuleika would one day mean to her, or what she meant to her now.

The first meeting of the council of war was held the following morning. Most of it was taken up with further discussion of the djinni's bewildering gifts, which were placed in the centre of the large tent set aside for the meeting. The council members sat around them in a circle while they talked. Gursoon told the story of the ruby again, and Zuleika repeated the conclusions she had reached about the significance of the pen and the word on Rem's arm, but they could make little of the other objects. They discussed the comb without success. Initially the stable yard key caused some excitement as a possible means of entering the palace, but this hope was dashed when Issi told them that the stable yard gates were locked from the inside.

"That leaves the water-skin," Gursoon said.

So far Jamal had been ignored by all present. His desire to speak had grown so strong by now that he swelled visibly with the pressure of his unspoken opinions. About most of the gifts he had as few ideas as did the rest of the council, though this had not dampened his urge to contribute to their discussions. On the subject of the water-skin, however, he had formed a decided view. It had been his gift, and he felt that this gave him a greater insight into its meaning. Now, he could contain himself no longer.

"I think I've divined what that means," he burst out. "When I accompanied the party who visited the djinni, I ran out of water. With nothing to drink, I became weak, and so vulnerable. The same logic works with an entire city." He paused, his face flushing a little with the brilliance of his deduction. "The djinni's will is clear enough: if we are to retake Bessa, we must poison its wells."

There was a communal intake of breath, followed by absolute silence. Jamal tried to suppress his smile of pride. He should, he felt, maintain an expression of solemnity during this weighty occasion. After all, now that he was finally taking his rightful place at the head of discussions, he must assume the role with the proper dignity. His level gaze faltered a little as he saw the shock and disgust on the faces that looked back at him.

"What is it?" he asked, in genuine surprise, "It seems obvious to me that—"

Gursoon's slap was not particularly forceful, but the shock of it nearly knocked Jamal over. He reeled in pain and astonishment, his mouth opening on a gasp of outrage.

"Jamal," Gursoon said fiercely, "you must never mention that repulsive idea again. Do you understand?"

"But—"

"I said never!" she roared. "A city without water is a city of ghosts. Nothing could justify such an act, and nothing could expiate it."

Jamal opened his mouth to protest further, but Gursoon cut him off. "I think it best that you leave this council now," she said icily. "There is nothing more you can say to us."

Jamal looked for support from the rest of the council, but found none; the eyes that met his gaze were cold and comfortless. No one, not even the most barbarous of the nomad tribes, who fed their enemies' innards to their dogs, would ever consider poisoning a well. Even the thought of it was taboo. Jamal would find no sympathy in the seraglio. He stood up, breathing hard. Though he had pretensions to the contrary, he was still a child, and for a moment his eyes filled with tears. Then, wiping his face with an aggressive motion, he walked shakily from the tent. The council watched him leave, their expressions varying from outrage to horror.

"That boy has a nasty mind," Issi muttered, his face dark.

Over the following months, the council of war met on alternate evenings. Zuleika divided her time between these gatherings and her reading lessons with Rem, but the best part of each day she devoted to training the army. It was a large force: all but the oldest women and the children of the seraglio, as well as Issi's camel-drivers and the bandits.

Zuleika started the fighters off with sword drills, teaching them the basic thrusts and parries before she moved on to more advanced techniques. For the first month, they drilled with wooden sticks rather than swords. This was partly because the trading parties whom Zuleika had sent to purchase weapons in Jawahir, Gharia, Perdondaris and Ibu Kim had not yet returned, and partly to limit the severity of any injuries sustained. In the early days of the training, such injuries occurred with moderate frequency, as each member of the army adjusted to the unfamiliar movements of combat. Even the thieves, who considered themselves competent swordsmen, had a lot to learn from Zuleika. Most of the women had never held a weapon before, let alone used one.

Gradually, however, a change was being wrought in the camp. While at first the women of the seraglio held their weapons nervously, eyeing them with a deep mistrust, soon they could wield them with the sort of practised ease which looks like carelessness to an untrained eye. A week

234

after the vernal equinox, Issi returned from a journey to Beyt Kirim with a cargo of longbows, and Zuleika began to instruct the fighters in archery as well as swordplay. Umayma proved particularly adept at this new discipline, her days of hunting oryx with Issi's boys having perfected her aim. But there were few in the army who found any of the skills Zuleika taught difficult to master. For the most part, they learned swiftly, growing in experience and confidence every day.

The same could not be said of the war council, where setbacks were numerous and progress slow. Although its meetings involved a much smaller number of people, and no weapons whatsoever, they were far more aggressive and easily twice as loud. Zuleika had envisaged the council as a way of gathering ideas, with all final decisions being hers alone, but she soon discovered that such an arrangement was much easier in theory than it was in practice. Once set in motion, the council of women had a momentum of its own which was difficult to arrest.

Zeinab had warned Zuleika that no one would follow her orders unquestioningly, and her prediction held true. Zuleika's tactics were disagreed with often and vocally, and almost every meeting featured at least one attempt to call a vote, usually led by Imtisar. The plan of attack was not developing smoothly; after several weeks of debate, the council had not even agreed upon the best direction from which to approach Bessa's walls.

The constant arguments and delays of the council frustrated Zuleika, and she looked forward more and more to those evenings that she spent with Rem. Though she found reading as difficult as ever, she liked and respected the librarian, who was patient with her mistakes, and as reserved in her nature as Zuleika herself.

Yet although Zuleika felt at ease in Rem's company, as the reading lessons continued she began to notice something distinctly strange in the other woman's manner. She seemed strained, somehow, self-conscious and constantly on edge. She sometimes lost her train of thought when they spoke, trailing off into silence and seeming to forget what it was she had been saying. She stiffened, almost imperceptibly, when Zuleika came near her. None of these reactions were obvious, but in Zuleika's line of work acute observation was second nature. She felt sure that she recognized something in Rem's behaviour, but she could not place it.

In the end, the answer came to her in one of those seamless shifts in perception that make optical illusions clear, the invisible rendered plain by the lifting of some barrier from behind Zuleika's own eyes. Rem quivered with unspent passion: she had been doing so for some time, but Zuleika had never noticed it before. Now, for the first time, she saw it in all its startling intensity.

Rem was not the first woman that Zuleika had encountered whose passions inclined towards others of her sex. Many of the concubines had lain together at some point in their lives, and Jumanah and Najla had been lovers ever since they arrived in the harem. In her early days with the seraglio, several women had made such advances to Zuleika, but she had declined them all, at first because any relationship she embarked on would interfere with her commission, and then, later, due to a simple lack of interest.

The thought of lying with Rem had never occurred to her before, but she could see now how the woman burned for her, and saw no reason not to satisfy her desire. Besides, it was beginning to interfere with the reading lessons.

The next time Rem came to Zuleika's tent, the incense which filled it was real. Zuleika met her outside. She slipped her hand into Rem's, tugging her gently towards the open tent flap. Rem's eyes widened. Zuleika seemed to sharpen into focus before her, the blurred images of her present and future selves suddenly coming into perfect alignment.

She followed Zuleika into the tent, and within its scented interior, for the first time since the library, she revealed the secrets of her body to another. Zuleika had expected to satisfy Rem's desire, not her own, but when their lips touched she felt again that dissolution of self that she had encountered the first time they kissed, and with it the stirrings of a hunger that surprised her with its strength. Rem's body, covered in its cursive script, fascinated and aroused Zuleika. That evening, her reading lesson was from the poetry that twined around Rem's arms and rose and fell on the slope of her breasts.

Long into the night, the tent was filled with murmurs, Rem's soft whispers merging with Zuleika's voice, musical yet hesitant as she stumbled over the new words on this new body, so unlike any she had lain with before.

After that day, a closeness sprung up between Rem and Zuleika such as neither of them had experienced before. They lay together frequently, their reading lessons melting into their lovemaking as evening melted into night. Together, they taught each other the pleasures of words and flesh that each had been denied, and each had surfeited on. Zuleika was surprised by how much she enjoyed her first embraces with Rem, and how strong her appetite became to renew them. She discovered a pleasure in Rem's company that she had forgone for so long she had forgotten its existence, and found, moreover, that she could talk to her as she had never done to the women of the seraglio.

The two women could converse for a watch at a time. They discussed the preparations for battle, spoke of their histories, and of their hopes. On many topics they differed considerably. Zuleika could not understand why Rem risked death to save the contents of Bessa's Library, while Rem was baffled and more than a little alarmed by Zuleika's casual mentions of her time as an assassin, and the complete lack of compunction she showed about the act of murder. Yet their conversations continued in spite of these differences, as did the joining of their flesh, so that by the time half a year had passed they thought of themselves as lovers, if that mysterious thing which lay between them could be given a name.

Meanwhile, the business of the camp went on. The fighters continued to train, and the council to argue. The impasse in the formation of tactics, however, gave way one day as suddenly as a break appearing in clouds. It was some months into the preparations for war, during a meeting of the council, and most of the women were engaged in a debate about the approach to Bessa.

"If we arrive at night, the guards will be less likely to see us," Issi was saying. "At any other time, the dust cloud will give us away."

The gifts exchanged at the djinni's cave remained in their place at the centre of the tent, and as Gursoon, half listening to the conversation going on around her, let her gaze play over them vacantly, her eye chanced to fall again on the wooden comb that Imtisar had given her. She looked at it with renewed interest, studying its long teeth and wooden handle with a thoughtful expression.

"Imtisar," she asked, cutting across the noise of the group, "what was it you said to me when you gave me this comb?"

"That it was useless," the courtesan replied, barely turning her attention from the debate in hand.

"That's not all you said," Gursoon murmured.

She thought a little longer, and then held up a hand for silence. When she had the attention of the rest of the council, she rose to her feet and spoke.

"We're planning this battle on too small a scale," she told them, "focusing on the city and forgetting the space around it. Bessa is surrounded by desert, nothing but flat sand for thousands of leagues. Those kind of distances can be deceptive."

Gursoon motioned for Rem to pass her the scroll of parchment she was using to record the decisions of the council, and a stylus. For a few moments there was only the noise of the pen scratching on the paper. Then she straightened up, and displayed what she had drawn to the watching group. They examined it.

"It looks like a salad tong," said Rem.

This observation was met with puzzled looks.

"It's a comb," Gursoon said, "and I think it may be the answer to our problems."

Gursoon explained her idea and it was greeted, for the first time in months, with general agreement on both its merits and its feasibility. Warudu was called, and the following day she constructed a prototype model from acacia wood. As per Gursoon's instructions, the shaft was about eight spans in length, and widened at the top into five immense tines, thick and curving. By the end of the month, mass production of the combs had begun, and the seraglio knew how they would take the city.

The only question remaining was that of the sultan's palace. All allowed that capturing it would be a gargantuan task. It was a stronghold, heavily fortified, and though its back wall formed part of the city's battlements, precautions had been taken to ensure that it was virtually inaccessible from Bessa's walls themselves. The sections of the city fortifications to either side of the palace were nothing but narrow, crenelated ramparts, no wider across than a single span.

The only way to take the palace from the outside would be through a prolonged and quite possibly bloody struggle, and it was here that contention arose in the council. Imtisar was of the opinion that a battle for the palace must be avoided at all costs, due to the massive loss of life it would entail on both sides. She argued for leaving the palace untouched and simply stationing soldiers around it, starving Hakkim and his guard of power and provisions, and so forcing their surrender.

Zuleika was equally adamant that this plan would be their downfall. A ruler under armed guard, she argued, was still a ruler, and in this case a trained assassin as well. The palace was large, and stocked to withstand a lengthy siege. Hakkim would mount a counterattack from within the safety of its walls, and defeat them even as they celebrated his overthrow.

As with the debate over how to take the city, ultimately it was one of the djinni's gifts that provided the council with a solution to their predicament. Ironically, it was Issi who first suggested that they use the stable yard key to enter the palace.

"I know that in our first meeting, I told you all that the key couldn't help us," he admitted, "but I've been thinking about it, and perhaps I was wrong. Our problem is that the palace is hard to breach from the outside, but it would be much easier for one person to get in than a whole army. If someone could do it—and I'm not saying I know how they might—but if they could do it, and get down to the stable yard in one piece, then they could unlock the gates and let everyone else inside. And then there'd be no siege."

His proposal was greeted with cautious optimism. "That's all very well," said Imtisar, "but it doesn't answer the question of how exactly someone would get inside the palace in the first place."

"Run the walls," Zuleika replied promptly. She had been considering the matter while Issi spoke. "The ramparts connecting the palace to the city fortifications. They're narrow, but it could be done. Then it would just be a matter of climbing in through one of the palace windows."

"What about the guards?" asked Zeinab.

"Zuleika and I could provide covering fire from the nearest watchtower," Umayma answered. "We'll take them all out before the runner even reaches the palace."

"Runners," Nafisah corrected her. "We'll need more than one if this plan is to have a chance of success."

There were nods of approval from Gursoon and some of the other women, but Imtisar remained unconvinced.

"Simply climbing through a palace window is not as easy as you make it sound," she said. "They're very small and narrow—there are not many of us who would be able to fit. Unless you were planning on using children?" she finished, with heavy sarcasm.

"I wouldn't rule it out," Zuleika shot back.

"I doubt that will be necessary." Rem spoke so seldom during council meetings that everyone turned to stare at her. "There are several women who are slight-figured enough to pass, I think," she continued. "I count myself amongst that number, so let me be the first to volunteer. I will run the wall."

It took Warudu a fortnight to construct the wooden platforms, each one an ell in length and placed a cubit apart along the sand. Zuleika weighted them down with stones, and oversaw their arrangement into a curve. They were to be the practice wall, and at their end a rectangular frame was placed, the practice window. Warudu had built it to the same rough dimensions as the windows of the palace, based on what the servants could remember of their size and shape.

The selection of the volunteers was more problematic. Imtisar wanted none but the adults of the seraglio to be considered for the task, but in spite of what Rem had said, only a few of the women, and none of the men, could fit through the narrow frame. On top of this, there were several amongst the seraglio children who offered to act as runners. Soraya and Huma came forward, arguing quite reasonably that they had both come into their change some months ago, and were more than old enough now to make their own decisions. Jamal, too, loudly and indignantly asserted his right to play a part in the overthrow of the treasonous Hakkim.

Eventually it was decided that all those over thirteen years of age could train to run the wall if they wished to, and that at the end of a month's space, those volunteers who had excelled far beyond the rest would be chosen as runners.

The next day, twenty or so volunteers gathered before the rough wooden wall to begin training. They ran the wall in small groups several times a day, with the council members watching carefully to see who among them showed the most promise.

Some had no aptitude at all for the task, and were swiftly persuaded to abandon the attempt. Others could balance well enough, but not run at the requisite speed, or vice versa. Taliyah sped along the wall so swiftly that she would have far outstripped the other runners every time, but invariably fell off the narrow ledge long before she reached the window. All these volunteers were turned away from the wall before the end of the week, until only the most agile members of the seraglio remained. Soraya and Huma were two of the better runners, as was Jamal's friend Zufir. Fernoush and Nasreen also rapidly distinguished themselves.

Jamal, however, outshone them all. He was swift, sure-footed and fearless, and never faltered in his balance. Time and again he reached the window frame and plunged through it without even slowing down, earning approving nods from many of the women watching the training, and even the occasional round of applause. Jamal basked in his newfound success, feeling that it repaid him in some wise for the humiliation that he had suffered when he had been thrown out of the council, and there was a swagger in his step as he strode through the camp.

The only other runner who showed enough skill to be considered for selection was Rem. Zuleika found that she was perturbed by this prospect, though Rem made light of it whenever she raised the subject.

"You're putting yourself in danger," Zuleika said, not for the first time, as they lay together in her tent one evening, Rem's head cradled on her arm.

"We're about to go to war. Every one of us is in danger," Rem replied.

Concern made Zuleika terse. "Yes, but you know you've chosen the riskiest role in this entire plan. You're putting yourself directly in the line of fire."

Rem raised her eyebrows. "I've got you to cover me, haven't I?"

"It's just as well," Zuleika grunted. "Your combat skills are appalling. I don't like the thought of you running around in the palace, especially armed. You'll be more of a danger to yourself than anyone else."

Rem laughed, and snuggled closer to Zuleika's chest. "Train me then. Go on, I've been giving you private lessons for the best part of a year now. It's about time you returned the favour!"

Zuleika smiled reluctantly, joining in with the game. "All right then, I will," she replied. "What do you want to learn?"

"The art . . . of murder," Rem said dramatically. She rolled away from Zuleika, sat up, and seized hold of her pack, which lay in the corner of the tent. "Let's see . . . where are the tools of your trade?"

Zuleika made a playful grab for the pack, but Rem jerked it out of the way, dangling it just out of her reach. She pulled a small grey box from the recesses of the bag, and flicked it open.

"What are these?"

They were ten tiny white spikes, each about as long as Rem's little finger, and wickedly sharp. Zuleika got up to look over her shoulder at them.

"They're finger daggers," she replied, "made of white zirconia—

virtually unnoticeable in a poor light. You stick them onto your nails with a special glue, use them like claws. I was going kill Al-Bokhari with them actually, before I changed my mind. They're a very useful weapon in situations where you can't carry arms."

Rem nodded in mock solemnity and snapped the box shut, carefully replacing it in Zuleika's pack. "My first lesson," she said sombrely, pulling Zuleika back down onto her bedroll and kissing her.

"You have far to go, my child," Zuleika replied, yielding to Rem's embrace.

The two women laughed, and turned to other games.

As the end of the month loomed, the volunteers who remained began to train with increasing energy and commitment. Jamal especially considered himself to be in open competition with the other runners, vying against them for a position in the army which would bring him both glory and a chance to avenge his father's death. Even Zufir, his closest companion amongst the seraglio children, found that the prince would no longer sit with him at meal times; Jamal considered him too much of a rival to associate with him, at least until the runners had been selected.

During practice runs, he began to run faster than he ever had before, urged on by the sense of admiring gazes fixed upon him. One day, in his enthusiasm, he ran too fast, and caught up to Zufir, who ran ahead of him. With a movement of impatience, he swept the other boy aside. Jamal was a strong child; Zufir toppled from the wall and crashed onto the sand below, landing awkwardly on his right arm. Jamal barely noticed that his friend had fallen. He bounded along the remaining crenelations, diving through the window at the end with more than his usual grace and rolling up onto his feet. For a moment, he fought down the ridiculous urge to bow, and a broad smile spread over his face.

His moment of triumph was short-lived, however. He looked behind him to see a cluster of concerned women gathered around Zufir, who was sniffling quietly. The boy had been more shocked than hurt by the fall. Still, he had grazed his arm on a stone, and it had left an angry red mark. Jamal glanced at him in contempt. "Stop crying, you baby," he said mockingly, "it's only a scratch." Umayma, kneeling by her son, fixed Jamal with a glare that could have stripped paint. He shrank back.

After that, any hopes Jamal might have had of being selected as a runner were dashed.

"Imagine if he had done that on the city wall," Umayma exclaimed in fury in the meeting that night. "My son would be dead by now!"

Zuleika spoke out in his defence, but there was little she could do but go and inform Jamal of the council's decision. She found him sitting by the practice wall, his expression morose.

"They've done it again, haven't they?" he said bitterly as Zuleika approached him, "Prevented me from playing my part. For one mistake!"

The disappointment was almost more than Jamal could bear. Zuleika maintained a tactful distance while his shoulders shook with sobs. Then she came and sat down beside him.

"The runners will be Soraya, Huma, Fernoush, Nasreen, Zufir and Rem," she said. "Had the decision been mine alone, it would not have fallen out thus. I'm sorry, Jamal."

He glared at her through tearful eyes. "I could have done this! I've fought before. I saved your life!"

"I have not forgotten that. No one has. And you should remember it too. Jamal, as far as I am concerned you don't need to fight in this battle to prove your bravery. It is a recognition you have already earned."

After sitting on beside Jamal for a few minutes longer, Zuleika rose stiffly to her feet and departed. But long after she had left, Jamal was still replaying her words in his mind.

The date set for the attack drew steadily nearer, and the day came when the fighters had all been trained, the last outsized wooden comb had been constructed, and the volunteers had practised running the wall until they could do it to Zuleika's satisfaction. Soon, the encampment at the caves would begin to empty out, the army departing for the posts assigned to them. It would be safest, Zuleika had decided, if they left in small groups, travelling at night and avoiding the major trade routes. Once, most of the concubines would have turned pale at such a prospect. Now, they were armed against the desert and the dangers it held, both with weapons and with the knowledge of how to use them. For the first time in most of their lives, the means of their deliverance had been placed into their own hands.

Zuleika agonised over the time of her own departure, torn between staying as long as possible to oversee the evacuation of the camp, or leaving with an early party to supervise the deployment of the army. Neither option was ideal; Zuleika hated having to choose in the first place. She had found it hard enough to delegate when her forces were all in the same location, and she could check on their progress as frequently as she wished. Now that the time had come for them to split up, she was infinitely frustrated that she could not be present to see the execution of every detail.

Eventually, and with great reluctance, she decided that she would go with the first group of fighters, leaving Gursoon in charge of the camp at the caves. She spent the day before her departure with Rem, training and reading, and at sunset they lay in each other's arms inside Zuleika's tent. The golden light seeped through the cloth, spilling over their entwined forms.

Rem looked at Zuleika steadily, drinking in the contours of her body, the lines and curves of her face, as if she could take hold of her with her gaze and keep her there. Zuleika ran her hands over the curling script across Rem's breasts and down her arms, pausing when she encountered her own name to give it a gentle squeeze. They clung to each other. They studied each other's faces. Neither of them spoke. They had said all that they could think of to say over the course of the day, and that was little enough. Silence flowed between them, richer than words.

When dusk fell, they parted, and Zuleika called the last full meeting of the seraglio. She stood on the same stone platform from which she had first spoken four years ago, and watched the women, bandits and camel men gathering before her. If they were successful, then this would be the last time they all met together until after they took the city. If they failed, there would never be another meeting. Tearful farewells were exchanged with the group of fighters due to leave, who would depart the next day before dawn. When the noise of the crowd had subsided, Zuleika spoke.

"A few months ago, our future was as frail as the memory of a dream after waking," she said, "but we whetted our swords upon it all the same." She was a black silhouette against the lighter black of the sky, her voice ringing out as if it were the only sound in the desert. Her words sank down into the valley like the cooling air and the gathering dark.

"We go forward because the path ahead is of our own crafting, and in the labour that forged it we also have been remade. When we left Bessa, we were a seraglio of silk and fragrance and soft music. Now the time has come to return, and we are become a seraglio of steel."

THE TAKING OF BESSA,
PART THE FIRST

Hakkim Mehdad was in the throne room when news of the approaching army was brought. "They'll be here in less than a watch, majesty," the watchman panted, "judging by the size of the dust cloud." The intelligence came as no surprise to the Ascetic leader. He employed many spies, not just to monitor the activities of those who posed a threat to his rule, but to identify those of his subjects who, whether through heresy, impiety or wantonness, threatened the supremacy of his doctrine.

Rumours of this attack had been circulating among the people of Bessa for months. Though his guards had not yet managed to arrest anyone who possessed knowledge of a more reliable provenance than what their brother's son had overheard at the market, Hakkim had learned enough to convince him that he would do well to prepare. He felt nothing so base as fear at the prospect that his city was soon to come under attack. Hakkim was armoured with the certainty of religious conviction, and besides, years of actively seeking conflict on a more personal level had inured him to any spasms of apprehension he might once have felt upon entering this larger fight. He would respond to it, as he responded to everything, without deviation or pause, following unflinchingly the way of the one Truth and cutting down whatever obstacles fate placed in the path. There was no hesitation in his voice as he replied.

"Summon Captain Ashraf," he said.

From the watchtower to the left of the Northern Gate, Zeinab looked out over Bessa and adjusted her helmet. It had taken her three months of constant pestering and a faked letter of recommendation from the watch captain of Saruqiy to get the position, but her persistence had paid off, and she was now employed, under the nom de guerre of Zahir, as junior watchman on the left north watchtower.

She had spotted the cloud of dust a short way into the afternoon watch, pausing before she alerted the more senior watchman on duty, a nervous man called Masood, to pull a red headscarf from her breastplate. While Masood sounded the three long blasts on the horn which signified that an enemy was approaching, she held the scarf over the edge of the tower so that it streamed out in the breeze. As she released it, a slight figure took off running. A little after that, Masood dispatched a guard from the right watchtower to the palace, and since then, Zeinab had been watching the city, tracking the currents of activity which carried its people to and fro. The sound of the warning bugle had cut through the normal hubbub of streets and squares, bringing the rhythms of leisure and commerce to a halt. Now, many people were scurrying into houses and packing up market stalls. Around the walls, the other gates were being closed and bolted, one by one. Only the Northern Gate remained open, ready to emit the troops that Zeinab could now see being massed in the palace courtyard. Every moment, more black-garbed soldiers were flowing through the city to join them.

Behind Zeinab, Masood peered anxiously at the cloud of dust on the horizon. Not for the first time, he rounded on his shift partner and wailed, "Zahir, you're looking the wrong way! In the name of the Increate, pay attention- there's an army coming towards us!"

Zeinab glanced round at the sound of his voice, then turned her attention back to the city. Technically, Masood was her superior, but after more than three months of sharing the afternoon shift with the fussy, timid man, she knew how little that counted for. She really felt rather sorry for him; any watchman who failed to notice that his own shift partner was a woman in disguise would probably be better off seeking other employment. Beneath her, Bessa spread its wonders, intricate and finely wrought as a tapestry. In the rapidly emptying market, two tiny figures haggled over loaves the size of peas. A crowd of black-veiled women hurried past them like gnats. Toy soldiers guarded the palace gates. From what used to be the seraglio compound, a man in a black headscarf strode rapidly toward the main palace.

"Zahir!" Masood shook his head in consternation. "For the last time, you're looking the wrong *way!*"

"That all depends on what you're looking for," Zeinab replied mildly.

Her eyes flicked to the street directly beneath the watchtower, where a steady trickle of people, mostly women, had been congregating since that morning. It was unusual to see such a crowd in public, especially since the Ascetics had taken the city, but such gatherings were not unheard of, even in these austere times. Traditional weddings in Bessa saw friends and relatives lining the street to the couple's new home and showering them with petals and comfits; many of the veiled women in the street carried covered baskets which could have been intended for just such a purpose. Hakkim Mehdad and his followers did not look kindly on such indecorous traditions, but the new sultan was too much occupied with other, more important matters to take the time to issue an outright ban on the practice. As Zeinab watched, one of the women readjusted the basket she carried, drawing the covering over whatever lay inside.

Masood gave a despairing sigh. He liked Zahir well enough most of the time: he was a good worker, quiet, and asked few questions. Today, though, he was being completely impossible. "Really," he said reproachfully, "you've never had trouble understanding your job before. I hope you're not being deliberately insolent." Still muttering, he turned back to his post.

Zeinab's cudgel hit him squarely in the back of the head. Glancing around to make sure that none of the guards on the other tower had seen, she knelt to tie his hands with a small sigh of relief. Knocking him out now had been a risk, one that could have endangered the success of everything they had worked for. But she had spent many months in Masood's company, and if he was obtuse and ineffectual, he was also polite and good-natured. When the storm hit, she wanted him out of harm's way.

Even had he been prone by nature to surprise, Captain Ashraf would not have been unduly alarmed by his urgent summons. Since its capture, Bessa's purification in the cleansing fires of the one Truth had been an ongoing process, unceasing by night as by day, and he had been called upon to perform his duties at far stranger times. He was with his men in their quarters, the former women's chambers, when the messenger reached him, so he arrived in the throne room minutes later. Hakkim began talking before the man had even straightened up from his low bow of obeisance. Ashraf's face darkened as he heard the report, but Hakkim had chosen his captain well, and he made no comments as he listened other than to inquire as to the Holy One's pleasure.

"How soon can your men be made ready?" Hakkim asked him.

"Immediately, Majesty. There are already archers patrolling the city walls, and I can have both infantry and cavalry regiments assemble on your order."

The sultan considered this for a few seconds before he gave his orders. The time which elapsed between Ashraf entering the throne room and Hakkim's commands passing his lips was not sufficient for a handshake, or the drawing of a sword from its scabbard. The entire force of the city of Bessa was nocked as to a bow, its trajectory decided in a bare moment. Armies fall and leaders are toppled from the honed edges of such moments. When he had assured the Holy One that his will would be executed, in this as in all things, Ashraf bowed again and departed.

In an alleyway beside the Eastern Gate, Rem's eyes widened. "I have to talk to Zuleika," she said abruptly, cutting through the whispered conversations of the women around her. Umayma glanced at her in puzzlement. "So? You don't have long to wait. She's due here for the second phase," she replied.

"No, you don't understand. We've made a mistake, she needs to know." Rem started to leave without waiting for a reply. Umayma dashed after her, grabbing her arm as she reached the mouth of the alley.

"Rem, you can't," she hissed. "The soldiers will be leaving any minute now. You're needed here. Whatever this is, it can wait."

Rem almost screamed with frustration. "No, it can't. I have to talk to her now, Umi!"

The urgency in her tone must have alarmed Umayma, for her grip slackened and she opened her mouth as if to enquire further. Rem immediately darted from her grasp and took off round the corner, calling back as she went, "I'll take a different route to the soldiers. They won't see me, I promise! I'll be back in plenty of time for the second phase!"

Umayma made as if to run after her, but stopped at the top of the street, torn between conflicting impulses. It would not be long now before the army marched out of the city. She could not abandon her post. Rem's footfalls died away as she hesitated, and she turned back to the other women, throwing up her hands in frustration.

"Do you think she saw something?" Bethi asked her as she returned to the bottom of the alley. "I mean—you know. *Saw* it?"

"She'd better have," Umayma growled. "For anything less, she's going to have a lot of explaining to do when she gets back."

Taliyah pounded up the street of Silversmiths, her breath sounding loud in her ears. She had been loitering outside the Northern Gate all morning, sweltering under her heavy robes as she watched for the little scrap of red cloth which was her signal.

When she saw it fall, she started off, along with the four other runners who had been assigned to carry the message to the other gatehouses. Nasreen was going to the Eastern Gate, Thana to the old Merchants' Gate and Reema to the Western Gate. Taliyah herself was bound for the water gate, the furthest away from their starting point, so she ran especially fast, fighting the urge to throw off her thick veil and feel the welcome coolness of a breeze on her face. Before the first of Hakkim's army had cleared the palace compound, she had reached the southern watchtowers, where Nafisah was waiting for her.

"The army has been sighted," Taliyah panted as she slowed.

Nafisah nodded, then motioned with her arm. From the alley to her right, a crowd of veiled women emerged. She turned to them. "We've had the signal," she announced. "We'll wait another few minutes, to give them time to clear the gates. Then we move."

Zeinab emerged from the door at the bottom of the guard tower and walked toward the nearest group of women. The tallest of them raised her head at her approach. "They're coming?" she asked softly.

"They're coming," Zeinab confirmed in the same undertone. "Heading towards us as we speak." Her words were taken up and repeated in whispers among the crowd.

"Then it's time," Zuleika replied. "Once they're outside the gate, they will stay close to the city walls and wait for the army's approach." Al-Bokhari had always done the same thing in his youth, whenever one of his quarrels brought an army to Bessa's walls.

"I've taken care of the other guard on my tower," Zeinab continued.

"You'll have to deal with the rest of them though." Zuleika acknowledged this with a curt nod. Not long after that, they heard the rhythmic tramp of boots on stone, and not long after that, the first row of soldiers appeared at the top of the wide street.

The soldiers marched by in grim silence. A long column of infantry marched behind a much shorter one of cavalry, who rode slowly so as to keep pace with the foot soldiers.

Captain Ashraf rode at their head, passing the veiled faces which lined the road without so much as a glance. If he thought of them at all, it was as citizens who had turned out onto the streets to see the soldiers march by. The crowd drew respectfully to the sides at the army's approach, as befitted those in the presence of the royal guard. Many of the men wore the blue garb and leather breastplates of city guard, but others were swathed in the black robes and headscarves of Hakkim's personal army. Regardless of their dress, all had their eyes fixed before them on the Northern Gate, which swept outward in the grandiose gesture of a ringmaster to the desert beyond.

If any of the soldiers had broken military protocol to glance to right or left, they might have noticed how the women surged in behind them as they passed, following them up the street. Even if they had, they would not have found anything disquieting in the sight. The guard were tasked with the defence of the city; most of them did not find it hard to believe that a crowd of grateful people might congregate to wish them well as they marched out to perform their duty. Perhaps the silence of the crowd was slightly unnerving, but then this was easily put down to fears for the safety of sons and brothers who marched in the force. The keenest mind in Ashraf's troop had all these assumptions ready to hand should he chance to look at the women in their inscrutable veils, and it so fell out that most did not look at them in any case.

Distances can be deceptive in the desert. From a couple of leagues away, a group of old women and children raking oversized combs through the sand can look a hell of a lot like an approaching army. The legions of Hakkim Mehdad marched out to face an enemy, strong in numbers, stout of heart, and armed to the teeth. They did not know that their foe was behind them, and as the last soldier passed out of Bessa, the first of the concubines were already breaking on the great wooden gates of that city like a tide.

The walls of Bessa were thick, so that each of the city's six gates was in reality twofold in nature, an inner and an outer gate separated by a barracks yard and flanked on either side by a tall watchtower like a sentry. First, the women pulled the outer gate closed, its great weight yielding easily to the force of many hands. While Zeinab and five other women hefted the great iron bar across it, the other members of the seraglio fell back to close the inner gate behind them. Those who carried baskets threw their coverings off as they went, producing daggers, cutlasses, bows and slingshots. Others shed voluminous shawls to reveal swords hanging at their waists, or sheaves of arrows on their backs.

The second bolt fell into place with a dull thud. The women were in the dim barracks yard, enclosed on all sides by the two sets of gates and the towering bulk of the watchtowers.

Their towers had been assigned to them before they arrived, so there was no confusion as the group split into two, Zuleika leading one half towards the door at the base of the right watchtower, while Zeinab took the rest towards the one on the left. The thin wooden doors gave easily, and the women poured inside. The ground floor was empty, the guards normally posted there having been drafted into the outgoing force. Followed by the rest of the women, Zuleika took the tightly spiralling staircase at a run, holding her sword before her. They met the first guard a few turns up. He was running too, so fast in fact that he had impaled himself on Zuleika's blade before he even registered the woman's presence. Najla gave an involuntary gasp of horror at the confusion and pain on the dying man's face, but Zuleika pushed him over the side of the staircase without breaking her stride.

It took only a few minutes to reach the top of the watchtower, and they met no one else. The remaining watchman on duty, who had been gazing vacantly at the departing troops, turned around when he heard the noise of feet on the stairway to see a crowd of women pouring into the guard post. He began to rise from his chair, reaching for his sword as he saw that they were armed. Then he realised several things at once.

Firstly, the scabbard at his belt was empty. Secondly, though he had intended to reach for the weapon that usually hung there, his arm had not in fact moved. His gaze flicked sideways. A woman, tall and terrifying, was standing over him, gripping his wrist with one of her hands. In her other hand she held a sword. He looked down, following the length of the blade. Its point had disappeared into his chest. He opened his mouth, raising the index finger of his free hand as if he desired to speak. Then he sank back into his seat with a broken sigh.

"You didn't have to do that," Jumanah whimpered to Zuleika, her eyes filling with tears. Zuleika only shrugged, and turned her attention to the walls beneath the tower. The rest of the concubines poured into the guard post and took up defensive positions around its sides.

Similar scenes were repeated at each of Bessa's watchtowers, though the details differed according to the temperaments of the fighters assigned to them.

On the left watchtower of the Eastern Gate, Umayma led the charge to the top with her hunting spear. She took out the two watchmen on duty there with a single throw, skewering both men through the chest. This feat both amazed and horrified the troops behind her. The right watchtower was laid to the charge of Bethi and Anwar Das, who achieved a more modest body count. The guards at the top of the tower were confronted not by a crowd of women and men with swords, but a single, ragged looking man. His eyes glinted with madness, and he held a young woman before him, a knife to her throat. "Don't move," he snarled, "or I'll bleed her out!" The watchmen hesitated a moment, hands wavering just above the hilt of their swords, but the woman wept so piteously, and her eyes were so wide with horror, that they could do nothing but submit to having their hands tied. They perhaps regretted this decision when her face brightened, all trace of fear vanishing, and she danced out of her captor's grip to retrieve the swords of both men from their scabbards.

As the other members of the seraglio spilled out into the guard post around them, Anwar Das complimented Bethi once again on her skills of deception. "That?" she said dismissively. "It would have been subtler if I'd just stabbed them." She turned, flashing him a broad grin. "I think we both know I've done better, Anwar, as have you."

On the plain below the city walls, Captain Ashraf surveyed his men with austere satisfaction. It never occurred to him to make them a rousing speech; they were a strong force, well arranged in columns straight as a ruled line, and thus ready for battle in all practical senses of the term. The concept of morale was an alien one to the Ascetics, who were doctrinally obliged to regard discontentment with material circumstances exactly as they regarded success, as one more illusion to withstand and ignore. Once satisfied, such worldly appetites only increased in their rapacity.

So Ashraf viewed any fear or apprehension in his men rather as he would the sulkiness of a small child, as emotions which would disperse naturally if their demands were ignored.

The shutting of the city gates had not startled him; far from it. It was natural that the sultan would give orders for the city to be made secure with a battle imminent.

Had Al-Bokhari still been sultan, he would have waited for the oncoming army to come to him, keeping his troops with the city to their backs, supported by archers from the walls. This was the traditional tactic employed by the desert cities when they came under attack, long held to for the simple reason that it generally worked, and there was no point in fixing a cart that still had four functioning wheels. From the outside, Bessa was almost impregnable, a vast fortress of stone and wood reinforced with steel. Thousands could throw themselves against its walls, and it would stand firm. The women had factored this into their strategy when they planned their attack on the city.

What they had never paused to consider was that the man at its head was the son of a shoemaker. Hakkim Mehdad had had no training in the old military traditions, and he had no especial sympathy for them. Indeed, in that knife's edge of time when he had paused to consider his course, the thought that he might order the troops to hug the city walls had occurred to him. But it was only one possibility in a sea of possibilities, unweighted by the old usage and familiarity that had always endeared it to the likes of Al-Bokhari, for whom the right decision had usually been whatever his father had decided before him. Hakkim, free from such legacies of military tradition, entertained the idea, and then dismissed it, choosing in the end a plan more suited to his general philosophy of nipping things in the bud.

Ashraf did not waste words as a rule. His army did not get a speech, but a word, barked out with terse precision. "Advance!"

Within minutes of the army passing out of the gates, the seraglio had taken the city walls. The watchtowers stood a full six feet above the battlements, so that the women had the advantage over the archers who patrolled below. They worked swiftly and methodically, one group sweeping the battlements, stripping the archers of their weapons and tying their hands, while another covered them from the nearest watchtower. Most of the guards were too intelligent to resist, making the process doubly quick. Zuleika was standing on the left guard post of the Northern Gate, covering the group of women currently securing the walls, when she felt a tug on her arm. It was Rem, panting and red faced.

"Rem? What are you doing here? You're supposed to—"

Rem cut her off. "They're marching away. Hakkim gave the order to advance on the enemy. I left as soon as it became clear to my sight, but it took so long to get to you!"

Zuleika's head whipped round to face the plains, properly examining the view for the first time. The army were already several hundred yards beyond the city walls, and travelling fast. She went still, her limbs and even her gaze freezing in place as if all the energy required to move them had been drained and channelled into her mind. Other women began to congregate at the edge of the guard post, alerted by Rem's presence to the fact that something was wrong. They stared at the departing troops in horror. Maysoon began to shake. She rounded on Zuleika.

"You said they'd stay here!" she yelled, "You said they'd stay by the walls. My little girl is out there, Zuleika!"

Zuleika did not appear to hear her. After what seemed an endless time, she turned and cast around the guard post until she saw the ivory bugle hanging from a hook by the stairway. She seized it, ran to the edge of the wall and blew, a flurry of harsh, urgent blasts. The riders at the head of the army slowed, halted, appeared to look back.

"It won't be enough," Rem said. "They're too far away to see that the walls have been taken. It will give them pause, but it won't stop them."

"What are we going to do?" Zeinab asked. In answer, Zuleika strung her bow and let fly an arrow towards the departing army. A figure in black crumpled to the ground. "Open fire," she commanded calmly. Zeinab was momentarily appalled. "But they have their backs to us!"

"Because they're heading towards your children. Open fire."

The women had been well trained, and dozens of men fell as the first wave of arrows rained down. Beneath them, the mass of soldiers writhed in sudden panic, casting around for an enemy they could not see. Every fallen man seemed to send a ripple through the troops nearest to him, distorting their strict formation and slowing the pace of the march. Some even began running back towards the city. But most of those hit were at the back of the column, and even as the soldiers nearest Bessa shouted out and turned, the front of the army pressed on, passing out of the range of the women's arrows without even knowing that they had come under attack.

The men who had turned back shifted their weapons from hand to hand, milling uncertainly before the city gates. Eventually, they would probably think to send a messenger to the vanguard to inform captain Ashraf of this development, but they were only foot soldiers, unused to taking control and faced with a situation that none of them had foreseen. Meanwhile the rest of the army marched on, already beginning to dwindle into the middle distance. Soon they would become a dust cloud on the horizon themselves, and soon after that, the two dust clouds would merge, and the plain would ring with distant screams.

Over one hundred women and children, and all of them had been in her care. For the first time in a long while, Zuleika felt something approaching panic.

"Open the gates," Maysoon said, fear draining her voice to a parched whisper. "Send someone to warn them."

"No," Zuleika replied, her eyes blazing. Opening the gates meant losing the city, and she would not do that, whatever the cost.

"Then they'll die!"

"No," Zuleika said again, more fiercely this time, as if willing it would make it so. Dropping her bow, she turned and ran down the steps from the guard tower to the main fortifications, crossing rapidly to where the women had left the prisoners, sitting against the side of the wall which faced the city. She seized one by the shoulders and dragged him to his feet, then forced him across the walkway to the outer battlements.

Confusion made the man sluggish, but he went docilely enough, reasoning that a ready submission to his captors' wills would go easier with him. As Zuleika bent and grasped his legs, the bewilderment on his face resolved into dread, and he began to shout and struggle. But his hands were bound, and however much he writhed, he could not free them to claw at the crenelated stone around him, or the garments of the woman who held him. Zuleika lifted him clear of the walls.

The scream of the man as he fell was enough to freeze Ashraf's remaining troops in their tracks. The cry, pregnant with the terror of death, carried far across the plain, arresting the motion of even the furthest riders. It was a long way from the battlements to the ground below. Most of the army missed the sight of the flailing figure as it plummeted from the city walls, but all had turned in time to see the next one.

By this point, the full import of what Zuleika had just done had sunk in to the other prisoners on the north wall, and the air began to fill with cries of hysterical entreaty. There was no need to do more; every man in the army was now running back towards Bessa. When she saw the cavalry reach the city gates, Zuleika stepped forward and brandished her sword in the air, her curved figure and long hair silhouetted in the fading light.

"You have been deceived," she shouted. "Here is the army you must face. There was never another!"

On the plain below, captain Ashraf's eyes narrowed. Clearly there was truth in what the woman had said. The situation was not as they had supposed, and it seemed more than likely that deception had played a part. Yet something in her words gnawed at him. In spite of being fairly new to the post of captain of the guard, Ashraf felt sure that he had been in this situation before.

It was a certain quality in the woman's voice, brazenness laced with something harder to define, that he recognized. He had been addressed in similar tones, though perhaps with more of desperation in them, when he purged the palace of the line of Al-Bokhari. Not everyone he killed had spoken to him thus. Some, like Oosa, had not had the chance to speak at all. But others, usually those who were with their sons or daughters when they were found, had attempted to reason or plead with him, offering bribes or making threats. When Ashraf came to the chambers of Al-Bokhari's third wife, he had found her son, though a grown man of twenty, hidden behind the rich drapery surrounding her bed. He recalled the mother's voice as she positioned herself between him and the entrance to her bedchamber, meeting his gaze as she assured him that this was not her son, but her lover, that there was no reason to end his life.

It was this lie that echoed in what he had just heard. If the woman on the battlements were telling the simple truth, then why go to such lengths to recall the army? No, the dust cloud contained no second force. What it very well might contain was a bargaining chip.

Ashraf called his lieutenant to him. "Take all the foot soldiers and half the cavalry, and try to retake the walls," he ordered the man. He nodded and rode forward, shouting orders. Ashraf gestured to a small group of riders to follow him. Then he wheeled round and began to gallop hard in the direction of the dust cloud.

Zuleika stared at the few horsemen as they galloped away, and then at the sea of men massing before the city gates. She had stopped all but a handful of them, and that was all that she would be able to do. Even if she had wanted to, she could not now open the gates to emit a messenger without endangering them all. It would be only moments, she knew, before the soldiers rallied and launched some form of counterattack.

She motioned to Zeinab. "Get the word out. Everyone is to come down off the walls and head for the palace."

Zeinab was rooted to the spot, her eyes glued to the two broken figures on the plain. "You threw them over," she murmured. "You threw them over the edge. Their hands were bound."

"Zeinab!" Zuleika shook her. "They will start to fire on the battlements. We do not want to be here when that happens."

Coming to herself, Zeinab ran back towards the guard tower, shouting as she went, "Fall back! To the palace!"

Zuleika took Rem's hand and pulled her toward the Eastern Gate. "I hope you're ready, because we just ran out of time. We need to start the second phase now."

Several leagues away, Warudu lowered her hand from her eyes, her face pale. "They're coming closer," she announced. Behind her, the group gave a collective moan of terror. They had put down the combs when Warudu noticed another cloud of dust, this one coming from the direction of the city. It had not taken long for them to guess what was happening. Hakkim's army was coming for them.

"Zuleika said the soldiers would wait outside the city walls." Efridah scowled at the plume of dust growing on the horizon. "And just think—this was supposed to be the safe job!"

"We all thought that," Farhat said grimly. She drew a group of children closer to her as she spoke, and they buried their faces in her arms. The younger ones had been excited when they began, helping each other to heft the unwieldy combs with shrieks of merriment. Now, although they did not yet understand what was going on, the fear in their aunties' voices frightened them. Many had begun to whimper softly.

"Perhaps they'll see we're just a bunch of old people and children, and leave us alone," Issi murmured.

"They'll start firing before they can even see us," Imtisar snapped back. "We're finished!" A chorus of angry voices shushed her as some of the youngest children began to wail, but she only became more strident in response. "What's the use in consoling them? An army is marching towards us, and when it arrives it will massacre us all!" she cried.

Prince Jamal, who alone out of the children of the seraglio had remained calm during all of these exchanges, raised his head at Imtisar's words, and gave the courtesan a thoughtful look.

"How do you know?" he asked.

"How do I know!?" she exploded. "What do you think they're going to do to us?"

"I mean, how do you know they're marching?"

"Marching, riding, flying. The manner of their approach matters little," Imtisar answered bitterly.

Jamal stared at the cloud of dust coming towards them. It was small, much smaller than their own had been. Then he looked at the pile of dust-raisers, left where they had been thrown in an untidy heap. He appeared to be working something out. When he turned back to the women, his eyes gleamed. "It does matter," he said, speaking loudly and to the whole group. For once, his arrogant tone and instant assumption of control were neither laughed at nor scolded. The women watched him and waited. "If they're infantry then there's nothing we can do," he continued, "but if they're cavalry, then we might have a chance."

The dust-raisers worked in tense silence, ears pricked for any sound of the approaching force. They had only minutes, but their task did not take long. Only the oldest of the women had been left with the fake army, but the ages of the children varied from toddlers of four summers to those on the cusp of manhood, such as Jamal. All joined in, and when they had finished, the adults and the older children drew their weapons and pushed the younger ones behind them, so that they would not see what was to come. Then they waited.

At the head of the group, Jamal stood, his teeth gritted and a dagger clutched in his trembling hands. The mounted men appeared as a dark smudge on the horizon, then a line of black specks. As the dull thud of hooves on sand, the slap and jingle of reins, began to drift towards the women on the evening breeze, many began to weep silent tears.

Eventually, they could see thirty or so distinct figures, growing steadily larger as they bore down upon the women with terrifying swiftness. Ashraf and his men rode quickly, fanning out in a semicircle as they neared the group of women. They were close enough now that they could clearly discern the huddled forms, in spite of the failing light.

Ashraf fixed his eyes on them, noting with quiet triumph how many of them seemed old or infirm. He thought he saw a small head peek from behind a woman's arm, and realised that there must be children in the party too. It was just as he had guessed. If they took even half of these wretches captive, it would be enough, he hoped, to buy the surrender of the women on the walls. Heartened by this prospect, he spurred on his horse, moving a little ahead of the rest of his men in his zeal to hasten the end of this attempted coup.

He was only ten feet away from the women when his horse broke its legs. The curved teeth of the dust-raisers, buried beneath the sand so that only their points broke the surface, tripped the beast as it ran, tangling its legs together into a twisted heap. It crashed heavily to its side, throwing Ashraf to the ground. He fell awkwardly, knocking his head on a stone, and lay still.

The man immediately behind him attempted to veer to avoid him, but his mount reared up in panic at the fallen beast in front of it, tipping its rider off backwards before it cantered away. Too fast to stop, and already too close to turn, the remainder of Ashraf's troop crashed into the tangled mesh of wooden teeth with sickening inevitability. Horses whinnied in pain, pinning their riders beneath them or throwing them off as they fell. The women charged.

There was nothing glorious about the battle, which was probably why they survived it. While dazed soldiers stumbled to their feet or vainly wrestled against the weight of crippled horses, the women of the seraglio ran at them with knives and rocks, terror giving them both strength and ruthlessness. When they had killed every man who could stand, those who were wounded or unable to move from beneath their steeds cast their weapons away and surrendered, though they had to scream until they were hoarse before the women seemed to hear them and ceased their attack. So driven were they by fear that it took many repetitions before the knowledge that they were safe could penetrate their minds.

As the women tied the hands of the surviving soldiers, Jamal noticed one of the fallen men begin to stir. It was the one who led the cavalry, the first to have been thrown from his horse. He had lain still till now, at a little distance from the main body of his troops, presumably knocked unconscious by his fall. As Jamal walked towards him, dagger at the ready, the man suddenly leapt to his feet. He stared about him with unfocused eyes. Jamal was standing closest to him, and it was Jamal that he fixed on. He charged unsteadily towards the boy, reaching for his sword as he went.

Jamal stood his ground until the man was a few feet away. Then, with a cry of mingled ferocity and terror, he launched himself forward and stabbed him in the chest. Captain Ashraf swayed for a moment, struggling to focus on the boy who stood shaking before him. He frowned, started to speak. Paused, tried again. "You're—" he slurred. Then he toppled forward, and Oosa's death was unwittingly avenged by her only son.

It was in this way that the army of Hakkim Mehdad, guardian of the one Truth, met its defeat at the hands of concubines, bandits and camel-drivers, and the city of Bessa was taken by a rabble of women. The sun which rose on the morning that Bessa fell had seen wonders enough, as all must agree. Yet its light still lingered in the sky when the army of women reached the sultan's palace, painting their faces with saffron and spilling golden pools onto the floors of empty rooms.

Though it had already witnessed sights both strange and terrible, they were far from the last that it would see that day.

The Cook's Story

1. Chicken with Millet

You will need between twelve and twenty chickens. If there are children eating, one chicken may suffice for eight people. When the girls have plucked and gutted the chickens, joint them carefully and lay on griddles over the fire pit to roast. Have some boys walk around the pit with long-handled ladles to catch the juices, which will be added to the sauce later.

Use a good handful of soaked millet for each person, and a few more for guests. Grind together pepper, cumin and cassia, also cardamom seeds if they can be spared. Chop up eight or ten onions, and five or six cloves of garlic. Fry these in oil for a few minutes, together with the millet, in as many pots as are needed. Then add enough water to each pot to cover the millet, and let them simmer until the millet is soft. While this is happening, prepare a sauce of dried limes, mint and fresh coriander with the juices from the chickens.

When the millet is almost cooked, stir in two or three handfuls of almonds and raisins to each pot. Serve the chicken on top of the millet, with bread enough for each person, and sauce at the side.

When the sultan entertained his guests, of course, they would eat the traditional feast of baby lambs stuffed with nuts, raisins and spices. But Rashad the cook prided himself on his ability to make a banquet just as fine out of cheaper ingredients. It was rare for the whole of the lower household to eat together, but on feast days, or for a special celebration as when Bokhari Al-Bokhari's eldest daughter was married, they would all crowd into the largest kitchen: the fire banked low, the giant pots and spits pushed to one side and every stool and bench in the palace assembled together, while the food was laid out on huge platters on the big chopping-table. The children were served first, and sent off to eat by the fire. Then each of the adults would fill his or her piece of bread, and they would eat at their leisure and praise the excellence of Rashad's art. The sultan never missed a little of his precious cardamom, or a few almonds; and a couple of Bessa's wine merchants would often attend as honoured guests, and never failed to bring a gift. Those were good days.

Sometimes the cook would make a smaller version of this feast with fish instead of chicken, at the urging of the Lady Gursoon, who said the flavours reminded her of her home. Rashad honoured all the ladies of the seraglio like his own sisters, since they had undertaken the care of his son. After his wife had died, Rashad had brought the boy into the heat and chaos of the kitchens every day, having no choice in the matter. But he was head cook—he could not neglect his duties to mind his son, still less to teach him. It was Gursoon who had discovered the child building a castle of cleavers on top of the whetstone, and had removed him to the relative safety of the women's quarters. And so whenever Gursoon took a fancy to taste the dried fish of her home village, Rashad would see to it that some was brought in from the market. Not too much: the sultan himself did not care for it. And to be honest, the feast tasted better with chicken.

2. Mahalabiyyah

Heat one small skin of new milk in a pot over the fire.

Pound four handfuls of rice in a mortar, and add a little less than a cup of water. When it is smooth, add this to the hot milk, taking care to stir it so that no lumps form. Add one handful of sugar, some drops of rose water and slivers of pistachio. When the pudding thickens, it is ready, but it should be cooled before serving. Decorate it well with nuts and rose petals: take care not to add the petals before the skin is quite cool.

This was the favourite pudding of sultan Bokhari Al-Bokhari. It became a tradition in the palace that whenever the sultan was annoyed or out of sorts, someone would send down to the kitchen for Mahalabiyyah. At first the order would always come from the seraglio, but in later days one of the queens themselves might request it, knowing the soothing effect of the dish.

In the last days of the sultan's reign the kitchen workers had many troubles. The followers of the Cult, with their strange and violent ways, had caused so much unrest in Bessa that the more reliable merchants stopped visiting the town altogether. Cucumbers and radishes were hard to get. There was no more rice, and the supply of saffron ceased altogether. Even fresh meat became uncertain in quality, and unreasonably expensive. All this, of course, made the sultan more bad-tempered than ever. The ladies of the seraglio worked valiantly to calm and reassure him, but there was more shouting, more stamping on the tiled floors and kicking of tables than the cook could ever remember.

His own little son, Dip, who had started to stay in the seraglio with his friends overnight, begged to sleep at home again—the master had been angry and scared them all, he said. He was a spindly, fragile child, with his mother's big eyes, and easily frightened. Rashad hated to see the boy unhappy, and tried to calm him with treats: cheese pastries or his favourite sesame sweets. But there was little time for making pastries. The sultan's guard now drilled constantly outside the palace, and had to be fed twice a day. The calls for Mahalabiyyah became ever more frequent.

Old Mahoor, who had been floor-sweeper since the days of the sultan's father, said that Al-Bokhari had shouted like this in the days of his youth, when he was at war with all his neighbours. Alas, the old man added darkly, he had lost the skills of war since then. All his soldiers would not be enough to protect the city now. And so it proved.

3. Lentil Porridge

Take a handful of split lentils for each person. Soak in water. When the water is absorbed add a little more, just enough to cover the lentils, and some salt. Put the pot on the fire and cook until the lentils are soft. Serve in bowls, with hard bread.

"And that's all?" Rashad had exclaimed, when the servants of Hakkim Mehdad came to him with orders for the new sultan's first meal in the palace. For a moment he could not disguise his shock. The second and third cooks stared in outrage.

It was not that any of them wished to celebrate. There had been flames and screaming for much of the night. Old Mahoor had picked up a cleaver and rushed out shouting, and had not returned. The two boys, full of idiot bravado, had tried to follow him, but Rashad had given them bread knives and told them to protect Adit and the kitchen girls, who had run to hide in the drying room. Then he had waited in the small kitchen with Karif and Suleiman, none of them speaking, staring at the walls as darkness fell. The screams outside became less frequent, and he tried to convince himself that none of them had been the voices of children, and that the invaders would not trouble to attack the seraglio.

When silence finally fell, and the light began to return, the three of them ventured out. The boys were sleeping by the drying room door, and there was no sound from within. They did not dare to go into the palace, from where most of the screams had come, so they looked out into the courtyard. It was as they had left it: the pots of herbs, the dew-catcher and the covered fire pit. They went behind the building, towards the smell of smoke, treading softly over the dark expanse of the exercise yard and through the arch to the prison and the guards' quarters.

Rashad stumbled upon the first body almost at once. He could not tell who it was; most of his face was gone. But the second was Faisal, one of the guards who sometimes loitered in the courtyard with his wine flask, and nearby was his friend, the fat one, whose name Rashad could never remember. The fourth dead man was Mahoor, lying face down with the cleaver still in his hand. All of them were cold. Rashad had worked with slaughtered animals all his life, but now he turned his eyes away from the wounds, like toothless mouths in their bare arms and throats. He had some idea of carrying the old man back to the kitchen, and gestured to Suleiman and Karif to help him, when they heard voices from the burned guard-house. They hid behind the arch and watched as armed men came out and took Mahoor and the others away.

Rashad could not think any more. His blood seemed to have set like jelly in his veins. As soon as the men had gone he followed his assistants back to the kitchen and waited there until morning. Then those same men had come in, black-clad and with their heads wrapped in scarves after the manner of the Cult, and told him that he was to prepare a meal for the new sultan.

But such a meal! Even through his numbness, he felt the inadequacy of it. A conqueror at the moment of his victory, with Mahoor's blood still on his hands: there should have been a herd slaughtered, a hundred barrels emptied, to match that enormity. But Hakkim Mehdad ate no meat, and drank only water. As the soldiers left, Rashad caught the look that passed between Suleiman and Karif behind their backs: what sort of master is this?

Rashad was staring down into the dull mass of soaking lentils while his assistants sulked in the corner, loudly wondering what was to become of them, when the Lady Zuleika crept into the kitchen to borrow knives. Everyone in the seraglio was safe, she told them. The children had been frightened in the night, but no one had been hurt and they were now sound asleep, Dip among them. The reassurance made a new man of the cook. For an hour the slaughter ceased to touch him—his son had been spared. He hastened to make up the porridge, though his professional pride led him to dress the lentils with butter and some spices before serving them. For this he was whipped later in the day, along with his assistants, to teach them the value of absolute obedience to their new master.

So it was that the last time Rashad saw his son, he was unavoidably short with him. It was not just the pain in his back, which burned like hot iron when he bent to embrace the boy. It was the shame of the punishment—to be whipped like an apprentice!—that made him gruff and somewhat distant. He felt that his son must see his humiliation in his face. If he had spoken any of his feelings, he might have wept. Instead he said, "Well, a man can live on dry bread too, eh?"—meaning it as a joke. Dip gazed at him with solemn, anxious eyes. The next day the seraglio, with their children, were sent away as a gift to the Caliph of Perdondaris. Dip went with them, and the cook watched him go with a desolate satisfaction: at least he would be safe. At least he would never see his father beaten.

4. Goat Stew

Skin and gut the goat. Keep the skin: there are many uses for it. The head and feet should be put aside for soup. Throw the rest of the meat into the great pot with some salt, cover with water and boil until soft. It is permitted to add vegetables or barley to the stew, but not spices.

Now there were no children in the kitchen, and no women either. Lame Adit, who scoured the pots, was sent away, and so were the three girls; from now on even the delicate work of plucking chickens would be in the rough hands of the boys. In the turmoil of those first few days Rashad did not realise the completeness of the new sultan's changes. There were hangings, and a mass burial—and then the remaining soldiers, who had been Bokhari Al-Bokhari's guard, were set to rebuild their old quarters, and became the guard of Hakkim Mehdad. But the black-robed men, Hakkim's special army, were quartered inside the palace, in what had been the ladies' house and the rooms of the women servants. From now on no woman was to enter the palace, Hakkim decreed; neither queen nor servant.

The kitchen became a place of silence. Rashad had often been irritated by the lame woman's gossip, and the girls' ceaseless chatter and giggling, but now he missed it all. The boys were sullen, and Karif and Suleiman blamed him for the beating of the first day. At the start all of them lived on a knife's edge while they tried to guess the mind of the new sultan, to discover which of their skills were still permissible and which would now be punished. There was no more roasting or basting with oil. Sweet stuff of all kinds, they learned, weakened the spirit, and spices were an invitation to the demons of artifice and falsehood. Alcohol was the worst of abominations: their second beating came when Karif was stopped with a skin of new wine, though it was meant only for a sauce. Eight soldiers carried out a search of the kitchens and cellar, and threw all of Bokhari Al-Bokhari's cherished wines into the fire pit. The jugs broke; the flasks were slashed with swords; and as the wine vapours filled the air, the soldiers threw in burning coals, which flared with a blue light and turned the sweet fumes to bitterness.

That night, Rashad painfully lifted down all the great jars of pepper, cardamom, cumin and cassia, wrapped them in oiled cloth and buried them deep in the ground behind the fire pit, which would not be used again.

Their work, at least, was undemanding. Lentils and dry bread made up most of the new sultan's diet and that of his trusted ministers. The soldiers, who needed to keep up their strength, were allowed meat three times a week, but this was to be goat, which was cheap and did not require haggling with the merchants for the best cuts. There was no good cut on a goat, Rashad considered. Three times a week he made huge pots of stew, and the rest of the time bread and pottage.

For a while he carried out small rebellions. He would find quails or pistachios or new carrots still on sale in the market and smuggle the precious ingredients back to make the old meals just for the five of them, cooking over the fire in the small kitchen so that the scents would not spread. He kept in his heart the hope that his son was safe and happy with the ladies, and that he might see them again one day. But no word ever came from Perdondaris, and rumours began to spread that the seraglio had not been sent to him after all, that they had all been abandoned in the desert, or killed there. As his hope faded, the small mouthfuls of freedom began to lose their taste for him. Soon, he feared, they would all be living on dry bread.

5. Baked Fish with Sauce

Take one fish for each man. If they are dried fish, soak them a little in water first, and do not use salt. Bake the fish in a pan, covering it so that the steam does not escape.

Make a thin paste of sesame seeds and oil. If there is yoghurt, this can be added. Garlic and lemon juice would also be good. When the fish are almost cooked, pour the sauce over them, then bake for a little longer, until browned at the edges. Serve with fried onions.

It had been a long time since fish of any kind had been seen in the market. As the rule of Hakkim Mehdad continued, more and more things disappeared: some outlawed, some whose sellers no longer came. There seemed to be fewer visitors to the city all the time; by the third year of Mehdad's reign, only traders—and precious few of those. And if trade had fallen off, so too had demand. The old fast and feast times were no longer observed—unless, as Suleiman sourly joked, they were now meant to take every day as a fast.

There would be no more quinces or medlars to make jam for the new-year cakes; no more sweets to throw to the dancers at midsummer. No more dancing or singing, come to that: either could get you whipped. It seemed there was a new prohibition every week, and the townspeople had started to throw angry looks at the palace, in which even the servants were included. Nothing could be said aloud, of course. But when the two boys came back from the market with mud on the flour-bags and Walid's eye blackening, Rashad decided that he would do the shopping from now on. He still had friends in the town, his wife's family and some of the grown-up children of the old sultan's ladies.

The marketplace was nearly deserted. Only the flour-seller and the blacksmith kept their old booths nearest the palace: most of the other merchants who had once fought for spots there had left, gone to other towns or different occupations. Those who remained preferred to lay out their oilcloths and blankets around the square, away from the shade of the awnings, but away too from the enclosed spaces where people could stand unseen. There were too many black-robed and scarfed men about, listening and watching for any sign of evil-doing—and others, without scarves and less visible, who listened just as hard.

Rashad bought cheese, milk and a sack of the hated lentils. Then he turned away from the palace, and walked down several side-streets, checking now and then to see that no one followed him. The house he made for had a prosperous look still; its owner had been a merchant. He had married the daughter of Lady Gursoon, and that alone would have made the cook think of him as a friend. But he had also been a wine-seller, one of Al-Bokhari's most valued suppliers, and a guest of the kitchen in the time when they had invited guests. Now he roamed the country, selling animal skins and embroidered blankets, and whatever else he could. And whenever he came home for a time, Rashad would visit him and hear his news of the world beyond Bessa.

The merchant's wife came to the door with her two young sons clinging to her legs. She greeted Rashad with a cry of pleasure, and unveiled once they were safely inside—they had known each other since her childhood. She had grown to be a striking woman, as tall as he was himself. Her husband looked tired, and older than Rashad remembered, but he jumped up instantly to embrace his friend.

They sat together and drank mint tea while the woman played with her twins in the other room. The sound of their shrill voices filled Rashad with sadness; they reminded him powerfully of Dip, the last time he had seen him. He would be twice their age now, if he still lived. But there had never been any news of the seraglio, and Rashad put the thought away from him. His friend had been to the north, he said, among the hill tribes, who fought constantly among themselves but were glad to buy his skins whenever they stopped. He thanked Rashad for the goat skins he had bought last time, which had fetched a good price. He offered him half of it, which Rashad refused, and the two men bickered amiably for a while. Both of them knew that a man with two secure meals a day does not take money from a man without, particularly a father of young children—but there were courtesies to be observed, which were more important than ever at a time like this, Rashad thought.

As they talked, it seemed to Rashad that the merchant was oddly constrained in his manner, even nervous, as if something were weighing on his mind which he did not like to mention. It was all too common a happening these days, but the cook was sorry to see his old friend so afflicted. Questioning delicately, he assured himself that the family were all in good health, and that the trip to the north had brought nothing more than a good profit. That meant that whatever troubled his friend had arisen in Bessa, and he would not speak of it to a man who lived in the palace. Rashad sighed, but he understood too well. He finished his tea, pressed the merchant's hand and took his leave.

The merchant's wife met him at the door, holding a package. Rashad could see at once that she was as tense as her husband had been; he said something meaningless and prepared to leave her, but she grasped his arm to prevent him. This was unheard of. If they were outside, the contact could have them both arrested. Rashad started and tried to pull away, but she held him fast, smiling into his face. And for a moment it seemed to him that she was a child again: little Mayisah with the green eyes, who had teased him and wheedled from him when he was a kitchen boy.

"This is for you," she said. "A present—to remember my mother."

Then she released his arm and he was outside in the street.

He did not dare look at what she had given him till he was safely back in the kitchen. It was one of the cloths she embroidered for her husband to sell: a small one, but intricately worked. And folded in it, a smaller package of oilcloth, with a familiar, pungent smell. He unwrapped it with shaking hands.

Dried fish from the river villages; five of them. He had not tasted one for years.

6. Bread and Onions

Slice the onions and fry them in a little fat. Serve with hard bread.

If there is no fat, or if a fire cannot be made, slice the onions very fine. Soak them in a little water to take away the worst of the sting, then add salt.

It was not that Gursoon's daughter had said anything to give him hope. She had told him only to remember her mother, which he did anyway, in friendship and sorrow. It was her smile, that look from their childhood. From that day, hope woke again in the cook, more painful than loss.

When he went out for supplies the streets seemed quieter each day, the market stalls less frequented as the patrolling men in black scarves became more arrogant in their power. Even women could be punished: one was beaten in the street for calling out to a young man; another for showing her hair. Blind Hama the beggar was hanged for using threatening words about the sultan, though everyone knew the old man was mad and would not kill a flea. And every now and then a man failed to turn up at his workshop or stall in the morning, and was not seen again. There were dark rumours of hidden prison cells, or worse—though perhaps, Rashad told himself, such men had simply left the city in search of a pleasanter life elsewhere. It was certain that Hakkim Mehdad was concerned about the traffic in and out of Bessa; some said that he feared attack from an outside enemy, though no one could say who it was. There were guards at the city gates, taking note of all who passed, peering into carts, and forbidding some to enter and others to leave.

For all that, there were still comings and goings. A few weeks after his visit to the merchant, Rashad went to the market and found the old flour-seller gone. His place was taken by a beardless boy who said he was old Abdullah's wife's sister's son, taking care of the stall while his aunt and uncle visited their family in another town. Rashad had known the old man for years and had never heard of a nephew, only a niece who had been one of the old sultan's ladies. But the boy was polite, and besides, had a familiar look to him. Rashad bought his flour and did not complain at the high price—he saw that there was less for sale than there had been even a week ago. Perhaps it was as well that people were managing to leave. Hakkim Mehdad's men somehow saw to it that grain and flour still arrived, and there were the goats: a herd of them had reduced the plain beyond the western gate to stubble. But there was little else, and many in the city were hungry. In the kitchen, the shelves were empty most of the time, and Rashad and the others lived on lentils like their master, or on bread and onions. Karif and Suleiman and he had become comrades-in-arms of a sort, trusting only each other and working by unspoken agreement to protect the two boys, who had grown into great gangly young men, not lazy, but headstrong and loud-mouthed. They were always incurring punishment of one sort or another, and seemed proud of the marks of their beatings. Rashad feared for them, but it seemed they could not be taught caution.

He bore it all in silence, hope and fear alike. But outside, in the streets or the marketplace, he felt that something was changing. There were still few people about; at least, few that he recognized. Perhaps there were more women, heavily veiled and averting their faces from all passers-by, not just the men in black scarves. He saw a few boys, none known to him, walking fast from one house to another. No one loitered on the streets; there was no stopping for greeting or conversation. Of course, people were cautious, and rightly so. But Rashad could feel something more, a sense of . . . purpose?

One day, as the year turned towards summer, he paid another visit to the house of his friend the wine merchant, and found it empty. He was about to leave when two women came down the street towards him, and one of them spoke to him as they passed. He recognized Mayisah's voice.

"My husband is away this week," she said, soft and rapid. "A business opportunity, he will be sorry to have missed you. My sons have gone with him."

She walked past the house as if it were not hers, and did not turn her head to say goodbye. But softly as she spoke, he heard three more words.

"Be careful, Rashad."

Back in the kitchen, Rashad gave the two boys ten dirham apiece and told them they were no longer needed. "Not for a week or two, at least," he said. "Go back to your parents and stay with them. I'll call for you if things change."

The boys were indignant, but it was little more than the truth; he himself ran most of their errands now, and no one would notice if the floors were swept less often. The money would feed their families for a few weeks. Suleiman and Karif looked on unhappily as the boys left, but neither spoke.

The attack came two days later. A column of dust appeared down the road leading to the main gate. Rumour said it was an army, perhaps from the hill-tribes, or some far-off enemy of Hakkim who had been biding his time till now. The soldiers were made ready with astonishing speed—before sunset a seemingly endless column of men in black scarves had assembled and marched out of the Northern Gate. A wave of townspeople ran to the walls to see them leave, and Rashad ran with them despite Mayisah's warning. Women crammed the gateway, many with their baskets from the market still on their arms. Then, as the last of the long column of men headed over the rise of ground and out of view, the women moved after them as one mass, into the gateway. Two of them pulled the gates shut and hoisted the heavy wooden bar across to seal them. More of the women followed, and some of them had pulled off their veils. They reached beneath their robes and into baskets, and the red sun flashed off metal. Rashad saw them splitting into two groups, pulling at the doors of the guard towers, before the inner gates clanged shut. From one of the towers there was a hoarse scream. From the other, only silence, then a dull thudding as of a body falling down stone stairs.

Rashad would have fled then, but his feet seemed unable to move. The crowds had melted away, but he scarcely noticed the emptiness around him, the sudden quiet. His whole mind was fixed on the towers, with their blind windows. And then there was shouting from the wall to the left, and two black-scarfed archers came running towards the towers—and dropped, both of them, without a sound, before either had loosed an arrow. One sprawled on the stones where he had fallen, a leg dangling high above Rashad's head. The other staggered, and plunged to the ground a few feet away. And a woman emerged from the tower with a sword to look down at them.

Rashad found himself running, his blood sounding in his ears like boiling water. It seemed to him he would never reach the palace walls, but he was there and through the wicket-gate which led to the kitchen. They had uncovered themselves, and killed Hakkim's men. They had had knives, swords. His head whirled so that he had to sit down on the stone floor. The tall woman who had appeared at the top of the tower . . . had that really been Lady Zuleika?

Once again, he sat with Karif and Suleiman as night fell, staring at the walls and wondering. But this time there were no flames, and they heard no screams. Just scuffling, running to and fro, and as the moon rose, a great yelling of women's voices.

7. Sesame Sweets

Heat two cups of white sugar with a cup of water until melted.

When the sweet smell begins to rise, take two good handfuls of sesame seeds and sprinkle them in, stirring until they are smoothly mixed. Add some pistachios and walnuts, if available.

Brush the sides of a broad, shallow bowl with nut oil and pour the mixture in till it covers the bottom. Leave to set. When it is cool, you can use a sharp knife to divide the mixture into squares or other shapes: when hard, it will break into sweets along the lines you have drawn.

Just before the sweets harden, decorate them with more nuts, or with sugar.

There was nothing to make a celebration, but Rashad felt that some gesture, at least, was essential. As soon as he knew it was safe to go outside, he walked to the homes of each of the kitchen boys and told them they had their jobs back. Then he sent them out—there would be no one yet in the market, but he knew people—to buy nuts and sesame and raisins. The big jar of sugar was still where it had been for the past four years, standing in its dark corner. He had told the soldiers it was a preservative.

Suleiman and Karif went out in the streets to join the festivities, but Rashad stayed in the kitchen. He would not admit even to himself that he was waiting, not until Lady Gursoon came in. She was shorter than he remembered, and her hair was entirely grey. Forgetting all propriety, he ran to embrace her.

"But see who I've brought, Rashad!" she said, and only then did he look behind her.

The boy was standing in the shadows, shy, taller than Rashad could have imagined. When they saw each other, his face lit with an uncertain smile. He still had his mother's eyes.

THE TAKING OF BESSA,
PART THE SECOND

Soraya, Zufir, Fernoush, Nasreen and Huma sat in tense silence at the bottom of the right-hand tower of the Eastern Gate, and listened to the sounds of the conflict above them. They had heard the long, terrible screams from the north watchtowers a few moments ago, and even though the voices of the dying had clearly been male, the knowledge had done little to reassure them. Zufir was rigid and trembling, and Soraya and Huma clutched each other in voiceless terror, flinching at each fresh shout. Nasreen and Fernoush sat in front of the younger girls and the boy, reviewing with them the details of the plan.

"Show me your keys," Nasreen instructed the group. Three trembling hands produced three keys from around necks and looped through belt strings.

"Good," Fernoush said, "very good." She caught sight of the fear on Zufir's face, and leant down to take his hand. "Don't worry," she told him softly, "Zuleika and Umi are going to cover us all the way. No one's going to get a shot at us while they're watching our backs."

"Yes," Nasreen chimed in with forced cheerfulness, "It's Hakkim's guards who should be worrying, not us!"

As the oldest of the volunteers, they were doing their best to reassure the others. But Nasreen and Fernoush were two of the youngest aunties, and the children had always looked on them more as older sisters than authority figures. Back in the seraglio they had been popular with the sons and daughters of the other concubines because of their willingness to join in with the younger ones' games, or take their part when an older auntie scolded them. Zufir had always revered Nasreen, with her shining waterfall of hair, and Fernoush's beautiful voice, far more than all the wisdom of stern old Gursoon. Here, however, both women seemed suddenly younger and less dependable, their smiles of comfort shaky and their embraces brittle with tension.

Umayma clattered down the stairs. "We've taken the walls," she announced, before she had even made it into the room. "Layla has an arrow in her leg, but no one's dead except the guards." At the sight of his mother, Zufir sagged to his knees, as if all that had been holding him upright was a string which her arrival had severed. His nervous tension flooded out in a sob of relief.

"Zeinab's fine," Umayma reassured Soraya as the girl stepped forward, her face taught with worry. "She came over from the Northern Gate just a moment ago, told us the order's going out to fall back."

Soraya's expression relaxed, though beside her Huma still fretted. Her mother was stationed on the water gate, and she would not hear news of her until the women had taken the palace.

"Everyone's pulling back to the palace now," Umayma continued, her arms wrapped around her son in an uncharacteristically fierce embrace, "so Zuleika should be here any minute."

"Have you seen Rem?" Fernoush asked her.

Umayma shook her head. "We're going to have to do this one runner short, I'm afraid."

Zuleika and Rem ran along the battlements, crouching low to avoid the arrows which occasionally made it over the high ramparts and onto the walkway at the top.

"Got your key?" Zuleika asked.

"What?" For a moment, Rem looked blank. Then her expression cleared. "Oh. Yes. It's here." She twitched her robe aside to reveal the key hanging from her belt. It was dwarfed by a sheathed sword, and partially eclipsed by three curved daggers. Zuleika looked at her curiously.

"Those weapons will throw you off balance," she cautioned. "And they're not necessary—I'm providing covering fire."

"I'll need something to protect myself with once I'm inside."

"True enough, but not all those. So many will slow you down."

"I'm just coming prepared."

"You have too many weapons," Zuleika repeated with emphasis.

"I know what I'm doing," Rem snapped back. Zuleika shot her a harassed look, but made no further comment. The wall curved round towards the Eastern Gate, and soon they had reached the watchtower where Umayma waited with Yusuf Razim to begin the second phase. She raised her eyebrows when she saw Rem.

"I'd started to think you weren't coming," she said. "What kept you?"

"Complications," Rem replied.

While Umayma ran back down the stairs to fetch the rest of the volunteers, Yusuf Razim got into position, kneeling at the side of the watchtower which bordered the wall to the palace. Zuleika touched Rem's arm, gently pulling her down into a crouch.

"We should stay low," she said softly, "in case the guards spot us."

Rem nodded, her face blank.

Zuleika looked at her, caressing Rem's right forearm where, underneath the dark cloth of her robe, she knew her name was written in shaky letters.

"In and out, remember," she said. "You go straight to the stable yard and open the gates. Don't try to fight."

"Don't worry," Rem replied, offhand, "I know the plan."

"Rem?" Zuleika pulled her closer, her brow creasing in concern. "Stick to what we agreed."

Rem saw the anxiety in Zuleika's eyes. Her own expression softened in response, and she leant in, taking Zuleika's free hand in hers and stroking it gently. Still, when she spoke, it was only to repeat what she had said before.

"I know the plan. Don't worry about me, Zuleika."

At this point, Umayma and the volunteers arrived at the top of the stairs, and the watchtower became a whirl of frenzied activity. Rem and Zuleika broke apart as the group raced to their stations, Rem and the other wall runners forming a line in front of Yusuf Razim while Zuleika and Umayma fitted arrows to their bows, training them on the single palace window which faced in their direction. It was from this window that the volunteers would come under heaviest attack from the palace guards within. It was also the one through which they would attempt to gain ingress. There was a breathless pause. Umayma gave Zufir an encouraging smile. Huma and Soraya glanced at one another. Rem, at the front of the line, readied herself to spring.

Then Zuleika spoke. "Go."

There were no steps connecting the right eastern watchtower to the battlements beneath it, so when Zuleika gave the signal to start, Yusuf Razim had to boost each of the volunteers over the parapet and onto the wall below. The first to go was Rem. She stumbled a little as she hit the ramparts and shot out her arms to steady herself, leaping from ridge to ridge on the crenelated wall as she had practised. When she had put five paces between herself and the watchtower, Nasreen followed. She swayed wildly from side to side for the first few steps, and it seemed that she would fall. After she jumped the first crenel, however, she regained her balance, straightening up just as an arrow flew past the spot where her head had been a moment before. The next arrow came so close to Rem that she felt the breeze as it whistled past her ear. Something warm trickled down the side of her face, and she knew that it had drawn blood. Zuleika was swift in her response, shooting the archer between the eyes before he had time to fire a third time. As she pulled another arrow from her quiver, the next guard stepped up to the window. Umayma hit him squarely in the chest, and he staggered backwards. Zuleika killed his replacement where he stood in the shadows of the room beyond, before he had even assumed his post.

This part of the seraglio's plan depended on Umayma and Zuleika killing as many of the palace archers as possible before the first of the volunteers reached the end of the wall. While one fired, the other readied her bow, dispatching the guards so quickly that few of them lived long enough to spot the two women firing on them from above. The runners kept going, only lowering their heads as the arrows whizzed past them, and Yusuf Razim continued boosting people over the side of the watchtower. After Nasreen came Soraya, who bounded along the wall with the agility of a young ibex. Next was Huma, less graceful but equally surefooted. The women ran carefully, never slowing enough to lose their footing, never going so fast as to catch each other up. The arrows from the palace were coming less frequently as Umayma and Zuleika got fairly into their stride. Zufir landed on the wall with a high-pitched squeak of terror. For the rest of the run, he was too full of gratitude that Jamal had not been around to hear him even to think about the archers and the sheer drop.

By the time Fernoush, the last of the runners, had cleared the parapet,

Rem had reached the palace window. She flung one leg over the sill and ducked inside, staring blindly into the room as her eyes adjusted to the dark interior. It was empty, except for the dead guards lying in a heap at her feet, but even as Rem set down her foot another man ran into the room from the stairs at the far end. He caught sight of her and raised his bow, and Rem threw herself to the ground. The arrow missed its mark, sailing through the window and along the wall. It took Nasreen through the throat. The girl's eyes widened in shock, and she gave a choked gasp. Slowly, her legs buckled beneath her. As she toppled sideways Soraya screamed, but Nasreen was already unconscious, and fell from the wall as into a swoon. She was there, her body flung out from the battlements at an impossible angle, and then she was gone. Umayma's next arrow hit the guard who had killed her in the eye. He staggered back, fell and lay still; no other men remained to pull his corpse away. Soraya witnessed all of this and kept running, too stunned to cry.

Rem, too, lay for a moment deprived of speech. As with all events in which she was a factor, her inward vision had been clouded and unclear. She had not seen this coming. Nasreen's body as it fell, twisted and transfixed by the arrow, was a vision she seemed unable to shake. It lingered before her eyes, an after-image of remembered horror, and wherever she turned it was before her.

Recovering herself slightly, she scrambled to her feet and glanced around her, checking the fallen guards for any signs of movement. She saw none, and scanned the room again, this time looking for the door. She found it at the far end of the narrow chamber, and darted towards it. Soraya was just reaching the window as Rem pulled the door closed behind her and raced down the stairs. She found herself in a corridor lined with doorways. From here Bethi, with her intricate knowledge of the palace, had plotted the volunteers a route through the servants' passages, narrow corridors which threaded the larger spaces reserved for the palace's richer inhabitants. They were ancient, and frequented only by servants, so Bethi reasoned that they were their best chance of getting through the palace unseen.

According to the map that Bethi had drawn on the inside of Rem's palm, the quickest way to reach the stable yard was to follow the corridor to its end, and take the winding stairs she found there. From there, a door on the right would lead to a further staircase, down to the level of the palace's immense dining hall. Thence, through a curtain on the left, to a final flight of stairs, this ending in a squat archway. Beyond this archway lay the kitchen gardens and the stable yard. The instructions Rem had been given were meticulous, and both she and the other volunteers had been drilled in them many times. So it was with deliberate care, rather than any confusion or uncertainty, that she turned from the path she had been shown and pushed open a large wooden door that lay directly to her left.

The day that Rem volunteered to join the runners, a thought she had long carried in her mind hardened into an intention. It was this intention, and not the purpose shared by the other volunteers, that she held before her as she trained to run the wall. She listened with patient attention to the plan she was to follow, but her mind was elsewhere, threading a different set of corridors to a different destination. When Soraya reached the bottom of the stairs to find the passage in front of her empty, she assumed that Rem had run on ahead of her. But Rem was long gone.

Hakkim Mehdad sat alone in the throne room. A little after he received word that Captain Ashraf's soldiers had departed for the Northern Gate, reports had started coming in about disturbances on the watchtowers. He dispatched a man to each of them, to identify the source of the unrest. When he heard the bugle blasts and then the screams from the Northern Gate, he dispatched another. A few moments later, the guard stationed at the top of the palace ran in to tell him that the walls had been breached. Hostile forces, he said, were attempting to enter the palace through the upper windows. Hakkim sent the remainder of his personal guard to deal with the aggressors. Neither his scouts nor his soldiers had returned. Clearly, the situation was degenerating, but Hakkim did not panic. He sat entirely still, and contemplated his position. There was a part of him that wanted to run outside and join the battle, to defend his rule with his own hands. He loathed this passive waiting for an outcome outside the sphere of his control. Yet he hesitated to leave the palace, not because he was afraid of death, but because he still had a mission to fulfil. It was imperative that he live to reveal the truth within him to the world.

As he sat thus in inner debate, a slight figure slipped through the curtain at the far end of the room. It was a woman, he saw and, aberrant as the sight was, she carried a sword. Hakkim was unarmed, but this did not worry him unduly. His training was such that he could kill just as readily with empty hands. He could turn the woman's blade upon herself or, if the mood took him, snap her neck or strangle her.

As she drew closer to him, something in her height and bearing made him think that he had seen her before. He studied her face. Four years had elapsed since he had last seen her, and he had passed sentence on many during that time, but still Hakkim recognized her as the heretic librarian, whom he had condemned to death when he seized control of the city. He checked his impulse of surprise, keeping his face expressionless as he regarded her.

"The concubines saved me," Rem said, answering Hakkim's question before he voiced it. "One of them was known to you already, as the cousin of Imad-Basur. She slit your guards' throats, and now I am come to slit yours. The desert is not so wide as you think."

She eyed him warily, gauging his reaction.

Hakkim rose to his feet. "If one of your number is trained in the assassin's art," he replied, never taking his eyes from her, "then why are you here, and not her?"

Rem walked slowly towards him.

"Because her grievance against you has been satisfied. You tried to kill her people and you drove her from her city. Well, now she has killed your people, and taken the city back. But what you took from me, I cannot retrieve. Your death will not make up for the loss of one thousandth of it."

She had drawn very close to him now, though not quite within easy striking distance. Hakkim scanned her form, noticing the awkward folds of her robe at the waist, which told his practised eye the location and number of the concealed weapons she carried.

"What did I take from you? You retained your life, did you not?"

"My scrolls. You burned them."

"They were lies, abominations. Things you should have been ashamed to live by." Hakkim gave a contemptuous snort. Rem's eyes flashed.

"And what do you live by, Hakkim?" she retorted. "Your rock is covered in moss on its underside. When it sat in your first master's garden, it was the home of ants and centipedes. You venerate it above the world, yet it is of the world, as much a part of the *qu'aha sul jidani* as you or I."

In spite of himself, Hakkim drew breath sharply. He had never told anyone about the boulder of negative thought, which he still kept behind a curtain in his bedchamber. It was a thing too precious, too personal, to be preached on; the lone, squat pillar upon which his faith rested. Rem saw with her inward sight the jolt of shock run through his mind, and lunged at him, drawing her sword to strike. Her attack was clumsy and slow; Hakkim evaded it with casual ease. Sidestepping the thrust, he stepped in towards Rem and jerked his arm up in a powerful blow to her left forearm which sent the blade flying from her hand. Rem jumped backwards, reaching for the smallest of the three daggers at her belt. She hurled it at Hakkim as if it were a throwing knife, but it went wide of its mark, clattering to the floor some feet away.

Hakkim did not bother to pick up these fallen weapons. Both were outside of easy reach, and it was clear enough that this woman posed no threat to him. He would wait until she disarmed herself through her own stupidity, and then he would finish her. He moved nearer to her, waiting patiently for her to attack a third time, and so expose herself.

Rem drew another dagger and swept out with it in a low, wide arc. It was an amateurish move, even easier to avoid than the first. Hakkim leant away from the blade, turned to the side, and drew back his leg. As Rem turned to slash at him a second time, he pivoted and kicked her, his foot connecting with her hand so that it snapped at the wrist. For a moment, her right hand bent backwards until it was parallel with her forearm.

Rem cried out, dropping the dagger as she had the sword. Gritting her teeth against the pain, she braced her broken wrist with her other hand, and reached down to her belt, trying to grasp the final weapon which hung there. But though she could, with difficulty, move her fingers, she could not make her hand into a fist with which to grip it, and it slipped from her grasp. She kicked the fallen weapon across the room. Hakkim considered snapping her neck where she stood, but Rem was unarmed now, and his was the overwhelming advantage. By rights she should have died years ago, and in a much slower and more painful manner than he had time to recreate in the present circumstances. Her crimes had been heinous at the time of her sentencing, and he had no doubt that she had only compounded them since. In recognition of her great evil, and the punishment that she had so undeservingly escaped, he felt that her death should be as protracted as he could make it.

He circled towards Rem again, making as if to strike. As she held up her hands to ward him off, he stepped in and seized her injured wrist.

Squeezing it until she screamed with the pain, he forced her to her knees, then kicked her so that she sprawled on her back.

He knelt on the woman's chest and put his hands to her throat. Rem struggled as his hands tightened around her neck, the wild hunger for air making her kick and flail. Hakkim pressed harder, feeling the ridged bones of the woman's throat beneath his thumbs. He gazed down on her slowly reddening face, varying the pressure of his hands in order to draw out the ordeal for as long as possible before she lost consciousness.

Abruptly, Rem began to cry. Black tears gathered in her eyes and spilled down her face in rivers of black. Her eyes themselves became wellsprings of darkness, their whites eclipsed by the sudden inky flow. Hakkim stared down at her, his eyes widening with the horror of recognition as he saw the black tide of his nightmares rising from her eyes. His grip became nerveless and slack.

"You misjudged your enemy, Hakkim," Rem rasped, "It is not the world. It's me." Though the Ascetic leader knelt on her chest, her arms were still free. Now, as he stared transfixed into her eyes, she raised her left hand, drawing back her fingers like claws. Each was tipped by a long nail, tapering at the end to a sharp point. White zirconia. Virtually unnoticeable in a poor light, Zuleika had said. She had been right. Rem drove her hand into Hakkim's neck.

Hakkim registered the pain, but at first he was so terrified by Rem's ghastly tears that he did not notice the other, more viscous liquid that had begun to mingle with them. It was not until he glanced down at his hands, intending to resume throttling his enemy, that he saw that they were drenched in blood. It flowed down his arms and pooled on the floor. He raised a hand to his throat, and tried with a convulsive movement to stem the blood which gushed there. It spurted between his fingers.

As his strength failed him, Rem managed to roll over so that she was on top of him. The tears still fell from her eyes into his, so that it seemed to Hakkim that his dream was coming to pass, the black flood embracing and whelming him. In his nightmare, he always woke at the last moment before he was consumed. This time, there was no redemption from the dark. Rem's tears occluded his sight as he died, and the blackness swallowed him whole.

Soraya careered down the final flight of stairs, the others on her heels. Through the archway she could see guards patrolling the gardens, but as Zuleika had predicted there did not seem to be very many of them, and in the flat, open spaces of the palace grounds no archers had been stationed. Fighting her instincts, she dashed through the archway and into full view of the armed men beyond. The guards looked at the group in surprise as they ran past, but made no movement to stop them. There was nothing inherently threatening in the sight of the four running figures, though the three girls were a mystery, since the sultan had dismissed all his female servants long ago. One hailed them, stepping towards them to ask their business. They ignored him, and he shouted again, a note of warning entering his voice. Fernoush, running behind the others, stumbled slightly. Her robe slipped sideways, and she pulled it back into place, but the watching guard had already seen the flash of steel at her belt. He called out once more, an order this time. Around him, the other soldiers drew their swords.

Soraya heard the shouts at her back, and knew they were pursued. She increased her pace, shooting past the kitchen gardens, the shady arbour, the paradise of a thousand scents, and registering each only as an indication of how close she drew to her goal.

When she finally turned onto the long pathway which led to the stables, she reached into her robe and pulled the key from around her neck, holding it before her as she ran. She knew how little time they had before the guards caught up with them, at which point they would have no hope. They had all volunteered for this task because they were small and light on their feet, not because they could fight. Fear, both for herself and for the women of the seraglio whose lives would be forfeit if she failed, gave Soraya strength. She reached the point where her legs lost all feeling, then the point where a brazier of hot knives seemed to blaze in her chest, and pushed past both, running the last stretch to the stable gates on adrenalin alone. She was too tired to check her momentum. She crashed into their wooden bulk with a dull thud, and as she did so she shoved her key into the rusty old padlock, and turned it with all the strength she had left. She held onto consciousness just long enough to hear the click as the catch released, but as she slid to the ground Zufir was at her side, tugging the heavy chain from the gates and throwing himself against them to make them open. Huma ran up next. She took her friend under the arms and pulled her to the side of the path, while Fernoush ran to help Zufir. Together, they flung themselves at the gates again and again. At the sound of the thumps coming from the other side, the army amassed outside the palace began pulling too. The gates creaked, shifted, gave at last with a grudging groan. The women of the seraglio poured in.

The fight was brief. Though Hakkim Mehdad's guards were better trained, the women far outstripped them in numbers. Many fled. A few surrendered. Those who fought managed to inflict some damage, but were swiftly overcome. When Zuleika and Umayma arrived from the Eastern Gate, the forces of the seraglio had taken the gardens, and were moving in a body towards the palace. As the mass of concubines, bandits and camel-drivers streamed past her, Zuleika scanned their faces with increasing anxiety. Rem was not among them. Catching sight of Soraya and the other volunteers sitting by the stable yard gates, she went up to them. They saw the question written on her face before she opened her mouth.

"I haven't seen Rem since we ran the wall," Soraya said. "I saw her climb through the window, but after that, nothing."

"She definitely got inside safely," Fernoush reassured Zuleika, "and none of us saw a body. Maybe she just—"

But Zuleika was already running to the palace, seized by a terrible suspicion. Her mind flew over the weapons she had seen at Rem's belt, her distant behaviour before she ran the wall, her guarded replies to Zuleika's questions. She ran through the corridors, glancing into every room and screaming Rem's name. She found her at last in the throne room, slumped beside the body of the sultan. Her head was bowed, her right hand broken, and breaths were as deep and ragged as if she had just run a marathon, but at the sound of Zuleika's voice she looked up, and managed a weak smile. Her face was covered in ink and blood. She held up her left hand, the elongated fingernails still dripping with gore.

"I stole them while you were asleep," she said, her voice hoarse. "Sorry. I needed a weapon that he wouldn't notice, and I didn't think you'd let me borrow them."

Zuleika stared at her wildly for a few heartbeats, her chest heaving as she tried and failed to control the flood of relief that threatened to overwhelm her. Then she burst into tears. "I told you to stick to the plan!" she sobbed, weeping and shouting at the same time. "Hakkim was a trained assassin—he could have killed you without even trying! You should be dead right now! Why did you do it, Rem? Why did you fight him?"

Rem was too tired to match the choked ferocity in Zuleika's tone. "He burned my scrolls, Zuleika. What else was I going to do?"

Zuleika wept with relief and incredulity. Her words came out in sharp gasps. "Scrolls? You did this because of your books?!"

Rem nodded wordlessly.

Zuleika ran to Rem's side and gathered her gingerly into her arms. Rem pressed her head against Zuleika's chest. As her wracking sobs subsided, Zuleika's breaths became deeper and slower. "Oh Rem," she whispered, "You should be dead. You should be dead." For a while, neither of them moved, locked together in the sweetness of reunion. Around them, the rule of Hakkim Mehdad ended, and the city of Bessa was reborn.

There remained but one enemy to face, and this one they could deal with entirely on their own terms. The army on the plains had long ago given up firing on the walls, and now sat or stood in small clusters at their base, casting occasional despondent glances at the fortifications above them. Captain Ashraf and his men had not returned from their charge on the dust cloud, and with every passing watch it became clearer to the waiting soldiers that the real battle had taken place in the city behind them, and that they had missed it. When Zuleika reappeared on the walls, the sky had grown dark. No one bothered to attack her. A few moments later, Gursoon came up to stand at her side. Unlike the rest of the older women, she had refused to form part of the dust cloud, instead entering Bessa in disguise with the rest of the army. There, she had gathered intelligence and helped to spread the rumours of the oncoming attack which reached Hakkim's ears. When the fighting started, she retired to Mayisah's house and waited it out. Now the two women stood on the walls and regarded the tiny figures below them.

"We can't just leave them there," Gursoon pointed out. "They don't have the provisions to make it to another city, and the dust-raisers would have to pass through them to get back to us. That could be a risk."

"We could just shoot them," Zuleika suggested.

Gursoon frowned. "No unnecessary bloodshed. We agreed that beforehand, Zuleika. Besides, we wouldn't be able to kill all of them. Some would get away, and then we'd have a party of angry exiles on our hands, constantly looking for a way to settle the score. We were in the same position once, and look how that worked out." She gestured at the city now under their control. "Better that we let them back inside, where we can keep an eye on them."

Zuleika considered her words. She knew they had wisdom in them, but she shook her head.

"We can't let them back in. They're Ascetics, and loyal to no one but Hakkim Mehdad. They would attack us as soon as they passed back through the gates."

"Not all of them," the older woman replied. "Only those with the black head scarves hold to that creed. The ones in blue are mostly the old guard of Al-Bokhari, who by their presence in this force I would guess are loyal to whoever can pay them a decent wage."

"Then I think we may reach a compromise." With these words, Zuleika picked up the warning bugle and blew a loud, long blast. The men clustered on the plains looked up at her.

"I think you've all realised by now that we have taken your city, and killed your leader," she called down. "We could kill you, too. If we fired on you from the battlements you wouldn't have a chance. You have no provisions with which to flee this place, and no siege weapons to regain it. But we are willing to let you live, and even to return. There is only one condition. Kill every man in a black headscarf."

Gursoon's eyes widened. Then she made a noise of disgust, and strode forward, shoving Zuleika aside. Zuleika staggered from the unexpected blow; though Gursoon was old, she was solid. She glared at Gursoon, but Gursoon paid her no heed.

"STOP!" she bellowed. "No man is to harm another!"

A few hands were guiltily removed from the hilts of swords, but for the most part the soldiers looked relieved. Al-Bokhari's old guard viewed the Ascetics with the resentment due to the favoured force of the new sultan, and the Ascetics in their turn kept aloof from the common soldiers, treating them with a certain amount of disdain. Still, they ate the same meals and drilled in the same courtyard, and what was more, each group of soldiers had seen the other split straw dummies in half with a single well-aimed sword swipe. Between a newborn feeling of camaraderie, and a healthy sense of self-preservation, the prospect of turning on one another was in no wise an attractive one.

"What are you doing?" Zuleika growled, when she had recovered from her initial shock.

"No one else is going to die here, by our hands or by others'," Gursoon shot back. "When you said compromise, I thought you intended to be reasonable."

She raised her voice again and addressed the army at large. "Many of you I know. Tell me, is Gamil still with the royal guard?"

After a brief pause, one figure detached itself from the rest and stepped forward.

"Hello, Gamil," Gursoon shouted cordially. "I'm sure you remember me. I am the Lady Gursoon, of Al-Bokhari's seraglio. I used to watch you and your friends training in the courtyard, and I stood lookout for you and Layla, when you two were lovers."

Gamil felt his face heat. A murmur of uneasy laughter rippled through the soldiers, but they remained wary of this friendly overture.

"You know me," Gursoon repeated, "just as you know the others who deposed Hakkim. Layla, too, is in our number, as are all the other ladies of the seraglio. Issi, the chief camel-driver, is here, and so is Bethi, who once styled the hair of Al-Bokhari's wives. Karam," she addressed a short, stocky man with dark hair, "your beloved Johara is here, and her child with her. Yusri, your—" Here, Gursoon was cut off. Another guard stepped forward, his eyes hard.

"Yusri is dead," he called out in a cold voice. "He was hit by one of your people's arrows."

Gursoon did not miss a beat. "Then that is a great tragedy, and I will grieve for him. But do not forget that a battle has just been fought. You fought us on the usurper's orders, and would have slain us all on those same orders." She glared at them, defying any man to contradict her.

"We all have dead to mourn," she continued. "The loss on both sides is the greater because some of those we fought against were our friends. We are not foreign aggressors. We're Bessans, all of us, and we came to liberate the city, not to steal it. Whatever the evils of this fight, I will not have them compounded in the name of revenge. The killing ends here, with a choice. Lay down your weapons on the plain and come back home. Or leave Bessa and never return there.

"If you choose the first option, there will be no reprisals against you, so long as you offer us none. If the second, then we will give you provisions for your journey, and dressings for your wounded. But whichever you choose, there is one thing you would do well to remember." Gursoon stared out at the army, fixing them with that falcon stare of hers. All the warmth had drained from her voice, and her eyes were like pebbles in her face. Those who had known her in the seraglio watched and listened for some trace of the Gursoon they knew, the amiable peacemaker who put people so effortlessly at their ease. They found none. Even Zuleika was surprised at the edge in her tone.

"That you fought against us, however unknowingly, is your first offence against the city of Bessa," she said, "and this your first warning. Give me cause to issue a second, and a vengeance will descend upon you so dark and so terrible that it blocks the daylight out. You will not take arms against us. You will not even begin to plan such a thing. Your regret, though short-lived, would be intense."

In the end, and after much discussion, all the soldiers decided to stay. As they filed back through the Northern Gate in single file, Gursoon and Zuleika noted down the name of each one, and the street in which he lived. If they remained peaceable for a period of five years, Gursoon told them, the list would be destroyed.

"I still think we should have shot them," Zuleika muttered, as the last man had trooped back into the city.

"Protected our interests by force, you mean," Gursoon replied. "We gained control in that manner, it is true, but we cannot hope to keep it in the same way. The city is free now, Zuleika. That freedom was born from chaos, but chaos will not sustain it. I think it is time we began planning for peace."

That night was filled with reunions, which would not wait until the daylight. The dust-raisers walked through the Northern Gate to a roar of joy and relief. Crowds of people thronged the street, watching for the return of their loved ones. Mothers rushed to embrace their children, friends searched anxiously for the faces of friends, shouting out to them across the sea of people when they were found. A tall, full-figured woman with a coil of dark hair burst into tears at the sight of Issi. She ran to him, closely followed by three gangly boys. Wife and sons reached the camel-driver at the same time and clung to him, the boys so much taller than their father that they almost obscured him from view. All that testified to Issi's presence in the group were his loud, laughing sobs, which rose occasionally above the loving murmurs and muffled prayers of his family.

Taliyah, not seeing her betrothed in the crowd, ran to his house as fast as she had run to the water gate earlier that day. On her way she heard her name cried many times, and in many tones, from the warm delight of friends to the wrenching joy in her mother's voice. She stopped for none of them, until she heard her name uttered in notes of rich mahogany and umber, and felt her dye-maker lover's arms fold round her.

Gursoon, after she had brought Dip back to his father, went to the palace stables. Night had fallen, but a full moon shone in the sky, and by its pale light, she could just make out a man leaning against one of the stable doors. He straightened up at her approach, and crossed over to her. His hair was greyer than when Gursoon had last seen him, but still tightly curled. His pale green eyes were just as she remembered them. The festivities in Bessa that night lasted until dawn. As the moon rose, people began to flood out into the streets, throwing dried rice and cheering. Gursoon walked with Fouad to the town square, and there she danced, just as she had when she was a girl. That night, she was lithe and graceful as a leaping salmon, in spite of her age. And Fouad watched her swoop and twirl from the side of the square, knowing that no man now could claim her against her will.

Rem found Zuleika where she knew she would be, standing at the top of the east watchtower and gazing out over Bessa, which shone with lanterns and seethed with activity as if it were a feast day. They looked down at the city for a while in silence. Then Rem took Zuleika's hand.

"There's something I need to do," she said. "Will you come with me?"

They walked hand in hand through the crowds until they reached the palace. Umayma and Zeinab were on guard outside the gates, and let them in with a friendly nod. The gardens were cool and quiet, and bathed in silver light. Rem led Zuleika through them to the palace, and then up the winding central stairs in the great hall. The throne room she passed without a glance; only Hakkim's body lay there, and that held no interest for her. She continued to climb until she reached the sultan's bedchamber, where she found what she was looking for behind a curtain in the corner of the room. With one broken hand, the boulder of negative thought was as difficult for Rem to lift as it had been for the young Hakkim, the day that he first felt its weight, and found in it his calling.

"What are you doing?" Zuleika asked her, as Rem strained and heaved at the stone.

"I'm killing an idea. I'll explain later."

"Ah."

Zuleika came to help her, and together the two women dragged the boulder over to the window and heaved it out. The bedchamber was near the top of the palace, so it had a long way to fall. It cracked the flagstones where it landed, producing a jagged pattern of fragments. For a moment, nothing else happened. Then, slowly, a hairline crack spread up the boulder from its base. It fell into two jagged halves, silently as a door opening on oiled hinges. To an insect, perhaps, the breaking of Hakkim's faith might have sounded like a calving glacier, or the earth cracking apart. To the lovers standing side by side at the window, any noise it made was drowned out by the singing and laughter drifting upwards from the bright city below.

BESSA, AT ONCE AND EVER

They built a city that shone like a vision, because it was born from a vision, a vision of stone and water and parchment. The stone was cut from the sun at dawn, the water shimmered like liquid fire, the parchment sang.

They did not tear anything down. They did not hold with tearing things down. They built. They built a Library out of gold, and they placed within it a scroll which contained all the knowledge of all the ages of the world.

In the centre of the city they built a fountain where the water spurts up to twice the height of a man. Where it flows, its colours changing with the colours of the sky, all may come and drink.

Joyful are the people who inhabit the city. Their voices sing, they dance in the streets. Their pageants are numerous and bright. It is a city of light and music. There is an embroiderer there, as I have heard, whose work is of such beauty that her own needle weeps to see it. A carver lives there whose statues come to life, so skilfully are they wrought. Many wondrous people dwell in the city: a woman who cries tears of ink, and a woman who has the golden touch and the death touch, and all in the city are blessed by the djinni with long life, and with many powers.

The walls of the city are high. They encompass it all around. Yet there is a gate in those walls, of burnished gold, and whosoever approaches it may enter if she will, for it stands always open. The gatekeepers are robed in saffron and red, and they welcome the traveller with these words: "Be weary no longer, and be no more oppressed. Lay down your burden of pain at the gate. Enter the city of women and rejoice!"

Gursoon

The library isn't made of gold. What a ridiculous idea! We're rich, but we aren't that rich.

And he's missed out the most important part. That's the House of Laws. It might not seem worth mentioning: it's fairly small. But it is the forge on which we make our city day by day.

Oh, we kept the sultan's palace. It's useful for quartering foreign dignitaries when they come to Bessa to see if we exist, and if we do, what we are about. But the real decision-making goes on in the Jidur, where any citizen may come to speak or to vote. And once the vote is taken, the House of Laws writes the decision up for the people's approval and—that granted—enacts it into our constitution.

The House is a former baker's shop. Rem found it. We enlarged it a bit. Then we moved in. It was very comfortable in there really, once we'd cleaned out the dead rats. It has large windows that let in great swathes of honey-coloured light. A bright, airy space. It also has an underground storeroom; perfect for storing the ever-expanding records and annals of our new state, and deliciously cool.

What we like best about it, though, is the peace and quiet. Somehow, after the desert, I think we all got used to silence, to drifting light with no walls to hem it in, to dark caves with a slight smell of dank mildew. A bakery on an unfrequented side street behind the Jidur isn't exactly the same, but it serves us well enough.

There's such a lot to do, it seems like we spend most of our time there, not just working out the wording of the new laws and writing them down but also making up lists of matters to be discussed in the next full council at the Jidur, writing letters to friends and allies in other cities, hosting meetings of groups assembled for specific tasks like cleaning the wells or rebuilding the houses of the lepers' quarter. It turns out, much to our surprise, that government when it's done properly is a full-time job.

Someone came into the shop to buy bread once: we'd never thought to remove the sign! He stayed to watch us at work, fascinated and bemused, and at the end of the day volunteered for the group that will dig a main sewer beneath the streets of the Samratani. After that, Fernoush started working in the front room baking bread. Her father was a baker, and she appreciates the chance to keep her hand in. She makes quite a profit by it as well, and it makes the place smell wonderful. It's nice, watching her work—feels almost like old times.

Those of us that stayed on to run the city after we had reclaimed it rarely have time to work with our hands now, not as we did in the desert. I'll sometimes stroll round the market place and catch Zeinab on a stall, haggling up the price of a bracelet with some trader's wife. Just for the joy of it. Issi is very proud of her. And Umayma still sneaks away to go hunting. Issi's boys go with her. I think half of them have a fancy for that girl, and all of them compete for her approval with a single-mindedness that's touching to see. She never was interested in them, though. Or only as hunting partners, anyway.

Yes, all of us who stayed in the council feel the need to steal away from time to time. Not all of us did stay, of course. Some joined the new palace guard. Others continued their work as artists and artisans. (I hear Maysoon has a nice little potter's shop in the centre of the city. I must go and visit her there.) Some simply took up the threads of their old lives, or those bits of them that were left. There's not much call for a royal seraglio anymore. There's no more royalty, for one thing. A neighbouring caliph once remarked that the inhabitants of Bessa are its sultans. He meant it for a jest, but it is the truth.

It was sad, too, seeing the army disband. In the desert, the four hundred of us were a city all on our own. None of us really considered it at the time, but on some level we all knew that we could not return to the city we left behind, and keep our own intact. There was no more comfortable seraglio to contain us. We dissolved into the new Bessa like sugar into water, and of necessity we spread out through it, and what we once had was lost. It's funny: we did it all for freedom, but in some ways, I know I will never be so free again as I was in that desert.

Oh, and of course we never call it "the city of women." Just as we never called the Bessa that was "the city of men." Ridiculous.

The rest? That's all true.

Farhat

People ask me who the girl in my tapestries is. The plain girl in the white dress. She's always there, in every one. Sometimes she dines with sultans in a great hall. Sometimes she fights dragons with a shining sword. Sometimes she is part of the story, and sometimes she watches from the crowd. She is not always smiling. She feels just as we feel. When the Seraglio was sent out into the desert, she wept little sapphire tears. When the city was reclaimed, she laughed with a mouth of scarlet and her eyes flashed emeralds. I cannot answer, when people ask, except to say that she is me, and all of us. She was a servant, and now she lives in a city where there are no servants. She can dine with sultans now, and count herself their equal. She never curtsies out of deference. She never begs anybody's pardon.

People recognize me in the streets, now that my embroidery has become popular. They sometimes curtsey or bow to me. Gursoon says that Bessa has no need for sultans, nor for queens; its figureheads are its artists, its craftswomen and its poets. I am happy with this, so long as we artists and poets never feel the need to emulate those symbols we have replaced. We overthrew them—this does not mean that we should follow them. We couldn't if we tried, anyway. We are different from them on a level that is always seen but rarely perceived, and really amounts to all that we are good for. I try to keep it before me always. Without it, this city would be brought to something worse than destruction—it would return to the way it was. The difference is this: almost everyone in Bessa is an artist, a craftswoman or a poet. They are sublimely simple things to be. You don't need fame, or even skill. Most importantly of all, you don't need birth. They are designations with no walls around them. Many people say many things about Bessa. I say this. And I raise people up, when they bow. I shake my head if they go to drop a curtsey. I look into their faces. I smile.

Fouad

Take our orders from women: why not? I did as Gursoon told me for years. She just has more of a head for some things than I do. And the women leave me free to follow my calling, which is all a man needs.

The last sultan, the fanatic, now, he was a hard one to live with. He sold my horses, all of them! Set me to tending camels and donkeys, and nursing sick goats. I should have followed the women; borrowed a horse and gone after her as I did before. But my daughter had not long had her twins, and my son . . . By rights I know Danyar is Bokhari's boy, but when did a sultan care for those sorts of rights? I'd taken him on as stable-boy and he was promising, a gentle hand with the beasts, and a fine rider already. But he was only thirteen then, and small for his age. I couldn't leave him.

When the women came back we didn't have much time to spend celebrating; there was too much to be done. Rashad had a few of us into the kitchens for a drink, and old Issi told us some of what they'd been up to. It was quite a story. My Gursoon has a way of turning a situation to her advantage; the others too, of course. I think Rashad had given up hope of ever seeing them again, but me—no.

What now? Well, it's as you see. I won't deny I miss the old horses, but these here are good beasts. My brother found them for me; he didn't undercharge me, either. Now I can teach my daughter to ride, and my grandsons, as a man should. And any others who want to learn. Of course women can ride, it was my mother who taught me. They have arms and legs the same as us, don't they?

I don't know if we'll marry. Gursoon might not have me—it was thirty years ago I last asked her. And we've managed well enough without it up till now. We'll go out riding together, though. She says she's too old, she's forgotten how, but you never forget.

I'm not a great one for words. But it's good to have her back. You know how it is after a storm, when everything goes back to how it should be, and you can stand up again and look around you? Yes, that's how it is. I can see properly again.

Taliyah

I missed him. I did. I spent most of my time in the desert pining for him. Every time I ground stone to make paint, I did it for him. We voted to go to war, but when I cast my lot I saw his face. It felt like a homecoming, not an invasion. For all of us, I think. We all carried the faces of loved ones in our minds like banners. Their names were our rallying cries. The others returned to Bessa for sons and daughters, for fathers and mothers and sisters. I came back a bride, and if a battlefield lay between me and my beloved, then so much the better if it was strewn with the corpses of those who had parted us. I thought he would be proud. *I* was proud. There was a desert and death between us, and I walked through both—for him!

And in my more mundane mind, I knew now that I had a craft, a livelihood. When I left I was an ignorant child, but now I was a grown woman. Do not believe that I had no fears. I had steeled myself for a cooling of feeling. In my darkest dreams I had seen him wed another, had seen that hair's breadth between joy and despair crossed, irrevocably, as he crossed the threshold into his wedding home. In my terror, I had even imagined his death. I came armed against these fears, ready for them. I was so afraid as I ran through the streets, one mischance after another pressing against my mind, that I was surprised by his embrace when it came. The relief of it nearly crushed me to the floor.

I was prepared for anything, except happiness. I returned to him a warrior. I fought my way to him through an army and across a desert, and arrived to find he had been waiting for me, with a house and a garden made ready. It should have made me glad. But I could not make him understand why the house felt like a cage.

He took my desire to work for mere restlessness at first, then for a lack of faith in him, a fear of relying on his skills. How could I rely on him? I lay on our bed through all those endless afternoons, and watched everything that I loved about myself drifting away like dust motes in the changeless light. He asked me if I was jealous, but I never doubted his fidelity. He brought me back fruits and necklaces from the market, and could not understand why I wept.

I cannot blame it all on his narrow-mindedness; he loved me the way he had always loved me, back when I was the daughter of a concubine, and had never dreamed of a greater joy for myself than the love he gave me. In the end, I grew up and he did not. I could not put my weapons down, and he wouldn't see that I never raised them against him. I couldn't make him understand that I left not because I thought his love had faded, but because it was not enough. He wanted me to feed on it and grow strong, but it was not enough, it could never be enough, to sustain me through a wasted life. In the end, I was prepared for anything except the thing I had crossed deserts to regain. So I left, to find out what I really came back for.

Warudu

The best part was seeing my children learn to read. I could never have afforded to apprentice them to a scholar, but after Rem built the schools, everyone learned to read.

Efridah

I suppose it was fifty years I worked here, since my husband died. I swept the floor for Al-Bokhari's father before him. Sometimes I thought the broom would stick to my hands. But it was a home, and the girls were kind, mostly. Then that murderer came. When he turned us out I thought, there's nothing to do now but pray for death. And death wouldn't have me.

And then it all got turned around. I came through the desert, lived in the mountains. I grew strong again. And now here I am back where I started, and it's all different. I don't have to hold a broom till I drop and then starve, or live off charity. They're even building me my own house. Think of that!

Well, I did think of it: I thought that after fifty years of slavery I would end my life as a queen. But no. It turns out they have more work in mind for me. Gursoon wants me to sit on their city council, and make laws.

I'm not sure. I did think they might let me rest at last. But it's only two days a week in that old bakery they've set up; they'll give you tea, and Fernoush bakes her pastries there, apparently. She's a nice girl and a good cook. So I might say yes. Perhaps I could insist that that bitch Imtisar brings me my tea.

At all events, someone else can do the sweeping.

Zeinab

The things you need to order to build a city: it's astonishing! Bricks, to rebuild the places Hakkim destroyed. Building tools; spades to dig sewers and plant seeds; pipes to carry water. And that precious material, wood—which turns out to cost nearly as much by weight as gold, but how else do you make cattle-yokes, spindles for scrolls or stools for students? I was in charge of finding it all, and working out how to get it back to us. Issi helped, of course, and ran the caravans, but I was the one who did the trading. And then after the building work, there were all the other tools. Needles and cloth. Chisels. Paints. Pens. And this new writing material that Rem loves so much: paper. You can make it from old cloth, or from wood shavings; we'll be able to produce our own soon. Rem says it takes ink better than skins, and it certainly smells less foul when you're preparing it.

We're going to be a trading centre, I can see it happening all around us. Sometimes I feel that my head can't take all the things I need to learn: the different grades of thread; the names and market rates for precious spices. I worry that I'll bring back too much or too little, that I'll be cheated or buy the wrong thing entirely, and wreck a vital project. But Gursoon says there's no one who's better qualified, and I suppose it is going well so far.

You know, it's strange. My parents were poor traders: they rejoiced when I was chosen by the sultan. They thought I'd be set up for life, and my daughter too, that nothing they had given me could compare. I wish they could see me now, see how I'm valued for the skills they taught me.

Soraya comes with me on some of the trading journeys: I want her to see how it's done. She doesn't have to follow in my father's footsteps. But she'll learn some kind of skill in Bessa. She'll have a trade.

Issi

Camel-man's a job for life, my father always told me. You'll always be needed. Well, I don't know about that. The past year or so I've been through more occupations than I knew there were. Nursemaid, farmer, builder. Trader and diplomat, now. Camel thief, too, though I haven't told my wife about that one. Still, I can't complain. I got back to her and the boys in one piece. And it seems I'm a big man in the city these days— they're always calling on me for something.

I don't know what the hurry is with all this trading. They sent us all the way to Sussurut last month just for a load of cloth and some spices. Zeinab got a good price, of course: the girl's a marvel. But she ought to have a rest, maybe settle down. A couple of the men have their eye on her, I know that. But you can't tell girls what to do, these days.

Anwar Das

I don't spend much time in Bessa. My work takes me to many places: Perdondaris, Agorath, Yrtsus, once or twice. I always smile when I hear I'm going there. They don't know what a lucky escape they've had.

All the cities I have visited are beautiful. Perdondaris has immense, spiralling prayer towers, and Agorath a magnificent gold-domed palace. Nor are they without their wonders. The vertical gardens of Jawahir bloom lush and green, and tower high above the arid desert all around. The sultan of Galal-Amin has carpeted the land round about his city for a mile on all sides with miniature date palms, so small they grow only to the height of one's ankles. Visitors walk among them and think themselves giants, while the city looms above, a mother of giants. I have seen this sight with my own eyes, and it is marvellous to behold.

More miraculous by far, however, is Lilliath, the siren-city. I see from your faces that you have never heard of this place. Few have, for its inhabitants all died long ago. It is a sad story:

A large tribe, wandering through the desert, came across an abundance of large rocks. They seemed uncommonly well-suited for use as a building material: thick, even slabs, flat and sturdy. Their only fault was a slight jaggedness at their edges, as though they had once been joined together and had since shattered.

The leaders of the people took these stones as a sign from the Increate, and used them to build a city, vast and mighty, on the site. They called it Lilliath, and for a time they prospered there, laying waste to the surrounding tribes and plundering their wealth. Their city, although it was perfect in all other respects, was dry as a bone, and the people had to fetch water from a spring far outside its gates.

One night, there was a great storm over Lilliath. The next morning, the city was filled with a low rumbling sound, quiet and ominous. At first, people thought the noise merely a continuation of the thunder from the night before. When they glanced out of their windows, and saw the sky was clear, they feared it was an earthquake. But the noise continued throughout the day, and the city stood firm.

Gradually, their terror turned to jubilation. Clearly, the rain had woken a dormant spring hidden beneath the streets. A source of water within the city gates! That evening, a vast crowd thronged through Lilliath, greedy for water. They reached the centre of the city, where the noise was loudest, and began at once to tear up the stones that paved the street there.

Once they had removed the stones, they dug deep into the sand, searching for the spring that they were sure lay just below the surface. They dug for a long time, and as they dug, the rumbling became louder. It had, they realised, a sort of rhythm to it. They kept digging. The rumbling rose in pitch, as if the water they sought was building in pressure on its way to the surface. Finally, a gaping hole opened beneath their fingers, and they stepped back, expecting at any moment a rushing fountain to appear. But it was no spring that the hungry rain had woken in the earth. Instead, from the dark hole, the people heard a voice. It sounded like no human voice they had ever heard, but it sang with such piercing sweetness that the crowd began to weep, at a beauty pitched to the intensity of pain. The voice gushed from the hole, filling the city with its ethereal notes, and now the buildings trembled, the ground shook. The inhabitants of Lilliath were so filled with the song pouring from the earth, that they did not notice. They did not think to run as their own city fell upon them and crushed them to death.

I myself have never been to Lilliath, for they say that all who hear the music that still flows from the ruins of that city are driven mad. I heard the tale from a cousin of mine, who the Increate saw fit to strike deaf as a young man. It was a bitter sorrow to his parents, but as you see, for every desert storm, a date palm!

I have, however, visited a place that was even stranger. You do not believe it is possible? Listen. Have you heard of Sah, the city of sand? You laugh: you think it no more than a fable. I did too, until experience taught me otherwise.

It was during a trip to Jawahir, and I was hopelessly lost. My water had run out the day before, and I staggered across the featureless desert, sure that death would be my lot if I did not find a spring or an oasis soon. I had just fallen, exhausted, to the ground, when a terrific sandstorm blew up around me. The dust stung my eyes, so I flung up an arm to shield my face.

When I risked a look to see if the storm had died down, where the swirling sands had been a great city stood, its gates just a few feet from where I lay. I walked up to it like a man in a dream, wondering that it did not crumble at my very breath. For I saw quite clearly that the pale material from which it was made was not stone but sand, gritty and fine. I ran my hand over the surface of its walls, and felt the tiny grains shift and stir beneath my fingers, much as they would if I ran my hand along the sand at my feet. Yet the city stood before me still, as real and sturdy as if it were built from granite.

I stepped back and surveyed it. Its whole surface seemed to shift and change, a motion I had taken to be an effect of the heat-haze at first. I could see now that it was the wind, rippling the surface of the city as it passed. The storm raged on, but the sand that it once moved had been transformed. These reflections occupied me for some moments, but as you can well imagine, by this point I had more pressing matters on my mind. A city, even a shimmering spirit-city borne through the desert by a sandstorm, might offer some source of water.

I stumbled through the deserted streets, calling out for help in a hoarse voice. The denizens of that strange place waited until dusk before they graced me with their presence. I saw several little drifts of sand rushing towards me, and a fragrant breeze caressed my cheek and ruffled my hair. The ribbons of blown sand seemed to fountain up into the air, and all at once I was surrounded by a crowd of ghostly forms, who peered at me with gentle interest.

They never spoke, but they laughed sometimes: rustling, whispering laughter. They were very welcoming, and wanted me to stay and marry the sultan's daughter (a story for another occasion, I think). I have to say, though, that their tastes were quite different from my own. All they drank was a curious wine, distilled from the desert heat haze, that seemed to bring about intoxication very quickly. They offered me a flask of it, and after I had taken it, and thanked them gratefully, the winds that blew perpetually outside the walls rushed in, and the entire place dissolved again into the sandstorm. It was gone before I could raise a hand to cover my eyes.

Thankfully, the contents of the flask were enough to last me the rest of my journey. I arrived in Jawahir, considerably inebriated but alive. Unfortunately, no one believed my strange tale, for the flask, as soon as I had drained its contents, crumbled back into the sand from which it had been crafted. I keep its remains still, in a bag which I carry always on my person. Have a look if you like, and witness for yourselves the truth of what I say.

Ah, my friends! I have visited Khyir, and eaten the fruits that grow there: the sun fruit, grown from seeds sown at dawn, and the moon fruit, harvested on the nights of the full. I have been to Fikri, the great city underground, and to Safa-al-Din, the city built on stilts. In Qismat, they hailed me as a hero, and I departed laden with many treasures, while in Tish-Barat they chased me with spears, and I barely escaped with my life. I could have settled in any one of those cities. Most (with perhaps the exception of Tish-Barat) would have welcomed me. On my travels, I have seen a thousand marvels, and I see more with every cycle of the moon.

But in every city I visit, when I tell the people there of the wonders of Bessa, their eyes go round and wide, and they listen like little children, struck dumb with amazement. And of all the beauties of all the cities I have ever seen, the best is the sight of Bessa's gates, standing open like great arms in the last light of the evening, welcoming me home. There is not another city like Bessa anywhere on this wide earth, my friends. Not a one.

Bethi

No doubt about it, life is more interesting now. But you know what, outside the palace there isn't nearly such a call for hairdressers as I thought there'd be.

A friend of mine says I have a talent for storytelling, that perhaps I could make a living that way. It's certainly a thought.

Rem

We are ahead of our time. So far ahead, that sometimes it seems we're in the wrong millennium entirely. It doesn't matter a damn. The city was built on a fault line, dropped into the middle of a spider's web. It shook things up, and the tremors of its coming reached backwards and forwards and out on all sides.

I always saw it, as a child, glowing in the distance as if in the desert at night, a day's journey away. Its light transfixed me then, and it has been drawing me to it ever since, across that desert of years. I see it still, now that I am living in it, and it flows over and around me like a river.

It is a masterpiece of fragments, spangled light and colour that fills my mouth with song and my eyes with tears. I can cry here, finally. I bottle the ink, give it to Zeinab to sell in the market. It is popular.

So are my poems. I sign them, as I sign everything, with an eye, proffering a single tear. Rem the weeper. One who fashions all things from her sorrow. I knew, I have always known, that I would one day be in a position to laugh at that prophecy. It does not deaden the sharpness of the joy I feel now. Nor does the knowledge that it will one day be fulfilled again deaden it. I have always known this to be the case.

The city shines in the centre of time, a solid ruby hung on a string of driftwood beads, floating in a landscape of black on black. Everything that came before was a crescendo, and everything that comes after a tailing off. It will fall, in the end, into that darkness, and all its works will turn to dust. It doesn't matter a damn. It exists now, it will always have existed. It is enough.

Zuleika

No one said it would be easy, and it wasn't. We did it anyway.

BOOK THE SECOND

The Gold of Anwar Das

"You know why I asked you to come, Anwar Das?"

"If I may speak my heart, Lady Gursoon, I think it's because the City of Women finds it expedient to have a man for its ambassador—and you don't know that many men who you actually trust."

"Do you think you could take on this role for us?"

"Of course. My previous job involved a great deal of diplomacy and protocol."

"You were a camel thief."

"Yes. The diplomacy and protocol arose more in the fencing of the camels afterwards. But tell me, lady. What does Bessa need most at this point in its trajectory? Wealth? Influence? Accurate intelligence as to its rivals' doings?"

"Stability, Anwar Das. We need something that will ensure we can survive, and thrive, in a future that is uncertain and likely to be stormy."

"And now I have my brief. Thank you, lady."

"Thank you, Anwar Das. When can you start?"

"I was on payroll, wise and beauteous one, from the moment when I bowed to you."

Arriving in Heqa'a on the back of a camel whose name was Muzra, the Whirlwind, Anwar Das of Bessa took up residence in the Imtil. From there, he sent gifts of wine and dates to the esteemed and noble house of Omran Injustari. He did not, at this time, present himself at that house, but announced his willingness to do so at a time that might be mutually convenient.

Only silence in reply, but Anwar Das was not discouraged. He obtained privy access to Injustari's sister, the celestially beautiful Siyah Sireyah. Extremely privy access: they made love for the best part of an afternoon, in a great variety of positions, and afterwards lay in each other's arms, spent and sweaty and highly satisfied with the day's labours.

"You are a strange man," Siyah Sireyah murmured.

"Am I?" Anwar Das affected dismay. "I thought I was a comparatively well formed one."

"Oh, as to that," the lady murmured, "I have no complaints. But it's strange that the City of Women should send us such a . . . what's the word? . . . such a *virile* ambassador."

Anwar Das frowned judiciously. "Bessa, lady, is far more than that sobriquet suggests," he told her. "A city whose populace were entirely female would be doomed to last only a generation, unless women like bees could find the secret of reproducing their kind without the intervention of the male sex. Until that happens, we men will always be at your side, ready at need to play our part in the propagation of the species."

"Such selfless devotion!" said Siyah Sireyah, caressing Das's manhood with warm affection. "This generosity of spirit must be rewarded!"

She rewarded it in a way that Das found impossible to argue with, and another hour or so passed without either of them looking at the glass or troubling to turn it. Then, regretfully, the lady began to dress. Her brother was extremely protective of her, she explained, and always charted her movements with scrupulous care. She had told him that she was abroad to visit friends, but he would look for her return before sunset.

"Lady, I have gifts for you," Anwar Das said. "Unless you think that gifts would profane the near-mystical communion we've just enjoyed."

"Not at all," Siyah Sireyah said, enthusiastically. "Next to the near-mystical communion we've just enjoyed, I enjoy presents best of all. Wheel them out!"

Anwar Das did so, and the lady's eyes became wide as she saw the beautiful things the Bessan envoy had brought her. Peerless silks, delicate brocades, silver necklaces and bracelets inset with coloured glass beads most cunningly wrought. Her breath caught, for a moment, in her throat.

"So lovely!" she sighed. "So lovely!"

"Their loveliness will be consummated when you wear them," Anwar Das said, kissing the lady's neck. And they took their leave of each other with many protestations of love.

The next day, Anwar Das sent gifts of pears and spiced meats to the esteemed and noble house of Omran Injustari, along with another discreetly worded suggestion that at some point, a meeting might be arranged to their mutual advantage. Silence again.

A lesser man might have been deterred. Anwar Das merely shrugged and went out on the town. In Heqa'a there is a house, the House Several, where musical performances are sometimes staged, and there he went. To the strains of buzuq, mijwiz and tanbur, he made the acquaintance of the Lady Afaf Nusain. It became an intimate acquaintance shortly afterwards, in one of the upper rooms of the House Several.

Kissing the lady's thighs and belly, after the immediate fires of passion had somewhat abated, Anwar Das asked her if she would be insulted to accept a gift from him. "Besides the gifts already proffered?" Afaf Nusain sighed contentedly.

"Of a different order," Anwar Das answered her.

"I should not be insulted, Ambassador. Not in the slightest."

Anwar Das gave her jewels and patterned cloths of great beauty, which she received with enormous pleasure. He begged her, when she wore them, to think of him, and she vouchsafed to do so—promising, besides, to spare him more than a passing thought when she took them off.

On his third day in Heqa'a, Anwar Das sent gifts of apricots and almonds to the esteemed and noble house of Omran Injustari, indicating in the accompanying letter that he wished to bend that gentleman's ear at some point before they both died of old age.

He expected no reply, and so was not disappointed.

That night he visited another noble house and met the wife and daughters of the Ibiri princeling, Namuz, in that royal gentleman's absence. There was no amorous play, but plenty of stories, in which—as in the act of love—Anwar Das was adept. The women were thrilled at his narrative skills, and the evening passed agreeably for all. Before leaving, Anwar Das presented all three of them with gifts of jewels and dresses of exquisite design, and they thanked him effusively. They asked if there were any way that they could show their gratitude, and he gave them the same answer he'd given the Lady Afaf Nusain—if they thought of him kindly, from time to time, he would be well rewarded.

On the fourth day, Anwar Das rested. That evening, Prince Namuz was hosting a party to which all the nobility of Heqa'a were invited, and Das, as envoy plenipotentiary of the city of Bessa, was naturally invited too.

In the course of the evening, he found occasion to sidle up close to the esteemed and noble Omran Injustari, and introduce himself.

"Oh," Injustari said, gruffly. "You're the one that's been bombarding me with fruit, aren't you? Well listen here, Ansul Bas, or whatever you call yourself. I don't need whatever it is you're selling, and throwing dates and apricots over my garden wall isn't going to change that. I've got profitable partnerships with every city west of Baram-Saal, and I'm not about to shake that tree while I'm standing under it, you understand me?"

Anwar Das confirmed that he did indeed understand, and turned the conversation to other things. As they spoke—about the shocking state of the city walls, and the best oasis to use between Stesh and Ibu Kim, and the chance of Abdul Mu'izz writing a decent poem one of these days—Injustari's attention kept wandering to the women who passed on every hand, dressed in uncommon splendour. Anwar Das noticed the frown that appeared on the great merchant's face, and could not forebear to smile.

Omran Injustari saw that smile, and slowly, its import dawned on him. "Yours," he said.

Anwar Das shrugged. "That depends on how you define these things," he replied.

"Bessan silk."

"No."

"Bessan silver."

"No."

"What, then?"

Anwar Das took a sip of wine, drawing out the moment. "Bessan weavers," he said at last. "Bessan silversmiths. Bessan carders and dyers and artists and glassblowers. We produce no raw materials, Excellency. We have no mines, and few farms. But we have the finest artisans in the region."

Injustari was silent, but many thoughts visibly pursued each other across his face.

"You're wondering," Anwar Das interpreted, "whether you can keep this secret, at least until you lock your current customers into longer-term agreements. Excellency, you cannot. Many of these ladies have husbands and fathers who are merchants in their own right, or who sell contracts on behalf of the Heqa'a principate. Each of them will by now have had a conversation which began with the words 'my dear, where did you get that?' The secret is not in your keeping, nor—any longer—in mine."

Injustari made a gesture—opening his fingers as though releasing some matter that, while annoying, was so insubstantial that it could be trusted to float away on the slightest breeze. "My contacts here are long established," he said. "They know me, and they're happy to trade with me."

Anwar Das nodded as if to say, *Of course, of course, and I have a bridge in a city not yet built which you might be interested in purchasing.*

"You offer me no threat," Injustari insisted.

Anwar Das threw out his hands. "I don't mean to," he said. "I'm only trying to find a market for these goods, which I'm sure you'll agree are superb. If, in so doing, I steal your client base away from you and leave you and your family in the most abject and unrelieved poverty, that will be regrettable and entirely unintended."

They stood side by side for some minutes, Anwar Das respecting the other man's profound inner struggle.

"How much do you want?" Injustari growled at last.

"For a five-year contract," Anwar Das said, "during which period Bessan goods will reach Heqa'a, Diwani and Perdondaris entirely via your trade caravans—for this, ten thousand in gold per year, rising to thirteen by annual increments, plus one half of all profits over twice the cost of manufacture, the books to be opened to your clerks whenever necessary and a review of these terms to be carried out twice per year or at any time during the life of the contract should either party realise profits which the other considers excessive."

Omran Injustari blinked.

"But . . ." he said at last.

"Yes, Excellency?"

"But those terms are entirely reasonable! What's the catch?"

"Ah," said Anwar Das. "The catch. I'm glad you asked."

From Heqa'a, the uncomplaining Muzra took Anwar Das at astonishing speed to Perdondaris, the white city of the north. Into the great metropolis, he fell as a single drop of water falls into Ocean, and is lost. But unlike that drop of water, he had letters of introduction from the esteemed and noble Omran Injustari, whose trade caravans wove in and out of Perdondaris's marbled streets every day of the year. And therefore, unlike that drop of water, he was admitted to a private audience with the Caliph.

It never rains in Perdondaris in any case, by the way, so it was a fatuous metaphor to start with.

The Caliph, the most Serene and Exalted Kephiz Bin Ezvahoun, was not surprised to see Anwar Das. He'd been tracking the Bessan ambassador's progress across the blessed hinterlands for a year and a half, wondering how and when he would finally thread the maze that led to Perdondaris's throne room. Now that Das had at last arrived, the Serene and Exalted felt moved to congratulate him.

"You had a bugger of a job," he said, "if you'll pardon my Turkish. The bureaucracy here has my official calendar sewn up five years in advance. In Perdondaris, spontaneity means only filling in seven forms before saying good morning instead of the usual eleven."

"Your Highness's jest is all the more amusing for being the literal bastard truth," Anwar Das said, performing a graceful and protracted salaam. "But is it your wish, this fine morning, to throw all that camel dung out of the window and be truly spontaneous?"

"Get yourself into a position you can sustain without a cramp," the Serene and Exalted invited him, "and give it your best shot."

Anwar Das settled into a more comfortable cross-legged posture and got to the point. "Perdondaris is like an elephant, Highness," he said. "It is great, and it is mighty, and everyone is impressed when they see it—but their choices, at the end of the day come down to two. They can ride on it, or they can stay well out from under its feet."

"A fair summary," the Caliph agreed.

"Some of your nearest neighbours, sadly, have been denied access to either of those options," Anwar Das pointed out.

"You mean Bessa?" the Serene and Exalted asked, slightly thrown. "Bessa is far enough away from us, I think, that she need not fear us."

"Your pardon, Excellency. I didn't mean Bessa, I meant Susurrut."

The Caliph's eyebrows rose. "Susurrut? That's much closer, certainly. You know there are factions within Perdondaris that view Susurrut as an unruly suburb."

Anwar Das knew this very well, but pursed his lips as though the folly of such a view pained him deeply. "Excellency," he said, "we're both men of the world and we're neither of us fools. You know as well as I that Perdondaris has conquered Susurrut three times in living memory, but never held it for longer than five years at a stretch. The irregular exercise of your subjects' wilder aspirations costs both cities dearly."

The Caliph stood. "We will continue this talk, he said, "in the gardens."

As they walked among the plenty of nature, sustained most unnaturally in this dry and thirsty place, the Caliph admitted Anwar Das's point—which was a lot easier than admitting it in the throne room, in the hearing of two dozen attendants and twice two dozen spies. "The cost to both cities of these futile skirmishes is indeed very high, Anwar Das. But it's a lot higher for the Akond of Susurrut than it is for me," he mused. "And in many ways, I prefer the war party here to be weakened and attenuated by the war draft and the war levy. I always make sure they pay more than their share."

The Serene and Exalted stopped on a terrace overlooking the sunset. Anwar Das stopped with him. That symbol of ending and endlessness made them both sombre.

"A man's life is like a wave that breaks on a beach," Anwar Das observed. "The water that was the wave rolls back down the strand to join the water of Ocean, and it has no knowledge of itself, any longer, as a separate thing. In the same way, a man's body joins the elements again and there is nothing left to show that he stood and thought and moved. Except for men like you, Excellency, whose lives touch the lives of others in myriad ways, and who may be remembered for their deeds long after their bodies are dust."

"You negotiate with philosophy," the Caliph said, "because your bag is empty."

"My bag is empty," Anwar Das countered, "because I would not insult so great a king with anything so paltry as a bribe. I would bribe you with history, Serene and Exalted One. I would bribe you with the words that will be spoken when you can no longer hear them."

"What words?" Kephiz Bin Ezvahoun asked.

"He took the fragile flower of peace and tied its stem to a stout stake, so that it grew stronger and stronger. Before him, Perdondaris and Susurrut exhausted themselves with war. Now they clasp each other in amity, and each is richer than it was before. The alliance between the two can never be broken, and neither need fear any enemy, for if any man rises against the one, the other will strike him down like the hammer of high heaven."

The Caliph laughed long and hard, but the glance he turned on Anwar Das was curious. "You have a fine line in camel dung yourself," he said.

"Your Excellency is too kind," Anwar Das said, bowing low.

"And if I said yes—ticking off the warmongers mightily—Bessa would be the broker of the peace?"

"A truly neutral party would be needed for such a delicate job. I would be honoured to act as mediator, and to lay out the terms of a suitable treaty for your own and the Akond of Susurrut's approval."

The Caliph grinned. "You want a crowbar," he summarised.

"Of the finest manufacture, tipped and filigreed with silver."

"What did you do before you were a politician?" Kephiz Bin Ezvahoun asked. "Were you by any chance a camel thief?"

For a moment, Anwar Das was discountenanced. "It was far south of here," he began. "I never stole from Perdondaris, Excellency, or from any of its . . ."

The Caliph roared with delighted laughter. "It was a joke, man! But you're telling me it's true? Oh, that's too wonderful!" He wiped tears from his eyes. "A thief! A bandit! Bessa appoints a bandit as her ambassador! But of course she does, because her soldiers are odalisques and her citizenry are sultans! Wonderful! By the Increate, truly wonderful!"

Recovering his composure a little, Anwar Das suggested that they might run up a rough draft for a possible treaty right there and then.

The Caliph shook his head vigorously. "Oh, the details I leave to you. Only make sure that they include the abandonment of the forts on the Yildriziah, and the re-opening of the Pass Paved with Iron. I need to have a few fig-leaves to flaunt in front of my fanatics." He was chuckling again by this point. "I meet so few camel thieves! If they're all like you, I'm surprised we have any camels left at all!"

They went back into the throne room, where spiced wine was brought. They talked for some turns of the glass about the many ways in which stealing camels and governing cities were not so dissimilar as might be thought, until at last Anwar Das took his leave, with effusive thanks for the Serene and Exalted's great generosity.

Thence to Susurrut, where Anwar Das arrived in the middle of the night. This being Susurrut, night or day made little difference: everything is for sale in that place so long as a man knows where to apply, and Anwar Das had old acquaintance there. Among them was Bethi, the former servant maid who had now become the most stalwart of his spies. She welcomed him with honeyed fruits, and with the sweeter gift of her embrace.

"How many times did you have to put out in Heqa'a?" she asked him teasingly, after they had pleasured each other.

"I am a loyal and uncomplaining servant of the Bessan polity," Anwar Das told her, his face grave.

Bethi marvelled. "That many times! Your poor manhood!"

Bethi's reasons for being in Susurrut included the clearing of the ground for a meeting between Anwar Das and Rudh Silmon, the merchant prince and so-called Keeper of the Fields of Gold. She had scattered bribes so judiciously and sweet-talked all interested parties with such address that Anwar Das was ushered, before noon of the next day, into the presence of the man himself.

Silmon was inspecting samples, as he did most mornings, sitting in a dark room with the windows barred and sniffing judiciously at dozens of dark-coloured powders arrayed in the recesses of a long tray built for that purpose alone.

"Anwar Das," Silmon said. *Sniff, sniff!* "The Bessan ambassador. *Sniff!* "Come with a shopping list, no doubt."

"The Keeper is as clear-sighted as he is morally irreproachable," Anwar Das said, civilly, and he handed Silmon a scroll. Silmon undid the ribbon, and the scroll fell open: it fell all the way to the floor, and had not completely unwound when it got there.

Silmon read the list, his lips moving as he silently recited its contents. Before he had got more than five lines into it, he set it down and stared at Anwar Das.

"Are you mad?" he asked him.

"I believe not," Anwar Das answered.

Silmon threw the scroll back across the table to his guest, in irritation or perhaps disgust. "You are wasting my time," he said, "and your own. I will sell you spices and scents in any quantity, assuming you have sufficient gold to pay my admittedly outrageous prices. But the items on this list I will not sell for a king's ransom."

"I have no such fortune," Anwar Das said, opening his hands to show his empty palms.

The Keeper glared at them. "Then you are an idiot, sir!

"But I have this." Anwar Das drew something slender and elongated from his belt. Silmon gasped and drew back, for a moment fearing an assassination attempt. Susurrut had enemies who would be only too happy to kill him, if they could do so without being found out.

But what Anwar Das handed him was only another scroll, broader but much shorter than the first. The Keeper stared at the seal, which was the seal of the most Serene and Exalted Kephiz Bin Ezvahoun, Caliph of Perdondaris.

"What is this?" he asked stupidly, his resources of speech and intellect briefly abandoning him. Perdondaris's whimsical pleasure and displeasure were the diastole and systole of life in Susurrut: Silmon could not regard that seal with equanimity.

"Read it," suggested Anwar Das," and see."

Silmon broke the seal and scanned the letter. Anwar Das stood silently and patiently by while the older man went through the requisite stages of awe, disbelief and violent perturbation.

"Peace?" he said at last, in a strangled gasp. "Peace with Perdondaris?"

"Well, a treaty with Perdondaris," Anwar Das corrected him scrupulously. "A treaty which guarantees peace for a period of . . . pardon me, I have misremembered the precise details."

"Ten years!" The Keeper ejaculated.

"Ten years. You are right. And the review to be carried out in the ninth year, by men of wisdom and goodwill from both cities, with a guarantee that if there have been no skirmishes or debacles in that time, a second period of not less than a further decade will be agreed. Susurrut must abandon the forts on the Yildriziah, and keep the Pass Paved with Iron open to all travellers and caravans of any provenance whatsoever. These are the only stipulations."

At this point, Anwar Das's greatest ally was time. Settling back in his chair, he took a pipe and tobacco from his pack, prepared a toke and lit up, while Rudh Silmon read and reread the entire screed from its initial fanfares to its closing pomposities. Das had written it himself, so he knew these flourishes were good and needed to be savoured. Moreover, he was aware that Silmon was weighing in his mind all the implications of a peace treaty with Perdondaris, and that this weighing was likely to be a complex and protracted process.

When he had almost finished his pipe, the older man set down the scroll and fixed him with a stare. "I'm no politician," he said, stating the obvious. "These matters are not for me to decide."

"No," Anwar Das agreed. "In this place, and at this time, they are for *me* to decide. I have won the ear of the Caliph Kephiz Bin Ezvahoun, and I don't mean in a game of hazard. For the time being—who knows how long it will last?—I have his permission to broker a peace on his behalf.

"But let us be clear, Rudh Silmon. These matters do have a direct bearing on your business. Peace with your great neighbour means an opening of trade routes kept closed for whole generations. Only imagine how far you could expand your empire, and how great the house of Silmon could become!"

Silmon was imagining precisely this: Anwar Das's words merely played, like the fingers of a skilled musician, across the already tautened strings of his thoughts.

Still, the Keeper rebelled against the price that was being demanded of him. "But what you're asking in return would threaten both the city and my enterprises!" he protested.

Anwar Das met this objection with a smiling countenance. "Only if Bessa entered into direct competition with you," he said. "A second treaty could easily be drawn up, not between Bessa and Susurrut but between Bessa's merchants and yourself. A treaty not of peace but of trade and commercial strategy. If the cities of the plain were imagined as one enormous confection, concocted of fruit and sugar and covered in glazed pastry, we could agree which slices went to you and which to Bessa."

Rudh Silmon examined this comparison, and found it both potent and suggestive. "That might be done," he agreed. "But once I give you what you ask for, you'd be bound by nothing but your word."

And there they were, at last, at the point which they had always been destined to reach. This time what Anwar Das took from his sash was indeed a knife, but in the numinous strangeness of that moment, Rudh Silmon did not quail from it. "We would be bound only by our word," Das agreed. "Excellency, let me show you what the word of Bessa means." He laid his right hand down upon the table, palm down, and poised the knife above it.

"I swear," Anwar Das said, "on my rank and eminence as Bessa's ambassador to Susurrut, that at your request I will cut any finger from this hand—including the forefinger, though it would be with some sadness because I play the buzuq in a small way and it's a lot harder to strum with that particular finger missing."

The Keeper looked from the hand to the knife, and thence to Anwar Das's face. He saw only calm, cold resolution there, and he did not doubt that the ambassador meant every word he said. "I am as serious in this," Das told him, "as I am in everything I've said to you. In the past, diplomats have been famed for their lies and equivocations. The diplomats of Bessa are as truthful as priests, and there are no priests in Bessa because the Increate has not decided yet what to make of us. You may believe everything I say, Rudh Silmon. My words follow my heart, and my deeds follow my words. I, who lived for years as a thief and a murderer, swear this to you in solemn sooth."

Silmon blinked.

"The—the forefinger then," he said.

Anwar Das's hand came down, and he began to carve.

"No! No!" Silmon cried, hastily. "I require no amputations, and the inlay on that table is of cedar and mahogany! I believe you, Anwar Das. I trust your word."

"I am heartily glad of it," Anwar Das said. The knife had already broken the flesh at the base of his finger, and a single drop of blood welled there like a ruby. "Then perhaps we might turn to the items on my list."

When he left Susurrut, Anwar Das rode at the head of a caravan of forty camels. They bore in their saddlebags many tens of thousands of seeds and seed pods, from which could be grown crops of cassia and cinnamon, marjoram and cumin, fennel, nutmeg and cardamom, and a dozen spices besides. Rudh Silmon had not stinted, and indeed had added in—after a visible struggle with himself—an additional pannier of unimpressive red-brown seeds which he forbore to name. "Give them," he had told Anwar Das, "to your sultana. Tell her it is a gift from the house of Silmon."

But since Bessa had no sultana, and since the Lady Gursoon didn't know a seed pod from a stamen, he gave the pannier instead to Farhat, who by this time was so busy setting up Bessa's trade guilds that she slept standing up and could not hold a conversation lasting longer than ten heartbeats.

When she saw the contents of the pannier, Farhat gave a small yelp, like the cry of a woman at the moment of sexual release, and looked up at Anwar Das with eyes into whose corners tears threatened to come.

"What are they?" Anwar Das asked, mystified at the vehemence of her reaction.

"Zaferan," she whispered. "Crocus seeds! Oh Anwar Das, you have done a great thing."

"And without losing a single finger," Anwar Das added, which mystified the lady considerably.

They sorted out the irrigation in the second winter after the fall of Hakkim, and in the third summer, there was a swathe of desert west of Bessa where the gold of endless sand gave way to the purple of crocus fields—and thence, by arcane ministrations, to the deeper, infinitely more precious gold of saffron.

And that is how Anwar Das fulfilled his commission.

The Uses of Diplomacy

Some years after the women began to rule Bessa, it happened that Suhayb bin Hassan, the sultan of Raza, took it into his mind to attack the city. He had delayed thus far in the expectation that one of Bessa's closer neighbours would undertake the task. The town might be small, but it was known to be prosperous and undiminished by wars; and how hard could it be to take such a trinket from the hands of women? However, the local sultans seemed content to leave the prize unclaimed, and one year, when his own lands were free from unrest, Suhayb decided to act. The town would be a welcome addition to his holdings, with its wells and grazing land; besides, it might provide a useful base from which to renew the attack on his ancient enemy Sahir bin Hussein, sultan of Gharia, which was as far from Bessa to the southeast as Raza was to the east. The two sultans were cousins, and bound to each other by a long family tradition of rancour and betrayal: this new acquisition would give him a decided advantage, Suhayb thought. So he laid his plans, and sent spies to Bessa to discover the town's weaknesses.

Now it happened by coincidence that Sahir bin Hussein, impelled perhaps by a family likeness to Suhayb in habits of thought, came to the same conclusion at the same time. So it was that Zuleika, chief of the city guard in Bessa, suddenly became aware of an influx of strangers asking suspicious questions in the markets and the Jidur. By offering hospitality and strong wine to some of the younger and more swaggering of the men, her agents quickly discovered the involvement of Raza. The sultan of Gharia was a cannier man, and his operatives were both fewer and better trained. But one of them had studied at the school of Assassins, and Zuleika recognized him as he stood quietly among the gossipers at the flour-merchant's stall, gazing about him in innocent interest and buying nothing. A few discreet enquiries furnished her with the name of his current employer. The next day she called a special meeting of Bessa's council and laid her information before them.

"So it seems we have two enemies," she concluded. "From what we know of the two cousins' histories they're unlikely to be allied against us; in fact it's most likely that neither knows of the other's interest."

"Certainly Ibrahim from Raza had no idea," put in Bethi, who had accompanied her. "He thought his master would walk in and take Bessa from us single-handed."

"He said that?"

"It was somewhat muffled," Bethi said reflectively. "But I'm sure those were his words."

"Our course is clear, then," said Anwar Das. "We let each of them know of the other's interest, arrange for a few insults, and let them fight it out between themselves."

"No," said Gursoon. "No one will go to war because of us. Besides, these things have a way of spreading. I think we must settle this by diplomacy."

"My father was a friend of the father of Suhayb bin Hassan," said Imtisar. "I met them both once, before I came to Bessa. If the council will permit me, I think I could make him see reason."

The Lady Imtisar set out in state a few days later, to pay a visit to the sultan of the city of Raza. The messengers sent ahead of the party informed him that their sultana had intended to send friendly embassies to all the cities around Bessa; affairs of state had prevented her from offering this courtesy to the illustrious Suhayb bin Hassan until now, and she was anxious to remedy the oversight.

Suhayb's first thought was to turn away the embassy: what empty pretension, in a city that was about to become his subject! But he reflected that he had not opened hostilities yet, and did not want to alert his prey too early; besides, the message was delivered with a very proper humility. "Illustrious" was an especially happy touch, he thought.

He was appalled, the following evening, to see what looked like an army approaching the city gates. The Bessan ambassador was flanked by a hundred armed men, all of whose beasts needed immediate stabling.

There were a further six camels bearing gifts for the sultan: bales of fine cloth, intricately worked tapestries and flasks of golden wine. The Ambassador herself, a tall and stately woman, was dressed in richly embroidered silks, a veil concealing all but her dark eyes. She was accompanied by six younger women, all of queenly bearing, whose more diaphanous veils half-revealed faces of dazzling beauty.

Imtisar had been very precise about these attendants. They included Jumanah, whom the ambassador had come to love almost as a daughter, and Jumanah's bosom companion Najla. There was also Binan, who was now in paid employment as hairdresser to the three ladies: a statuesque young woman of surpassing skill in her profession but very few words. "Binan? Are you sure?" Zuleika had asked. "I don't see her as a diplomat."

"Trust me," Imtisar replied.

The six ladies stood demurely behind the Ambassador, maintaining propriety, as she sat with the sultan in his audience chamber and accepted from his servant a cup of her own city's wine. Suhayb was finding himself somewhat at a loss. There was a protocol for such meetings—ritual courtesies followed by empty promises; threats, veiled or otherwise; competitive displays of wealth or force leading to the climbdown and acquiescence of one side, usually the guest. But the Bessan Ambassador was not adhering to the rules. She smiled and asked him about the grain crop in Raza, which had been bountiful that year. She seemed genuinely interested, and none of Suhayb's conversational sallies could distract her. Worse, whenever for a moment his eyes strayed from those of the Ambassador, he could not avoid the sight of her retinue: standing like guards, but with the faces and bodies of peris. The very air of his chamber seemed full of a subtle and insidious perfume.

"So, lady," he said, essaying for the third or fourth time to turn the conversation his own way. "Your guard . . . an impressive body of men, and well turned out. But such a force: are you not taking from your city's defences?"

The Ambassador laughed, like the tinkling of little bells. "Oh, it's true, I suppose," she said. "I begged them not to send so many, but Bessa values the safety of its envoys. But we have many more. And then, of course, there's always the citizen army."

"The citizen . . . ?" said Suhayb, gripped by a sudden unease.

"Oh yes," said the lady. "Had you not heard? Every man and woman in the city is a trained soldier. And every child over fourteen. That's how we took the city in the first place, of course. And in recognition of their victory, the sultana decreed that everyone would have a say in making the laws of the city, through the Jidur; so now the citizens will defend her with their lives. It's worked very well, we found."

The sultan was momentarily speechless. The young women behind the Ambassador, as if sensing his discomfort, stood a little more to attention: he saw the breasts of the tallest shifting beneath her tight tunic. "Your . . . attendants too?" he managed. "They fight?"

The lady laughed again. "Trained soldiers, every one of them," she assured him. "Though a friend such as yourself, Excellency, will never see them doing anything so ungentle."

"It must be a barbarous place!" the sultan exclaimed. Strangely, the monstrous knowledge did not make the young women one whit less attractive. The tallest of them bared a flash of teeth in what looked like a smile, and for a moment Suhayb's gaze was caught in hers like a fly in amber.

"Somewhat barbarous," the Ambassador agreed cheerfully. "But very safe. And also most comfortable." She raised her cup to him, and the sultan signalled his servant for more: it was, indeed, excellent wine. "I entreat you to be our guest soon, Excellency; you must allow us to return your hospitality."

This time the tallest of the women did smile at him, in a way that indicated he would be made very welcome indeed.

When the delegation left the next day, the sultan was unwontedly thoughtful. It seemed to him, on mature reflection, that Bessa might, after all, have its uses as an ally. Of course, he could not agree a treaty with women—not in his own house—and the lady had shown too much delicacy to suggest such a thing. Nevertheless, he resolved that he would indeed visit Bessa, and soon. The promised welcome of the tall young woman should not be spurned. And who knew how many others like her the city might hold?

So, from a combination of caution and lust, the sultan of Raza suspended his plans to attack the city.

The Lady Imtisar's approach to Sahir bin-Hussein, sultan of Gharia, was more circumspect. The initial messengers were less florid in their greetings; the gifts were fewer, the trappings of the embassy less rich, and while the escort of a hundred men was still felt to be prudent, Imtisar was accompanied by only two ladies.

As before, the sultan received the Ambassador and her attendants in a private audience chamber. He kept his vizier with him, however, the same graduate of the assassins' school that Zuleika had recognized back in the market of Bessa. This man was his chief adviser, and had been the subject of much discussion between Imtisar, Zuleika and Gursoon before the second embassy was dispatched.

"He's known as Kedr," Zuleika told them. "It's not the name he had when I knew him, but that's usual in his profession."

"Which is?"

Zuleika shrugged. "Fixer. Enforcer. One who removes the barriers to a man's ambition, for a high price. He was known as a sneaky little bastard even by the assassins' standards, and particularly mercenary. If he is the one making Gharia's policy, the sultan must value profit above all else."

"Is he clever?" Gursoon asked.

"Up to a point. He trusts no one and does his own investigating; that's bad. But he has his blind spots. He thinks everyone is stupider than himself. And in the market that day I looked him in the face, and he didn't know me."

In the sultan's audience room, the vizier looked at the Ambassador with a professional indifference, and at her ladies not at all. The sultan himself seemed barely more impressed, though he spared Najla an appraising glance. But he greeted the women civilly enough, and responded to the Ambassador's queries about harvests and prices, while plying her with her own wine.

"We are forging trade links with all our neighbours," she told him, accepting her fourth cup. "Free trade is so important, don't you think?"

"Indeed, lady," the sultan said. "Though I fear that our current suppliers will not welcome the competition."

The Ambassador seemed not to hear him. "For instance," she went on, her speech slurring a little in her enthusiasm, "I probably shouldn't tell you this, but we're about to form an alliance with the city of your cousin, the esteemed Suhayb bin Hassan."

"Indeed," answered Sahir, whose spies had reported no such thing. He glanced briefly at his vizier, who gave a fractional shake of the head. Behind the Ambassador, her two attendants exchanged dismayed looks, and one stepped forward, laying her hand on her mistress's shoulder.

"My lady . . ." she began.

"Not now, Jumanah," the Ambassador said, removing the hand. She turned back to Sahir, her eyes bright with eagerness. The sultan motioned to his servant to fill her cup again. "Do tell me more, lady," he said.

"Well," she said. "It's a matter of the utmost secrecy, but since you and he are family . . . You know that Raza has a huge corn surplus this year?"

Sahir did indeed know this, and had been watching the resultant fall in prices with interest, but he shook his head. The lady drained her cup and leaned forward.

"It's worked out so well for us," she confided. "Our harvest this year was poor—the dust storms came early, and nearly half was spoiled." Her voice dropped. "We've kept it quiet till now. But the truth is, there's nothing left in the granaries. We were staring famine in the face. And then we heard that Raza has a surplus! How wonderful! Our envoys are heading there right now, prepared to pay full price for their entire crop. You see what I mean, Excellency? The benefits of trade. We are saved from our little difficulty. And your cousin avoids a fall in price which would impoverish his merchants, and ultimately the whole city."

The vizier stepped forward and spoke into his master's ear.

"You are indeed fortunate," Sahir said. "And when does this sale take place?"

Both of the Ambassador's attendants stepped forward. Jumanah touched her mistress on the shoulder again.

"My lady," she said quietly. "It grows late. "Do you think that perhaps . . . ?"

The Lady Imtisar could make a hiccup sound decorous.

"Is it so late, dear?" she said. "Just one more cup, then. You'll join me, Excellency?"

"And drink to free trade," said the sultan gravely.

The Ambassador and her ladies slept late the next morning. Long before they had roused themselves and assembled their men, the vizier Kedr had departed on the sultan's fastest camel for Raza, where he astonished the chief corn merchant by offering full price for the city's entire stock. So much did he buy that Raza itself was left with local shortages for some weeks afterwards.

Several notable events resulted from the Lady Imtisar's second embassy.

Sahir bin-Hussein readied his armies and waited several weeks for news of famine and unrest in Bessa, which would be his signal to advance. Hearing nothing, he sent his spies again to the city, who returned bewildered to report its continued peace and prosperity. Sahir turned his fury on his vizier, and in the resulting quarrel Kedr left the sultan's service for new employment.

On that same day an unexpected message arrived from Raza. Suhayb bin Hassan had learned of Sahir's purchase of the grain surplus, and could find no other motive for it than a friendly overture. Mystified, he concluded that his cousin had suffered a softening of the brain, and after some thought, decided to take advantage of this weakness through an overture of his own. He offered a good price for some of Gharia's longhorn sheep, which he had long coveted. A rapprochement ensued between the cousins, which lasted for several years.

The Bessan embassy returned home quietly. A few weeks later, when news arrived of the vizier Kedr's departure from Gharia, a party of celebration was held in the former baker's shop. The dancing spilled out into the square, and heroic quantities of wine were drunk.

"Of all your manifold achievements, lady," Anwar Das said to Imtisar, "this is the one that most fills me with admiration. You drank seven cups of the three-year-old wine, and could still walk? And talk?"

"Seven cups," confirmed Jumanah, with some pride.

"I have a good head," said Imtisar complacently. "Of course, this helped a little."

She held up a leather pouch, wide-lipped and suspended from two strings. "I had it concealed beneath my veil. The girls and I designed it together: with a little practice you can dispose of the drink very neatly. We shared it on the way home."

The final consequence of these events was perhaps the strangest. For a full year the city of Gharia experienced a glut of flour, which led several enterprising tradesmen to set up shop as bakers. As a result, the city developed a flourishing trade in pies and baked goods, for which it became famous. A distinctive knobbly pastry named the Suhayb was celebrated throughout the region for a hundred years afterwards: in fact it became one of Gharia's staple trading items with the city of Bessa.

REVOLUTIONS

There was once a prince, who became something less than a prince; or at least, something different. He became a citizen; a man with no honorifics; an equal, lost from sight among his equals. It was not what he had sought, or what he had expected, and it took a heavy toll on him. In the end, it placed a strain on him that was beyond his endurance, and it turned him into something else again.

The prince's name, as you've probably already guessed, was Jamal.

He was the son of a sultan—Bokhari Al-Bokhari, the ruler of Bessa—but it was not to be expected that he would ever become a sultan himself. His mother, Oosa, was the youngest of the sultan's wives, and therefore, in the palace's strict pecking order, the least of them. Jamal had seventeen legitimate brothers, all older than him and higher in the strict ranks of succession. His lot in life was to be pampered, to be cared for, to be pleasured, to be deferred to by the lower orders, and beyond that to be ignored.

But Jamal's nature was both curious and restless, and he did not submit to that fate as willingly as you might imagine. Imprisoned within the palace walls for most of his waking life, he explored as much of that little world as he could. He visited the ostlers in the stables, the cooks and acaters in the kitchen, the soldiers in the guard house, the falconers in the mews, the viziers and diplomats in the chancellery, the turnkeys in the oubliette, the scribes in the scriptorium, the smiths and potters and silkmakers and horners and lapidaries in their various workshops. All of these persons were, of course, obliged to receive him courteously, and to answer his questions, so in each place he learned; and in some, perhaps, more than in others.

Jamal also spent a great deal of time in the seraglio, with his illegitimate half-brothers and half-sisters—the children of the concubines. These bastards could not inherit and therefore were mostly invisible, passed over in the palace intrigues that so engrossed those born on the right side of the sheets. Being eighteenth in line, Jamal was almost as negligible as they, but still he had the cachet of being able, when he chose, to enter the royal apartments without being challenged—and to summon or dismiss a guard. The bastard children, though they tried their best to hide it, were impressed by these appurtenances of power and prestige—and Jamal, for his part, found in their grudging admiration a welcome relief from the indifference, bordering on contempt, that he met from the other royal princes.

It was a strange childhood, and it probably wasn't going anywhere good. The death of the sultan, when it came, was likely to precipitate a great bloodletting among his heirs, and if civil strife was to be avoided, only one could be allowed to survive and flourish. Jamal could not hope to be that one, unless his father survived for long enough for him to reach his majority, and so death or exile would most likely be his fate.

But then came the rise of the Ascetics, and of their terrifying leader, Hakkim Mehdad. The city was torn apart by sudden and unexpected insurgency. Suddenly, all bets were off. The upside of that was that all the other princes of the royal bloodline were killed in a single day; the downside was that Jamal was obliged to flee the city in the company of the concubines and the bastards. He was first in line, but to a throne that now harboured the hindquarters of a usurper.

It was an upheaval beyond anything the boy could have imagined. He was then but twelve years old, and it was as if he had been plucked physically out of the life that he had known, erased and rewound, scraped like a manuscript whose surface must now bear fresh inscription.

Against all the odds, he found the strength within himself to resist that dissolution. He held on to his sense of who he was, though there was nobody with whom he could discuss it.

As himself, he wielded his sling to save the warrior-whore, Zuleika, from the usurper's soldiery.

As himself, he trained the children in the desert to defend themselves against attack, and helped with the building of the dust-raisers.

As himself, he rode in the vanguard of the false army, when his petition to fight in the true one had been denied.

And the city was recaptured, the usurper cast down, and that was the end of it all, or should have been. But the women seemed determined to see it as a beginning.

On the day of victory, after the death of the accursed Hakkim, there were many tasks that Jamal felt were incumbent on him to perform.

The first was the despoiling of the usurper's body. Jamal found the ex-sultan in his throne room, sprawled across the lowest steps that led up to the throne itself. Nobody had stayed to watch over it once he was dead, which shocked and angered Jamal. It could so easily have been stolen by one of the fleeing Ascetics, and afterwards given decent burial. It could have become a place of pilgrimage.

Whatever Rem had done to Hakkim had left him whole, though the look of horror on his frozen features was certainly gratifying. With a sharp knife, Jamal first blinded the corpse in both its eyes, thereby blinding the spirit also. Then, steeling himself for the repellent task, he slit open the belly, found after a few moments' groping the nested whorls of the dead man's intestines and hauled them out. In the process he must have punctured them slightly, for a foul smell washed over Jamal and made him nauseous; he had to bend his head to his knees and draw a few shallow, shuddering breaths of cleaner air. The usurper's tongue and the usurper's manhood had both to be dealt with, but the boy's eyes were swimming and his arms felt nerveless and weak.

The tongue. He knew, in theory, what was to be done. You made an incision across the throat and dragged the tongue out at its base, so that it lay across the chest like a scarf or a blazon. But the throat was already damaged, mangled, and he couldn't find the tongue: though he delved and rummaged deeply, there was nothing within the blood-black pit he'd hacked out with his blade that would yield to being pulled forth. In the end, his hands trembling now, Jamal was forced to reach into the mouth, cut away the portion of the tongue that he could reach and lay it on the chest like the fleshy petal of a ruined flower.

The manhood was easier, but there was nowhere to burn it once it was cut away. Jamal wandered around the royal apartments, looking for a brazier that was still lit and becoming ever more frantic and furious when he failed to find one.

Zuleika found him there, at last, with Hakkim's sawn-off pizzle dangling forlornly in his grip and submerged tears shaking his frame. She took in the scene, and knew at once what it was he had meant to do. Finding oil and a tinder, she quickly made a pyre in a bowl that had held scented water, and then stepped back from it.

"Whenever you're ready," she told Jamal.

When the rest of the concubines entered a minute or so later, they found the woman and the boy standing side by side over the bowl of burning oil, within which something black and shapeless fried. The air was filled with a smell that belonged in equal parts to the charnel house and the kitchen.

"What has he done?" Gursoon asked Zuleika. Her voice was tight with repressed anger.

"He's despoiled the body," Zuleika explained. "Hakkim killed his father and his mother. There was a blood-debt to be paid."

Gursoon frowned. "I had meant to give the body to his followers," she said. "It would have been the best way to soothe their feelings, and might have headed off further bloodletting. Now we can't even let them see him, and they'll know why."

"There was a blood-debt," Zuleika repeated.

"And now there'll be more of them."

"Perhaps. Yes."

Jamal's next duty, he decided, should be to oversee the execution of the Ascetics and palace guards who had been taken alive. He said as much, as soon as he felt sure that his voice would not shake. But here he came up against Gursoon's will in a more direct way, and he did not carry it.

"There'll be no massacres," the older woman told him, grimly. "We didn't come here for that. And we didn't cast Hakkim down so that we could become Hakkim in our turn." She looked to Zuleika, as though she expected to be challenged. Zuleika only shrugged: she had her own opinions, clearly, but she did not voice them.

The question of what to do with the prisoners was shelved, for the time being. That left Jamal's address to his loyal subjects, and here, too, he was overruled.

"Why would you wish to speak to them?" Gursoon asked him. "What do you think has happened here?"

"The usurper has been cast down," Jamal said. "The bloodline has been restored. Why? What do you think has happened?"

Surprisingly, it was not Gursoon but Zuleika who answered him.

"Bessa has been liberated," she said. "It belongs to no one now, but only to itself. That is what we said we'd do, and that is what we've done. Jamal, there is no bloodline. There is no sultan. Nobody here wants to invent one."

On some level, he had already known this. It was a forlorn and weak part of him that had hoped—or rather pretended—that the past could somehow be restored. It couldn't: the past was dead, along with so much else. He made no protest, and indeed no answer at all. In any event, no answer seemed to be required. Gursoon and the armed women with her went on with their task of securing the palace compound, which they intended to use as a base. They paid Jamal no further heed.

Zuleika went with him to find his parents' graves, and he was grateful to her for that, but it was a gratitude that held itself—by necessity— aloof. He couldn't permit himself to depend on her any more, as he had in the desert. It was not clear to him yet what he would become, in this new morning that smelled of blood and spilled incense. Himself, of course— but he had a child's intuition that there might be many versions of him, a breath or a thought away from incarnation, and that any commitments he might make now would be voided when one or other of these Jamals was born. Better to look inwards, and wait.

In the event, there were no graves. Whatever Hakkim had done with the bodies of Bokhari Al-Bokhari, his wives, and the royal princes and princesses, he had left no trace. There was a fire pit, too far from the kitchen to be of any practical use in cooking, and it had seen extensive use; there was nothing else, and the bones in the pit had been smashed into pieces so small that they might have been anything.

"I'm sorry," Zuleika said.

Jamal bowed his head, and she let her hand rest on his shoulder. He wanted to tell her how he had felt, first when he watched her fighting in the desert, a storm of violent possibilities discharging in such a narrow space, and then again, later, when he saw her naked in the water. But this was not the time. So he stood in silence, mourning his mother more than his father, and perhaps himself more than either of them. Finally Zuleika left him there, to work through the logic of his grief.

He had plenty of time to do this, in the five years that followed, but in many ways the project evaded him. It was as though his feelings remained in that state of suspension which his twelve-year-old self had thought was momentary: as though he still stood beside the fire pit, staring at bones which told no tales and cast no auguries. Alone among those who had fled into the desert—or at least, so it seemed to him—Jamal found no point of attachment to this new Bessa to which they had returned. He could not seem to find a map of it within his mind.

Discouraged and even a little shamed by that incapacity, he sank into a kind of depression, or a paralysis which was not quite depression because within it all emotions, even grief, seemed dulled and unreal. His life had stopped, and it was clearly in no hurry to resume. He even contemplated suicide, and purchased from a former Ascetic a poison of such potency—allegedly—that a single drop of it would kill a great multitude. But Jamal's will was paralysed. All he ever did with the poison was to take it out and look at it from time to time, touch his lips to the glass and tilt the bottle so that it seemed as though he was sipping from it. A man cannot die from such things; in their default, he dies from other things that work more slowly.

In the wider world around Jamal, many things of great import happened. The concubines formed a government, which considered by its own lights did reasonably well—it took a chaotic situation and introduced a modicum of order into it. But that was all it could do, ultimately. It could not remove the chaos, because it depended on the arbitrary interplay of too many different personalities. The women refused to nominate a leader: worse, whether naively or knowingly, they instituted rules and customs which prevented a leader from emerging.

Jamal tried to explain this once, to the librarian, Rem, who chronicled the debates in the Jidur and composed the wording of the written laws on which the women placed such fanatical emphasis. Rem seemed to understand what Jamal was trying to say, but not to sympathise.

"So you're talking about a model where one person gets to run the state and embodies its laws?"

"Yes."

"Sorry, Jamal. It's shit. It happens a lot, but it's shit every time. The trouble is, the one person who gets to run things is just as conflicted—just as big a mess—as any random man or woman you pass in the street. You say committees lead to chaos? Well, every one of us is a committee inside—lots of desires and instincts and ideas and unexamined beliefs, all pulling in different directions. Every king is a committee. The trick isn't to eliminate the conflict, it's to make a machine—a state—that allows every idea to be fed into the hopper and somehow winnows out the ones that are crazy or sick or stupid or unworkable. That's what the Jidur is. What we want it to be, anyway."

She tried to explain to Jamal the functioning of a device she called a centrifuge, but the words mostly washed over him. Watching her speak, but not really listening, he was amazed at how she had changed from the silent and tentative creature they had saved in the desert. Where had this confidence, this eloquence, come from?

Wherever it had come from, it was resistant to reason. It was the antithesis of reason, in most respects: the concatenation of words in defence of nonsense and error. But to rebut her required more effort and persistence than he could sustain, and it would have served no purpose in any case, even if his words were as sharp as caltrops. The whole city was moving, on a vector he could deplore but not alter: you could throw caltrops in front of a man on a galloping camel, but not in front of a city.

By this time, Jamal was living in a single room above the street of the silversmiths. Most of its extent was taken up by his bed roll, and the rest, by a few scrolls, a few amphoras of wine, a brace of swords and two of daggers, the sling with which he had once saved Zuleika's life, and whatever girl he was currently sleeping with. The source of his income—and the reason for his lodgings—was a mass of silver plates and goblets, exquisitely worked, that he had taken from the palace on the day of its sacking and now sold at a judicious rate. Because he did not take any of his lovers into his trust, the silver was hidden in the roof space above the apartment's ceiling, covered with a rotting curtain.

He seemed to be the only one of the desert company who had been reduced to such degrading circumstances. The bastard princelings and their bastard half-sisters had mostly thrown themselves into the service of the new state with great enthusiasm. Jamal saw them sometimes, striding through the streets with letters in their hands and purposeful looks on their faces, or reading proclamations in the streets about some or other piece of newly minted morality: no citizen to be beaten, whether by employer, husband or guard; selling of brides to be outlawed; price of grain to be fixed by strict tariff, and public granaries to be maintained against times of famine. It was an industry. They were industrious. He was anything but.

His real link to the world—to a world that still moved and meant— was Zuleika. She would visit him once every few days, drink a glass or two of wine with him, and tell him about the many trials involved in folding the remnants of the old palace guard and the many raw recruits into a new citizen militia; turning human ploughshares into swords; weeding out Ascetic cells still loyal to Hakkim; squeezing money for new fortifications from an appropriations committee more interested in schools and lazarets.

He listened, commiserated with her complaints, laughed at her jokes, and told her nothing in return about his own life—because what there was to tell was what she could see all around her. There was no more.

One night, finally, after more of these chaste visits than Jamal could count and more (it seemed) than he could endure, he yielded to half-drunken desire and kissed her. She didn't resist, but neither did she respond. When he broke the contact, looking at her for some clue as to whether or not he should continue, she put her hand to his cheek and met his gaze in silence for a few seconds.

"It wouldn't work," she said at last.

"Why not?" Jamal blurted, both hurt and piqued by her indifference. "You were a concubine. I presume you know how."

Zuleika nodded. "Oh yes. But I was bedded by your father. And I knew you when you were a child. There's a line of poetry somewhere . . . How does it go? *We do not sow the flower, or eat the seed.*"

"It's *sow the rose,*" Jamal corrected her coldly. "And I'm hardly a seed. And in any case, since when do you quote poetry? I thought the only poetry you made was with something sharp in your hands."

"A stylus is sharp," Zuleika said. She said it lightly, smiling, but some distance had fallen between them. Jamal knew that it would take more than words to bridge it, but her rejection had closed off all other options. Words would have to do.

"I feel a kinship with you," he told her, urgently. "I've felt it ever since we met. Ever since the desert. I think if I had you, I could be happy even here."

She raised an eyebrow. "Even here?"

He raised both hands to indicate the room, the contents of the room, the narrow confines of his life. But he meant more than that, and he knew that she had read more into it.

Zuleika drained her glass and stood. "Better get back to the barracks," she said. "If there's anything left of it by this time."

"Very well," Jamal said stiffly. "I'll see you."

She took up her sword belt from where it lay on the floor beside her, and put it on. She always removed it when she sat with him—a gesture which (given that this was Zuleika) had about it a thrilling intimacy.

"I'll see you," she echoed him.

But she did not return, either that week or the next. Then the dark of the moon came and went without her visiting him. Jamal knew that his kiss—or else his words, or else some combination of both—had precipitated a crisis, and that it had resolved in the wrong way for him. Sleepless in his narrow bed, he replayed the embrace and the conversation again and again, both as it had happened and with more satisfactory outcomes. Sometimes he forced Zuleika and she yielded to him, at first reluctantly but then with ever-increasing ardour; sometimes he did not kiss her at all. Either way, the world he rose to the next morning was one in which he was alone on a mattress drenched not with the sweat of love but with that of summer insomnia.

Jamal was prey to his own obsessions: he had no work to shield him from their heat. He went to the barracks, and walked endlessly past its closed doors in the hope that he might accidentally meet her coming out. Then he asked a soldier where she lodged, and was given an address near the spice market. So he went and loitered there instead.

And there, on the third night, he saw her. It was very late; after moonrise. He was leaning in a doorway, in deep shadow, half-dozing, when the sound of footsteps echoing on stone roused him. Looking up, he saw her coming towards him. She was only a silhouette, lit from behind by the light of a watchman's brazier, but she was still unmistakeable: nobody else walked with such a mixture of unselfconscious grace and predatory alertness. A shorter and slighter figure walked beside her, and now rested his head upon Zuleika's shoulder in a way that made Jamal's pulse stammer unpleasantly.

They stopped almost directly opposite him, at the door of the house: so close that he could have leaned forward and touched them.

"I think you're drunk," Zuleika told her companion.

"On a single glass of wine!" the other protested. Jamal knew the voice, but the street was lighter here and he had already recognized her: it was the librarian.

"Perhaps you're one of those people who can't handle their drink," Zuleika said. They were facing each other now, and very close.

"I haven't sobered up since I met you," Rem said, and pulled her closer still. There was no kiss: he might have fled or cried out or attacked them if there had been a kiss. But the librarian merely laid her cheek alongside Zuleika's cheek, and for a moment or two, in silence, they breathed the same air.

"Stay with me tonight," Zuleika suggested.

"I can't," Rem whispered. "I've got two bills to write for tomorrow's session."

"But you write the agenda, too."

"So?"

"So put them last."

Rem laughed, scandalised, compromised, surrendering. They went inside together and Jamal stepped out of the dark as though drawn after them on a string: stepped up to the closed door and laid his palms against it. The wood was hot under his hands. Just the day's heat locked in the wood, for the building faced west, but he imagined for a dizzying moment that it was the heat of their bodies he felt, radiating outwards through the substance of the building.

Jamal had a vision, then. His mind filled with images and ideas, which—though they broke and reformed like the glitter of light on wind-whipped water—all seemed inextricably and profoundly connected: the city; his father; the usurper; Gursoon; the last embrace his mother had given him, and the knife he had wielded to make Hakkim Mehdad's body unfit for paradise; Zuleika's lips, and the stone he had fired in the desert. He looked inward, and saw his destiny written where it had always been, upon the vaulted inner surfaces of his own skull.

When at last he turned away from the door, he did so with the slow, exploratory steps of a man carrying a heavy weight that threatened to overbalance him. It seemed as though fate and history bore in upon him from either side, and he had to balance their opposed forces with each rise and fall of his own encumbered feet.

Jamal would describe, later, a dream he had that night. In the dream he wandered a vast desert, with a blindfold upon his eyes and his hands bound before him at the wrists. Then a voice—he thought it was his father's—spoke in his ear. "You are not bound," it said, "if you choose to be free."

Whereupon the ropes and the blindfold fell away. And from the tears of his eyes, an oasis sprang. And cradled in his hands, when he opened them, was a city, which grew to fill his vision. And he laughed, even as he slept, because he knew in his innermost heart that this was no dream at all but a vision, like the visions vouchsafed to marabouts and madmen. It was ordained: in the fullness of time, Bessa would be his.

All of this was true: and when Jamal spoke of it, the truth spilled from his eyes as the water had spilled in the dream, so that few found the will to doubt him. But whenever he retold this, he omitted one detail. In his vision, when he entered the gates of the city and walked in triumph through its streets, he found it peopled only with the dead—and though they bowed and salaamed to him, they did so in a dread and intimidating silence.

From the next day, Jamal began the process of recruiting an army, his purpose being to reclaim the city of his forefathers from the concubines who had stolen it.

He made slow progress at first. The memory of Hakkim's rule was fresh in people's minds, and most were well aware that the state in which they lived now—the rule of all, through the messy and wondrous mechanism of the Jidur—was far better than that which they had known before. It's hard to foment revolution in a time of peace and plenty.

Hard, but not impossible. Even in Heaven there will be malcontents, and Bessa (though the concubinate strove mightily and continuously) was not Heaven. Some men who were bemused by the prominence of women's voices in the Jidur found in this anomaly a plausible explanation for the failure of their own enterprises, whether romantic or commercial. Some had done well out of the old regime—that is to say the old, old regime of Al-Bokhari—and wanted it restored. Some were drawn in by Jamal's eloquence, or by the suasion of their friends, or by a love of adventure and intrigue for their own sake. Some, no doubt, wished only to make mischief, or hoped to thrive on the chaos that war brings in its wake.

So, by inches and ounces, Jamal filled out his muster, and began to cut and shape them to the great purpose of revolution. Most were thwart and unpromising, it must be said, but revolutions require dry tinder as well as flame. And there was flame enough in some of those who signed on with him to make of Bessa a furnace: the crucible into which the present, being cast, sighs forth its dross and so becomes the future.

The garnering of funds, the procuring of a base of operations in a disused cloaca, the purchase and smuggling in of weapons, the drilling of his cohorts in the use of said weapons, the reconnoitring and planning, the assignment of tasks and responsibilities, all things were spun out of

Jamal's relentless will as a spider spins silk out of its innards. Nothing happened without his word. All things bore his imprint, and in their turn they imprinted him.

It was a mystery. He had seemed to himself for years now, ever since the day of the concubines' triumphant return, a man made out of shadow. He had hoped that Zuleika might make him real again, and in a sense she had—but only by rejecting him. His project of violence and insurrection was now become the solid core of him, a knot of purpose intertwined endlessly with the knot of his grief and the knot of his unspoken love.

The day was set, and the plans laid. Some of Jamal's lieutenants had seen the Jidur as the main target, and had assumed that their primary goal would be to occupy and hold it. He told them to dismiss it from their minds: not only was the great square, with so many arteries opening off it, almost impossible to defend, it was also completely irrelevant, except as a symbol—and symbolism could wait.

The targets for the first phase of the day's action, he told them, would be the former bakers' shop where the lawmakers met and the headquarters and satellite stations of the city militia—in that order.

At the house of the lawmakers they would find Gursoon, along with most or perhaps all of her inner circle of planners and advisers: isolating them would ensure that there would be no citywide response to his insurrection until it was too late. The librarian would be there too, of course, but that was a matter of far less importance. For all her arcane knowledge and unsettling insights, Rem spoke seldom. Her role in the business of state was mostly as a recorder, and today, Jamal mused pleasantly, he would provide plenty of matter for her pen.

Zuleika's well-drilled militia squads, meanwhile, would respond with speed to any threat: Jamal had factored that readiness and efficiency into his plans. The rebels would set up plausible crises—fires, vandalism, random affrays—in many parts of the city. The sites for these provocations had been carefully chosen; when the militia units responded, they would find themselves trapped in blind alleys or other indefensible spaces. Archers and slingmen would pin them down, and slaughter them if they refused to drop their weapons and yield.

The second phase would be to secure the palace—the guards there were mostly volunteers, with a purely symbolic function, and they would offer no resistance. Jamal would install himself there, and from that beachhead he would send messengers abroad to reassure the citizenry. He wanted no general riot, and as few civilian casualties as could be managed. The guards aside, he wanted this to be a bloodless coup. He saw it in his mind's eye as an act of surgery, a therapeutic intervention into the city's life, and a surgery could not be counted successful if—in the course of excising a cancer, say—the patient died. No doubt, too, he was mindful of his dream, and wished to avoid the direst of its predictions, the transformation of Bessa into a citywide mausoleum populated only by the dead.

The day came. Jamal and his lieutenants met for the last time, and he gave them the word for which they waited so long: "Begin." They went forth, each man (he had chosen to recruit no women) to his separate station. Jamal remained behind at his headquarters, from where he would communicate with his lieutenants by means of swift runners; in the second phase, he would command the composite force that attacked the palace, but in the first place, when there were so many separate actions to orchestrate, he kept aloof from all so that he could command and amend any one at need.

The preordained moment was the start of the fifth watch, when shadows having lengthened start to join and the sun dips his head into the bowl of night to be washed clean for the morrow morn. That moment came and went in silence, as of course it would: the decimation of the city guard and the mass arrest of the lawmakers were now in train, but they were happening in other parts of the city. Jamal felt a prickling in his scalp and at the nape of his neck as he watched the last grains of sand slide through the hourglass, and as he picked it up to turn it. The hour just ended was the last of the old dispensation: the hour whose first grains were now starting to spill was the first of a new age.

There were eight runners, four of whom had remained behind with Jamal while the other four went with the most important of the ambush parties. This arrangement seemed to Jamal to offer the maximum flexibility, allowing him to send an immediate response to any situation that arose, while still allowing the incoming runner a few moments' respite before requiring him to take to his feet again.

But the minutes passed, the sand trickled down through the glass, and no runners came. At first, Jamal was encouraged by this: it seemed to vindicate the excessive detail of his planning. But soon doubts began to assail him. It was inconceivable that everything should have gone off without a single setback or complication; much more likely that his lieutenants had broken discipline and were improvising on the fly rather than using the runners to report to him and take instruction.

In the end, his restlessness and curiosity got the better of him; he couldn't just sit there while the battles were being fought, and his fate decided, in scattered places throughout the city. He sent the runners to four of his ambush squads to tell them that he would be with the fifth, at the Eastern Gate. Then he set off through the darkening streets at a rapid walk.

Long before he drew near his destination, Jamal knew for certain that something was wrong. The people walking by in the street were too calm, and too intent upon their own business. By now, the rumours of armed clashes, of fires, of mayhem and murder, should have begun to spread. Panic or prurience, away from the violence or towards it, there should be no movement that was not full of purpose. The heartbeat of the city was healthful and measured, when it should be pounding like a war drum.

At the Eastern Gate there was nothing. Jamal's ambush squad was nowhere to be seen, and he could see no evidence that they had ever been there. The shed they were meant to have torched stood untouched, still stacked with tinder and barrels of oil.

Jamal went to the site of the second ambush, although it had already occurred to him by now that he should have met his own runner coming back; emptiness and silence once again met his eyes, and he could not hide from the obvious conclusion. All had miscarried, in some inexplicable way. There was no point even in returning to the sewer to await his squads' return, since if they had been intercepted they would only return to lead the militia to his door, and if they had reneged out of fear they would not return at all.

He went instead to his own rooms, intending to gather the few belongings he deemed worth saving and the pieces of palace silver he had not yet sold. It was full night when he arrived there, and as silent as the grave. The day of revolution had come and gone, and the city had not even noticed it. Full to the brim with bitter sorrow, he threw open his door and walked inside, registering a moment too late that the lamp was already lit.

Zuleika was sitting on the divan, where he had so often imagined her. In his imaginings, though, she had almost never held a naked sword in her hand.

Jamal took a step back, not from fear but from surprise, and then hesitated on the brink of flight.

"How far do you think you'd get?" Zuleika asked him. "Seriously?"

Jamal shrugged and sat down, choosing—since the divan was already taken—a wooden stool that stood beneath the open window. He poured himself a goblet of wine from an amphora he'd opened four days ago. It had already spoiled in the heat, but he wasn't thirsty in any case—the only merit the gesture had was its threadbare bravado.

"So you had a spy among my people," he guessed.

"We had seven spies among your people," Zuleika corrected him. "And two more among the merchants you bought your weapons from."

Jamal took a sip of the sour wine, and forced it down. "Then why not move against me sooner?" he demanded, fighting the urge to retch.

Zuleika made a small gesture with the sword—a gesture that implied the cutting of a thread. "It suited me to know who was unhappy," she said. "Unhappy enough to take up arms, I mean. The ones who oppose us in the Jidur are at liberty to do so, Gursoon says. Personally, I'd cut all of their throats, but the tenor of the times is against such things."

"So?" Jamal asked. He put down his glass and readied himself. If he took the vinegar taste of that wine down into the underworld with him, so be it: there was nothing of sweetness left in him anyway.

"So," Zuleika said. "The ringleaders will be exiled, without pardon or remission. The rank and file will be pardoned, but will be given to understand that they've used up all the goodwill we care to give them."

"And me?"

Zuleika stood, and faced him. "My orders are that you are to be taken alive, and tried in the Jidur," she told him. "The citizens will decide your fate. In other words—"

Jamal rose too, his hand on the hilt of his blade. "In other words, you're to bring me in alive so they can vote on how to kill me."

"It's not my wish, nor Gursoon's. It was decided by the council that deals with city security. We're not the government, Jamal. The people are the government."

Jamal expressed with an obscene oath what he thought of that proposition. Suddenly, he remembered the pharmacon—the poison which he had never used, because the right state of mind had always evaded him. A wild scheme rose in his mind, inchoate and foul. "Drink with me?" he asked Zuleika. "One last time?"

Zuleika stared at him for a long moment. "I'm not thirsty," she said at last.

No. Of course not. Only in stories do warriors trust their enemies to that extent. And perhaps, now, he had revealed something of his soul to her that she hadn't seen before. He felt ashamed, and in some way that he didn't understand, the shame gave him strength. He drew his sword and beckoned her to come. "It will be here, then," he said, between bared teeth. "And it will be now."

But Zuleika slid her own blade back into its sheath, and dropped her hands to her sides. "Indeed," she said. "It would have been here, and it would have been now. But when I came to your house, expecting that you might return there, I found that you'd already been and gone. The place was stripped bare, indicating that you had no intention of ever returning. It's personally shaming to me that I didn't think to station a guard or two there to detain you. But nobody is infallible, I suppose."

She stepped within the reach of Jamal's sword, and he couldn't decide in that surreal, frightening moment whether it was a gesture of trust or one of contempt—whether she knew he would not strike her or was only certain that if he tried she could disarm him before he offered her any hurt.

She kissed him on the cheek.

"Be well," she said. "Find a place a long way from here. Marry, and have children. Try out what life is like, before you flirt with other people's deaths again."

He laughed—or at least, he made a sound that started out as a laugh. "An assassin tells me that!" he said.

Her hand caressed the back of his neck, and for a moment he was a twelve-year-old boy again, howling and weeping to the night sky because the stone in his sling had just stopped a man's breath forever. He shuddered at the touch of that unwelcome spectre, the ghost of his own childhood.

"A friend tells you that," Zuleika murmured in his ear. "Goodbye, Jamal. And good fortune follow you—so long as your steps don't lead you anywhere within ten miles of Bessa."

He was barely aware of her leaving. And he had forgotten, now, about the silver he had come here to collect. He remembered the bottle of poison, though, and took it with him: he felt that the right state of mind might not be too far away now.

He left the city by the Southern gate, unchallenged and seemingly unnoticed: either his description had not been given out, or else Zuleika had ordered that he should not be accosted.

In Ibu Kim, where he fetched up after six months of wandering, the roughnecks he took up with called him *Bir Hatain*, the Two-Faced Man, because he seemed to alternate between two states: stasis (which they thought was somnolence) and savagery (which they thought was courage). They misread him on both counts, but the name pleased Jamal, and he affected it for a while.

But he knew there was a third face in him somewhere, not yet revealed.

In the Fullness of Time

It's an expression. A commonplace. It comes close to being a metaphor. Time is envisioned as a seed that flowers; a moon waxing to its final, perfect roundness; a woman who gives birth.

But the fullness of time is only ever perceived in its aftermath: fullness is defined by endings, and known retrospectively.

Bessa grew, and was great, and its fame spread. Seasons came and went, and although no man or woman can ever know the paradise of the Increate, where loss and suffering are inconceivable, still most things were good. And this goodness lasted long enough that it came to seem, at last, like the natural state of affairs. Peace and plenty stood over Bessa like invisible caryatids, holding up the sky.

In remembering that time, I hold it in my cupped hands like water: I drink from it, and I feel as though I can never be thirsty again. But as to how long it endured, I cannot truly say. I who see all things can still sometimes refuse to see certain things in their true relations. Bessa is timeless for me. I choose to keep it so.

Yes, the calendar was different in those days. So was the span of human life. Upheavals in the way we perceive the universal dance upset, too, our perspective upon our own lives. The geological revolutions that stand in your past and my future make my past as intangible to you as your future. When you reach for us, you find that the water has shown you only your own reflection. When I speak to you, my voice is distorted by our mutual incomprehension, our irreconcilable alterity.

So long we lived. So bright.

So soon it ended.

CORRESPONDENCE

There came a day when Fouad went out for an evening ride and came back to Bessa slumped over the neck of his favourite horse. "I'm dizzy," he said, and was dead before they pulled him from the saddle.

Issi finally stepped away from the body, shaking his head. "I told the old fool not to go out galloping on his own!" he said, his voice unsteady.

"Never too old," said Gursoon quietly.

She sent word to Fouad's tribe, and a surprising number of cousins, nephews and nieces came to the city. They gave their kinsmen a splendid funeral, with drums, songs and loud keening. His last surviving brother, bent and grey, lit the pyre, and kissed Gursoon on both cheeks before riding back into the desert to scatter his brother's ashes, as befitted a nomad.

After that, the Jidur and the House of Laws became Gursoon's home. She would leave her lodgings at dawn, have breakfast with one of her grandchildren and spend the morning at work, meeting trade delegates, discussing building projects with the council, and once a week acting as judge in the city's disputes. In the afternoon she wrote letters, or helped her daughter in the school she ran in the old seraglio quarters. But when the sun dipped behind the dome of the old palace, it was her signal to stop for the day.

There was always more work to be done, of course. But on occasion she could permit herself to rest and look about her. These were, many said, the glory days of the city. Their cloths, their embroidery, their works in metal, clay and above all, ink, were sought throughout the region. Local sultanates were so eager to trade with them that Zeinab and her daughter Soraya were offered fair prices at the start of negotiations. Bessan poets, musicians and dancers (for whom Gursoon had set up a practice room in the old palace) were prized performers in the festivals of other cities. And the harvests flourished. Bessa had become the chief trader of saffron: Walid and Dip, the city's chief cooks, had invented so many dishes featuring the spice that old Imtisar complained she was sick of the colour yellow.

Imtisar herself had never been busier. It was she, along with Anwar Das in his rather different way, who was most responsible for what they thought of as the city's public face. Known envoys, from established trading partners, would deal with Gursoon directly, or with Issi or Zeinab, who could give immediate answers to practical questions. But the new approaches, the tentative diplomatic initiatives from the further cities, or from the sultans who had hoped until now that this wild freak of nature, a city ruled by women, might simply vanish, given time . . . they were met by Imtisar. She would entertain the bemused ambassadors to wine and cakes: queenly in her silks and jewels, impeccable in her courtesy and concern for her guests' prickly feelings, and so effortlessly in control that neither condescension nor threat seemed possible in her presence. To such men, Gursoon never appeared. Imtisar would sometimes refer to her as "our sultana," suggesting a being as regal as herself, but more forbidding. In reality, Gursoon was known in Bessa simply as the Speaker of the Council, a title that seemed appropriate to one who now, by tradition, opened each meeting—though, as she sometimes complained, that might be the only time she was able to speak before the final vote.

She had been feeling her age, Gursoon admitted to herself. She could no longer move quickly, and had begun to suffer from shortness of breath. Nafisah, the oldest of the town's physicians and a veteran of the desert days, believed that she was ill, but thought the malady a slow-moving one. She advised little treatment beyond rest and regular meals; counsel which Gursoon was happy to take.

She sat with Farhat outside the bakery at the side of the council house, sipping coffee and eating Fernoush's pastries as they looked over the square in the late-afternoon light. It was the favourite haunt of many of the older women, though fewer were left each year of those who had first gone out into the desert. Warudu, Adiya, the old councillor Efridah, even Maysoon the potter had succumbed to old age, passing on their work to their children or apprentices. Gursoon was grateful that her old friend at least had been spared to her.

She was tired that day, and uneasy. She had foregone her midday rest to help out at the school, where Hayat needed someone to help the little ones recite their numbers while she took an older group. She had visited the kitchen to talk of old times with Rashad, who insisted on helping his son to cook the midday meal for the children though he was supposed to have retired years before. And she had dealt with the day's letters. It was one of these that was causing her concern; she handed it to Farhat now.

"What do you make of this?" she asked.

Her friend turned the letter over in her hands. There were two sheets: one of poor-quality parchment, closely written on both sides; the other, which had enclosed the first, on much finer-grade vellum, with a single line of greeting. Farhat whistled when she saw the seal.

"Kephiz Bin Ezvahoun!" she said.

Honoured lady, the Caliph had written,

My agents have intercepted this, which I believe will entertain you. I trust, as always, in your continued health and prosperity.

"A very polite message!" said Farhat, eyebrows raised. Gursoon did not return her smile.

"Read the letter," she said.

The writing was crabbed and tiny; Farhat had to squint at first to make it out. Her eyebrows rose again as she read.

Report on the Polity of the City of Bessa

My Lord,

In furtherance of my commission, I here submit a full account of the individuals most responsible for the workings of this unnatural city. My regrets that some of the matter I must submit will be, of necessity, unseemly.

First, Lord, you must know that the women employ a number of male operatives to extend their web of corruption outside the bounds of the city itself. In Agorath I was frequently told of one Mir Hussein, who works to establish ever more lucrative trading agreements between the merchants there and those of Bessa. In Saruquy a similar function is performed by one Abdullah Rafiq.

Farhat looked up. "Who are these men he talks of? I've never heard of them."

Gursoon smiled briefly. "Oh, they're both Anwar Das. He feels some areas of his work are best kept separate."

I met one of these agents briefly in Heqa'a: a man named Bashar Hudhayfah.

"And Hudhayfah?" Farhat asked.

Gursoon nodded. "That's one of his."

The man was shabbily dressed but plausible, and seemed astonishingly well-connected. He ran it seemed, a stable of whores—your pardon, Lord— the better to bring the weaker-minded traders under his control. I myself was accosted by one of these women, a brazen creature of many wiles and considerable persistence. I need not say that her blandishments had no effect on me.

"Needn't he, though?" Farhat said. "Our Bethi doesn't give up that easily."

Within the city, the obstacles to our endeavour are more clear-cut.

First, the sultana herself. Few are permitted to see her: it is said that she is a woman of ferocious character but siren-like beauty, whose very face, if unveiled, would cause a man to lose his wits. Her name is Gursoon. I have heard that in the inner circle of the city she is given a different, more arcane title, but I could not learn what this was.

She is represented in the audience chamber by her regent Imtisar, an older lady, but still possessed of considerable grace and beauty. She is an effective ambassador, Lord: she has the manners and the modesty of a great lady of our own city, and while speaking to her it is easy to forget the abominations which must occur daily within Bessa's walls. In the event of an invasion of the city, I would recommend that this lady and her maidens be captured if possible, and not killed.

The leader of the army is a different creature entirely: a madwoman, it seems, more beast than woman, who is reliably reported to have killed over a dozen men. I saw her with my own eyes, lining up women and men together to drill with swords. She is immensely tall and well-formed, and seemed indeed to be capable of fighting like a man. She must be our chief target; but when your generals encounter her I would advise caution. She has no notion of mercy, nor yet of decency. The name of this harridan is Zuleika.

These are the main individuals we must consider. There are some three or four others, of lesser risk to us. The woman-general is supported by another female named Umayma, scarcely less witch-like in demeanour, who is also said to be a terrible fighter. She too would need to be killed expeditiously. An old man named Issi arranges many of the trading missions from the city, and is treated with unusual respect: I surmise that he may be responsible for the network of agents in other cities with which I began this report. His deputy appears to be a woman named Zeinab: a hard-faced market haggler as brazen as her sisters, but no threat as a warrior.

The women are also reputed to be served by a prophetess, who warns them of future dangers, but I saw no sign of such a one during my visit. Those claiming to have consulted her went not to the palace, nor even to a temple, but to the city's library, where as far as I could see they did nothing more than speak to one of the women working there, sometimes staying to consult a book. (The promiscuous teaching of reading to the whole population is one of the more alarming signs of this city's complete fall from good order.) I believe that the talk of prophecy is merely a bluff put about by the sultana to frighten the city's enemies, and can be discounted as a factor which might influence our plans.

Lastly, Lord, you instructed me to report on the council chamber of Bessa, and to determine which of these women it is who makes their laws. This was both simpler and more difficult than I had anticipated. They meet in a single-roomed building next to the Jidur, unadorned, with neither dignity nor defences. I needed no concealment: anyone is allowed into their discussions, without distinction of rank or even age. I saw one day a group of school-children sitting on benches at the back of the chamber, for all the world as if they were attending to the debate.

But for the debate itself: such a name can scarcely be applied to the chaos I witnessed there. The noise was that of a cattle market, rivalling the Jidur outside; and indeed, I heard many of the same arguments and proposals advanced in both, sometimes even by the same people. There was neither leadership nor decorum, so that I could form no judgement of who, in fact, was making the decisions. There were never fewer than ten people present, and sometimes seven or eight times that number. Women and men alike would raise their voices; the only order was provided by a little fat woman at one side who allotted turns to the speakers, though she seldom spoke herself. When it seemed all had spoken their fill the little woman would call for a vote, and all present would raise their hands, or not. Then another woman wrote down what they had agreed.

This daily meeting, for I could learn of no others, is the means by which Bessa is governed. I was left astonished, as I am sure you, Lord, will be astonished, that the city has survived for as long as it has. If it is your will to invade this singular place, be assured that they have no ruler capable of resisting you.

I kiss the ground before your feet, my Lord, and eagerly await my summons to return to your presence.

Farhat had begun laughing halfway through the letter. By the time she reached the end, her shoulders were shaking.

"It's wonderful!" she managed, wiping her eyes. Do we know who sent it?"

"No." Gursoon was smiling in spite of herself, but her tone was serious. "If the Caliph had found out, he would have told me. You notice there's no address or signature."

"Well, we can't show it to Imtisar, that's for sure. Grace and beauty! She'd never let us forget it. And you!" Her shoulders shook again, but a look at Gursoon's face sobered her. "You don't think it's funny?"

"This one won't hurt us," Gursoon conceded. "But it worries me that after all these years there are still people who want to make war on us. We've done nothing to harm his master, whoever he is. Maybe lost him a trade agreement, but that happens everywhere. It seems he wants to snuff us out simply for what we are."

Farhat was serious again. "You're not really concerned are you? The Caliph himself saw it as a joke; look at his note to you."

"Kephiz Bin Ezvahoun might do well to joke a little less," Gursoon said darkly. From what Anwar Das tells me, even his own power may not be as secure as it once was." She leaned back in her seat, turning away from the thought. "But you're right, Farhat. We have strong allies, and I'm not truly worried that some distant sultan with a grudge could be a threat to us. Our own trading partners would dissuade him, if it came to it. Only . . . Zuleika has never dropped her guard, in all the time the city has been ours. She still drills the army, and still keeps the weapons store full. And Anwar Das is still making his enquiries, looking for possible threats to the city, though we've been at peace now for years. I just wonder if, perhaps, I've allowed myself to become too complacent. If we are ever threatened again, how would I deal with it?

"That's easy," Farhat said. She took the pot and poured more coffee for them both. "Raise your veil and blast them with the beauty of your face!"

The cheerful sounds of the square were all about them, and the city glowed in the golden light. Gursoon allowed herself to be soothed into laughter, and the two women sat peaceably together, chatting about other things as the evening fell.

The Lion of the Desert

Rumours arose at this time of a bandit king called the Lion of the Desert. He was both ruthless and ambitious, it was said, and had already united several existing companies of thieves under his own rule, in most cases by defeating and killing their existing leaders in single combat.

These reports were for the most part ignored in Bessa: bandits and rumours were alike perennial, and could be relied on to go away if you didn't turn your head to acknowledge them.

But the Lion did not go away, and the rumours turned into inconvenient fact. Trade caravans travelling from Bessa toward Perdondaris were waylaid and did not return. Nobody survived these encounters, so the Lion's involvement remained a matter of hearsay and whisper, but it seemed safe to say that there was a new power in the land—a roving, mobile power, unlike the powers that ruled from behind city walls.

Zuleika's janissaries went out into the desert and the mountains on wide patrols, hoping to find the Lion's lair or else to meet his cohorts in the field. They were unsuccessful: this bandit king, if he existed, knew better than to engage a trained military unit in the open, and no one seemed to know where he was hiding.

After a summer of such provocations, Zuleika made the decision to send a company of her soldiers along with each caravan. The attacks became less frequent, but they did not stop. Several caravans, in spite of their armed escorts, found themselves encircled at night by hostile forces who rained arrows on them out of the desert, night after night. Then, when the guard company were diminished and demoralised by this skirmishing, the bandits would mount an ambush and fight them to the death. In every case where this happened, the guards and camel-drivers were slaughtered and left to lie where they had fallen. There were never any bodies belonging to the attacking force.

Zuleika saw this for what it was—the Lion of the Desert, or whoever was leading these raiders, wished to tell Bessa as little as possible about who they were fighting: their weapons, their tactics, their numbers. Perhaps he was also hoping to weaken the morale of the Bessan forces by creating the myth that his fighters were indestructible. It was a clever trick, and Zuleika had to admire the care with which it was executed; the dead soldiers had also been stripped of their weapons, so it was impossible to prove that they had drawn blood, and the sand had been raked over with branches so there was no battle sign left for her to read.

After consultation with Gursoon and a full debate in the Jidur, she doubled the guard contingents. It was important that the trade caravans continued. Bessa needed to keep her obligations to her neighbour cities, and to continue to expand her economic activity to cover the massive spending that was underway on the city's infrastructure. Schools and lazarets, public gardens and slum clearances all cost money.

But the cohorts of the city guard were finite too, and all of this meant that they were spread more thinly than Zuleika liked. In retrospect, she was playing into the Lion's hands, as she realised when the next attack came not on the caravans but on the crocus fields.

Ever since Anwar Das's great coup in Susurrut, and the bargain he had struck with Rudh Silmon, the refining and sale of saffron had been the city's sheet anchor, raising more revenue than all her other crops combined. That was so, at least, until the day when the people of Bessa woke under a choking black blanket, to find the crocus fields on fire. The bittersweet smoke stung the eyes of the citizens and made them weep, and there was plenty to weep about. Farhat was obsessively protective of the crocuses, and had cool storerooms filled with seed pods already laid aside for next year, but the entire harvest was destroyed, and a precisely calculable fortune lost to Bessa's treasury.

The general assembly in the Jidur seemed paralysed for once; they proposed a motion ordering Zuleika to triple the guards on the fields. She explained, coldly but calmly, that this would only be possible if she removed most of the armed escorts from the caravans, which would only encourage further depredations.

"Then what do you propose?" one of the speakers demanded. "We do nothing, and allow our wealth to be consumed?" It was a man who said this: Ereth En-Sadim, a cousin of the En-Sadim who Zuleika had murdered on the day when the seraglio escaped into the desert. He had heard, of course, of how his kinsman had died, but had never seemed to hold it against Zuleika. He was all about the bottom line.

"I'm not suggesting we do nothing," Zuleika answered him, when her turn came to speak. "But this bandit clearly has a plan, and our own actions and decisions are factored into it. If we keep on reacting blindly to each stab, each feint, then when the knife is drawn across our throats we won't see it coming."

This speech caused perturbation, and the perturbation caused more debate, which caused more edicts. A recruitment drive for the city guard was decreed, but this was meaningless; Knowing as much as she did about the secret ways in and out of cities, and the covert methods sometimes used to topple them, Zuleika had already doubled the size of the guard and increased its effectiveness by ten times. But as far as this went, Bessa was a victim of her own affluence: there was full employment, a trade boom and (as a consequence) more wealth, shared more equally, than anyone had ever known. The reserve pool of citizens who desperately wanted to be guards wasn't big enough to make the planned expansion feasible.

Other edicts were more controversial, and more scattershot. A curfew was imposed, and then withdrawn again almost immediately—the crisis was outside the city gates, not inside. Letters were drafted to the neighbour cities asking them to confirm their trading agreements with Bessa and commit to their continuance, but the letters were never sent, because Farhat knew better than to sow panic by groping after security. The city announced a zero tolerance policy for bandits, and it was suggested that Anwar Das, along with the other surviving members of his own cohort, should be questioned in secret conclave about his past activities and present allegiances. Gursoon scuppered this decree by threatening to walk away from the Jidur for good if it were ever put into force, and such was the respect in which she was held that the idea was dropped immediately.

Zuleika, meanwhile, consulted with Das in a very private garden on the roof of the old palace: their conversation centred on what practical measures they could take on their own initiative.

"I believe this is a time for subtlety and indirection," Das said. "You were right when you told the Jidur they were reacting blindly, and a great many of our problems stem from that blindness—I mean, from a lack of information."

"Agreed," said Zuleika. "So . . . ?"

"So. I'd like to walk abroad a little, incognito, and see what I can find out about this Lion of the Desert by listening in insalubrious places."

Zuleika favoured him with a searching glance. "And how does a Bessan diplomat go incognito?"

Anwar Das made a great show of admiring the scent of a yellow rose. "Are you asking in your official role as head of the city guard," he asked her, "or in a more private and casual capacity, out of innocent curiosity? I ask because these are difficult times, and my probity has come into question."

Zuleika gestured impatiently. "Private. Casual. That one. All right, it was a stupid question."

Das answered it anyway. "When I was with the bandits," he told her, "I used to dress as a leper so that I could loiter unseen in the stables and marketplaces of the Southern cities. It worked reasonably well, but I was limited to what I could discover by passive eavesdropping, because who would answer the questions of a leper?

"Consequently, when I came into the city's employ, I set up a number of aliases—one or more in each of the cities I've dealt with on Bessa's behalf. These false identities range from petty criminals to merchants, and mostly require little upkeep. I've found them useful on a score of occasions, and I've encouraged my spies to copy my example. Bethi took to it at once: her aliases probably outnumber mine at this point."

"You've ruined that girl," Zuleika said, darkly.

Anwar Das acknowledged the compliment with a grave bow.

He left the same night, alone, and was gone for three weeks. In that time, two more caravans were attacked. The first was wiped out to the last man and woman. In the second, though, the drivers and merchants were all guardsmen and guardswomen in mufti, and the curtained howdah at the head of the train held not a pampered merchant but Zuleika.

The trap had been very carefully prepared. Each evening when the train stopped and encamped, Zuleika would wait for dark to fall and then send fully half of her cohort out on wide patrols around the camp, charging them to rejoin the caravan just before dawn.

The first two nights were without incident. On the third, the bandits struck—and then were struck in their turn, finding themselves trapped between their erstwhile victims and a phalanx of skilled fighters descending on them out of the dark.

The bandits were tough and experienced, and they fought with a silent ferocity that amazed Zuleika. They must have known, after she turned up at their backs, that their position was hopeless, but it didn't occur to any of them to surrender. They sold their lives as dearly as they could, and when they were finally overwhelmed their leader killed the last two of his own fighters still standing with two strokes of his scimitar, before turning his dagger on himself.

There was a survivor, though: a wounded man, younger than most of the contingent, who was brought to Zuleika after a search brought him to light. He had been hit by three arrows, one of which had embedded itself deeply in his lower abdomen, so he could not be saved; but she had the wounds bound, gave him water and a bed, and sat with him until he died.

Zuleika didn't interrogate the man in any formal way, but she plied him with small kindnesses in the way that a torturer would have plied him with thumbscrews. She told him her name, held his hand, and stroked his brow. The man knew that he was dying, and that hers was the last face he would ever see. She needed, in the end, no more pressure or leverage than that. When she finally asked him who he was, and who he served, he answered freely, though through teeth clenched tight in pain.

"We are the Claws of the Lion," he groaned. "Colder—than melt-ice is our hate, and harder our hearts than the edge of steel."

"Really?" Zuleika asked. "And who is it that you hate?"

"We hate—you. We hate Bessa. Because you are an obscenity. A city founded on injustice, steeped in lies. A blasphemy!"

These words did not surprise Zuleika; she knew there were many who saw the existence of the Bessan polity in these terms—either because it was run by women or because it was run by commoners. Still, the declaration made her eyes narrow and her jaw set. These bandits had motives beyond pure profit, then—and a bandit who has motives beyond pure profit is a soldier, whether he admits it or not.

"Is that what your master says?" she asked the young man, voicing none of this.

"My master doesn't—need to," he gasped. "The truth of it—cries out to all the world. And that's all he asks. That we serve truth!"

"He sounds like a noble and an upright man," Zuleika observed.

"He is my king. And your king, too."

With these words, the man died. But with these words, Zuleika knew.

Anwar Das returned to Bessa three days after this conversation, and found Zuleika at the guard barracks, drilling a most unpromising batch of new recruits. Fresh from the road, standing in his own sweat and in the dust and sand that had adhered to him along the way, he nonetheless waited quietly, watching the proceedings, until Zuleika reached a point where her charges could be left to practise alone. Then she beckoned him into the spartan room she maintained for the nights when she had to sleep at the barracks, and he closed the door behind him.

"The news is all bad," he warned her in advance.

Zuleika poured two glasses of wine laced with brandy, handed one to him and then sat. She made no reply, knowing that he would tell the story in his own way and in his own time. But he paced a while, and fastened the wooden shutters across the window, too, before he spoke again.

"In Ibu Kim," he said, "I found Bessan goods for sale in bazaars we never use. Inquiring as Medruk Nifahr, a petty thief, I ascertained soon enough that these were wares brought into the city by the Lion's men, to be resold there. But that led me to wonder how it was that stolen goods with our makers' marks upon them could be sold so freely in a city with which we have a trade agreement. So I made a second pass, as Indrusain Irumi, a prosperous merchant with suspect acquaintances including the aforementioned Medruk Nifahr. Bethi posed as my wife, and had several intimate conversations with the younger son of Ibu Kim's sultan. He was profligate with his words."

"I'll bet he was."

Das took a sip of the fortified wine, and wiped his mouth with the back of his hand, leaving a cleaner smear across his dust-masked face. "It became apparent," he told her, "that this was a franchised operation, carried out with the blessing of Ibu Kim's viziers. The Lion of the Desert sells what he steals from us at half the price we normally ask, and the profits are shared equally between him and the sultan.

"Moreover, Ibu Kim is not the only city with whom the Lion has made this arrangement. I found the same pattern in Ashurai and Sebun. You'll note that these are currently the furthest cities with whom we regularly trade. I don't think that's coincidental. The Lion has chosen to begin at the edges of our perception and steal in upon us slowly—with the long-term aim, it seems, of sabotaging our economy, disrupting our alliances, and leaving us comprehensively isolated."

Zuleika nodded, her face grimly set. "Which in turn is instrumental to a further aim—that of attacking and conquering the city."

Anwar Das stared at her. His cup, which was halfway to his mouth, did not reach it. "How did you know that?" he demanded, looking both surprised and chagrined. "I travelled a hundred leagues and risked my neck more times than a chook has feathers to find that out!"

"I'm sorry, Anwar Das. Your revelation first, then mine."

"No," he insisted. "I intend to have the last word on this. You go first."

"The Lion," Zuleika told him, "is Jamal."

Anwar Das's eyebrows rose a trifle. "Your former prince, and would-be insurrectionist."

"Yes."

"Whose throat you forbore to slit, despite my earnest pleading."

"Even him."

"So divine a thing is mercy."

"Go ahead and gloat."

They drank in silence for a minute or two, musing on the implications of this. Then Anwar Das resumed.

"Depressing as that is, it's not the worst news," he said. "From Ibu Kim, I followed the Lion's trail westward."

"Westward? There's nothing west of Ibu Kim but the sea."

"Aye, exactly. And on the sea, a fishing port, so small it doesn't even have a name. And yet, in that negligible place, I met a great many slab-faced men with their own weapons and armour, not one of whom could get his tongue around a simple 'good morning.' I know, because I am uncommonly polite and exchanged the time of day with dozens of them. Whatever their native language was, it was not one I knew. Some of them may not even have had a native language."

Zuleika so far lost control of herself that she stood, and took an involuntary step towards Anwar Das. "Mercenaries," she said.

"Barbarians," he countered coldly. "Call them what they are. Men from the lands north of the Tigris, who never knew until now that civilization resumed beyond the desert's reach. How our young Lion made contact with them in the first place, we may not guess—still less, how he was able to negotiate with them or in what coin he pays them. But he has bought himself an army, nonetheless, and an army of indecent size. He hasn't bought it to let it lie unused.

"He will bring it here. He will bring it against us. I think he only waits now because in the plan he has formulated he will come to Bessa when Bessa is already on its knees—and for the moment, though we stagger, we still stand."

Zuleika put her free hand to the hilt of her sword, and half-drew it from its sheath. Her own words from another time rose in her mind. "We must become once again the seraglio of steel," she said.

"Ah," said Anwar Das. "But that was another battle, against a lesser enemy. Will steel suffice, this time? I think it may not."

"Then we'll become that thing on which steel breaks," Zuleika said.

THE MAKING READY

Even though Anwar Das had located and identified Jamal's army, it was no easy matter for the Bessan polity to chart its progress. At first, Zuleika sent agents into the field to locate and follow the horde; she abandoned this approach after the third such agent failed to report back. Clearly, whatever else they were, the barbarians whose loyalty Jamal was renting were no fools. They had scouts out around the main body, and the scouts had sufficient experience to blood their own tracks.

The next attempt, which entailed trying to get one or more of her people recruited into Jamal's forces, fared no better. Anwar Das had heard rumours that the Lion of the Desert had been recruiting followers from Ibu Kim and Susurrut, but it was soon evident that his muster was full. Zuleika's agents wasted weeks trawling the taverns and whorehouses of those cities, without encountering a single press gang or even a bandit on a weekend pass.

The truth was that Zuleika's skills, as far as warfare went, had always been tactical rather than strategic. Gifted though she was with intelligence and animal cunning, it still didn't come naturally to her to think on these scales. It took a combination of the four of them, Gursoon as well as Anwar Das, Rem alongside Zuleika, to find a way past this impasse. It was unsubtle, but it was effective, providing an accurate picture of Jamal's forces which—though it came with a built-in time delay—entailed no risk.

It worked in this wise: Zuleika set her spies to wait at the waterholes, and to ask the refugees who came through there, fleeing ahead of the horde, from whence they had come and for how long they had travelled.

There were more than enough people there to ask, for though the Lion's forces did not lay siege to any of the cities they passed, and indeed skirted as wide of them as was feasible, they had no choice but to live off the land. Their quartermasters and acaters pillaged the goat herds of the mountain peoples and the tent villages of the plains nomads, and those people moved on before them in a great wave of the displaced and the pauperised.

Debates ensued in the Jidur as to whether these refugees should be offered sanctuary.

Farhat: I don't think we can let them go on into the deep desert. They're exhausted already. They won't survive.

Khelia: But we have no room. Where would they live?

Imtisar: Some of them could live in the barracks. Don't we need soldiers? Well, here are soldiers in plenty.

Zuleika: Untrained, undernourished, and terrified. They wouldn't be soldiers, they'd be oxen in a fire pit, waiting to be roasted. Take them in, by all means, but if you're thinking of enlisting them into the city guard, then you might as well save time and effort by cutting their throats as soon as they sign their names.

Issi: We should at least make the offer. Compassion demands that we take them in, if they want to come here.

Gursoon: There's no compassion in inviting these wretches into a war zone.

This last was unanswerably true. Judging by the combined accounts of the refugees, there could no longer be any doubt: the Lion's army was heading towards Bessa, steadily and directly. Even its slow progress was bad news rather than good, because Gursoon and her lawmakers knew exactly what it meant. An army that wanted only to raid, as some of the plains tribesmen had once raided across the northern reaches of *As-Sahra* , could move with spectacular speed and be at the gates of a city almost before the watchmen had raised a cry. But an army that meant to lay siege required solid lines of supply, and therefore moved more slowly, cementing in place the support structures that would later keep it alive. Jamal's measured progress was an indication that he meant business.

More handwringing and heart-searching in the Jidur, but on this point very little argument.

Risheah: This is our home, and we love it. Of course we'll fight for it, and die for it. If we lose Bessa, that will be like death in any case.

Lying at Zuleika's side, Rem listened in silence to long accounts of the preparations that she already had in train. She had a score of fletchers turning out arrows, and two score blacksmiths forging swords at a fantastic rate, and despite her sour words about making untrained people fight, she had instituted a voluntary training regime for the ordinary people of the city, who were being drilled in the use of these newly delivered weapons by sergeants selected and overseen by Zuleika herself.

There was an unspoken question in all of this, which Zuleika forbore to ask. Do we win? Do we prevail here, and go on as we have done before, or do we end now in blood and fire?

Rem could not answer. Because her own survival was directly involved, and because of the inverse square law already described elsewhere in this narrative, the answer changed from moment to moment and seemed to hinge on things that made no sense to her. So she did not speak but only listened, her head resting in the crook of Zuleika's shoulder, breathing in the musk of her sweat and watching the rise and fall of her breasts as she breathed. Before the library fell, it had been the place of all her happiness. Now the place of all her happiness was here, in this room, in this bed, and in these arms. If a word she could speak would save the city, or save Zuleika though the city burned, she would speak that word though it burst her lungs and cleft her heart.

But there was no word. All of her visions agreed on the blood, the pain, the slaughter that was to come. All converged on a scene in which Jamal, older but still recognizable, walked through Bessa's streets and was met at every door post, every turning, by the bodies of the dead. With that sight painted on her inner eye, Rem was blind to all else and mute in the face of Zuleika's logistical commentaries.

Their lovemaking, also, was desperate and clumsy, as though they had forgotten the rhythms of each other's desire. They had not forgotten, but the future lay like a pit between them: fearful of falling into it, they misjudged every word and foreshortened every gesture. It was a terrible time.

The response of the city at large, meanwhile, was more equivocal or at least more nuanced than Zuleika's. There were still some speakers in the Jidur who believed that a truce of some kind might still be possible, and that negotiators should be sent to meet Jamal's armies on their way. Gursoon did not subscribe to this view, but the vote went against her and she dutifully assembled and sent forth a diplomatic legation. Jamal's old friend from their desert-wandering days, Zufir, volunteered to lead it, and after some discussion was allowed to do so. But when fourteen days had passed and the delegation still hadn't returned, even the most optimistic began to see war as inevitable.

It was at this point that the city suffered another blow.

Gursoon's illness had been advancing slowly, leaving her each week a little stiffer, a little more easily tired. Her mind was as sharp as ever, but much of the day to day running of the city she now left to her trusted lieutenants. Anwar Das handled most of the diplomatic missions, Zeinab the trading agreements (her mentor Issi having long since retired), while the public works were overseen by Huma, who had a remarkable head for figures, and Mir Bin Shah, one of the chief builders. Gursoon's opinion was still valued, and her good sense and experience as an arbiter were as much in demand as ever. But she spent more of her time than before drinking coffee outside the bakery, or walking the streets of the city, stopping every now and then as if to fix some familiar scene more firmly in her mind.

The week after the delegation had been expected to return, the council sat as usual, discussing matters both weighty and mundane. A motion to send a second party after Zufir's was defeated; there were too many reasons to fear the worst. A report on the state of the city's provisions was satisfactory: the year's grain and date harvest looked promising, and the weapons-store was well maintained. The small schoolhouse to the east of the city needed pens and a wooden bench, and a new sewer was required by the cattle-market. The meeting broke up early, with the uncertain fate of Zufir and his party weighing heavy on everyone's mind. The other council members clustered around Umayma, Zufir's mother, as they left the house, offering what cheer and reassurance they could. But Gursoon remained in her seat, and Zeinab returned to see what the matter was.

"Zeinab," the old woman said in a low voice, "I can't move."

They made her up a bed in the House of the Lawmakers. Nafisah was called at once, along with Gursoon's son and daughter. Farhat, grey-faced, ran to the spice warehouse and scrabbled through the jars and sacks for remedial herbs. But before nightfall it was clear that the Lady Gursoon was dying.

She could still speak. She called Zeinab to her first, then Huma.

Zeinab's daughter Soraya, who had just returned from a trading journey, accompanied them. Gursoon was propped on pillows, with her daughter Mayisah and Farhat at her sides to hold her upright. She gave each of her two lieutenants instructions on the matters she thought most urgent— securing the crops and looking to the repair of the city walls—then fell back against her attendants, closing her eyes. "Thank you, my dears, for everything," she whispered. The three women kissed her and left weeping. It was only Soraya who replied.

"Thank you, Auntie, for your stories."

Gursoon's interview with Anwar Das was shorter, and she sent away her daughter and her friend while she spoke to him. He left stony-faced, and would tell no one what she had said. By this time the square had filled with people, friends and gawpers in equal measures. Among them were the crowd of Gursoon's grandchildren and great-grandchildren, but even the youngest waited patiently until they were called, knowing that their grandmother had a duty to the whole city.

"She wants to see you," Anwar Das said shortly to Rem and Zuleika as he emerged. He did not indicate which of them he meant, so they went in together.

Gursoon was still alone, leaning against her pillows, eyes closed. But as they approached they heard her gasp, as if in pain. It came to Rem with a sudden horror that the old woman was crying, and she left Zuleika's side and ran to embrace her.

"How can I leave you?" Gursoon sobbed. "War is coming again— after all I tried to do—and I don't think we can keep them out. I could have done more. Why must I go now?"

She looked into Rem's face, and Rem knew she was asking for reassurance. She wished with all her heart that she could lie convincingly.

"We won't . . . the future's not fixed," she stammered. "We may yet drive Jamal off."

Zuleika knelt at Gursoon's other side. "It's no time to despair," she said with surprising gentleness. "We have a strong army, we're well supplied, and we have good people, who will make the right decisions and know what to do. You've taught us well. You've built a city that can go on without you."

Gursoon seemed a little comforted. She had stopped sobbing, but her eyes were still bright with tears.

"It's true," she said. "And yet, Bessa will fall."

"Yes," Rem said.

Zuleika looked at her in shock. But she knew what to say now. The words flowed from her as smoothly as prophecy.

"It will fall, in time, as all things fall, and the sand will close over it. That happens to all cities. But Bessa is not like other cities: nothing like it was ever seen before. It won't be forgotten. We've brought a new possibility into the world; that's your achievement."

Gursoon sighed.

"I spent my life holding back the sandstorm," she said. "I suppose that's an achievement too." Her voice was growing weaker. "Well, then, that's how it will be." She gave an irritable twitch. "But I can't move my arm. Wipe my eyes for me, dear. And then send my family in."

Lady Gursoon, Speaker of the Council, was given the kind of funeral previously reserved for sultans. All of Bessa, it seemed, wanted to attend. The procession wound through the four main streets and finished in the Jidur, with addresses by the council, her daughter and friends, and anyone else who wished to speak.

"She said not to make a fuss," Danyar complained as he watched the crowd file past his mother's body. "She didn't want any of this carrying-on. No more did my dad!"

His eldest granddaughter, who had been clinging to his hand with both her own, turned up a tearstained face.

"But everyone else wants to honour them," she said. "And they both deserved it."

Imtisar came out of the crowd, walking slowly on two sticks. Mayisah came forward and helped her to a seat beside them.

"Thank you for your generous words, just now," Danyar said to Imtisar.

The old woman made a dismissive gesture. "No more than her due. I have something for you here." She fumbled in her clothes, and handed something to Mayisah. "I always meant to give it back to her. I delayed too long. But it was only ever borrowed."

"Her ruby," Mayisah said in wonder. "The one the sultan gave her."

Imtisar nodded. "The diplomacy stone," she said. "Did your mother ever tell you the story of how it came to her? It could have no better owner."

The mourning had to be short-lived: there was too much work to be done. Zeinab took over Gursoon's role as Speaker, and she and Huma consulted widely on the state of Bessa's defences. In some ways, they were robust. The palace, though it had been allowed to fall somewhat into disrepair, was still for the most part intact. With the Jidur's approval, Huma commissioned repairs so that it could serve as a final redoubt if the need arose. The walls, though, were another story: they had been neglected during the long years of the peace, as other civic building programmes continually took precedence. Now that there was so little time left to work in, it became apparent that in some areas the damage and dilapidation were more severe than had ever been imagined. The Southern gate, which at one point had been converted into a cock-fighting pit by one of the city's dodgier entrepreneurs, was scarcely defensible.

There was the problem of the water supply, too, but here it seemed little could be done. As the city's population had grown, it had come more and more to depend on three new wells dug some quarter of a mile outside the walls. Those wells would become unreachable on the first day of a siege, and from that day onward the city's daily needs would outstrip its secure supply by some two thousand gallons.

Zeinab gave orders for water to be drawn from the external wells and stored in tanks and jars in the warehouses left depleted by the Lion's raids. Grain not yet quite ripe was nonetheless being harvested and stored too, and rationing had already been introduced in anticipation of the coming siege.

All was bustle and activity, and on the surface it was hopeful and purposeful enough. Beneath that surface, though, and not a long way beneath, there was a great knot of fears and forebodings, a sense that the city was facing a crisis it was ill-equipped to weather, and that the Increate (for whatever inscrutable reasons) had turned His face from Bessa.

"Bugger the Increate with an iron bar," Zuleika snarled when she heard such thoughts expressed. "The Increate doesn't live locally." Because she was much admired, it was an opinion that was much quoted. But the fears and forebodings persisted, nonetheless.

On the day before the Lion's army was expected to come into sight, Zuleika held a final meeting. It was closed to those outside the circle of the lawmakers, not because there was any great fear of spies within the city but because some of what was on the agenda had profound implications for morale. Present were Zuleika herself, Imtisar, Anwar Das, Farhat, Zeinab, Huma, Umayma (by then Zuleika's deputy) and the master builder Mir Bin Shah, who had been made responsible for overseeing the repairs to the walls and fortifications.

Mir reported first, and the others heard him out without interruption. He was a somewhat overweight man in his late forties, with a hectic red complexion and a tendency to sweat heavily, which combined to give him, perpetually, the look of a man who had just finished a five-mile run—but since his alarming appearance was matched by a keen mind and an absolute discretion, he had come in recent weeks to inherit a set of responsibilities far outside his usual area of expertise.

"We've got a good ways along with the walls," he told them. "To the north and east, they're sound—very sound. The other stretches are all fair, even the west reach by the cattle market that was more or less down. That's all built up new, and with a few more months to bed in, it'd be stronger than the old stuff. But the mortar dries in three stages, the masons told me, and the last stage needs a summer and a winter before you can say for sure it's done. So right now, though it looks solid, they're afraid that if someone hits it hard enough, it might give more easily than the rest. So we followed the advice of the ambassador here—" with a nod to Anwar Das "—and that seems to have done some good."

"What advice was that?" Imtisar demanded.

Anwar Das shrugged. "I suggested that buckets of slops from the inns and eating houses on the streets adjacent to that stretch—and dung from the cattle market—should be dumped over the wall and allowed to accrete there. The staining to the wall makes it less obvious from a distance that it's new, and the noisome mound at its base discourages closer inspection. It's a crude ruse, but it might work."

"There were also some buildings over in the west there," Mir resumed, "what had gone up outside the wall and touching onto it. Like ladders, it was—like we'd already put up siege ladders for them to climb. We tore them all down, and we took the rubble inside the city, so there's nothing there that could be used against us."

Umayma raised her eyebrows, and seemed to be about to raise her voice, too. "We compensated the people who lived there," Zeinab told her. "And we moved them all inside the walls. Nobody was made homeless." She nodded to Mir to go on.

"Then there's the gates," he said, "and the news isn't so good there. If they come at the South Gate with anything more than a harsh word, it'll give. We've repaired the obvious damage, and we've banked it up inside with timber baulks, but the whole structure's rotten and there wasn't anything like time to tear it down and rebuild. To do the job properly would have taken months, so we did what we could and there's nothing left to do now but pray."

Anwar Das shot Zuleika a surreptitious glance. He had heard her current opinion of the Increate, and wondered if she would offer any remarks upon the subject of the efficacy of prayer, but she let that comment sail by without acknowledgement. "With regard to our military readiness," she said, her voice clipped and cold, "we have two thousand guard who I would be happy to call trained and ready. We have, besides, almost one thousand raw recruits, who range in training and readiness from some who are rough but plausible to others who are unable to lace up their own sandals without sustaining a nosebleed. If you were to call our full muster two and a half thousand, that would be fairly accurate."

"Three thousand," Anwar Das said, and Farhat, Zeinab and Huma gasped in fervent relief. Since the answer was obviously coming in any case, Zuleika didn't ask the question, but Imtisar stiffened and stared at Anwar Das. "What have you done?" she demanded.

"Ten days ago," the ambassador said, "I entered into negotiations with the Caliph of Perdondaris."

"Kephiz Bin Ezvahoun," Umayma said.

"Alas, no. That worthy man is now in his final sickness, and his nephew, Garudh, has selflessly stepped in to supply his place." Anwar Das's expression and tone had an exemplary blandness about them, and he met nobody's gaze while he spoke these words. But he cleared his throat, as though they might have stuck there for a moment, a little unpleasantly. "The subject of my discussion with the . . . *acting* Caliph was the purchase, or as it might be the hire, of mercenary soldiery."

The faces around the table now all mirrored Anwar Das's careful lack of expression. Taking on mercenaries had been discussed for many hours in the Jidur—hours of bitter argument, furious denunciation, shameless attacks on character and reputation and at least one actual fist fight. For many in that assembly, the thought of emptying the public purse to purchase the services of killers (Zuleika was never considered under that heading) was anathema; for just as many, the thought of allowing foreign fighters inside the city walls to examine its approaches and defences was just as distasteful. Between the conscience of the former and the paranoia of the latter, the debate had stalled. Therefore, any words that Anwar Das had exchanged on this topic with the Caliph of Perdondaris, or with his nephew, had been unauthorised adventurism of a kind that could easily lose him his post.

But there was no arguing with results.

"Five hundred mercenaries," Zuleika mused. "If they're seasoned, they'll be well worth having. I'm assuming the price was pretty steep, though?"

Anwar Das shook his head, looking a little grave now. "You mistake me, Zuleika. The Caliph's answer was no. He refused to become entangled in our small war—perhaps fearing that to offer us aid might turn the attention of the Lion towards himself."

"But Perdondaris could roll over the Lion and squash him flat!" Imtisar protested.

"That's most likely true. But the assessment of risk is a subjective science. And why take on any risk at all, when you don't need to? The Caliph weighed the money I was offering against the benefits of strict neutrality, and went with the latter."

"Dirty yellow bastard," muttered Umayma.

"But in that case," Zuleika asked Anwar Das, "where did these five hundred fighters come from?"

"I'm glad you asked," the ambassador said gravely. "I followed a hint given to me by the Lady Gursoon."

There was silence for a moment. The loss of Gursoon was still raw— it seemed outrageous to invoke her name lightly, in support of a scheme that might still prove disastrous. Both Imtisar and Farhat looked ready to protest. But Anwar Das held up a hand.

"I spoke to her just before she died," he said. "She suspected I would make an advance to Perdondaris, and advised against it; she had, perhaps, a clearer understanding of the situation there than I. But she made another suggestion. You remember that Fouad was a member of a nomad tribe: his family often came here to trade, and she met them several times after his death. She reminded me how many of the nomads, Fouad's people and others, have had to move aside as the Lion's army passed, or flee ahead of it. How many have lost their livelihoods—the goats they herded, the horses they bred, the tents they lived in. And she reminded me of what Fouad used to say, that should you quarrel with a plains nomad, you'd better have ten good men to back you up if you want to go home with both ears.

"So when the Caliph turned me down I took a circuitous route back to the city, through a dozen or so of the largest encampments I could find. Most, obviously, were on the move, and had scant time to listen to my tenders. Still, in each I was given at least a cursory hearing. I promised that any man or woman who agreed to fight for Bessa in this conflict would be given afterwards if he or she survived ten goats or three horses and a sum equal to the yearly pay of a labourer. If they died, a like sum would be paid to their families. And in each case, after I'd spoken, a few people came to me and joined my train—two here, three there, perhaps as many as ten in the larger camps."

"Ten times a dozen doesn't add up to five hundred," Zuleika pointed out. She was staring hard at Anwar Das.

"No," he agreed. "It doesn't. But one morning, having retired to sleep at the usual time and after consuming only a moderate amount of wine to quench the fires of the day, I awoke to find my tent surrounded by silent, grim-faced warriors on horseback. They were dressed in jerkins and breechcloths of faded leather, without adornment. They wore no swords at their sides, but each instead had three long spears strapped to his back. At least, the men were so accoutred; as for the women, each bore a curved dagger and a leather bolas. Their skin was so dark it was more black than brown, and therewithal it shone like polished wood. Their faces were like the death masks of princes: fine of feature, but with a cold and forbidding immobility. They outnumbered my retinue by more than ten to one, so as you may imagine I waited most politely to hear what they had to say for themselves.

"And what they said was *la im sa'ika we ahlaam shede*."

"*Sign me up*," Zuleika translated. "By the gods, Anwar Das! The Yeagir! You've brought us Yeagir horsehusbands!"

"And horsewives," Anwar Das reminded her. "To the number of five hundred. It seems the word had spread from oasis to oasis, and these— the proudest and most reclusive people of *As-Sahra* —had come to hear of our need."

Silence around the table as the implications of this sank in. The Yeagir were a law unto themselves: arrogant and insular, a tribe whose full complement was also its royal family, since for any Yeagir to cede sovereignty to any other was impossible. All knew of them, but few had ever met one. Fewer still had walked away from such a meeting.

"And what's their price?" Imtisar asked, when she deemed the silence had lasted long enough.

"They ask no price," Anwar Das said.

"What? But then, to take on someone else's fight—"

"That's not what they've agreed to, lady. Apparently, the lion's men killed a young boy from one of the Yeagir meinies, having met him at a waterhole and quarrelled with him when he refused to stand aside and let them drink. Now that insult has to be wiped out in blood. They have come to fight for Bessa because they consider it a more condign revenge to thwart the Lion in his goals than to kill a few of his people in a pointless bloodletting. All this they explained to me that night. And then they followed on behind me as I rode back toward the city, forbearing to share the amenities of my camp. Now they await us at the Well of Sparrows, due north of here, and we have six turns of the glass to tell them our decision."

"Our decision is yes," Zuleika said instantly.

"But the Jidur knows nothing about this!" Imtisar protested, horrified. "And it's not as though they could be hidden. Once they enter the city, the lawmakers will know that you went behind their backs."

"Then if we all survive, they can hang us," Zuleika said. "The Lion has, at a conservative estimate, some twenty thousand soldiers. It may be as many as thirty thousand, since he's careful to break up the companies when he marches to make counting difficult. In a pitched battle, he'd swallow us like a drunken man swallows a sherbet, in one gulp. And these desert riders—if you lop off their arms in a fight, they'll fight on with the dagger in their teeth. They'll be troublesome to handle, but by the devil's hairy balls, they'll earn their keep!"

The meeting broke up, after some further discussion of ways and means, and Anwar Das was despatched to invite the Yeagir within the city walls. Because they came in by night, only the guards on the Northern Gate saw them arrive: but word of their presence had already spread by morning, and the citizenry of Bessa came down to stare at these silent and intimidating strangers as they boiled their tea over copper braziers and oiled their hair and skin with unguents that smelled of horseshit.

The Yeagir bore this awed scrutiny with stolid indifference. And then, shortly before midday, swirls of dust on the horizon announced the imminent arrival of the Lion's army, drawing off the crowd as the ocean is drawn by the moon.

At first they stared from the battlements and from the plain in front of the Eastern Gate. Then as the dust rose—even as the sun did—towards the zenith of the sky, Zuleika gave orders for the city to be sealed, and they went inside without demur.

The Lion was methodical: his troops arrived in perfect order to deploy around the curve of the city's eastern walls. Later, of course, they would move to encircle it completely: this was a show of strength, intended to impress upon the people of the city the hopelessness of their position.

After some minutes, a single figure rode forward from the host, seated on a white stallion and robed in white so that beast and rider seemed at first to be one entity. He stood before the walls in silence for a while, waiting for some answering figure to appear on the battlements above him: none did.

"You brought this on yourselves," the Lion of the Desert called up to the silent walls, when it was clear no interlocutor would step forward. "This city had a ruler once—a just and a fair one. He was overthrown by a monster, and then in the fullness of time, when the monster was cast down in his turn, the rightful prince appeared to claim his birthright. But you stood against right and against nature—against man's law, and the Increate's. You refused the yoke, and therefore chose the sword. You roused the lion. Today the lion has come to chastise you."

He paused for an answer. No answer came.

"Look out upon this multitude," the Lion called. "If you put a sword in the hand of every man, woman and child in that city—and such is your perversity, I judge that possible—you would still be outnumbered by my host. You cannot fight me, and you cannot entreat my mercy. I have none. Throw open your gates now, and throw down your swords, and even then, many of you will die: chiefly, the women of my father's harem, the concubinate, along with their families and hangers-on. The rest of you will live, but will be punished in strict proportion to your participation in the civic life of Bessa. By how much you helped with hands and hearts and minds to turn the city where I was born into the obscenity it has now become, by so much will you suffer. No one will escape my rod. No one. So decide, and answer me."

He fell silent again, and again the silence grew.

"Is nobody brave enough even to speak?" the Lion bellowed at last. "Are you all so cowed, so beaten down by the rule of whores that you have no voices left to plead or treat with me?"

Only silence. Only stillness.

He turned his horse around at last, and rode back towards his own ranks. "Then you'll get my answer in due course," he shouted over his shoulder.

There was a lull of some minutes, perhaps half a turn of the glass, while mechanisms of some sort were assembled in the foremost ranks of the Lion's forces, from baulks of wood laboriously dragged by whole chains of draught camels. This was another reason, presumably, for the slow progress of the army as it marched on Bessa. The machines were siege bows and ballistas, and as soon as they were complete, the first rocks and arrows began to sail over the walls.

Along with the first volley came the severed heads of the peace delegation.

MUSHIN'S TALE

The forces of the Lion of the Desert, the unconquerable Jamal, moved across the face of *As-Sahra* like a louse across the armpit of God.

That was the trouble with the desert, Mushin thought. This must surely be the mightiest host that had ever been assembled in the world's long history—fully thirty thousand men at arms, with horses and camels and siege engines so huge that they had to be carried along in separate pieces and only assembled when they were to be used—and yet, once they had left the coastal plain and were properly embarked upon their journey, their numbers seemed suddenly negligible. *As-Sahra* made you look small, no matter what you did.

Mushin was now a fully grown man of eighteen summers—a scion of Ibu Kim, with light fingers and a lighter heart, who had earned his bread by thieving, just as his father had done before him, and asked no greater gift from God than that he kept on allowing men to drink more than was good for them and to look the other way while their purse-strings were being cut.

But then he had met Jamal, and heard Jamal's story—the story of a prince cozened by evil women, and beaten and cast into exile when he remonstrated with them. These were potent ideas, but it was not the story so much as the man telling it: a prince who drank at the common tap with common men, and stood his round, and laughed at coarse jokes and told a few of his own. It was hard not to love such a man, and then once you loved him you believed in him. You could see it in his eyes, anyway, in case you were ever inclined to doubt. His eyes were haunted by a great tragedy, and when he spoke you could see it moving there behind those two dark windows, barely contained.

And so it was that when Jamal asked Mushin to join him in a brave enterprise, he accepted at once. Others did, too—more than two dozen of them—but Mushin spoke up before any other and so Jamal named him as his lieutenant.

"A lieutenant!" he told his mother, when she called him fool and bade him stay where he belonged. "Not a common cutpurse any more, mother, for you to berate and disrespect. I'm an officer, now, and the privilege of rank is . . . is . . . is for you to shut up, unless you salute when you speak to me!"

Instead of saluting, Mushin's mother—who had two inches and forty pounds on her wayward son—beat him with a broom handle and threw him out onto the street. But that mattered little, since Jamal was leaving the city the next morning in any case, bound for Susurrut. Mushin marched out of the wagon gate without a backward glance, and did not miss his home until almost lunchtime.

Jamal's business in Susurrut was the same as his business in Ibu Kim: recruitment. He trawled the inns of Copper Street and Forgotten Lane from one end to the other, drinking—or at least clinking glasses, for Mushin noticed now that his new master drank but little himself—with all the local rowdies, swapping stories and punches, arm wrestling, gambling, kissing the whores on the hand and talking to them as though they were princesses, and ever and always laying his money down.

These methods met with much success, and the Lion's numbers swelled in Susurrut. Among the new recruits was one Tayqullah, who when first he walked into the warehouse that was their current lodging introduced himself as Jamal's lieutenant.

Mushin stood, realising as he did so that Tayqullah had more of an advantage over him in height and mass even than his mother had. Nonetheless, he spoke up boldly. "I'm Jamal's lieutenant," he told the big man. "And you'd do well to—"

He woke up some hours later, with the lower half of his face so swollen and bruised that he couldn't talk or eat for three days. At that, he was told by some others among the new men, he was lucky; Tayqullah had been known to break a man's neck with that punch of his.

When he finally regained the use of speech, Mushin asked Jamal to sort out this small matter of the line of command. Jamal explained the situation to him. The precise terms of the explanation were complicated and extensive, but the nub of it was that Mushin and Tayqullah were both Jamal's lieutenants. Tayqullah was the lieutenant when it came to making decisions, having ideas and giving orders: Mushin was the lieutenant in terms of prestige and trust and being able to call himself one, except when Tayqullah was in earshot.

After Susurrut, they got to work in earnest—and in spite of what Mushin had told his mother about moving up in the world, most of the work was robbery. And the part of the work that wasn't robbery was murder.

Mushin didn't mind robbery, but found murder upsetting. It was one thing to stick a knife in a man who was trying to stick one in you; it was, indefinably but definitely, a different thing to cut the throat of a man (or woman) whose arms two other men were holding. After the first three raids on Bessan caravans had gone down in this way, Mushin found an opportunity to talk to Jamal in private, and offered as a suggestion that they should take the camel-drivers and merchants alive and ransom them back to Bessa. "And then we get even more of their money, don't we, Jamal? It's like we rob them twice, every time. Genius!"

But Jamal didn't think it was genius. He reminded Mushin that having ideas wasn't in his job description, and explained to him— patiently, for the most part—why it was necessary at this stage to kill every man and woman in the caravans. "Some of them might know me by sight. Even if they don't, others might recognize me from their description. Better, for now, if they don't have the faintest idea who their enemy is. The fires of our imaginations, Mushin, unlike most fires, burn brightest if you starve them of fuel. So, for now, flailing in the dark against an enemy who could be near or far, the lawmakers of Bessa will injure only themselves. This is the first phase in a grand plan, my friend. Stay with me, and watch it work itself out."

Tayqullah took a more direct approach. At the next raid he had three prisoners—a man, a woman and a boy of eight or nine years—brought before Mushin, bound and gagged, and gave him a blade. "These three are yours," he told Mushin coldly. "Kill them."

Mushin looked around him, and saw no face that he knew. The men closest to him were all of them Tayqullah's cronies from Susurrut, and they all had their hands on the hilts of their swords. It was clear what fate awaited him if he refused to carry out these killings—and yet his hands trembled and his mind faltered.

Desperate, he considered attacking Tayqullah instead. He would lose, of course, and die, but he might inflict some damage before he fell. But that would change nothing, except to add one more body to the pyre: these three would die, regardless.

Mushin had once heard a marabout say that the Increate, when we die, weighs our souls against a feather: and if the weight of our sins is enough to tip the scales, he casts us into Hell. Mushin knew well that even if the counterweight was a reasonably sized ox, his chances of Heaven had been forfeited long since. But for some sins, the Increate hurls you down hard enough that you crash through the floor of Hell and keep on going.

Mushin saw off the man with a single stroke, drawing the blade quickly across his throat. The woman, seeing this, struggled against him when he came to her, and her death was worse: messier, and more drawn out, despite his efforts. In the one-sided struggle, the gag slipped from her mouth.

"My son!" she wailed. "My little boy! Please don't hurt my—"

Mushin lowered the bloody dagger, his hand shaking as though with a palsy. This was the worst moment of his life. Fervently, even devoutly, he wished that he had never signed on with Jamal, that he had continued to live the desperate and yet comparatively carefree life of a cutpurse. In his mind's eye he saw his past life in Ibu Kim as though down a long corridor: its squalors were tinged with surprising splendour.

Finally, he turned to Tayqullah.

"I'll keep this lad for myself," he said. "I need a catamite."

Tayqullah blinked. He wasn't used to being disobeyed, and didn't seem to like it. "I told you to kill him," he growled. "Do it."

Mushin made no move. "I've claimed him," he repeated.

Tayqullah sighed, and shook his head, but he was smiling as he did it. "I knew you wouldn't disappoint me," he said. His scimitar cleared its scabbard and he whirled it around his hand in a series of tight arcs as he advanced on Mushin. With only the dagger in hand, Mushin waited. The certainty of death brought with it a strange calm.

"Let him have the boy," Jamal said from behind him. They all turned to face him, and Tayqullah paused with his sword still aloft. There was a moment of expectant silence. Jamal walked up to them and met the big man's gaze. "It is my wish."

"Then so shall it be," Tayqullah muttered. He walked away, the steel still unsheathed in his hand. The others waited for a few moments, presumably uncertain as to whether further orders would be forthcoming, but Jamal dismissed them with a nod, and they left hurriedly.

"You saw how she pleaded with you," Jamal said. "Not for herself. For the boy." He wasn't looking at Mushin, and Mushin therefore could not be sure that he was being addressed. In any case, he had no idea what he should reply, so he merely waited, his legs feeling suddenly nerveless and weak, until Jamal spoke again. "She reminded me of someone. A little. Only a little. What you did . . . there was a rightness to it, in my mind, and I honour you for it. But all the same, you should from henceforth do all the things that are asked of you, without hesitation or argument. Otherwise, Tayqullah will kill you, and I will say nothing."

And then he, too, walked away.

Mushin removed the ropes that bound the boy's hands, and the gag from his mouth. The boy was so terrified, still, that he seemed unable to move of his own volition. Mushin had to carry him. He took him to the tent he shared with seven other men, offered him water and food (although he took neither) and gave him a bedroll to sleep on.

"I didn't mean that about needing a catamite," he assured the boy. "I'm not going to fuck you." The boy didn't seem to understand, or to care. He only wept, and Mushin knew that he had not altered the weight of his soul by a thousandth of a grain. He had destroyed this child's life, and then only failed to deliver the coup de grace. Outfaced, unmanned, he fled.

But he kept the child with him in his tent from that day forward, and looked out for him as best he could. Since the boy refused to speak, even to give himself a name, Mushin invented a name for him: Abidal. The other men in the tent ignored the lad at first, until Mushin, in a burst of inspiration, began to have conversations with him in which he supplied both sides of the discourse, with Abidal's persona that of a gruff-voiced tough of whom the more timid Mushin was afraid. This relationship, played out in a number of *ad hoc* scenarios, caused great hilarity among the other soldiers, and led them to adopt the boy as some kind of a mascot. They kitted him out in a black djelaba, gave him a dagger to wear as a sword, and generally played along with the idea that he was a pint-sized berserker who grown men were afraid of offending.

Mushin's goal in this way was to keep the boy alive and unmolested, but he had no idea whether Abidal knew this or cared about it one way or another. The boy's demeanour was either solemn or impassive, depending on how you looked at it. He never spoke, and bore Mushin's comedic monologues in stolid silence. When the men marched, he marched until he dropped, and then Mushin carried him on his shoulders. When they camped, he stayed in the tent, alone with his thoughts.

So it went until the army came to the City of Women, and the fighting began. And after that, there was scant time for joking.

Mushin would not see all of the siege of Bessa, but he would see enough of it to learn for certain what by then he already suspected: that the tragedy he had once read in Jamal's eyes was not, as he had thought, in the distant past—but one that Jamal had incubated inside himself for many years, and was now bringing to birth.

SEVEN DAYS OF SIEGE

Bessa was a paradox: ripe to fall, yet hard to crack.

The armies of the Lion of the Desert broke over it in waves, assailing the walls alternately with stones flung from siege catapults and then with living tides of armed men.

The defenders cast down the scaling ladders, shored up the breaches with rubble and wooden baulks, stitched empty air with skeins of arrows and poured libations of burning oil on the attackers' heads.

At the end of the first day, the city stood. Its walls were piebald with running repairs, the crenelations of its gates gap-toothed, its battlements puddled with congealed blood, but it stood. And for every Bessan who had fallen, two or three of the Lion's men had fallen too.

The second day was no different, except that the assaults began earlier and finished later: for fully fifteen hours the bombardments and massed charges continued. The defenders were at full stretch, because the attacks came at all points around the city walls: Jamal was able to rotate different cohorts into his front lines, ensuring a continual supply of fresh fighters, but the warriors of the City of Women enjoyed no such luxury. They were tied to the stake, and must endure.

The fighting was bloodier, as well as longer. When the Lion's troops withdrew, they left the sand strewn with hundreds of their dead. But Jamal was well satisfied, nonetheless. He had discussed with Nussau, the gaunt and weathered captain of his mercenary division, the arithmetic that governed sieges—he felt that his losses were within acceptable bounds, and knew that he could sustain them for far longer than Bessa could.

The third and fourth days followed the same pattern. The defenders succeeded in keeping the Lion's soldiery off the walls, but they succeeded by the thickness of a hair. With each fresh assault, it seemed a miracle that they did not succumb. With each fresh bombardment, the walls creaked and groaned like living things, and though they did not fall they showed every sign of wanting to. Meanwhile, stones that missed their mark sailed over the walls to wreak havoc within.

In the course of the fifth day, one of the city gates to the South was all but breached, and only desperate manoeuvres by the defenders had kept it standing. On the following day it would certainly fall. To the western reach, also, there was a stretch of wall that had taken more damage from the catapults than any other. Despite appearances, it seemed to be of recent and hasty manufacture, and was not sufficiently braced to withstand the fifty-pound stones that were being hurled against it.

On the sixth day, therefore, the Lion's tactics were different. All of his catapults were lined up along the western wall, keeping up a relentless barrage against a stretch of stonework perhaps two hundred yards long. Initially firing at random, the engineers paused every half hour or so to read the wall and interpret the patterns of damage they saw there, increasingly concentrating their barrage where it would do the most harm. It was like doing a jigsaw puzzle in reverse, taking out at each stage the pieces that seemed the most promising.

Meanwhile, foot soldiers ran against the Southern gate with heavy battering rams—wooden logs thirty feet long with the forward end lapped in iron. They were protected by their comrades, who held aloft body-length shields as wide as an outstretched arm, so the arrows and spilled oil of the defenders told but little on their momentum.

By mid-morning, the gate was off its hinges and only standing because of the improvised scaffolding thrown up behind it.

By noon, it hung at so louche an angle, a running man could have sprinted to the top of it and stepped off onto the battlements.

And a little while after that, it fell.

Jamal's foot soldiers, well-drilled, moved quickly aside to right and left, and his cavalry charged into the breach. Three hundred men on stallions—better far than camels once they were on paved stone—galloped through the gaping portal five abreast, their scimitars whirling like the skirts of dancers.

These were the elite of Jamal's army: the cream of the northern mercenaries whom he had travelled so far and paid so much to acquire. They were practised killers, as much at home in the saddle as on the ground, and so proficient with a sword that if two men had stood at arm's length to the left and right of a rider as he advanced, the rider could have cut both throats *en passant* without unseating himself.

But no men—and no women—opposed them. They rode into a narrow avenue, high-walled on either side, and followed it for perhaps a hundred yards before they realised that they had ridden into a trap. Behind the problematic gate, before the battle had even begun, the city's masons under Zuleika's instructions had built a killing ground, enclosed by tall, uneven stone ramparts (the rubble from the demolished buildings outside Bessa's walls had been put to good use).

From these ramparts, now, arrows rained in unsettling profusion. The archers were not the city's trained soldiery, nor yet the Yeagir volunteers: they were the young and the old of Bessa, who could not serve on the walls but could at least string a bow. In such narrow confines, it wasn't necessary for them to be able to aim.

Jamal's cavalry turned en masse with skill and address, and rode hell for leather back towards the gate. But from the barricades above them, more rubble now fell to crush them and block their path. Between the hail of arrows and the rain of stone, barely a dozen of the three hundred made it alive back through the portal through which they had charged only a minute before.

The defenders on the walls cheered and called out to the men below, inviting them to come back for another visit, to bring their friends, to stay the night if they liked. Jamal's troops milled and murmured, their spirits dismayed by the massacre; but only for a time. Before the glass was turned, they renewed their assault—only this time they didn't try to enter the city by its Southern gate.

The sixth day, then, went to Bessa. When the sun went down, the western walls were still intact, and Jamal had suffered the first serious setback of his campaign.

The seventh day did not go so well. The greater numbers of the attackers began to tell more and more, and the beleaguered and exhausted defenders could not be everywhere at once. Close by the modest entrance known as the water gate, three or four siege ladders remained upright long enough to disgorge a small but determined group of fighters onto the battlements. These in turn sold their lives one grain at a time, like misers, and by the time they fell two score more had taken their place. The defenders were forced to turn now and face the enemy on their own level, which meant that they had less attention to spare for the enemy below. The rams came forward and the water gate fell.

Here there was no killing ground. Charging into the city, Jamal's cavalry found nothing and nobody in its path. The riders fanned out quickly, torching buildings and putting any citizens they found to the sword. Within a few short minutes they cut a terrible swathe through Bessa's undefended avenues.

On the street of the silversmiths, though, they were met—by a force much smaller than their own. A few dozen men and women on horseback, wearing no armour, blocked the way ahead of them. The ranking officer (it was that Tayqullah whose name has already appeared in these annals) gave the signal to charge, expecting that this ragtag force would melt away before them.

But the defenders were the Yeagir horsehusbands and their grim-faced womenfolk; therefore, they charged too, full into the face of the much more numerous enemy. The women raised their arms as though in some barbaric salute, and flung their bolases all at the same time. The bolases were just lengths of horsehide weighted at either end with a stone, but the women threw them with such skill and force that the air made a sound at their passage like the cracking of a flag in a gale.

Every bolas found its target. Some wrapped around the throats of the riders, breaking their necks or pitching them backwards off their mounts. Most encircled the horses' legs, and folding tightly around them, hobbled and broke them in a violent instant. The front rank of Jamal's cavalry went down in its entirely, the horses stopped so abruptly that some of them turned somersaults, crushing their riders as they fell.

The fall of the first rank brought down the second, tangled up in the dying and the already dead. The riders further back had halted their headlong career by then, and would have rallied—except that at that point, presented with such easy and tempting targets, the Yeagir men hurled their spears. Rider after rider fell, pierced through chest or neck; then the horsewives came among them, employing their daggers now, as their nimble mounts danced between the fallen men and beasts of the Lion's ruined cavalry.

It was a rout. Tayqullah would have been ashamed to return to his chief and report it, except that he lay among the fallen, his throat slit from ear to ear by a horsewife so coolly detached she might have been peeling an apple.

But the merchants' quarter was burning by that time, and there were few at hand to put out the flames. And up on the battlements, it had cost Zuleika more than she could afford to demolish Jamal's beachhead and reclaim the walls. She had been forced to throw into that skirmish all the half-trained troops she had been holding in reserve. She had led them herself, and in the end they had triumphed. To the very few who survived, that was a source of some pride. But Zuleika was heartsick: she felt as if she had used the blood of her volunteers as a builder uses mortar.

That was the first of three such incursions. The second was across a narrower stretch of wall, and was quickly contained. None of the gates was breached. The third was even bloodier than the first, and the defenders only survived it because Zuleika sent twenty archers to the roof of a high grain warehouse that faced the city walls across a small courtyard. That accident of geography allowed her to direct a crossfire against the attacking troops and wipe them out before they could consolidate their position.

As the sun sank in the sky, it was obscured by ragged sheets of red-brown haze in the middle distance. A storm was coming, throwing sand into the faces of attacker and defender alike. Uncertain of their advantage, the Lion's forces withdrew as the wind rose.

But just before the sun's red eye was lost from view, the western wall, across an area twenty paces wide, sagged like the belly of a spavined horse and readied itself to fall.

THE STORM

In the camp of Jamal, this:

The Lion inspected his troops, who after seven days of battle were both dirtier and grimmer than they had been erewhile. There were fewer of them, too, as was only to be expected. Where there had been thirty cohorts of a thousand each, now there were perhaps twenty-seven. It was a loss without meaning: a few grains of sand from the storm that he had brought against Bessa. Although an hourglass perhaps made a better comparison, since each man in fighting and dying marked an increment in an inevitable process. As the sand poured out, Jamal came closer and closer to his inheritance and to his destiny.

Certainly Nussau, the mercenary captain, saw things in this wise. He could afford to be sanguine, since (apart from that one incident by the Southern gate) Jamal's losses had come overwhelmingly from his homegrown troops rather than from the better trained and better fed soldiers-for-hire who bulked out his numbers. Nussau had consulted with his junior officers, and he was confident that the city would fall on the morrow. He congratulated Jamal on how well the campaign had gone so far, and even haggled about the division of the spoils when the city was sacked. Jamal had agreed that Nussau would take half of any wealth that was found; now Nussau contended that this should be raised to six parts in ten, and Jamal, after some circumambulation, agreed.

When they retired to their tents, their mood was sanguine.

In the night, however, the storm reached its height and a keening wind woke Jamal from a troubled sleep. He could not remember his dreams, but felt that they had been unpleasant. Some of their mood now seeped, unbidden, into his waking mind.

The omens were good, but he was far from happy. He had not expected Bessa to stand for a full week, and though in absolute numbers he was still strong, the utter loss of two wings of cavalry disturbed him greatly. So did the fact that the concubinate had not attempted to parley. He remembered his abortive rebellion, and how Zuleika had descended on him out of a clear sky, knowing everything he intended to do while concealing her own stratagems perfectly.

Was it possible that she had a plan which encompassed all that had happened so far? That despite all the indications of success, and the massive odds in his favour, she was about to destroy him in a way that was as absolute and unexpected as the ruination of his previous schemes?

Reason said no. But reason could not raise its voice above the wind's screaming.

Like a man still in the grip of a dream, Jamal left his tent. His bodyguards made to follow him, but he stayed them with a gesture. He walked away from the camp and the watchfires, his own soldiers eyeing him curiously as he passed them unseeing.

He was a child of Bessa: he knew that there were wells outside the walls, and he knew where they were. He went to the largest of them now, and peered into its lightless depths as though he were interrogating his own heart.

Then he took from the sabretache he wore at his waist a small bottle he had not touched nor even thought about for many months. It contained the poison he had bought from dead Hakkim's disciple. The cap twisted in his hand, the wax seal giving with a sound like a sigh.

The bottle upended itself, and the poison dribbled sluggishly from its neck, down into the well.

Jamal watched his own hand with something like unease. The movement had come ahead of the decision, or at least ahead of the conscious realisation. But he knew exactly what it was he was doing. It was just that his hands had known it first.

As he replaced the stopper and put the empty bottle back into his sabretache, he became aware that he was being watched. He turned and saw one of his own men staring at him from a few yards away. The man was squatting to shit—presumably the reason why he had come so far from the camp's perimeter. His eyes were wide, and his mouth hung open.

Mushin. The man's name was Mushin. He was one of the first; the men Jamal had recruited in Ibu Kim, before he left that pestilential place forever.

For some reason, possibly arising from the lingering atmosphere of the dream, Jamal felt the urge to explain his actions, though he knew that Mushin probably could not be made to understand them.

"It's one more assurance," he said, controlling with some difficulty the tremor in his voice. That was not enough: Mushin still gaped like a dead fish. "One more guarantee that we'll bring them down. If they survive this siege, it won't matter. This well draws from the same aquifers as those in the western part of the city. They'll fall, now. They'll have a choice between dying of thirst or dying by poison. Even if the walls hold, they'll still fall."

No response from Mushin, whose face seemed fixed forever in that mask of horror and mental incapacity.

"It won't matter. When we take the city, we'll dig new wells. They'll be further from the walls, but that's only a hardship to the idle. Nothing is lost by this." Jamal had run out of words, so he fell back on repetition. "Nothing is lost."

Finally, Mushin got his lower jaw back into its customary position, stood and adjusted his robes. He still said nothing, though, and only watched Jamal as if afraid that his chief would attack or berate him. Jamal had no intention of doing either.

"Tell the soldiers," he ordered Mushin. "This well is forbidden. All the wells on this side of the city—they shouldn't be used. A single sip will kill."

He expected a salute, and possibly a "Yes, Jamal," but clearly that was too much to ask for from this dullard. "Tell them," Jamal said again, then he turned his back and walked back towards the distant campfires, barely visible through the swirling sand.

The storm raged through the entire night, and he did not sleep again. But in the morning, the wind fell and the sand sank back to the desert floor like the falling of a curtain.

What it revealed made the soldiers of the Lion wish that it had stayed.

Within the walls of Bessa, this:

The seventh day was unlike the others they had endured. Each in its

389

turn had wrought darkly on the city and its defenders; each in its turn had scattered tragedies and disasters with a liberal hand, ending lives and loves, unmaking friendships and betrothals, changing the human geography of Bessa as profoundly as its material substance. But the seventh day was the day when Zuleika knew for sure that Bessa could not stand.

It was also the day when Bethi died. She was no soldier, and had no illusions that she could become one. She had sought out the place where she could do the most good, and had organised two parallel groups of citizens both to supply the soldiers on the walls with food and water and to carry messages between the various towers and guard posts.

She was on the street when the third and largest of the breaches occurred, and went down under the hooves of a group of riders. The message she was carrying when she died warned that such an incursion was imminent.

Bethi was one of Zuleika's closest friends, and Anwar Das's beloved. Three times he had asked for her hand, and been rebuffed—for though she loved him as fervently as he loved her, she was also as promiscuous as he by nature and inclination. She had told him they would wed, at last, when no man or woman else would look at them.

Now he knelt by her catafalque in the numb silence of grief. He had nothing to say in response to the clumsy words of mourning and comfort offered by his friends. All words had deserted him, and he cared not in the darkness of that moment whether he ever spoke again. Zuleika respected his speechlessness, and only held him, mute, as they wept together.

Then she gathered herself for what must now be done.

Though a night attack was far from being out of the question, she posted a skeletal watch on the walls and called an open meeting in the Jidur. There were things she wished to discuss not just with the lawmakers and strategists but with all of the people in the city, and they would not wait until the morning.

The storm frustrated her, initially: the wind ripped the breath from her mouth, and raised its own voice over hers. It quickly became clear that the meeting would have to move indoors, and the throne room in the palace was chosen as the venue, since it was the only space that was big enough to contain them all.

The room had not been entered since the day of Hakkim's death.

Zuleika ascended the steps of the throne, treading through inch-thick dust, and turned to face her audience. There was utter silence in the room. She knew that Rem was standing behind her, carefully out of her line of sight—afraid, as always, that her own reactions would spark some change of heart in her lover, and so weave her into the unfolding of events in ways that would be traumatic and unbearable. Zuleika took some comfort from her presence, but given what she was about to suggest, she yearned for more tangible support.

"We persuaded ourselves against all reason that the city could hold," she said. She spoke in the same ringing voice she would have used in the Jidur, but here it wasn't needed: the room's perfect acoustics brought her voice to the ear of everyone present. "And we've made that ridiculous argument good for seven days. But reason gets the last word, my sisters and my brothers. Tomorrow, or the next day, or the day after that, Bessa will fall. Thereafter, the Lion will kill those of us he cares to kill and take the rest into a servitude worse than that you knew under Al-Bokhari—because now you've tasted freedom, and the taste will never leave your lips."

Zuleika paused. The emotions welling within her made it difficult for her to speak. But nobody interrupted her, and in due course she took up her theme again.

"We decided to make our stand here because we felt that to lose Bessa was the same as death. I spoke those words myself, and I applauded when others spoke them. But it was a lie, and I should have known better. Death is the end of every hope and every possibility. To flee with your lives is not the same, even if you're scattered like dust across *As-Sahra*. Hope remains. Possibility remains. Bessa is its people, not its stones. If the stones fall and the people live, Bessa may live again. If you die here, Bessa dies with you.

"So I stand before you now to urge the exact opposite of what I urged erewhile. The streets and towers you love are now a trap that holds you. I want you to consider ways in which you might escape from that trap."

This time, when Zuleika paused, the spell of silence was broken. A hundred voices answered her, and then a thousand. The citizens forgot the discipline of the Jidur, for this was not the Jidur, and they forgot the courtesies of the everyday because they felt their distance from the everyday as one might feel the pain of a wound.

Zuleika weathered the bombardment of voices, until Imtisar stood and quelled them: Imtisar, who was so old and frail now that she was barely able to stand at all. She did it with a gesture—fingers of one hand folded into the palm of the other—which she sometimes used in the Jidur to mean "this discourse is against the purpose of the debate." It worked. All voices were stilled again, and those who wished to speak stood, waiting to be recognized by the chair—a role that Imtisar had assumed by means of that very gesture.

Many responded, and at first the responses were all of the same tenor: *We swore we would stand to the last man and woman, and we mean to be true to what we swore.* But the certainty of death weighed on them all, and by some magic the many iterations of this theme began to change it from within into its own opposite. It is hard enough to love death in the abstract; nobody wants to die when death is before them.

But when all had spoken, Rem stood. Within the prism of her inward sight, a possibility so remote it could barely be made out at all had come into clear focus—had become, in the space of a few heartbeats, an actuality. Rem's agitation prevented her, for a moment, from even speaking.

"Rem is recognized," Imtisar said, in a quavering voice.

"He poisons the water!" Rem cried, her arms waving in front of her face as though she was trying to draw the horrific scene on the empty air. "Jamal! He has a bottle in his hand! He pours it into the well, and poisons the city's water. Two hours from now, he did this. Does this. It can't be stopped. It happened . . . it would have happened . . . because we stood against him for so long, we made this thing inevitable. He can't be stopped. He couldn't ever have been stopped!"

She faltered; almost, she fell. Zuleika supported her and helped her to sit again, her hands still jerking spasmodically.

There was shocked silence at first. All who had heard Rem speak knew now that their position was hopeless. One by one they stared into the abyss and made their accommodation with what they found there.

From heroic defiance, the speeches modulated into arguments about feasibility. How could they flee, when the city was surrounded by armed men? Even if they escaped, Jamal would hunt them down—his cavalry was much faster than a column fleeing on foot with all its worldly goods—and take them into servitude, if he did not simply slaughter them on the spot. Then, too, they would be fleeing into the mouth of a raging sandstorm, which would blind and scatter them, slow them still further, and quite possibly kill a great many of them before their flight had fairly begun.

Backwards and forwards the arguments swayed, like a spinning plate balanced on the end of a stake. And as with the plate, irreparable damage seemed the most likely outcome wherever in its orbit it finally slowed.

Now that Zuleika had spoken, Rem felt safe to go to her. They sat on the steps of the throne, their hands clasped together, and listened as one after another rose and spoke.

The last to speak was Anwar Das. He had come direct from Bethi's bier, and he walked like a man already dead. His words are not recorded.

The storm died out just before dawn, and the sun rose at last on an altered landscape.

This is the way of things, after a sandstorm. Valleys and ridges move their places by as much as a mile, level plains shrug themselves into hillocks, and once-familiar places must be learned all over again.

In this case, the human landscape had been similarly transformed.

True, there were still warriors, men and women alike, on the walls of Bessa. And true, an army still faced them on the plain.

But the Lion's forces were a third of their former size: a core of eight or nine thousand remained from the vast horde of the day before. Mushin had gone among the fighters from the desert cities, and told the tale of the poisoning of the wells. Those pragmatic people had few taboos, but this was the strongest of them; they had fled their former chief in the night, even while the storm was at its height, and there was now no sign of them. Only Jamal's mercenary troops, who cared a great deal more about the spoils of the soon-to-be-sacked city than they did about poisoned water, had stayed in their places.

In their place, though, another army—an army of strangers—faced Jamal's across a half-mile of wind-rucked sand.

How the City Was Unmade

Jamal and Nussau surveyed the newcomers with troubled hearts and grim faces.

At first, Jamal thought that they were the deserters from his own army, intending not to leave his service but to renegotiate the terms on which they fought. A second, longer glance told him that this was not so; wherever it had come from, this new-arrived force was not local, and not his. The swarthy complexions and richly coloured robes of the warriors told a different story.

An hour passed, and then a second hour, and the newcomers did not move. Nussau's mercenaries began to grow restive, since their chief had not yet ordered them to renew their assault on the besieged city. Jamal had expected them to be more dismayed by the desertions, but if anything they seemed to be pleased that they would not have to break the spoils of fallen Bessa into quite so many shares. Certainly, they harboured no doubts about their ability to take the city, which was clearly now on the very brink of falling.

But it would be folly to launch an assault with—potentially—a fresh enemy at their rear. At last, Jamal and Nussau both went out to meet the newcomers, taking with them only half a dozen handpicked warriors. They rode to a midway point between the two armies, and there waited.

From the newcomers, only two men rode out.

At closer quarters, their strangeness was even more apparent. One of the two was as dark as ebony, but his face was daubed with white paint into the likeness of a skull. His teeth, exposed in an almost ceaseless grimace, had been painted red. Red was the colour of his robes, too, except where strips of tanned animal hide had been tied like brown ribbons around his upper arms and the calves of his legs. Overall, he looked like a piece of half-cured meat. But the scimitar that hung from his saddle horn was fully three feet long—a weapon designed for a berserker who did not need to worry, when he charged, about the safety of those around him. Even the man's horse was barbarically appointed, its mane dyed black, and black nails hammered into its pawing hooves.

At this man's side rode a second man whose manner was less alarming but equally exotic. His face was painted pure white, and the word "speaker" was written in red upon his brow. On his chest, further characters appeared, spelling out the two words "unto infidels." He was naked except for a breach-clout, he bore no weapon, and he rode without a saddle.

"Greetings unto you," Jamal said, bluntly. "What brings you here?"

The dark man spoke tersely in a tongue Jamal had never heard, and his white-faced companion, after a short silence, said "We came because of the war." His voice was high and fluting, almost effeminate. Evidently he was acting as translator.

"Because of the war?" Jamal repeated. "What do you mean? Are you emissaries from one of the cities of the plain?" Clearly they were no such thing, but Jamal preferred to let them state their business in their own words; he offered this unlikely scenario for them to disagree with it, and so define themselves.

Again, the dark man spoke, his utterances sounding almost like the barking of a dog.

"We offer our services," the white-faced man said. "If we fight beside you, you will win. We are the Misreia, unbeaten in battle. We number five thousand, and each of us is worth fifty. Our blades sing in the air with the voices of those we have slain—a choir louder than the angels of Heaven."

Jamal blinked, and Nussau looked grave. "You're mercenaries, then," the mercenary captain said. He said it with a profound lack of enthusiasm, but Jamal's interest quickened. He had just lost a large number of fighting men—he wasn't going to reject new recruits out of hand.

The white-faced man translated. His companion—or more likely his master—made a harsh sound and spat. Then he spoke at greater length.

"We do not fight for money," the white-faced man parsed, "or for any material reward. Only our god demands recompense."

"And how much does your god charge?" Nussau asked, with heavy sarcasm.

"Our god is great."

"Evidently."

"Greater, far, than other gods."

"And therefore?"

"Two-thirds of any bounty taken from the city will be due to Him. And two-thirds of the city's people, to be His slaves and serve His chosen."

"Unacceptable," Nussau said.

It was an absurd price to ask; presumably it was intended as the opening gambit in a protracted bout of haggling. But it would be difficult for Jamal to haggle with Nussau beside him, defending his own men's share of the spoils. Reluctantly, he shook his head. "Your god's price, though he be greater than any other god, is too high. We can't afford him."

The white-painted man conferred with his master and then looked up again, staring meaningfully over Jamal's left shoulder at the city. "Then we're free to offer our services elsewhere," he said, his tone pitched between a statement and a question.

"By no means," Jamal said. "If you try to enter the city, we'll be obliged to turn and fight you."

Nussau, being of a more practical turn of mind, added a further argument. "They'd never let you in, in any case. They'd be bound to assume you were with us, and that your offer was a subterfuge. Any sane man would come to the same conclusion."

"And how could they agree to pay you in the coin of their own citizenry?" Jamal asked. "Nobody would fight alongside you, for the privilege of being your slave—so you'd stand alone on those walls, and as you can probably see even from here, they wouldn't hold your weight for very long."

All of these points were passed along to the red-robed chieftain, who digested them with scant pleasure. He spoke again, what sounded like a single word.

"A half of the spoils," the white-painted man said.

"No," said Nussau again.

"The timing of these negotiations," Jamal said, "is unpropitious. You say you number five thousand. We have many more than that number, and though we obviously wish to retain them all for the final assault on the city, we will if it proves necessary turn from our task long enough to gut you like dogs and water the desert with your blood. I say this with all due respect."

The chieftain, apprised of this assertion, looked thunderous, but said nothing. For twenty heartbeats, he and Jamal merely stared at each other, as though each was waiting for the other to blink.

Finally the chieftain spoke again, for a final time. Before his companion had even begun to translate, he wheeled his horse about and galloped away.

"We will withdraw," the white-faced man said. "If you prevail, you will not see us again. If you lose, we will harry you as you retreat, and rape and murder your soldiers. We will do these things, however many you number. This is my Lord's promise to you."

Jamal reached for his sword, but Nussau clamped a heavy hand on his forearm and stayed him from drawing it. "If we're forced to retreat," he said, "although that won't happen, we'll be short of horses and provisions. We'll take your mounts for both, your robes for wash-cloths, and leave you to walk home naked across *As-Sahra*. This is my promise to your Lord."

The white-painted man dipped his head in a perfunctory bow and rode away.

"Why didn't you let me kill him?" Jamal snarled.

Nussau gave a coarse laugh. "Those insults meant nothing," he said. "They merely allowed that jackass to withdraw without loss of face. But a decapitated messenger would have forced him to fight. You've much to learn about human nature, Jamal."

And it certainly seemed that the mercenary captain was right. The strangers decamped immediately, and they did not look back. Ever cautious, Nussau had them followed for some several miles by three of his best scouts: they did not turn back, or split their forces, or even look behind them. They headed due north, towards the mountains, and presumably beyond them to their distant homeland.

The way was clear for the final assault on Bessa. It now transpired that Jamal's deserters, in leaving, had sabotaged most of the siege catapults with judiciously laid fires, but Nussau greeted this discovery with only mild irritation. There was little need, at this stage, to pound the walls further: the breaches already made offered doorways enough.

But Bessa did not fall that day. Perhaps it was because the reduction in the numbers of the attacking forces forced them to make their forays across a narrower front, where the walls were weakest. Or perhaps it was because the tall, slender woman whom Nussau's soldiers called "the demon" was so very prominent in that day's fighting, hurling herself again and again into lost positions, only to win out and buy her people a second or a minute's advantage. However it was, though they came against the walls with might and main, and wreaked red havoc among the defenders, the Lion's cohorts did not gain a single good foothold throughout what remained of the eighth day of the siege.

At night, there was muttering. Some among the mercenary officers felt aggrieved that they were now bearing the full weight of this conflict alone, when the contract to which they had assented saw them as the mercenary wing of a greater force. They had been happier when Jamal's expendables were taking most of the pounding, and acting as a human bulwark against their own losses.

Nussau went among them and rallied them with words both sweet and stern. He reminded them of the booty to be won on the morrow, when the walls finally fell. He reminded them, too, that any man who defaulted in his duty would lose all pay accrued during this campaign, as well as a goodly portion of the skin on his back.

These exhortations had their effect. On the ninth day, the attackers launched themselves on the ruined walls and the all-but-ruined defenders with the ferocity of madmen and the fervour of marabouts. Under this onslaught, the Bessan soldiery fell back rapidly, and then with unexpected suddenness a section of the damaged west wall fell, not under any direct assault but from the damage previously inflicted on it.

The defenders had presumably planned to fall back on the palace when the walls were breached, but this instantaneous collapse prevented them from doing so. As Jamal's troops charged through the breach, the beleaguered Bessans fled under heavy fire to a tall structure with walls of pink stone—the only nearby building that was even remotely defensible.

This was, by now, the only real front. Elsewhere on the walls, surprisingly small pockets of defenders were wiped out with ease as the besieging troops took control of stretch after stretch of the battlements. The defenders, men and women alike, fought until they dropped—

but they dropped quickly as the spread of Jamal's troops across the battlements allowed more and more fire to be trained on them. What had been a pitched battle now devolved into a series of localised culls, which the mercenaries carried out with brisk efficiency.

By the time the main gate was broached by the battering rams, there was silence across the rest of the city. Apart from that one building, where a few of Zuleika's janissaries had managed to go to ground, nothing moved.

Jamal entered Bessa in state, riding a white stallion through the jubilant ranks of the mercenaries. They cheered him to the skies, and he accepted their homage with some considerable satisfaction.

But the sight that met his eyes sobered him somewhat. The streets of Bessa were mostly empty—its citizens presumably hiding in their houses and waiting for the worst. What citizens he did see were uniformed and dead, but there were not many even of these. His eyes lingered on each corpse as he rode past it. The silence which had announced his victory scant minutes before now seemed somehow funereal.

A scar-faced sergeant led him to the pink building where the last defenders had taken refuge. Though it was a formality, Nussau, with a fine tact, allowed the Lion of the Desert the privilege of directing the last engagement of the campaign. But Jamal seemed in no hurry to do so.

"What is this place?" he asked the sergeant.

"Sign over the door calls it the House of Pleasant Fires, sir," the sergeant answered, with a brisk salute. "Looks like a brothel. Should we mount a charge, sir? Looks like they're all out of arrows, else they wouldn't let us get so close."

"A moment," Jamal said. He rode his horse a little closer to the building. It stood in a small square, with the blind sides of other buildings to right and left and the city walls facing it. Nothing moved inside.

"The city has fallen," Jamal called out loudly. "Come out with empty hands, and throw yourselves on my mercy."

"Do you have any mercy, Jamal?" Zuleika answered him from inside the building. "You've kept it well hidden until now."

Jamal's heart raced. He realised then that when he had examined the dead bodies in the streets he had been looking for hers—and had been glad not to find it. Zuleika's death should not, could not be anonymous. It mattered too much.

"Oil and arrows," he ordered. "Burn them out."

Cavalrymen galloped past the front of the house, hurling clay jars full of oil in through the windows to shatter on the stone floors inside. Then they withdrew and the archers fired arrows whose heads had been wrapped in oily rags and set ablaze.

Inside of a minute, the inside of the House of Pleasant Fires was belying its name, its interior a flesh-broiling inferno.

The defenders began to sprint through the front door and to dive from the windows of the house. Backlit as they were by the bright flames, they made easy targets. Jamal's archers took them at their leisure.

He knew her when she came. She did not run, but strode through the doorway with her sword in her hand, her steps even and her head high. The first arrow took her in the shoulder and the second low down in the side. She fell to her knees as a third pierced her right hand. The sword fell from her grip and clattered on the flags.

"Stop firing!" Jamal cried. "Stop firing!"

A few more arrows were launched, but they went wide. Jamal's order was relayed by the sergeant in a cattle market bellow, and the archers lowered their bows.

Jamal dismounted and went to her, kneeling before her to stare into her eyes. They were open, but dulled with shock. Blood was trickling from the corner of her mouth, and her breathing was so shallow it was scarcely visible.

"Zuleika," he said to her, gently.

"Jamal," she said, her voice almost a whisper.

"How goes it with you, lady?"

She did not answer this sally. Presumably she had too few breaths left to waste any of them on badinage. Her eyes met his, but they did not focus. Her expression was unreadable. He wanted more from her than just his name.

"Your city has fallen," he told her. "Your soldiers are dead."

Disconcertingly, Zuleika smiled. "My city . . ." she breathed. "My city left this place two days ago."

It happened in this wise.

As Anwar Das had suggested, the people of Bessa went from the palace back to their homes, where they quickly gathered as many of their possessions as they could carry, as well as water and provisions. They were fleeing from a death they knew was certain. Jamal's poisoning of the wells, two scant hours in their future, was a sentence of execution pending over every one of them. The people assembled again in the Jidur. The storm was at its height, and the shrieking of the air, added to their own state of restlessness and urgency, caused some to faint and many to weep.

The evacuation of the city's civilian population was to be total. Among the soldiery, it was decided that the issue of who should stay and who should go would be settled in the first instance by asking for volunteers. Zuleika believed that two hundred men and women, judiciously positioned, would be sufficient to maintain the illusion that the walls were fully defended, and to have some reasonable chance of holding them, at least for a few hours, against Jamal's assaults. Each soldier, then, would place a scrip into a jar passed around by Zuleika herself. The scrip would contain either the soldier's name, if the soldier wished to volunteer, or else a cross or some other random mark if the soldier did not. Only if fewer than two hundred names were given would Zuleika ask—or order—specific people to stay.

Rem watched as Zuleika read the names aloud. They were the names of friends, making compact to die so that other friends might (if the Increate willed it) live. They were the names of heroes, who would have no other memorial.

Umayma was called first, and she saluted her chief with closed fists as though this in itself were victory. Rihan, Dalal, Najla, Firdoos, all were named: and each name carried a full freight of memories—for Rem, memories not only of the past but of the futures that would not now be lived.

The tally reached one hundred, sixty and seven. Zuleika pronounced herself satisfied with this number, but old Issi stood, shaking his head sternly. "The lady said two hundred," he said to the room at large, his voice as strong as ever. "Are we to be shamed in this way? To send her into this lost battle with a smaller muster than she asked for? No! Never! Not while I live!" Issi's eyes shone with tears as he stared round him, meeting every gaze in turn. "You know what they said of us. That every citizen of Bessa was a sultan. That was us. That was ours. And today, every citizen of Bessa is a soldier. I demand the right to add my name to Zuleika's muster!"

"I demand the right to add my name!" another old man echoed, rising to his feet.

"I demand the right to add my name!" cried a woman from the other end of the hall. It was Halima, who had said once that she could not kill if called upon.

"I demand the right to add my name!" came from all sides of the hall, and Zuleika raised her hands in surrender.

"I will refuse no one," she said. "Step forward, then, all those not of the city guard, who wish now to stand with the guard in its extremity."

Three or four dozen stood, and walked towards her. Among them was Imtisar, leaning heavily on the arm of Jumanah. Zuleika put a hand on the old woman's shoulder. "You're sure this is what you want?" she whispered.

"This is my home," Imtisar said with energy. "No rabble will throw me out of it. And I'll take a few of them down, as well."

"I'm staying too," Jumanah said. "With Imtisar, and Najla. My place is here with them."

When the tally was finally made, the muster stood at two hundred and seventeen. Zuleika gave order that the new recruits should be given weapons and breastplates. Zeinab, whose name had not been called, came to her friend Umayma with the best sword and scabbard she could find.

"It shouldn't end like this," she wept, as the two friends embraced.

Umayma did not weep.

"I buried my son's head, a week ago," she said, her voice hard. "Where his body lies, I know not. My life is over, Zeinab, but I give my death freely, for whatever it may be worth."

While the volunteers were armed, Zuleika came to Rem to say her farewells.

Zuleika was accustomed to keeping her emotions in check. It was the first thing that an assassin learned, and it was a lesson that was revisited, in a sense, with every subsequent killing. Still, when she embraced Rem, she did not trust herself to speak. Her hands were steady; her voice, she knew, would not be.

Rem made no pretensions to stoicism. She clung to Zuleika in an access of despair. "I can't," she wept. "I can't live without you! Don't make me! Don't make me!"

"I'll follow you," Zuleika whispered, stroking her hair. "I'll follow you, Rem. If we can hold through today and tomorrow, those of us who are left will do then exactly what you're doing now. We'll only be two days behind you."

Rem knew that these were lies, and was not soothed by them. It was not her foresight that told her this, but remorseless logic. Only the storm gave this current plan the smallest chance of succeeding, and whatever passed now, nobody left in the city would follow. This was the last time that she and Zuleika would ever touch. But she knew, too, that what she said and did now would affect Zuleika's spirits for good or ill, and so she said no more, but held to her beloved as if her muscles had locked and her flesh had petrified. Whereas it was only her heart that had suffered this fate.

"Lady," Anwar Das said at last, gently. "We must leave."

And they broke apart, and went their ways, their suffering a mirror to the lamentations played out all around them by friends and families sundered now forever: those about to leave pulled unwilling and weeping from the arms of those who had chosen to stay.

The procession that wended its way to the cattle market gate made up the vast majority of the city's population, along with five hundred able-bodied fighters who would protect them from casual predation on their journey. From Jamal's army, if Jamal realised what was happening, there could be no protection.

They left the city in total silence. Only four or five abreast, they walked in a long, straight column out from Bessa and onto the plain. In front came the children, schooled not to speak, carried by mothers and fathers or led by their teachers Hayat, Laila, Mahmud and Mayisah. Old Rashad, who had been begged by his son and grandchildren not to stay behind, walked in tears, held up by Dip and Walid; he had left his old deputy, Karif, to die on the city walls. Beside him came Farhat, leaning heavily on the arm of Huma.

Behind the old, the young and the infirm came the able-bodied women and men. The members of the Artisan's Guild walked behind Farhat, holding those of their works they could not bear to leave behind: Taliyah carried a roll of paintings, while Maysoon's daughter Suri and her apprentice had wrapped their most precious pots for safekeeping in Farhat's tapestries. Those that walked in the rear of the column led horses and camels, all muzzled, gentling them with strokes and whispered words.

They passed between two of Jamal's encampments, close enough on either side to have called out to the men in both and been heard—but the air was in turmoil, the rent veils of the storm sliding over everything and its voice booming over all other voices. They would not have found their way at all, except that Rem led them, and she knew in advance the position—both relative and absolute—of each of her footfalls. She did not walk through the storm: eyes closed, she walked through the stillness that was and would be again.

When they were almost a mile out, the Bessans turned half-about, and under the direction of Zuleika's most experienced officers formed themselves into a phalanx. Those who were actual soldiers, and whose bearing was therefore the most convincing, stood in the van. They had darkened their skin with henna and tangled their hair with tar: in place of the tunics and breastplates they had been wont to wear on Bessa's walls, they stood (or rode) mostly naked, with only jerkins and breach-clouts made up hastily from uncured leather. Close at hand, they looked like maniacs or ecstatics lined up with implausible discipline. From a distance, they hoped to pass for a foreign army.

They waited out the storm, and then the sun. And on the morrow, when Jamal and Nussau rode towards them, it was Anwar Das, white-painted, who rode halfway to meet them. The man at his side was a Yeagir, though his speeches were chants in the sing-song nonsense language used to send small infants to sleep. Anwar Das, for his part, disguised his voice by forcing it into a shriller register, and trusted to the painted words on his brow and on his body to prevent Jamal from looking too closely at his face. Another could have been sent, but Anwar Das's heroic deceitfulness was legendary: who else could have been trusted to sell such a lie?

So he made his offer to Jamal—an offer that Jamal obligingly refused—and then he rode away, back to the ranks of the Bessan refugees. They turned again, setting Bessa at their backs, and began their long march. At first they were followed by Jamal's scouts, but after a few hours these fell away and they were alone.

Their goal was the mountains, and the caves of the bandits which they had left so many years before. But that was only a staging post on a much longer journey.

Jamal did not at first understand what it was that Zuleika had said. But then certain thoughts and images cohered in his mind in a sudden, abstract wash of thought, and enlightenment came. He knew, then, why the streets were so empty, and why the Bessan defenders had failed, at the end, to fall back to the palace and bar themselves in. There were too few left, by then, to maintain a line as they retreated, or to cover each other's backs as they crossed open squares and piazzas: all they could do was run, and they had not run far.

He knew, too, who it was he had spoken to out on the plain on the morning after the storm, how he had been fooled into allowing the people of Bessa to escape the siege unmolested—and how, therefore, he had come to inherit, as in his nightmare of yesteryear, a city of the dead, with no populace, no farmlands and no safe water.

He had won the war, and at the same time defeated himself utterly: grasped after the substance, and caught the shadow.

All that was left of his victory was Zuleika. And Zuleika was still smiling. It was not a deliberate taunt—she was thinking of her lover, safe and away and two days gone; of the city of women turned into a seed on the wind, that might take root elsewhere. She smiled because she was not a concubine any more, nor yet an assassin, but a soldier who has done her duty and could now hope to rest.

But to Jamal, the smile was salt in wounds both old and new. He kicked out in a rage, sending Zuleika sprawling to the ground, and then he kicked her again and again as she lay. When she raised her right arm to ward off the blows, his foot connected with the arrow that had transfixed her right hand, and the shaft snapped in two.

Around him, his troops watched the beating in stolid silence, without much interest. But Nussau, arriving then, viewed it with irritation. He had found to his horror that the spoils on which he and his men had placed such store were not to be had. Bessa had been emptied not only of its people but of most of its portable wealth. The granaries were empty, the shops and warehouses—those that had not been burned in previous incursions—stripped down to bare wood and cool stone. Bessa hosted nothing, now, save corpses and ruin.

In dark mood, therefore, and impatient of Jamal's self-indulgence, the barbarian captain drew his sword and stepped in to finish Zuleika with a single sword-thrust. To his annoyance, Jamal laid a hand on his sword-arm and shook his head.

"No," he said. "She's mine."

"We need to talk about payment," Nussau said brusquely. "And provisioning."

"We will talk," Jamal told him. "But this must come first."

With curt gestures, he made the watching soldiers back away. "Nobody is to intervene," he ordered. "Nobody touches her, but me. Nobody speaks to her, but me." Then he stood over Zuleika and nudged her with the toe of his boot. At first she did not stir, but finally she raised her head—her lips split and bleeding, one eye already swelling shut from the beating he had given her. With the other eye alone, she met his gaze.

"Fight me," he invited her. "You heard what I told them. Fight me and win, and you'll be free. That's all you have to do."

He waited. He was not a patient man, but for this, and this alone, he found an unexpected reserve of patience in the fervid cauldron of his soul.

Slowly—terribly slowly—Zuleika gathered herself. She struggled up onto her knees, using her left arm to support her weight. Once on her knees, she was able to grasp her sword in her left hand and then to rise to her feet, though she staggered and almost fell again.

"It will be here," Jamal told her, "and it will be now."

She nodded, acknowledging the remembered words.

Jamal's sword flicked from side to side as he moved in toward her, and Zuleika raised her own blade to block him, but there was no strength left in her. Jamal swept the sword aside with a tremendous stroke, and stabbed her in the stomach. He didn't drive the sword in deeply; he did not wish, just yet, to deliver a killing blow. An inch or two only, then out and up, en garde, as he stepped back from a counterattack that didn't come.

Three more times he repeated this: advancing on Zuleika, beating down her defence with ease and then wounding her lightly before withdrawing. The wounds bled freely, and the areas of saturated cloth spread and merged until Zuleika was robed in red. That she managed to keep her footing was something of a marvel to the men watching, who already knew of the Demon and had extended her their grudging admiration.

"Finish it," Nussau grunted, in something like disgust.

Jamal did not wish to do so, did not relish the thought of turning from this cathartic killing to the other, more problematic aspects of his victory. But he bowed to the inevitable. Attacking once more, he stepped inside Zuleika's guard, turned his blade deftly and raised it in a lateral flick that severed the tendon of Zuleika's left arm. She dropped her sword again, the arm now even more useless than the right.

He waited for her to fall, but she did not fall. No matter. He backed away a step and readied his blade for the *coup de grace*. But he could not forbear from one final taunt. "You see where you are?" he asked her, indicating with his sword-tip the blazing building at their backs. "Your heroic last stand was in a brothel. Your life came full circle, my lady, and you ended where you were always meant to be. A house of copulation. By such means does the Increate teach us our lessons."

He made ready to strike, and then realised that Zuleika was still staring over his shoulder at the inferno which the House of Pleasant Fires had become. He turned to look in the same direction, standing away from her at the same time in case this was some trick—even without a weapon, even dying on her feet, Zuleika presented a clear and present danger.

But it was not a trick. Haloed by flames, a figure stood in the doorway of the burning house, as though fire was her home. She was very slight, and the intensity of the light behind her ate into the edges of her silhouette, making her slighter still—superhumanly attenuated into the merest ribbon of flesh between the fire and the fire.

"*Imir Nussau,*" the figure said. "*Min he Shara insulleh han mu'neana kulheyin. B'rabatha me kuth imal han. Drueh in neru keli mu'neana ha.*"

The words were low and harsh, throat-spoken. Nussau stiffened, his eyes opening a little wider. It had taken Jamal thus far to recognize the dialect of the northern tribes, though the captain and his officers spoke it to each other each night around the campfires, as did the common soldiers on the few occasions when he walked among them.

"What is she saying?" he demanded, unsettled not by the apparition nor by her words, but by captain Nussau's reaction of hackles-up surprise.

Still speaking, or perhaps reciting, the figure came forward a few paces. Still backlit, her features were invisible, but she looked more human now—to Jamal, at least. But clearly the soldiers around him were less reassured.

This was because they could understand her speech, as Jamal could not.

"Captain Nussau," she had said. "Your wife, Shara, writhes and screams now in childbirth. Half out of her, half in, your son hangs between life and death. The Increate watches you, and His hand is poised."

Nussau had left his wife in the fifth month of her pregnancy, and he could count as well as the next man; he knew that her time was now upon her. His gaze was fixed on the half-invisible figure as she walked out of the fire, directly towards him.

"The Increate watches, and His hand has fallen. Born into death, your son's eyes never open. The next child, a girl, lives to be six, dies then by drowning. There is no third. Your name dies with you."

An explosive gasp escaped from Nussau's chest.

The fire-woman spoke next unto the sergeant—a man so solid, a man of such girth and sinew, you'd think to see him standing still that he had never moved. "Sergeant Drutha," she called. "The blood in your shit is an omen of death. By winter you are shrivelled to a husk, eaten from within like a cankered fruit. The poison is in your veins and crawling toward your heart."

The sergeant swore, and drew his sword. The fire-woman didn't even turn to acknowledge him. But the soldier standing nearest to the sergeant ran toward her with a spear pointed at her breast.

"You die now," she told him, still without turning. And he did, though none saw what killed him. He just fell, suddenly, to his knees and then full length, and lay forlornly at the woman's feet—an unintended tribute, which she ignored utterly.

"Manasih Rey," she continued, still advancing on the soldiers step by measured step. "Your betrothed fucks another in the bed you built for her. And the man she ruts with is mad, and kills her for the money in her purse. For three gold pieces she lies torn and opened—not now, but two months hence. However quickly you run back along the line of your marching, she's dead and stinking when you open your front door. The sight will never leave you.

"Qusid Apheli, your family is well, but you don't see them again. Running from this place, you're knocked aside by a stronger man and your skull breaks when you hit the ground. Uncaring, comrades kick and trample you. When all is done, your body is a smear like the smear of a dog crushed by many cart wheels.

"Adir Beg, death does not even have to stoop to pick you up. The despair you carry inside you is his doorway, and the dagger at your waist is his key. You slit your wrists, three years from now, just as your older brother Yushif did before you. Your corpse lies at the side of a road until some stranger, passing by, drags it to a ravine and rolls it over the edge. Kites eat your body. Jackals fight for the bones."

It must have been the voice that did it. The details were circumstantial enough that every man addressed knew what he was hearing for the truth, and was struck dumb by it, but for the others . . . it was the voice. They heard the blade of a relentless fate grinding against their souls as against a strop, and they feared to be there when the blade was finally raised to chastise them.

They fled.

Only a few, at first, but a few is all it takes. Seeing their comrades running, others ran too. The sergeant was the last to move, Captain Nussau among the first. Within seconds, the soldiers were barging and climbing over each other in their haste to reach the gates again and get out of this cursed city. Qusid was not the only one who was trampled in that panic flight, but his fate was exactly as the woman had told him it would be.

Within a few seconds, only Jamal remained. The voice was as forbidding to him as to any man, but the words were gibberish, and the silhouette was close enough and clear enough now that he recognized it. This was Rem, the librarian: he knew her too well to fear her. Moreover, he knew her as the woman who had won Zuleika when he had desired her himself.

He strode toward her, his sword drawn back, his mouth fixed in a rictus snarl.

The two blows that killed him came simultaneously.

Rem had been carrying a crossbow, low down at her side. Zuleika had drilled her in the weapon's use during long hours. She knew that one must hold it as level as possible when firing, and pull on the trigger with a single, coaxing movement of the index finger, removing the sear cleanly from the string. Her aim was true, and her hand did not falter.

Zuleika, for her part, had taken advantage of Rem's prophetic tirade to grip in her teeth the shaft of the arrow that had pierced her right hand. Jamal's kick had snapped off the head, so she was able to draw it through her wounded flesh. Of the three daggers in her belt, she chose the heaviest, because it would fly straight despite the trembling of her hand and the spasming of her muscles.

The quarrel entered Jamal's heart: the dagger, which was hiltless, buried itself to the fullness of its length in the back of his neck.

He continued to move toward Rem, his own momentum carrying him. She stepped aside, and he fell at her feet, face down.

His death removed him from the future, as a factor that might touch Rem or be touched by her. Instantly, in the kaleidoscope of her inward sight, he went from blurry incoherence into pin-sharp focus. She saw the lives he might have lived, and how few of them were good. A wasteland had surrounded him from birth. It would have taken a much stronger man to find a way across it.

"Oh, Jamal," she murmured, her voice thick with tears.

On the cusp of death, he heard those words—the pity in them filled him with a horror greater than the dark into which he fell.

Kneeling quickly by Zuleika's side, Rem stripped off her shirt and tore it into strips to dress her beloved's wounds. Zuleika had slipped by this time into a shallow unconsciousness, barely aware of what was happening to her.

Rem, conscious of everything, gazed down at her in something like envy.

She had managed a full day's march away from Bessa, and every moment of that day had been a torment.

The future broke into the present like a tidal wave infinitely renewed and sustained. With each breath, it brought a fresh lading of ruin. She was aware of every death, every ending: the unmaking of the city, the labour of all those years uncannily and cruelly reversed.

She saw Rihan and Firdoos fall, back to back, and she saw horsemen trample them—Rihan still alive for a few moments as the hooves pounded her.

She saw Umayma shooting arrow after arrow until none were left; saw her take an arrow herself in the heart, another in the belly, and then saw her scream Zufir's name as she threw herself from the battlements onto the head of a startled soldier below, killing him even as she died.

She saw old Issi split a man's skull with a thrown axe; gentle Halima embed a slingshot stone in the socket of a cavalryman's eye; stolid Dalal scream like a berserker as she hacked at the top of a scaling ladder and sought to topple it on the heads of the enemy who climbed it. And in each case, saw the death that followed: the extinguishing, as Zuleika had said, of all hope and all possibility.

Imtisar's end she also saw. Equivocating to the last, the old politician had set a banquet for herself in the Jidur, on a carpet she, Jumanah and Najla hauled laboriously from her own house. Wine and fruit there was, and honeyed cake. She took a tearful farewell of the younger women, who would die together at the wall an hour later, and settled herself on the most comfortable of the seats. When the soldiers arrived, she was eating a piece of cake. She raised her eyes and greeted them with level gaze.

"I enjoy our plenty to the last," she told them sternly. "But all you locusts will eat is dust."

The nearest man clubbed her down with the pommel of his sword. Another man ran her through with a spear, and she died there, on the spot where she had made so many speeches. Her blood ran as freely as her words had run, and had its own eloquence.

The soldiers ignored the fruit, but stopped to share the jug of wine— which Imtisar had diluted with water freshly drawn from a well by the Western Gate. By the time they flung the jug down to shatter on the pink stones, the gripes had already begun in their stomachs and some had fallen to their knees. They died in the same place as their victim, but in a manner more protracted.

All these things Rem saw, with the clarity of certain fact. But Zuleika's death she could not see: a veil hung over it, as it hung over all things that were too close to Rem's own fate to be disentangled from it. The thought that Zuleika might be dying right then, and she herself walking away from her, her face resolutely set in the opposite direction, was like the heated tip of a poker in her mind, stirring her thoughts into burning steam.

She had reasoned it out. Zuleika needed to know that her beloved was safe, and would be made stronger by that knowledge. For that reason alone, Rem had agreed to leave. But the belief would bolster Zuleika just as well if it were false, and if Zuleika were to die as she purposed, the world could afford Rem no more comfort than to die in the same place, as soon afterwards as was possible, and so to lie with the woman she loved in death as she had lain with her in life.

So at the end of that first day, when the refugee column had made camp beside the oasis known as Al Teif, Rem slipped away. She intended to walk back to Bessa, and to do so alone, but she had not gone a hundred paces from the camp when she realised that she was followed.

Turning, she saw Anwar Das. He held the reins of two camels.

"My part in this is played," he said gravely. "I'm not needed here. And like you, lady, I find it hard to walk away from a fight before it's finished. Will it please you to take the larger of these two beasts? Despite appearances, he is also the more placid of temperament."

They rode through the night, sleepless, making up in three hours the distance that had taken them a day to march. From the dunes to the west of Bessa they watched the siege's last hours, but could not gain entrance until the walls fell and Jamal's soldiery moved from the plain into the city. Then they crept down, having tethered their camels to the remains of one of the attacking army's ruined war machines, and made their ingress through the water gate (which had now been breached for the second time).

Anwar Das had no clear goal in mind. He meant to help the defenders if he could, and to stand by their side; finding no defenders left, he was uncertain how to proceed. But Rem headed at a run to the square where Zuleika was, and Das followed her at a distance. His dagger it was that took through the heart the man who tried to kill Rem at spear-point. The brightness of the flames concealed both his blade and his position.

And at last, when Nussau and his men had fled, and the two women were alone, he came out and joined them.

There was no question of moving Zuleika: she was far too weak. They cleaned and dressed her wounds, as gently as they could, then used a carpet as a travois to carry her into a neighbouring house.

They lived in the city of the dead for the three weeks that followed. Anwar Das foraged each day for water, taking it from jugs and bottles in already ransacked kitchens. When these supplies ran low, he supplemented them with wine.

In those days, while Zuleika reclaimed by tiny increments the strength she had had before, Rem and Anwar Das went around the city with a wagon and collected the bodies of the defenders. They brought them to the Jidur, where Imtisar already lay along with the soldiers who had unwillingly joined her in her final libation. They built a pyre, using mostly the doors and shutters from surrounding buildings, and the oil from a thousand lamps.

They spoke in the silence of their hearts what prayers they were able to muster. And they burned the bodies, friend and enemy alike.

While they burned, Rem walked to the city gate. The acrid smoke that came to her on the wind stung her eyes and made her weep, which was all to the good. Standing to the right of that great arch, she dipped her index finger in the tears that coursed down her cheek and began to write upon the white stone the names of those who had died in Bessa's defence. The task took her four hours, but the blaze and her tears lasted long enough for the task. When she paused at last, the names were spread across twenty yards of stonework. Because of the hot sun, and because of the ash that had fallen down from the sky to blot it, the ink on that strange memorial was already dry. No amount of weathering would ever erase it.

The day came at last when Zuleika was able to stand, and then to walk, and then to ride. They provisioned themselves as well as they could and set off from Bessa just before dawn. Zuleika rode on one of the two camels, and the other held their supplies. Rem and Anwar Das both walked.

It was a clear day, and cool at first, though it would be fiercely hot later. At the top of a rise, some half a mile from the city walls, they turned to look back on the city. The first rays of the sun were by then touching its towers, and it looked like any city about to wake: held in the stillness not of death but of anticipation. It seemed that at any moment a marabout or a market trader might begin to cry his wares, and the business of the city, both secular and sacred, would resume.

Tears coursed down the cheeks of the two women and of the man as they watched, and remembered.

The Tale of a Man and a Boy

Mushin returned to Ibu Kim, where his mother berated him bitterly both for leaving without telling her and for returning without any gold from the pillaging of so great a city as Bessa.

She reproached him, too, for bringing back another mouth to feed, in the form of the boy, Abidal. Only her son, she lamented, would walk past pavilions of gold and jewels and snatch a child—and a mute child, at that. If it were raining money, she opined, Mushin would somehow contrive to stay dry.

Mushin endured these verbal batterings without complaint, so thankful was he to be home again. In any case, they did not last. In his mother's fearsome bullying and hectoring there was a thread of great kindness, and she responded to the sorrow and fear she read in Abidal's eyes as to a challenge: she would make him feel happy and safe if it killed the both of them.

She made him oat porridge to fatten him and honey cake to delight his palate. She told him stories of djinni and foreign kings, to which Abidal listened with fascination disguised as indifference. She took him to the bazaar and bought him whatever he chanced to pick up there, or if she could not afford it, stole it for him. In short, she did everything for this unwished-for stepson that she had never done for the fruit of her own womb, and seemed to take a huge amount of pleasure in the doing of it.

After two years of this benign tyranny, Abidal remembered how to speak. Scenes of great rejoicing followed, and Mushin's mother showed the lad off as proudly as if he had mastered some astonishing and exacting discipline.

When the initial fuss had died down, Mushin asked the child, with as much trepidation as curiosity, what his real name was. The boy seemed mystified by the question. "Abidal," he said with a shrug.

Mushin was not a brave man; in many ways, he was an abject coward. That was as far as he took his questioning. But he drew from the boy's answer a hope that he might have forgotten, along with his given name, some of the details of how they had first met.

Whether he was right or wrong in this belief, only the Increate may say. But man and boy lived long together, bullied and cosseted respectively by the old lady, who when asked would introduce them both as her sons.

THE TALE OF THE BOOK

Some centuries after the time of Rem the Archivist there lived, in a cold northern city, a young woman of learning. This was an unusual thing in her place and time; but her mother had grown up in the desert lands, in a family which placed as much importance on the education of daughters as sons. Accordingly, the woman taught her daughters to read, both in her native tongue and in that of the land where her husband, an enterprising merchant, had taken her to live. The merchant loved his wife, and since his business prospered he was in a position to indulge her whims. So the girls learned languages, and the elder—who had a particular gift for the study—could write, by the time she was twelve, in a fine flowing hand.

Her father's prosperity did not last. By the time the three sons were set up in trades of their own, there was no money left for dowries, and the elder daughter did not have beauty enough to make a dowry unnecessary. Furthermore, the family's acquaintances agreed, she lacked those qualities of humility and obedience that make an ideal wife. So after her mother died, her father placed her in an enclosed order of nuns. For this life too, some financial settlement is usually made by the postulant's family, but here they were lucky: the very learning that had proved a barrier to the girl's marriage was a recommendation. The convent owned a library which had recently been swollen by a behest from a scholar's widow, and the nuns were in need of scholars and scribes.

So the girl became a nun. After her grief for her mother's death had abated, she did not repine at her fate—the convent was small but rich, and the work to which she was put suited both her talents and her disposition. When her younger sister, who was fair-faced, was married to one of their father's business friends, she sent the couple a passage of scripture that she had written out and decorated with her own hand: *a good wife is worth more than rubies*, she wrote. But she secretly considered that she had had the better end of the bargain.

The library of the convent was chiefly famed for its antiquity. Indeed several of its books were scrolls, some of them in scripts too old or too faint to be deciphered. The Abbess did not consider this a reason to discard them. On the contrary, she reasoned, their very age made them precious, for one day some great scholar might learn from them the lost wisdom of the ancients. They were kept in the very heart of the convent's main building, where the air was driest and the temperature most constant. Meanwhile, it had to be admitted, the harvest of wisdom, old or new, to be garnered from the library was small. The most valuable books had long ago been taken for safekeeping to the houses of one of the men's enclosed orders, where the buildings were more secure; likewise the more weighty volumes of theology and philosophy, so that they could be pored over by doctors and divines. The books that were left were something of a ragbag: apocrypha, chronicles, old tales, songs and household saws; accounts, receipts and remedies, sometimes all bound together in the same codex. Many were in languages unknown to the nuns, and it was these that the young woman was first set to study, to copy if they were faint and to translate if she could.

Sitting in the close darkness, poring over her lines of text by the light of a lamp, she came across a book one day that seemed to her unlike any of the others. It was one of the oldest she had seen: though a bound volume, the script—or scripts, for it was in several hands—were clearly so ancient that no one had been able to read it. She had found it at the bottom of a pile of similarly obscure books, carefully stacked but covered in dust. The volume was small, thick and undistinguished-looking, with no illustration save for a single symbol at the very end. It was made up of sheets of different weights and thicknesses, roughly sewn together, and the ink in which it was written was unusual. In each of the different hands, firm or spidery, it was the same colour—far blacker and more distinct than it should be in such an ancient document.

The young woman's interest was piqued. Though the book's script was archaic, she did not at once lay it aside, and a more careful study revealed that some of the characters were familiar to her from her mother's teaching: this was a language from the lands of the south and east. Other discoveries quickly followed; she was able to make out words, and guess at whole sentences. Sometimes the layout of a page would help her. As in other books, there were lists of materials and prices; poems; recipes. But most of the volume seemed to be made up of tales, of a group of women lost and wandering in the desert, of wars and bandits, and a lost city.

She studied the book into the night, missing the evening meal and arriving late for prayer, for which she earned a severe reproof, tempered only slightly by the Abbess's respect for the pursuit of knowledge. After that the little volume became her pastime. She wrapped it in a cloth and laid it at the back of her desk, and sometimes when the day's work was done and the other women left to walk for a while in the chill evening air, she would remain in her place and carry out a little more of her translation.

She understood the outlines of the language very rapidly; its details came more slowly, and it took her many months, drawing on other texts for comparison, before she had fully completed her translation of the first of the stories. The chief speaker in the book, the writer of more than half the pages, was a woman, in some ways very like the scribe herself: she declared that she never married, and chose to spend her life among books. But she was also, it had to be said, mad. She wrote wildly of demons and monsters, of visions of the future, of a world in which people flew in the bellies of iron dragons and lived in towers of glass which reached to the clouds. She claimed to have dressed in men's clothes, to have survived death by vultures in the desert, to have killed a tyrant single-handed. Clearly, the scribe realised, the tales in this book were of a profane nature, of no spiritual value to her sisters in the convent. She could not translate it as part of her daily work. And yet the book exerted a hold on her. It reminded her strongly of the stories she had heard from her mother as a child.

And the work helped to speed her in her official duties; as she mastered its language, she found she was able to decipher a number of texts which had never been read by the nuns before, and uncovered treasures including a physician's book of remedies and a treatise on astronomy. She became known as an expert on arcane languages, and the other scribes began to come to her with their own perplexities.

And whenever she brought a translation to a close, or finished a job of copying, she would allow herself an hour or two to work on the little book of stories.

After some two years of study, she was satisfied she could read it all. By then she had been promoted to chief scribe, and with the authority this brought her she took it on herself to translate the book for the library. It could not be a full translation. For all her work, there were some passages that still made no sense to her—she was certain that she understood each of the words, but not what they meant together. For each of these passages she did her best to produce a possible meaning, and added a footnote giving the original phrase, to aid better scholars who might come after her. Other passages were indecent, or spoke of commerce with demons, and these she regretfully omitted, since their discovery by certain dignitaries might cause both the translation and its original to be destroyed.

The stories that gave her the most trouble portrayed women who acted in unwomanly ways: they met unchaperoned with men to trade in the markets, chose or rejected husbands, even fought as soldiers. One, it seemed, took money for committing murders, and was never punished, or even blamed. After much thought she left out the tale of the murderess, but retained most of the others, adding a note to remind her readers that these tales told of heathen times and lives long gone.

She showed the finished work to her sister scribes, and was relieved to find that they were neither shocked nor disgusted by it. They laughed at the stories of the women who tricked a cave-full of bandits, and the young man who won his life back with a tall tale. Some even wept at the final story, in which many of the women fought and died defending their city against the invader who destroyed it. The stories of the city of women became part of their daily conversation when they were alone in the scriptorium. The women in the tales were brazen and violent: the nuns talked of them with giggles, as people who could not exist in real life. But every now and then, there was a note in their voices of something like envy.

When their own troubles came, the nuns were anything but warlike in their response. Barbarians invaded their city. They came at night and sacked the convent, took away the great silver cross and chalices and burned the building to the ground. By then the women were long gone; they had known about the invasion for months, and had received warning two days before that the hordes were close.

They did not stay to fight. They packed all the belongings they could carry on carts, and joined the procession leaving the city. The most valuable books, the Bibles and tomes of theology, were packed in great brass-and-wood chests, as befitted their importance. But the chief scribe carried a package of her own, holding the profane volumes that she would not leave behind: the treatises on the stars and on medicine, some volumes of songs and poetry, and the book of the City of Women, with her translation.

She kept the book with her for the rest of her life. She and her sister nuns found another convent to take them in, small and poor enough to avoid the notice of the barbarians, and resumed their work there. When peace was finally restored, many of her sisters moved to larger houses, but the chief scribe remained where she was, and after many years, rose to be Abbess there. Before her sight failed, she took up the little book once more and made a second translation, full and complete this time, as a gift for her youngest niece, who was shortly to be married to a rich man three times her age. The Abbess had no advice to give the girl on the subject of marriage, but hoped that the book of stories would bring her comfort, or at least a distraction.

Her niece visited her the following year, bringing with her the book and also her baby daughter.

"I'll tell her all the stories when she's old enough," she promised. "But I hoped you could show me the original volume, in my grandmother's language."

The old woman nodded and went to fetch the book. They pored over it together, the old one squinting in an effort to make out the black writing that had been so clear to her in her youth, as she pointed out this or that familiar word, and showed how the meanings of the whole had first begun to appear to her. The younger woman listened and looked attentively, while the baby dabbed a fat finger at each page in turn.

When they reached the final page, the young woman exclaimed in pleasure.

"There's a picture! You didn't tell me, Auntie."

"It's the only one," the old woman said. "That's the sign of the writer."

The book ended with a list of names, in tight columns taking up a page *and most of its reverse.* Below them the first writer had added:

These gave their lives so that the people would live. The story of Bessa is their story, and we who live on keep them alive in the telling.

And to this I give my name.

The page was signed with one symbol: a weeping eye.

The old woman sighed. "Of course," she said, "it's all just a fable. A tale of heathen folk and far-off lands."

"Perhaps," said the young woman. "But she might come to read it differently."

"Ma," added the baby, and tapped the book with a soft hand.

THE TALE OF TALES

The mechanism by which stories are transmitted is a strange one. My tears survive, but my story will be refracted into many stories. They will call me the woman who cried tears which turned to pearls. They will call me she whose tears restored sight to the blind. They will say that where my tears fell, flowers grew. They will say that my weeping filled oceans and drowned cities. All of these tales are true, and none of them are. The only thing that has ever sprung from my grief was words. They were the only thing, and all things. And they are what endures, now that my tears have finally ceased.

Many stories are told about what became of the inhabitants of the City of Women. There are those who ascribe to the outlandish theory that they never left Bessa at all. They live still within its walls, hiding from sight in a series of underground tunnels of ingenious design. They have grown resistant to the poison which the Lion cast into their wells, but as a result of drinking it every day they are all become monstrous in stature and rapacious in desire, and prey on incautious male travellers to gratify their concupiscence. This tale is mostly repeated in slurred accents in the many drinking dens of Ibu Kim, where for some reason the thought of tall, feral women with insatiable sexual appetites has a certain appeal.

More conservative commentators aver that the Bessans disbanded, trickling in dribs and drabs into Perdondaris, Agorath, Jawahir and Gharia. Those who tell this story add, with a knowing look, that if you know where to go in those great cities, you may still be able to purchase yourself a shawl of Bessan weave, an embroidered tapestry or a book of poetry.

Some say that they wandered in the wilderness until their food and water were spent, and that the desert was their last resting place.

Others tell the same tale in a different way: the people of Bessa never dispersed to settle in other cities, nor did they die on their wanderings. Instead, they became a desert nation, roaming the wastes without cease and earning their living by trading with the travellers they met on their way. Bandits sitting around the fire in the deep desert, when the flames dip low and the world becomes a dark bowl filled with stars, will speak in hushed tones of the city of the heat haze, whose buildings and people seem to emanate from the sand itself. It springs up to offer comfort to the weary wayfarer, a city of dust and incense. And its inhabitants are, according to some, of the city of Bessa, and according to others this is a lie, and the two cities have no connection.

All the storytellers agree on one detail. The standing stones of Bessa's main gate, on which the archivist and librarian of Bessa inscribed the names of the dead, are standing still. Millennia may pass, and their ink will not fade.

All else of truth is shrouded in darkness. Those who know most, say least.

Zuleika and I bade goodbye to Anwar Das on the outskirts of Perdondaris, and purchased a small house outside the walls of that city. We live there now. There is a pleasing completeness to it—we arrived in the place the concubines were bound for, only many years later, and on our own terms. Our house is quiet, and there is plenty of room for those scrolls I managed to bring with me. Most, of course, remain in Bessa's Library. It is still intact: it was built to stand through many sieges, though there will be no more. I have seen its fate. The next incursion into Bessa is a wave of scavengers, who find the Library and its scrolls largely untouched, and sell the latter to the cities nearby for a tidy profit. The Library stands on, forlorn and imposing in a city of ruin and rubble. Eventually, it is the last building left. Travellers passing that way will look upon it, and on the standing stones of the city gates, and grow thoughtful, thinking of things that were and things which might have been.

Our days are passed in quiet joy, though that joy is often tinged with sadness. We read each other poetry, and I write still, but Zuleika will never regain the use of her left arm. Our home is a delight to us, and over the years our conversations, loud with laughter in the evenings or whispered across the pillows at night, have seeped into its walls like incense into wood, so that everything in it seems to bear the signature of our happiness. Still, there are days when the angle of the light, or the scent of spices on the breeze, or a certain quality in the voices we hear in the market, will recall to the both of us the home that we lost. Then we walk through Perdondaris in silence, our minds traversing the streets and squares of another city, a city which exists no longer in wood and stone, but in thoughts and memories, ink and parchment.

Bessa was scattered on the wind, destroyed, yet also sown, like those plants whose seeds are released only by the ravages of fire. Its words survive, borne in minds and on lips, lying dormant in dreams. I end this tale here, but it is but a thread in the vast tapestry of tales, which has no end. From the weeper, tears. From the City of Women, a diaspora. Moving slowly through the desert of ages, traversing those distances of space and time. They may be far off, or they may be yet to come.

Baraha, barahinei.

ACKNOWLEDGEMENTS

This book wouldn't have happened at all if it hadn't been for a fortuitous encounter at Eastercon 2010 between us (well, two of the three of us) and Sandra Kasturi and Brett Savory, of ChiZine. The encouragement and practical help they gave us in shaping what was then a fairly fuzzy and vestigial idea into a fully working book with actual words and punctuation marks goes beyond praise. The rest of the ChiZine posse (Helen and Laura Marshall, Sam Beiko) are similarly amazing. To paraphrase Isaac Walton, the time you spend with them is not deducted from your lifespan.

ABOUT THE AUTHORS

Linda, Louise and Mike Carey are three writers living in North London. Sometimes they write together, sometimes alone.

Louise wrote *The Diary of a London Schoolgirl* for the website of the London Metropolitan Archive. She also co-wrote the graphic novel *Confessions of a Blabbermouth* with Mike.

Linda, writing as A.J. Lake, authored the *Darkest Age* fantasy trilogy. She has also written for TV, most notably for the German fantasy animation series *Meadowlands*.

Mike has written extensively in the comics field, where his credits include *Lucifer*, *Hellblazer*, *X-Men* and *The Unwritten* (nominated for both the Eisner and Hugo Awards). He is also the author of the *Felix Castor* novels, and of the *X-Men Destiny* console game for Activision. He is currently writing a movie screenplay, *Silent War*, for Slingshot Studios and Intrepid Pictures.

They share their crowded house with two other writers/artists, a cat, and several stick insects.

ABOUT THE ARTIST

Nimit Malavia is an award-winning illustrator from Ottawa, Canada. Born in 1987, he received his degree in illustration from Sheridan College. Nimit has produced work for clients including Marvel Comics, Shopify, *The National Post* and 20th Century Fox. He has also exhibited internationally in galleries in Berlin, London, Los Angeles, Miami and Toronto. He works to live, but really, it's more like he lives to work. You can find more information about Nimit at www.nimitmalavia.com.

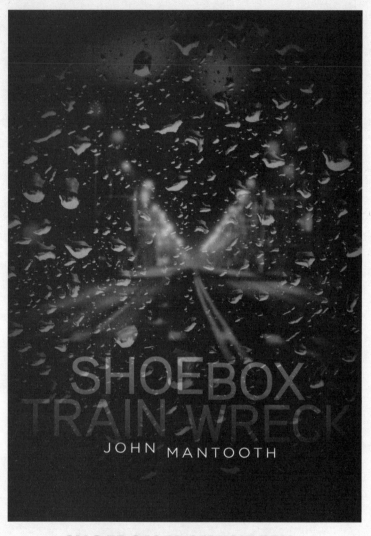

SHOEBOX TRAINWRECK
JOHN MANTOOTH

AVAILABLE MARCH 15, 2012
FROM CHIZINE PUBLICATIONS

978-1-926851-54-9

WESTLAKE SOUL
RIO YOUERS

AVAILABLE APRIL 15, 2012
FROM CHIZINE PUBLICATIONS

978-1-926851-55-6

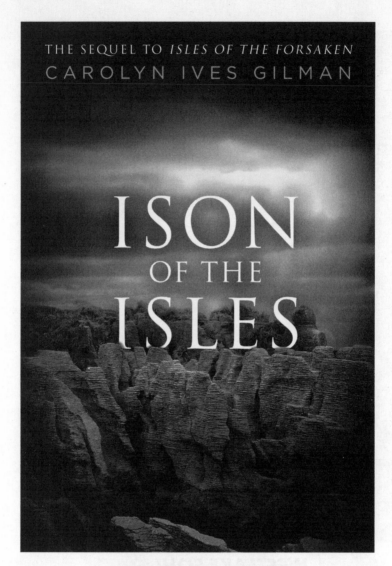

THE SEQUEL TO *ISLES OF THE FORSAKEN*
CAROLYN IVES GILMAN

ISON
OF THE
ISLES

ISON OF THE ISLES
CAROLYN IVES GILMAN

AVAILABLE APRIL 15, 2012
FROM CHIZINE PUBLICATIONS

978-1-926851-56-3

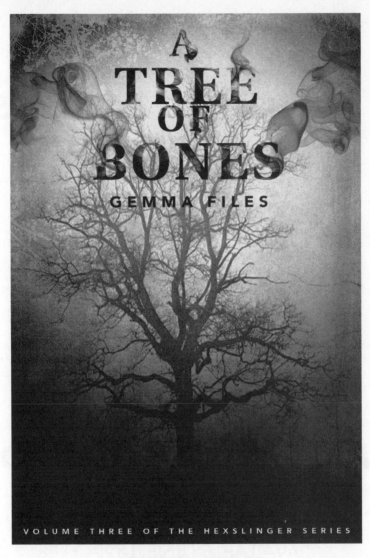

A TREE OF BONES

VOLUME THREE OF THE HEXSLINGER SERIES

GEMMA FILES

AVAILABLE MAY 15, 2012
FROM CHIZINE PUBLICATIONS

978-1-926851-57-0

NINJA VS. PIRATE FEATURING ZOMBIES

JAMES MARSHALL

AVAILABLE MAY 15, 2011
FROM CHIZINE PUBLICATIONS

978-1-926851-59-4

RASPUTIN'S BASTARDS

DAVID NICKLE

AVAILABLE JUNE 15, 2011
FROM CHIZINE PUBLICATIONS

978-1-926851-58-7

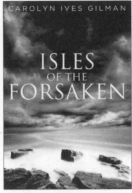

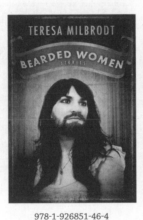

978-1-926851-10-5

TOM PICCIRILLI

EVERY SHALLOW CUT

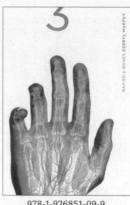

978-1-926851-09-9

DERRYL MURPHY

NAPIER'S BONES

978-1-926851-11-2

DAVID NICKLE

EUTOPIA

978-1-926851-12-9

CLAUDE LALUMIÈRE

THE DOOR TO LOST PAGES

978-1-926851-13-6

BRENT HAYWARD

THE FECUND'S MELANCHOLY DAUGHTER

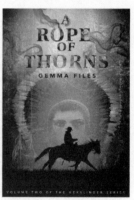

978-1-926851-14-3

GEMMA FILES

A ROPE OF THORNS

ALSO AVAILABLE FROM CHIZINE PUBLICATIONS

978-0-9813746-6-6

GORD ZAJAC

MAJOR KARNAGE

978-0-9813746-8-0

ROBERT BOYCZUK

NEXUS: ASCENSION

978-1-926851-00-6

CRAIG DAVIDSON

SARAH COURT

978-1-926851-06-8

PAUL TREMBLAY

**IN THE
MEAN TIME**

978-1-926851-02-0

HALLI VILLEGAS

**THE HAIR WREATH
AND OTHER STORIES**

978-1-926851-04-4

TONY BURGESS

**PEOPLE LIVE STILL
IN CASHTOWN
CORNERS**

CHIZINEPUB.COM   CZP

978-0-9812978-9-7

TIM LEBBON

**THE THIEF OF
BROKEN TOYS**

978-0-9812978-8-0

PHILIP NUTMAN

CITIES OF NIGHT

978-0-9812978-7-3

SIMON LOGAN

**KATJA FROM THE
PUNK BAND**

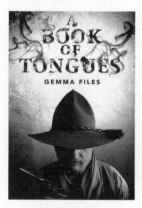

978-0-9812978-6-6

GEMMA FILES

**A BOOK OF
TONGUES**

978-0-9812978-5-9

DOUGLAS SMITH

CHIMERASCOPE

978-0-9812978-4-2

NICHOLAS KAUFMANN

**CHASING THE
DRAGON**

"IF YOUR TASTE IN FICTION RUNS TO THE DISTURBING, DARK, AND AT LEAST PAR-
TIALLY WEIRD, CHANCES ARE YOU'VE HEARD OF CHIZINE PUBLICATIONS—CZP—A
YOUNG IMPRINT THAT IS NONETHELESS PRODUCING STARTLINGLY BEAUTIFUL
BOOKS OF STARKLY, DARKLY LITERARY QUALITY."
—DAVID MIDDLETON, *JANUARY MAGAZINE*

ALSO AVAILABLE FROM CHIZINE PUBLICATIONS

978-0-9809410-9-8

ROBERT J. WIERSEMA

**THE WORLD MORE
FULL OF WEEPING**

978-0-9812978-2-8

CLAUDE LALUMIÈRE

**OBJECTS OF
WORSHIP**

978-0-9809410-7-4

DANIEL A. RABUZZI

THE CHOIR BOATS

978-0-9809410-5-0

TIDHAR AND NIR YANIV

**THE TEL AVIV
DOSSIER**

978-0-9809410-3-6

ROBERT BOYCZUK

**HORROR STORY
AND OTHER
HORROR STORIES**

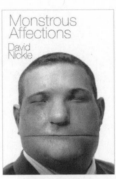

978-0-9812978-3-5

DAVID NICKLE

**MONSTROUS
AFFECTIONS**

978-0-9809410-1-2

BRENT HAYWARD

FILARIA

"CHIZINE PUBLICATIONS REPRESENTS SOMETHING WHICH IS COMMON IN THE MUSIC INDUSTRY BUT SADLY RARER WITHIN THE PUBLISHING INDUSTRY: THAT A CLEVER INDEPENDENT CAN RUN RINGS ROUND THE MAJORS IN TERMS OF STYLE AND CONTENT."

—MARTIN LEWIS, *SF SITE*

CHIZINEPUB.COM CZP